Dear Reader,

We are delighted to welcome you to this wonderful volume of two complete and satisfying books in one cover.

This year we concentrated on finding you eight wonderful books with strong, single dads in them as our first initial focus, and when we came to think about which books to put together the pairings were instantly self-evident. This book just had to be the volume that took a look at dads and their daughters—how they interact and how they cope with each other. We loved the picture of the strong protective hero dealing with his burgeoning females! Very few of us *ever* understand the opposite sex, so these dads had to call in some help. Suddenly we weren't just talking about dads and daughters, but families!

Happy reading,

The Editors

*First published in Great Britain 2000
by Harlequin Mills & Boon Limited,
Eton House, 18-24 Paradise Road,
Richmond, Surrey TW9 1SR*

JACOB'S GIRLS © Tara Lee Reames 1995
A FATHER'S PLACE © Joan Kilby 1998

ISBN 0 373 04675 8

20-1000

*Printed and bound in Spain
by Litografia Rosés S.A., Barcelona*

Jacob's Girls

TARA TAYLOR QUINN

HARLEQUIN®

TORONTO • NEW YORK • LONDON
AMSTERDAM • PARIS • SYDNEY • HAMBURG
STOCKHOLM • ATHENS • TOKYO • MILAN • MADRID
PRAGUE • WARSAW • BUDAPEST • AUCKLAND

To Agnes Mary Keller Gumser

For having the courage to follow your heart
when others were against you.
The stubbornness to prevail
when your heart didn't seem to be enough.
The strength to do what was right
when right wasn't easy.
The fairness to forgive those
who didn't have the strength
and the unselfishness to keep giving
during those years when you didn't receive.
May I someday be half the woman you are…
Thanks, Mum.

* * *

Thanks to Beth McDonald and Bill Austin
of KESZ Radio, 99.9 FM in Phoenix, Arizona,
for their technical support.

CHAPTER ONE

"I DON'T KNOW about you, but that woman can sing to me anytime. That was Celine Dion with 'The Power of Love' on KOLR as we get you to work on time. I'm Jacob Ryan..."

"...and I'm Michelle Colby, on 'color,' your station at the end of the rainbow."

"You wanna do the weather or shall I?"

"You go ahead. You do it so well."

"So I've been told."

"The weather, Jacob, the weather."

"Yeah, well, it looks like it's going to be a hot one today, folks..." He grinned at Michelle. She grinned back. What the...? Hell, it was happening again.

Jacob finished the weather report, but he was shaken. For a second there he'd actually wished their sexual banter was more than an act for the show. The prospect of his upcoming meeting this morning must have had him more off kilter than he'd realized.

While Michelle announced a giveaway, he glanced at the AP bulletin that had just come over the wire. Then he leaned toward his mike. "For all of you heading into work this gorgeous Monday morning, let's check in with Officer Barb Jansen in the traffic 'copter. You there, Barb?'' he asked.

"I'm here, Jacob, and we've got some good news this morning…'' Barb's voice piped into the sound booth. Jacob shut her off. They had three minutes until they were on again. He needed some peace and quiet.

"YOU OKAY?''

Michelle was watching him, a pair of scissors in one hand as she clipped an article out of the local newspaper spread in front of her.

"Couldn't be better,'' he said. It wasn't true, but confiding in people wasn't something that came easily to him. He picked up the *Wall Street Journal,* looking for anything that might interest their listeners.

"You seem a little preoccupied.''

Damn her for noticing. And damn her even more for letting him know she'd noticed. They were casual friends, workmates, but that was all. "Hey, who wouldn't seem a little preoccupied at six o'clock in the morning? It's called 'not awake yet,''' he said lightly.

She gave him a pointed look, telling him she wasn't buying it, but she went back to clipping news articles for them to use on the show. And that was when he realized he was actually tempted to tell her about Friday's phone call, to ask her opinion. What the hell was wrong with him these days?

"IT'S EIGHT-O-NINE on this gorgeous January morning, and in just a few minutes we'll be talking with football superstar Joe Montana, so keep your dial right where it is on ninety-four-point-five, KOLR. But first we have a special anniversary wish to send out...." Jacob clicked off his mike and half listened while Michelle took over to congratulate a couple of Los Angeles natives on their fiftieth wedding anniversary.

Only another hour and he'd be on his way to Lomen Elementary School to tackle whatever crisis awaited him there. The next time they called him from school asking for a conference he was going to insist on meeting with the principal immediately. He'd been driving himself crazy all weekend with possible scenarios of the triple trouble his daughters could have concocted. But really, how bad could it be? They were only seven years old. It wasn't as if they were at an age to skip classes or be caught smoking in the locker room....

"What do you think, Jacob? A day at the beach sound good?" Michelle's voice cut into his ruminations.

He reached automatically for the button that would turn on his mike. "With you?" he asked, a standard comeback. But for once he really thought about what he was saying. He could imagine a lot worse things than a day at the beach with Michelle.

"That depends," she said.

"On what?" he asked, reminding himself that

they'd been trading this kind of banter for almost three years, that it meant nothing.

"On whether or not you plan to wear those ridiculous boxer trunks you wore to the company picnic last summer. I gotta tell you, they didn't do anything for your legs."

"They hung down to my knees. You couldn't see my legs." She was looking at him, but she wasn't laughing the way she usually did when they played their on-air roles. For the first time in three years, the sound booth seemed small to him.

"My point exactly." She stuck out her tongue and grinned. So that was that. She'd just been playing with him—as usual.

"Well, I'd love to fill you in on this little racing suit I've got, but it's time to get Joe Montana on the line," Jacob said, a tad peeved. Which was ridiculous. Michelle was doing the same professional job she'd done ever since they'd started cohosting the morning show. He was the one acting weird.

He punched in the blinking button on the phone and looked to Michelle.

"Joe? Michelle Colby here on KOLR. We're on the air...."

Jacob sat back, disgusted with himself. Not only was Michelle his partner, she was a married woman. And while Jacob enjoyed the company of many women, he stayed away from the married ones—always. Besides, however casual, Michelle was his friend, and Jacob never slept with his friends—ever.

HE STOPPED HOME after the show to change his sweats for a pair of off-white cotton slacks. Stepping over three little pairs of sandy beach shoes in the garage, he was glad to be away from the station. His reaction to Michelle that morning was still bothering him. They worked well together. And no matter how beautiful she was, he wasn't going to let his libido mess up a good thing.

He passed through the kitchen, clean except for the cereal bowls, through the living room cluttered with Dr. Seuss books, past a huge bedroom with three unmade beds, to the master bedroom in the back of his beach house. Of course if he was to be honest with himself he'd have to admit that what was bothering him most was how close he'd come to pouring out his concerns over the triplets to Michelle when he was perfectly capable of handling his children's problems on his own.

His sweats landed in the general vicinity of the laundry basket. He tucked the KOLR T-shirt into the waistband of his slacks and slipped on a pair of canvas loafers. Glancing in the mirror over his sink, he wondered if he looked as tired as he felt. His hair, dark and a little too long, was slightly mussed but it would do. He was ready to take whatever the school principal had to dish out.

MICHELLE SPED along the 405 toward Long Beach, weaving in and out of the traffic with the ease of a

California native. She had to get home, far away from Jacob Ryan.

Not once, in all the years since she'd met Brian Colby, had she been seriously tempted by another man. She was in love with her husband, and damn Jacob's cocky, sexy-as-hell attitude for making her forget that—even for a minute.

She exited the 405, past the car dealership where Brian had taken her to buy her first new car, the Thunderbird she still drove. He'd planned the car as a surprise for her college graduation, and he'd preened like a rooster as he'd handed her the keys. They'd driven for hours that night, taking turns at the wheel as they'd traveled along the California coastline.

And then, sometime after midnight, they'd pulled into a deserted cove, climbed into the back seat and made love till dawn. Brian was a tender lover, always thinking about her pleasure as much as his own. He'd made love to her slowly, savoring every second, and afterward they'd fallen asleep in each other's arms, cramped in the back seat. Michelle could still almost feel that warm safe haven they'd created, with Brian on one side of her, and the seat back, smelling of new leather, on the other. And then, when the sky had changed from black to purple to a hazy gray, he'd made love to her again, caressing every inch of her body, telling her with his hands how much he adored her. Their bodies had still been linked when the sun finally rose, and Brian had teased her that nice girls didn't romp all night in the back seats of cars. Then, his eyes having grown serious, he'd whispered her name. And he'd promised to love her forever.

Tears blurred Michelle's vision as she turned into her neighborhood, and she hurriedly blinked them away. She'd promised to love Brian forever, too. Which was why she had no business flirting with another man—especially not Jacob Ryan. If there was one thing Michelle had learned from her parents long happy marriage it was that loyalty was everything. Jacob didn't know the meaning of the word. As much as she valued his friendship, she despised his womanizing. His liaisons were too casual to be considered relationships. He never dated the same woman twice in a row—twice in a week, perhaps, but not twice in a row.

Maybe that was why her body had responded to him this morning. After five years of silence, she finally had a small lead on Brian's whereabouts. She was geared up, coming alive again. And Jacob was safe. Lusting after him was safe. He'd never take her up on it. He never slept with women he had to see in the morning.

She pulled the Thunderbird into her cracked driveway, trying not to notice how run-down the neighborhood had become in the past couple of years. She'd had the house painted. She had her lawn mowed once a week. But while she could certainly afford to have the driveway repaved, she knew that any money she put into the place was money wasted. It was time to move. And she would—just as soon as she found Brian. Until then, she wasn't budging from the tiny home they'd bought together.

Fumbling with the dead bolt on her front door, she swore softly, anxious to get inside and check her answering machine. Frank Steele, the private detective she'd hired several months before was in Egypt. Brian had been working as a foreign correspondent in Cairo at the time of his disappearance, and Frank thought he'd found someone who might have a lead on his whereabouts. It was the first time she'd heard anything of her husband since he'd ordered breakfast from room service five years ago.

The minute she was in the door her fluffy white cat wrapped herself around Michelle's legs. No one had ever told Noby that cats were supposed to be standoffish. Michelle scooped the Persian up, rubbing her face in Noby's soft fur as she hurried to the little bedroom she'd converted into a den.

The red light on her answering machine wasn't blinking. No messages. Michelle ran the machine through its cycle, anyway, just to be certain it was still working.

''This is the Colbys. We're not here right n—''

Noby put her soft front paws on Michelle's cheeks, kneading and purring, as Michelle clicked off the message Brian had recorded so many years ago. Frank had said he'd call as soon as he had something. And unlike the government officials who'd finally given up and pronounced Brian legally dead, Frank Steele *had* to call her. She was paying him a good portion of her salary to do so. It was just a matter of waiting until he had something to report.

JACOB LOVED WOMEN. They intrigued him. Introduce him to a woman, young or old, fat or skinny, and he could usually find something about her to like.

Not this time. From the moment Lomen Elementary School principal Eleanor Wilson ushered him into her office, Jacob didn't like her. She reminded him of his mother—impossible to please.

But unlike his mother, Ms. Wilson had the power to make Jacob's life difficult. Which was why he immediately took the seat she indicated, a hard-backed, walnut-colored torture device set directly in front of her slate gray desk. Feeling like he was twelve again, he folded his hands in his lap.

"Mr. Ryan, there are several situations I feel I must make you aware of concerning your daughters."

Ms. Wilson's short dark hair looked as stern as she did. Jacob sat up straight and smiled encouragingly. After all, they were on the same side, weren't they?

"In the past month, Alison, Jessica and Meghan have been to the nurse's office a total of thirteen times."

"Thirteen times? That's crazy. They haven't been sick."

"A couple of times Allie brought Jessie in from the playground."

Jacob tried to relax. "She fell out of the swing again, right? That kid can't hold on and pump at the same time. She's too busy creating fairy tales in her head. I swear that Jessie's going to be a writer some day.''

Ms. Wilson pursed her pale lips. ''She didn't fall out of a swing, Mr. Ryan. They've all three been complaining about stomachaches....''

''But that's ridiculous. They've never once told me their stomachs hurt and they're eating like a pack of hogs,'' Jacob said, thoroughly confused.

''They've also had sore throats, headaches, cramps and fatigue.''

Jacob's hands fell to his sides. ''Cramps and fatigue? Fatigue? Are we talking about the same bundles of energy that have my house trashed ten minutes after they come home from school?''

Ms. Wilson tapped a pencil against the top of her desk. ''They're a little young for cramps, too, unless you know something we don't?''

''What? Oh,'' Jacob said, feeling stupid. ''No, I mean, yes, they're too young for that.''

''Well, as you can imagine, we've become quite concerned—''

''Wait just a minute here.'' Jacob leaned forward, placing his palms on the edge of her desk. ''Are you implying that I'm not taking proper care of my daughters? Because if you are you can stop right there. Meggie, Allie and Jessie are all healthy as horses. You just have to spend an hour playing with them to know that. Even the sea gulls run for cover when the girls are on the beach. And why am I just hearing about this now after it's already reached the point where you're *concerned?* Isn't it standard to notify a child's parent when the child isn't feeling well?''

Ms. Wilson's lips softened, her eyes filling with something close to sympathy as she nodded. So maybe he'd been mistaken about her resemblance to his mother. ''And we would have called, but each time we started to the symptoms mysteriously disappeared, leaving us no reason to contact you.''

''Disappeared?'' Jacob sat back, frowning. The hard wooden slats of the chair dug into his back.

''Your daughters aren't sick, Mr. Ryan. They're looking for attention.''

Jacob froze. He knew he wasn't good at relationships, but surely he wasn't failing his own daughters.

''I give the girls more attention than most kids receive in a household with two parents,'' he said, knowing he was right. He spent all of his free time with them. It had to be enough.

''I know you do. You're to be commended for the effort you put into being a father. The girls benefit greatly from your guidance and love. But they're girls. And I suspect that they need some feminine influence, too.''

Jacob gritted his teeth. ''Before you suggest it, I'm not about to go out and find another wife just to be a companion to my daughters. They've done all right without one for the past four years. This is probably just another stage they're going through. I'm sure it'll pass like the others have.'' Jacob stood up. ''I'll talk to them about visits to the nurse. I can assure you it won't happen again.''

"Sit down, Mr. Ryan.''

Jacob took one look at the woman's serious expression and sat.

"Alison is organizing her teacher to death. As you know, this is the first year she's been separated from her sisters, and she's lost without them. Instead of playing with the kids in her class, she spends her days making suggestions about what the other students should be doing and trying to help the teacher give them their instructions.''

"She's always had a lot of initiative. That, combined with her incessant drive to organize, is going to serve her well in life.'' He knew he sounded rather pompous, but he didn't need this. His triplets were the one thing he'd done right.

"Initiative is good, I agree, but not when it's taken to such an extreme. Not only is it disruptive to the rest of the class, but we'd be remiss to ignore what appears to us to be Alison's cry for help. Last Friday, she sneaked out of the lunch room, tricked her way into the staff lounge by saying she had an emergency and proceeded to inform her teacher that they needed to rearrange the classroom seating—put the students in alphabetical order, she said—and if the teacher liked, she'd be willing to stay in at recess to help her do it.''

Jacob shrugged, wondering if the principal wasn't overreacting a bit. "So she's a little obsessive. We'll work on it. I fail to see how this points to a need for female guidance.''

''Not even when Alison's plan would've given her a recess period alone with her teacher *and* put her in the seat right next to the teacher's desk?''

Jacob rubbed his forehead. He hadn't realized that Allie was so fond of her teacher. ''Like I said, I'll talk to them.''

''Jessica's crying has become much too frequent.''

There was more? Jacob stared at the principal as worry crept past his defenses and started to knot his stomach. He was facing what every parent dreaded—a child with problems. Only apparently he had three of them.

Ms. Wilson came around to the front of the desk, crossing her arms. ''The reasons for her tears are always different—bumping her leg on a desk, catching her finger in the pencil sharpener, getting a bad grade on a paper—but the pattern is always the same. With a hug from her teacher, the tears stop immediately. Lately it's been happening almost daily. We believe that Jessica, like her sister, is reacting to a need for a woman's love.''

''Maybe. Or maybe—''

''She's more forgetful than normal, too. She's had to get her lunch money from Alison three times in the past week, and she's forgotten several assignments. I'm afraid her grades are dropping, Mr. Ryan.''

''Jessie's a normal seven-year-old girl. She's taken

up with fantasies right now, but just wait until she masters reading. She'll be more studious than both of her sisters, mark my words.''

"I'm not saying any of your children are abnormal, Mr. Ryan. I'm saying they're sending out signs and it's our job to recognize. Meghan has become almost reclusive. In class she refuses to work or play with anyone but Jessica. And if Jessica's busy, Meghan occupies herself on her own. She resists any attempts her teacher makes to include her in games with the other children.''

Jacob's gut clenched. This wasn't something he could rationalize away. He'd been concerned for a while now about Meggie's holding herself apart. He'd tried to give her some extra attention, to cuddle her a little more, but nothing seemed to be working.

At a complete loss he stared at Ms. Wilson. Meggie's behavior worried him. Unlike Jessie, who lived in a dreamworld much of the time, Meggie seemed just plain lonely to him, which was ridiculous considering she had two identical sisters around her practically twenty-four hours a day.

"A couple of weeks ago, the teacher put her arm around Meghan while she was explaining a math problem," Ms. Wilson continued. "Meghan jerked away and told her teacher not to touch her—ever.''

Jacob studied the pearl buttons running the length of Ms. Wilson's blue-flowered dress. He had a problem. Okay, he'd faced that much. Now what in hell was he going to do about it?

"Have the girls said anything to you about the try-outs for the spring play?" Ms. Wilson asked, returning to her seat.

Jacob shook his head, surprised by the change in subject. "Come to think of it, they haven't. Which is odd, since that's all they talked about over Christmas break. They love acting."

"They're very good at it, too," Ms. Wilson said with a nod. "And that's why it concerned us when they started telling anyone who'd listen that acting is dumb."

"My girls are saying that? But why?"

"I suspect it has to do with the costumes. The school doesn't have money for costumes this year. Instead of canceling the play, we decided that each actor or actress would be responsible for his or her own costume. And to keep things fair, they all have to be homemade."

Jacob was beginning to get the picture. Out of necessity he'd mastered a lot of skills over the past several years. But he knew nothing about sewing. And his daughters were well aware of it. He'd made it into something of a joke so they wouldn't feel as if he was incapable of caring for them.

"You got any suggestions?" Jacob asked, meeting Ms. Wilson's concerned gaze. The bottom line was, he'd do whatever it took to keep his girls happy.

She folded her hands together. "One you may not want to hear, Mr. Ryan. Your daughters need a woman in their lives. From several things the girls have said, their teachers and I believe they're blaming themselves for the fact that there isn't one. I'm not suggesting you rush out and get married, but apparently you aren't even in the habit of bringing your dates home to meet them. They think it's because they're too much trouble.''

Jacob felt sick. All he'd hoped to do was protect his girls from further desertion. He'd had no idea they'd misconstrued things so completely. ''I'll talk to them,'' he said again.

''You need to do more than talk, Mr. Ryan. If you don't have a current woman friend to introduce them to, hire a housekeeper, but I wouldn't put this off.''

''I have a perfectly good housekeeper. Nonnie Moore has been keeping house for fifty years and she's damn good at it. She comes in twice a week like clockwork, and any other time I need her to help out. They have a baby-sitter, too. Laurie's a nice responsible teenager and she loves the girls.''

''They've mentioned Laurie, and I've seen Nonnie a time or two when she's come for the girls. I assumed she was their grandmother. Apparently she doesn't hear as well as she used to.''

''She's seventy-five years old, but she takes excellent care of us.''

''I'm not doubting that, Mr. Ryan. But a seventy-five-year-old woman is hardly companion material for three lively seven-year-olds. And a teenager, however sweet, can't give the guidance of a grown woman. I must tell you, the next step we take here on an official level is the school counselor.''

''Are you threatening me?'' Jacob asked, rising to his full six foot one.

''Absolutely not,'' Ms. Wilson said, not intimidated by Jacob's glare.

''No one's going to take my daughters away from me. You can call in all the officials in the state. Call in the whole damn army if you want but my daughters stay with me. I'm a damn good father, and I'll hire the best lawyer in the country if I have to to prove it.''

Ms. Wilson's thin hand descended on Jacob's arm, giving it a gentle squeeze. ''I wish all fathers were as conscientious, as caring, as you are, Mr. Ryan. The last thing the school wants to do is break up your home. We're only trying to help avoid more serious behavioral problems somewhere down the road. Your daughters are young. They're psyches are still being molded. Now's the time to give them the very best in all possible ways.''

Jacob nodded, covering the principal's hand with his own. ''I'll talk to them,'' he said.

Ms. Wilson sighed as she watched him leave her office. The man was what her older students would call a hunk. His chocolate brown eyes and irresistible grin exuded sex appeal and charm with every breath he took. There must be thousands of women in L.A. who'd be only too happy to set up housekeeping with him, even it meant taking on a set of triplets as impish as the Ryan girls. Jacob Ryan even made *her* heart beat a little faster, and it had been more years than Eleanor could count since that had happened.

She liked Mr. Ryan. She admired and respected him for raising those three girls on his own. But more importantly she was fond of his daughters, and worried about them. It wasn't proper for a school principal to play favorites, but Eleanor knew that, just this once, she was. Still, there was only so much she could do. The rest was up to their father.

CHAPTER TWO

MICHELLE KEPT HER EYE on the little black ball. Her arms ached, her lungs were burning, but her gaze never wavered. The court echoed as the ball smacked against the front wall. Michelle dove, flinging her racket out to her right just in time to see the ball fly over her outstretched arm. Damn! He'd put a back spin on it. She landed with a crash on the wooden floor.

"Nice match, sweetheart. You gave me a run for my money on that last set." James Walker reached out a hand to help his daughter up off the floor.

Michelle grinned ruefully. He was barely even sweating.

"Someone's got to keep you in your place," she said, rising and giving him a quick kiss on the cheek before she gathered her gear. "Meet you out front in twenty minutes?" she asked, water bottle, racket and towel in hand.

He held the door open for her. "Make it fifteen, and I'll buy you a soda."

"You're on."

Michelle turned toward the women's locker room but not before she'd seen the appreciative glance a young woman in the hall had sent her father's way. At forty-eight, James Walker would have been considered quite a catch if he hadn't already been caught thirty years before. Tall and lean, he still had a full head of blond hair that blended well with the few strands of gray that were starting to filter through it. Ever since Michelle could remember he'd attracted attention from the opposite sex, but not once had it crossed Michelle's mind to wonder if he might be interested in following up on some of the more overt glances. After thirty years of marriage, James Walker was still so entranced with his wife it would have been laughable if it weren't so darn sweet.

"HOW WAS YOUR GAME?" Grace Walker asked as her family came in through the back door forty-five minutes later. Gray-haired and plain, she was busy at the counter chopping vegetables for the Mexican feast the three of them shared every Tuesday evening after James wore Michelle out on the racquetball court.

"I would've beat him, but I decided to be nice today," Michelle said, giving her mother a kiss.

Grace's gaze met her husband's, her soft blue eyes alight with humor. "Did you trounce her?"

He smiled, leaning down to kiss his wife before helping himself to the pile of shredded cheese. "It won't be long before she's trouncing *me*," he said, stealing one more lingering kiss from his wife before he left the room.

"Right," Michelle said. "The day I win my first

game with Dad, I'm going to announce it on the air.''
She filled a glass with ice and popped the top on a
can of diet cola.

Then she hoisted herself onto one of the stools at
the breakfast bar and asked, ''So how were things at
the clinic?'' Every Tuesday afternoon, while Michelle
and her father battled it out on the racquetball court,
Dr. Grace Walker donated her time to a free clinic in
a part of L.A. that tourists never saw.

''Busy as usual, but nothing too terrible turned up.
A couple of ear infections, a strep infection and the
usual cases of head lice. All easily remedied.''

''Did Amanda Blake show up for her prenatal
check?''

''Yep. That's three in a row. We just may get that
baby born healthy yet.''

''So you think she's staying clean?''

Grace shrugged her slim shoulders. ''She's either
clean or hiding the evidence miraculously well. The
baby's heartbeat is steady and strong. I think we have
a fighting chance.''

''And afterward?'' Michelle knew her mother
wouldn't be able to deliver the baby and then just
forget it.

''Amanda wants this baby. That's half the battle
won. If she stays clean for the next four months,
we're well on our way to winning the second half.''

Grace finished chopping the onions and lettuce,
popped the tortillas in the oven and stirred the refried
beans. Michelle got up to set the table.

"Any more word from Frank Steele?" Grace asked.

"Nope."

Grace brought the condiments, arranged in a sectioned serving tray, to the table. "How much longer are you going to give him?"

"As long as it takes," Michelle said, putting out napkins.

"Do you think that's wise?"

Michelle stared at her mother. "How can you ask that, Mom? You of all people know I don't have any other choice."

Grace's brow creased with concern and she reached out to smooth Michelle's hair back from her face. "I don't like what this is doing to you, honey. You have no life anymore, no friends."

"I have a life, Mom. I work out at the gym three times a week, I play racquetball every Tuesday, I have a job I love—a job that lets me go places and meet people—I have my crafts, and I have Noby."

"Noby aside, those are just *activities,* honey. They may fill up your time, but they won't fill you up inside. I'm afraid your soul is going to wither, and one day you'll wake up and find out it's gone."

"I have you and Dad."

Grace's lips tightened. "It's not the same, Michelle. You know it's not. You used to have so many friends I couldn't keep track of them. Every time I talked to you, you were running off to help one of them or on your way to a party. You thrive on people, just like I do. Needlework, no matter how beautiful, and jobs, no matter how satisfying, can't take the place of people in your heart.''

"I gave my heart to Brian. As long as there's a chance he's alive, it's not mine to take back.''

"He has only a part of your heart, honey. What about the rest? What happened to Sarah and Jaime? I haven't heard you mention either of them in months.''

"I still talk to Sarah, but with her new job, any free time she has she likes to spend with Roger. It's the same with Jaime. She's on a husband hunt again and inevitably has some guy in tow. I'm always the odd one out. Believe me, I'm happier at home with Noby than feeling like a fifth wheel every time I leave my house. Besides, I don't think they understand about Brian. Ever since he was declared dead they've been after me to start dating again.''

Grace bent to take the tortillas out of the oven. "And maybe you should.''

"What?'' Michelle's shock was evident in her voice.

"You're twenty-eight years old, Michelle. Brian's been missing for more than five years. At some point you're going to have to either get on with your life or die right along with him.''

Michelle paled. "How can you say that? I finally have word on Brian and all of a sudden you want me to give up on him?''

"The word is three years old, honey.''

"But it's still more than I had a month ago.''

"I'm just afraid this is going to drag out forever, Michelle, with a word here and there, just enough to keep you hoping. And then one day you'll realize your whole life has passed you by. You've always wanted a family more than anything else—you'd be a wonderful mother. But it's never going to happen if you don't lay the past to rest and start building a future for yourself."

"You're saying I should just call Frank Steele and tell him thanks but no thanks. That I should forget Brian, forget the vows I made to him, the love we shared, and go find some other man to father my children?" Michelle's voice was clogged with tears.

"I'd never suggest that you forget any of it, sweetheart. I know how much you loved Brian. Your father and I loved him, too. I'm only saying that maybe it's time for you to consider the possibility that Brian isn't coming back."

Michelle looked at her mother. "Would you, Mom? If it was Dad missing, would you give up, ever, if there was one iota of hope?"

Grace held her daughter's gaze for a long second and then turned away. "If you run low on money to pay Frank's fees, let us know. Your father and I will give you whatever you need."

JACOB WAS WAITING, already in his swim trunks, when the girls got home from school. He knew they'd want to take advantage of the unseasonably warm weather with a swim in the ocean.

"What's for a snack?" Allie asked as she led the line coming in through the front door of the beach house. Her long dark hair was falling loose from the ponytail he'd put it in that morning.

"I want peanut butter," Jessie said, following right behind her sister. She was missing a barrette.

"Hi, Daddy," Meggie said, dropping her book bag on the floor as she headed for the refrigerator. She'd braided her hair sometime after he'd left them that morning. There were straggling pieces sticking out all over her head.

"How was school?" Jacob asked, depositing three granola bars on the table. He reached past Meggie to grab the milk, then shut the refrigerator.

"Okay. Billy Martin spilled his juice at lunch and cried. Only babies cry, don't they, Daddy?" Allie said as the three girls slipped into their chairs at the table. He used to have a smoked-glass tabletop. Now he had Formica. It was a breeze to clean and easily replaceable.

"It's not babyish to cry, is it, Daddy?" Jessie asked, waiting while Jacob opened her granola bar for her.

"Babies *do* cry," Meggie said, using her teeth to rip open her snack.

First talk, coming up. Jacob poured three glasses of milk, glad he could start with an easy one. "Of course babies cry. It's their only form of communication. But there are other reasons for crying, too. If you're sad or lonely or hurt you might cry. There are times when it's best to get those feelings out, so they don't bother you anymore. But sometimes people cry just because they don't control their feelings very well, like if they're mad or embarrassed or disappointed. If all goes well you learn to express those emotions differently as you grow up.''

"We're grown-up, Daddy, aren't we, you guys?" Allie looked at her sisters, her mouth full of granola bar.

Jessie and Meggie nodded dutifully. And suddenly Jacob was faced with three sets of solemn brown eyes as the girls waited for his confirmation.

"Well, darlin's, grown-ups work before they play, so I guess that means you have to make your beds *before* you put on your bathing suits. You better hurry up if you want to be outside while it's still high tide.''

Jacob smiled at the three identical little faces scowling up at him. His daughters slid from their chairs and left the room, clearly unamused. He rinsed the milk glasses and wiped the crumbs from the table. And two minutes later he was shaking his head in resignation. The noise coming from the triplets' room was only one level below deafening. They were singing, if you could call it that, the L.A. Lakers Jam Session rap song at the top of their lungs.

THE OCEAN WAS TOO COLD, in spite of the January heat wave, for any real swimming, but the girls managed to get soaked, anyway. They did a fairly good job of soaking their father, too. Jacob finally retreated to sit well out of reach of their splashing. He watched his daughters play for a while, grinning at their happy squeals as they ran from the waves. All three of them wore fluorescent green, one-piece swimsuits; he remembered when he'd bought them. The girls had complained about the ''gross'' color. ''All the better to see you with, my dears,'' he'd growled, and they'd giggled, just like he'd expected them to do. They didn't need to know how serious he'd been about his reason for the blindingly bright suits.

Jacob stretched his legs out in front of him, leaning back on his hands, watching while Allie organized a sand-castle construction crew. Jessie and Meggie played along, apparently content to be her laborers. God, how he loved them.

The muscles in his gut tightened as he watched them play together. How did a man tell his daughters that he wasn't as perfect as they thought he was? That he'd driven his wife away just as he had his parents before her? How did he convince them that their mother loved them, even though she'd left them? Eleanor Wilson had said that the girls thought they were too much trouble, but that wasn't true. Not to him. Never to him. Somehow he had to convince them of that.

Jessie darted over, bobbing up and down in front of him. ''I have to go.''

''Be sure to clean your feet before you go in,'' he said. He kept one eye on Allie and Meggie at the edge of the ocean while he watched Jessie run up the beach to their cottage. She stepped into the small tub of clean water he kept by the door, wiped one foot on the mat beside the tub and raced into the house. Oh, well, the floor could withstand a few wet footprints.

"What's for supper?" Allie asked half an hour later. She plopped down in the sand beside Jacob, playing with the dark hairs on his forearm.

"Macaroni and cheese, but I want to talk to you guys first. Get your sisters for me, please?"

"JESSIE! MEGGIE! DADDY WANTS YOU!" Allie hollered.

Jacob covered his ears. "I could've done that myself," he told Allie, giving her what he hoped was a look of disapproval.

Jessie ran over and sat on Jacob's other side, spraying him with sand and seawater as she leaned her arm against his outspread thigh. "Wadja want?" she asked, grinning at him.

"What?" Meggie asked, bringing up the rear. She sat in front of Jacob, her expression serious.

"I've been thinking, since you guys are so grown-up now and all, that maybe it was time we talked about your mother."

His stomach sank when he intercepted the worried looks that passed between his daughters. Ms. Wilson had been right on the mark. The girls' motherless state was bothering them more than they'd let on to him.

They stared up at him silently, expectantly.

"Your mother is a very beautiful woman," he said,

wondering where on earth he was going to go from there. "You guys take after her."

Jessie smiled. Allie fiddled with the hair on his arm again. Meggie still stared silently. Jacob would've given just about anything to know what they were thinking.

"She loves all of you very much," he said, telling the lie without flinching. He'd grown up without the security of his parents' love. His children weren't going to suffer the same fate.

"Then why doesn't she ever come to see us?" Allie asked, her brows drawn together in a frown.

"She lives and works very far away from here."

"How far?" Meggie asked.

"All the way across the United States. She's a senator's, um, aide, at the White House."

Jessie tapped his leg. "What's an umaide, Daddy?"

Jacob took a deep breath. He should have guessed that the girls wouldn't be satisfied with the vague answers he'd hoped to give them.

"Aide, Jess. It's someone who stays close to a senator and helps him with things so that he can do his job better." At least Jacob hoped Ellen helped Senator Keller with something more than undressing at night.

"What kind of things?"

"Well, Al, things like entertaining prominent people and maybe writing important letters. Stuff like that."

"Can we go visit her sometime?" Meggie's small face was virtually expressionless.

"Maybe sometime. When you get a little older and don't need a baby-sitter, in case she has to go out and meet someone important for dinner or something."

"Weren't we important enough, Daddy? Is that why she left us?" Jessie's big brown eyes were filling with tears. Jacob felt sick, and he floundered for words as he hugged Jessie against his side. Her wet, sand-covered suit grated against his skin, but he couldn't have cared less about the discomfort.

"You guys are the most important people I know," he said, pinning each of them with his "I mean it" stare. "Your mommy didn't leave you. She left *me*. I wanted her to be someone she wasn't. Senator Keller liked her just as she was."

"Didn't you like her at all?"

Jacob pulled Meggie onto his lap and hugged Allie to his other side. "Of course I liked her, honey. I chose her to be your mommy, didn't I? But I wanted a different kind of wife than she wanted to be, and I guess I'm just a little too hardheaded sometimes. I wouldn't give in, and as much as she tried, your mommy couldn't be happy with me," Jacob wondered if he was making any sense.

"You're not hard in the head, Daddy. You're the best daddy in the whole world," Meggie said, laying her cheek against him. Her long black hair fell around her shoulders, tickling his chest.

"And I love being your daddy more than anything

in the world, Meg, but your mommy and I just wanted to live our lives in two different ways. My way made her unhappy. You wouldn't want her to be unhappy would you?''

All three girls shook their heads. ''Well, I didn't want to make her unhappy, either. So when Senator Keller asked her to go to Washington and she wanted to go, I told her it was okay with me.''

''Did you miss her when she was gone?'' Jessie's question was soft, hesitant.

''For a while, but I had you guys to keep me company, and we've done all right, don't you think?''

Meggie sat up. ''Did you love Mommy a lot?''

''Not like I love you three,'' he said, though in his heart he didn't know how he could have loved a woman more than he had Ellen McCormick.

''Maybe we were bad, Daddy. Maybe we cried too much and she just didn't want to tell you,'' Allie said, her little face dejected.

''And we probably didn't pick up our toys, either,'' Jessie added.

''Yeah, and I'll bet we spilled stuff a lot, 'cause we were only babies then,'' Meggie said.

Impotent rage swept through Jacob as he realized that his words were falling on three sets of deaf ears. The thoughts the girls were expressing were obviously not new to them. And worse, in spite of all he'd said, they still believed them. So how the hell did he convince them of anything different?

''You guys were great babies. You loved to eat.

And you slept a lot, too, giving us lots of time to keep up with stuff. Your mother used to love to take you out and show you off.'' The showing-off part was true. If only Ellen hadn't been so overwhelmed by getting three babies ready to go and in their car seats all at once.

''Where did she take us, Daddy?''

''To the mall. She liked to shop.''

''Then why didn't she get a job at the mall and take us there every day? Wouldn't that have made her happy?''

I'm blowing it. ''Because she couldn't work all the time, and when she came home to me she would've been unhappy. If we'd been madly in love like mommies and daddies should be, then she wouldn't have left even if we had a whole houseful of kids.

''Don't you love your girlfriends enough, either, Daddy? Is that why you never bring them home?''

''It's because of us, Jess,'' Meggie said, sounding far more adult than a seven-year-old had any business sounding. ''Remember Jennie? She didn't want to be our mommy, either.''

''That's not true!'' Jacob said, knowing he was failing miserably, but still finding himself without divine inspiration. The girls had taken his breakup with Jennie, his former on-air partner, hard at the time— she'd been the first woman he'd dated after Ellen left—but he'd had no idea they still remembered her.

''Yes, it is true, Daddy. Katie Walters's mother

says we're a handful. She said if she'd had three to take care of all at once, she'd probably have left, too. We heard her tell that to Bobbie's mommy.''

Jacob bit back the curse that sprang to his lips. Just wait until he saw Katie Walters's mother.

''Katie Walters's mother doesn't know what she's talking about,'' he said. ''Jennie just wasn't in love with me. That's why we quit seeing each other. Believe me, it had nothing to do with you guys. Doing for three is just as easy as doing for one. It takes a little longer, that's all.''

Allie stood up suddenly. ''Can we eat now, Daddy? My stomach's shocking it's so hungry.''

Jacob knew they weren't finished, not by a long shot, but it was probably best to do these things in small doses. He figured the girls had had enough for now; he knew he had.

''Last one to the shower has to load the dishwasher,'' he called, jumping up to race his daughters to the house.

Meggie was the first one to reach the outside shower head he'd installed right after the girls had learned to walk. It had only taken one houseful of sand to convince him he'd either have to rig up some outdoor plumbing or move. Meggie stood under the stinging spray, offering only a token argument when her sisters crowded in on her. Jacob knew she had to have an awful lot on her mind to put up with that without a fuss. He was in for a long haul.

ALLIE ENDED UP having to load the dishwasher, but only after Jacob declared that he didn't count since he'd made the dinner. At Jacob's urging, Jessie and Meggie helped their sister by clearing the table and rinsing the dishes. Jacob had the job of storing the leftovers.

"What's happening with that play—*Cinderella*—everyone was so excited about after Christmas?" he asked as he opened the refrigerator.

Jessie dropped a fork and looked at Allie. Meggie stopped spraying and looked at Allie. Allie stood with a dripping plate in her hand.

Jacob found a place for the container of macaroni. "Did they call it off or something?"

"Uh-uh," Allie finally found her voice. "The trying-out part is next week."

"So who's trying out for what?"

Jessie and Meggie resumed their duties, glancing furtively at Allie.

"We're not sure yet," Allie said. Her voice was an octave higher than usual.

"We don't have costumes, Daddy," Jessie blurted, then dropped a knife covered with butter in the middle of the floor. Jacob watched as she took a wadded up napkin from the table and smeared the butter over the linoleum. Thank God for washable floors.

"If you get a part, we'll get you a costume," he told her.

"They have to be homemade, Daddy," Meggie said. She and Allie exchanged glances.

"Then we'll make them."

"They have to be *sewn*," Allie said.

"We'll handle it, girls. Have I ever let you down before?"

Three heads shook vigorously.

"Now, what parts are you trying out for?"

"Cinderella," Jessie said.

"And her two evil stepsisters," Allie and Meggie chorused.

LIGHTS-OUT WAS at eight o'clock sharp. It used to be at seven o'clock, but Daddy had added an hour after they turned seven. They were almost all grown-up now, and everybody knew that staying up late was part of the deal. Allie snuggled under her covers and waited for Daddy to kiss Jessie and Meggie goodnight. He'd already done her. He would turn off their light on his way out the door, and then he'd tell them that he was right down the hall if they needed him. She never had figured what he thought they might need him for when they were sleeping, but it was kinda good hearing him say it, anyway.

"I'm right down the hall if you need me." The words came just as Allie had known they would.

"'Night, Daddy," she said.

"'Night, Daddy." Jessie was always next.

"'Night, Daddy," Meggie said last, just like every night.

Allie waited until she heard Daddy's shower start

and then climbed out of bed. She tapped Jessie on the shoulder.

"What?" Jessie's eyes looked funny, like she'd been asleep already.

"Come on." Allie tugged Jessie up and pulled her over to Meggie's bed. They always had their meetings on Meggie's bed.

Meggie sat up and made room for them.

"Daddy seemed pretty sad today," Allie said.

"Probably because he was talking about Mommy," Meggie said, picking at the foot of her sleeper.

"Do you think he's mad at us for making Mommy leave him?" Jessie asked, her lips all shaky like she was gonna cry. Allie exchanged a glance with Meggie. Daddy would get them for sure if they made Jessie cry.

"Shh." Allie scooted over to give Jessie a hug. "You don't want Daddy to hear us. I don't think he's mad at us, but we better really be gooder just in case." Allie looked at both of her sisters, making sure they were paying close attention to her. "We don't want to make him mad enough to leave us, too."

Meggie and Jessie nodded. Allie patted Jessie's hair. "And if we're going to have to do the trying outs, then we're just gonna have to try not to be too good."

Jessie frowned. "But, Allie, it's okay now. Daddy said he'd make—"

"Daddy can't sew, Jess, you know that." Meghan frowned at her sister.

"But he said—"

"Jessie—" Allie drew out the name like she'd heard Daddy do "—it's Daddy's job to say those things."

Meggie nodded and after a couple of seconds Jessie did, too. But she didn't seem convinced.

Allie hoped her sister wasn't going to screw things up. She didn't even want to think about making more trouble for Daddy. She just wanted Daddy to be happy living with her and Jessie and Meggie. She lay back down in her own bed, wishing she hadn't messed up Daddy's tuck-in. She wondered if Daddy knew that she'd been wishing for a mother. Feeling guilty and ashamed, she looked across at her sisters. She was afraid her wish might ruin everything.

JACOB STOOD under the shower until the water turned cold, but it did nothing to ease his worries. Ms. Wilson's suggestion that he find a woman for the girls sounded valid, but he knew in his heart that a woman wasn't the answer to his problems. He'd already tried that route shortly after Ellen had left him. And all he'd managed to accomplish was to confuse his daughters more. Maybe he'd wanted it too badly. Maybe he'd tried too hard. Or maybe he'd just expected more than anyone could give him. All he knew for sure was that he wasn't going to expose his girls to the possibility of further rejection. Twice in seven years was already too much, or they wouldn't be having the problems they were having now.

Walking into his bedroom, he rummaged in his drawer for a pair of boxer shorts and pulled them on, thinking back to the years of his own growing up. He still had scars from those years, albeit invisible ones. His real mother, a teen-pregnancy statistic, had given him up at birth. And after his adoptive parents divorced and subsequently remarried, they'd each had children of their own. They'd passed him back and forth between them as if they couldn't get rid of him fast enough.

Wandering out to the deck off his bedroom, he looked out at a light blinking on the ocean, remembering. The time he'd asked for a first-baseman's mitt had been one of the worst. He'd been so excited when his Little League coach had given him, a fifth grader, the honor of playing first base. Everyone knew a first baseman was one of the most important players on the defensive team. But when he'd asked his mom for a mitt, she'd told him to wait for his father to get it the following week. And when he'd been with his father, he'd been told that his mother would have to handle that one. As it turned out, the coach had lent him a mitt. He'd only been eleven at the time, but Jacob had felt the humiliation clear to his bones. He'd been barely able to make himself go to practice once his coach knew he wasn't worth enough to warrant a stupid baseball mitt.

He'd learned the lesson over and over again

through his teenage years. There were celebrations for his half siblings' birthdays, while his were either forgotten or acknowledged with a card. There were school trips he couldn't take because his parents' "real" children always came first. By the time his high school graduation arrived, it hardly hurt at all when the seats reserved for his family were empty.

Jacob left the deck, walking through his silent house to the kitchen. He reached into the cupboard above the refrigerator, pulled out his bottle of scotch and poured himself a shot. Stopping only long enough to wipe the butter from the floor, he carried the glass back to his bedroom, looking in on the girls as he passed their open door. They hadn't been asleep long. Jessie's bear was still tucked in beside her and Meggie's covers were on top where they belonged. Satisfied that everything was as it should be, he returned to the deck and stretched out on the padded lounge. His kids were not going to grow up the way he had. They might have only one parent, but at least that parent loved them to distraction.

He took a sip of the scotch, savoring the taste, thinking suddenly of Michelle. Now there was a woman worth having. She was loyal to the core. It was too bad that the man she honored with her loyalty wasn't around to know what a lucky son of a bitch he was. If Jacob could ever find a woman who loved him the way Michelle loved Brian Colby…

Jacob stood up and tossed the rest of the scotch over the deck rail. He was getting maudlin. He had all the women he could handle, in miniature, sleeping right down the hall from him. They needed him and he needed to be there for them. He'd long since given up wanting anything more.

CHAPTER THREE

"I'M GOING TO BE a little late getting home today, but I'll make it up to you, Noby, I promise." Michelle gazed into the blue eyes across the table from her and refused to allow their unblinking stare to make her feel guilty. She took a sip of diet cola, her version of morning coffee, and picked up the Wednesday-morning newspaper. It was a rare treat for her to still be at home when the paper was delivered.

She read one headline before the newspaper was smashed to her lap. Those eyes were a lot closer—and demanding an explanation.

"Jacob and I are doing a remote broadcast at the new mall off La Cienega. I'm meeting him at the station at eight, we're driving over together, and we'll be done by two. That should put me home before four—in plenty of time for dinner."

Michelle took another sip of cola. The blue-eyed stare was relentless.

"You're not going to let me read my paper, are you?"

Still nothing but that silent stare.

"You're spoiled rotten." Michelle leaned over to

plant a kiss between Noby's knowing blue eyes.
"And I don't know what I'd do without you."

"AND THERE YOU HAVE IT, folks. Jacob Ryan and
Michelle Colby are secretly involved in a wildly passionate relationship, which is open now for your
viewing pleasure," Jacob muttered under his breath.

"Jacob." Michelle punched him playfully in the
shoulder as they cleared the papers off their table in
the main entrance of the mall. "It wasn't that bad."

Jacob unplugged their microphones, handing them
to one of the KOLR technicians. "Admit it, Michelle.
You just like having all those people drooling over
me and envying you for having me."

"In your dreams, Ryan."

"Yeah, there, too," Jacob mumbled, reminded all
too clearly of the dreams he'd had Monday night.
Erotic dreams he could deal with. They came with the
territory of the single man. But erotic dreams featur-
ing Michelle Colby were something else entirely. As
he'd told himself in no uncertain terms early Tuesday
morning.

They finished clearing up, stopping several times
to sign autographs, and in a matter of minutes were
saying goodbye to the technicians who would drive
the KOLR van back to the station. Jacob had to admit,
if only to himself, that the broadcast had come off
better than he'd hoped. Not because he'd had any
doubts about his or Michelle's performance, but be-

cause for the past two days he'd had doubts about himself.

After all these years of working with Michelle, he was suddenly finding her more attractive than filet mignon. It made no sense. She certainly wasn't encouraging him. Hell, she wore her wide gold wedding band like a suit of armor. The woman was so tied up with a memory she probably wouldn't know what to do with a flesh-and-blood man if she had one. Or at least that was what he told himself.

And this morning it seemed to have worked. His libido was practically asleep.

"Would you mind if we made a quick stop before heading back?" he asked Michelle as she waved off the van. "I need to pick up something for the girls."

"I'm not in a hurry," Michelle replied, as easygoing as ever. Her blond hair swung over her shoulders as she turned toward the mall. In Jacob's dream it had been spread over his pillow.

He made a beeline for the department store where he did all his shopping for the girls. They'd had a minor crisis this morning, and he'd promised Allie he'd take care of it today.

"What are we looking for?" Michelle asked as she followed him into the store. He seemed to know exactly where he was going.

"Wednesday panties."

She looked to see if he was pulling her leg. "Pardon me?" she asked, trying to keep the laughter out of her voice when she saw he was serious.

"Allie couldn't find any Wednesday panties this morning. I don't know what happened to them, but they weren't in her drawer or in the laundry. I had a hell of a time getting her to go to school."

She could see the girls' department straight ahead.

"Uh, Jacob? What are Wednesday panties?"

"They're underwear with Wednesday written on them. There's a pair for every day of the week. Allie's obsessive about wearing the right pair on the right day."

"Oh." If anyone had ever told Michelle that she would be following Jacob Ryan into the girls' department to buy underwear, she'd have laughed them out of the city. "So how'd you get her to go to school?"

"Convinced her that if she wore both Tuesday and Thursday they'd average out to Wednesday."

Michelle burst out laughing and Jacob sent her an understanding grin. "I know. It's not the smartest thing I've ever come up with, but it was the best I could do on short notice."

He stopped in front of a rack of packages of pastel-colored underwear. Michelle watched as Jacob chose two packages of size-seven panties and four size-six ones. He obviously didn't realize that each package had an entire week's worth. Michelle smiled.

"Jacob? That's forty-two pairs of underwear," she said, trying to be gentle about educating him.

He just nodded as he moved through the department carrying all six packages. "I only go through each crisis once if I can help it. I'm going to put an extra day per person away in *my* underwear drawer.''

Shying from thoughts of Jacob's underwear, Michelle wasn't sure which touched her the most, the ease with which he moved among the racks of miniature feminine apparel or the competent way he handled being a single father to three little girls. She did know that she envied him more than she'd have thought possible.

"Look at these." Jacob stopped by a rack of child-size Lakers jerseys. "They're great! The girls'll love them. Help me find two six-X's and a seven," he said, riffling through the shirts on the rack.

Michelle helped him find the sizes he needed and then followed along as he searched for three pairs of jeans to match. She was seeing a whole new side to Jacob Ryan. A side she liked far too much.

He took his choices to the register and handed over his credit card. "How are you today, Mr. Ryan?" the middle-aged clerk asked.

"Just fine, Joan, and you? Did you enjoy your trip to Florida?"

The clerk kept up her end of the conversation as she completed the transaction, but Michelle couldn't help but notice the glances she kept sending her. The glances weren't surprising. After all, she was used to speculation about Jacob and her. What shocked her was how disappointed she felt that there was absolutely nothing for the clerk to speculate about. Mi-

chelle had no business wishing she and Jacob *were*
an item, and buying clothes for *their* children.

"You know, Jacob, if you end up with all this
when you're just going after a single pair of underwear, I'd hate to see what happens when you shop
for school clothes," Michelle said as they headed to
his vehicle.

Unlocking Michelle's door before storing his package in the back of the Explorer, Jacob said, "A way
to a woman's heart is through the clothes department." At least he hoped the new clothes would help.

"Where'd you ever hear something like that?"
Michelle asked, grinning at him as he climbed behind
the wheel.

"God knows Ellen sure bought enough of them.
And I can remember my half sister's pleasure every
time my mother surprised her with something new."
He turned his key in the ignition. He'd always told
himself it was because girls loved getting new clothes
that none of those surprises had ever been for him.

"So what have you done to upset your daughters?"

Jacob shot her a startled glance. "Why would you
think I've upset them?" he asked, turning out into the
city traffic. Was he that transparent? Or worse, did
she know him that well?

"Why else would you think you need to buy your
way into their hearts?"

He could feel her looking at him. Really looking
at him. And he found himself wanting to tell her.
What could it hurt? She'd been a good buddy over

the years. And she was so tenaciously married to her memory she was no threat to *him.*

"I think my place in their hearts is pretty much a given. Though I'm not so sure it'll still be that way a few years from now when they want to start wearing crap on their faces and talk on the phone all the time." He paused, wondering if he should stop right there. He couldn't remember the last time he'd confided in anyone—not about something that mattered.

"So you just like to spoil them?" she asked.

Jacob shook his head, well aware of the danger of overindulgence. "As a general rule they think I'm stingy with the goodies. But right now I don't want them feeling like they're missing out on anything." He turned onto La Cienega Boulevard, heading back toward the station. "I guess the jeans were a little overboard, considering that they already have enough clothes to get us through two weeks without doing laundry. I just wanted to do something to make them feel special."

Michelle was surprised by the concerned tone in Jacob's voice. He always seemed so invulnerable. She'd pretty much figured that if life ever did dare throw him problems, he'd just tackle them—or hire someone else to do it for him. But he'd been unusually preoccupied on Monday, too.

"Are you having some difficulties with the girls?" she asked, feeling rather tentative. Jacob wasn't the type one usually offered a shoulder to.

He shifted in his seat. "I don't know that I'd call

it that exactly, but there seems to be a misunderstanding or two we need to clear up. The girls' principal called me last Friday. It seems there've been a few minor problems at school which they're attributing to a lack of feminine guidance in the girls' lives. Ms. Wilson seems to think that my daughters are blaming themselves for my divorce and subsequent single state.''

''Did you talk with them about it?''

''Yeah. I talked. But I'm not sure they heard. In fact, I'm pretty sure they didn't.''

''Did their principal have any suggestions?''

''Not really.''

''She referred you to someone else?''

''No, though she did mention calling in a school counselor if things don't get better.''

''So how does she expect that to happen?''

''The most obvious answer would be for me to marry again.''

''Oh.'' Michelle didn't know why she should feel so deflated. ''I guess that wouldn't be too difficult. Considering the number of women you've dated in the past year, you should have at least a hundred to choose from.''

Jacob glanced at her oddly, and Michelle realized how she must have sounded. After all, why should she care if Jacob dated every eligible woman in the state of California? ''I haven't dated a hundred women in the past *five* years, Colby.''

''Fifty then.''

"Thirty. Maybe. And since when have you been counting?"

"I'm not counting obviously." Michelle flushed with embarrassment, glad that at least half his attention was on the traffic. "So what'd you tell the principal?"

"That I'd talk to the girls."

"Which didn't work."

"Not yet, but it will. Like everything else, these things take time."

"I'd be glad to help out if they need anything meanwhile, Jacob. You know that, don't you?"

Jacob glanced over at her, his sexy brown eyes piercing. "What, you wanna marry me?"

For a split second the idea held way too much appeal, leaving her strangely depressed as she replied, "I'm already married."

"Hey, I was only teasing, Colby. Lighten up."

"I know you were. But I meant it about your girls, Jacob. I've only met them a couple of times, but they seem like great kids. I could spend some time with them. You know, do girl things. It'd be fun."

"Thanks, but that won't be necessary." Jacob answered so quickly Michelle knew he hadn't even considered her suggestion. "We've managed on our own thus far and we'll get through this, too. All they need is a little extra love and attention, and their insecurities will vanish just like their wet diapers did."

"Hey, I never meant to imply that you won't do just fine. It's obvious you have things well under control. But until Brian's home I've got time on my hands, and I can see where three little girls might benefit from having a woman around now and then. There are bound to be things that are understood differently from a female point of view. You know, like the importance of feeling pretty and falling in love with teddy bears.''

"Just because I'll never feel some things doesn't mean I can't recognize or understand them. I'm not the first single father on earth, Michelle, and I damn sure won't be the last. Others have coped. So can I. But thanks for the offer. I appreciate it.''

Michelle knew a brick wall when she smacked into one. After all, she knew Jacob. What she hadn't realized until right then was just how much she would've enjoyed doing something for his children. For a brief moment there, when she'd heard herself offering to take Jacob's daughters under her wing, she'd felt almost excited. She had a gaping hole inside her that could use some filling up. And Jacob's children were safe. They belonged to him, not to her. She couldn't lose what she didn't have.

ELEANOR WILSON'S JOB was her life. She felt more at home in the school building than she did in her little two-bedroom bungalow a couple of blocks away. And as for her students, she loved them all, though admittedly some more than others. But she'd never felt as deep a fondness for any of them as she felt for the Ryan girls. Being triplets was enough of an oddity to make them stand out. Being beautiful, precious little girls made them easy to like. But being motherless bought them their special place in Eleanor's heart.

Which was the only reason she made it a point to attend the auditions for the spring play. Normally Eleanor avoided these auditions like the plague. In most cities children grew up encouraged to be doctors or lawyers. Not in L.A. Eleanor hated what the lure of Hollywood did to her students, but mostly she hated what it did to their parents. It seemed that for some, no sacrifice was too great if it meant their child might one day be on TV or in the movies. Several students at Lomen Elementary had agents already and missed school to go on auditions. And the parents of those who were just starting out weren't necessarily above attempting to bribe the school principal to get their children stage experience.

To be fair, some of the children were good. It wasn't that uncommon for Eleanor to see one of her students on a television commercial while she sat at home in the evenings. She'd watch with a twinge of pride while they tried to sell her cereal or tennis shoes or clothes freshener. Some of them were even convincing. But never had she seen three children just plain love acting the way Allie, Meggie and Jessie did. She wanted them in the school play.

She sneaked into the back of the auditorium and sat in the last row, not wanting to draw attention to herself. Slipping off her half-inch pumps, she swore to herself she'd just be an observer. She wasn't going to play favorites. She had faith that the triplets would win their parts all by themselves.

She watched myriad Prince Charmings amble onto the stage, some of them shy and quiet, some of them shouting lines that should have been heartfelt. But there were a couple of boys who were perfect for the part. She was glad she wasn't the one who had to decide between them.

And then it was time to look for Cinderella's two evil stepsisters. The first pair of girls out on the stage did nothing but giggle. The next two couldn't read all their lines. Two more little girls came out and read the lines in a monotone. Eleanor couldn't find anything wrong with the next pair, except that they just weren't right for the parts. And then Allie and Meggie Ryan came onstage. Eleanor felt as stiff as the starch in her collar as she waited for them to begin. So much rested on the outcome of this afternoon. Jacob Ryan would be forced to provide his daughters with a little female companionship if they got the parts. She'd seen the panic flare in his eyes when she'd mentioned costumes. He might have mastered things a lot of men never tackle, but she'd bet ten years of her life that he couldn't sew.

Allie stumbled over her first line. Ms. Thomas, this year's casting director, had to help her with the word "and." Eleanor's brow creased. For a second Allie seemed more interested in the stage lights than the play, but then she started to read again. The word "sister" came out without a hitch, yet she couldn't sound out "but." Eleanor slipped her feet back into her shoes. Allie continued, getting caught up in her part for a line or two. Then, as if remembering something, she faltered briefly. When she began again, she imposed enough sugar on an evil passage to raise the casting director's eyebrows. Meggie giggled throughout the audition, a forced unnatural sound. Eleanor stood up.

Jessie Ryan was onstage, a potential Cinderella, by the time Eleanor made it backstage. She watched Jessie trip over her feet, pick a fight with her prince and lose her place in her script. Ms. Thomas had to tell Jessie to speak up at least twice, and Eleanor was frustrated enough to cry.

The auditions were finally completed; as the children were leaving, Ms. Thomas reminded them that she'd be making her choices within the week. Eleanor couldn't stand still another minute. She grabbed Jessie as the little girl walked past, then rounded up Allie and Meggie. One look at their principal, and their guilt was written all over their young faces. They stood in a line before her, shoulders slumped.

"Okay, gang. Who wants to tell me what's going on?"

Meggie and Jessie looked toward Allie, whose face wore her determination like a cloak. "We just did our trying outs, Ms. Wilson," Allie said innocently enough. But her lips were so tightly pursed her chin was solid dimples.

Eleanor looked from one pair of big brown eyes to the next and almost gave in. Blowing the auditions meant a lot to them. But they were wrong if they thought that was going to solve their problems.

She pinned Jessie with her sternest stare, knowing that the affectionate little girl would be the one most likely to cave in. Jessie's lips started to tremble and she burst into tears. But she honored whatever pact she'd made with her sisters.

"Meggie?" Eleanor said, going for the other sibling who wasn't quite as forceful as their leader.

Meggie stared back solemnly, doing a perfect imitation of a deaf mute.

Eleanor's heart ached as she faced the threesome, but she reminded herself, not for the first time, that sometimes tough love was the only answer.

"Girls," she said in a no-nonsense tone, "I know what you're doing here. And I think I have pretty good idea why. But do you really think your daddy will be happy to hear that you didn't get picked for the play?"

"He won't be mad at us," Allie said, looking at her sisters.

"He will be when he realizes that you blew the auditions on purpose."

Three horrified gazes locked onto Eleanor's face. "Please don't tell him, Ms. Wilson," Allie begged, confirming Eleanor's suspicions. "Daddy's got troubles right now. Please don't make him worried. We'll be good, we promise. Won't we, you guys?'' Allie looked at her siblings.

Meggie and Jessie both nodded, Jessie's eyes flooding with tears again. Meggie studied her tennis shoes.

Eleanor wanted to hug all three of them. ''Do you promise me you'll always try your best at whatever you do from now on?'' she asked, keeping her tone properly firm.

''Yes, ma'am,'' Allie answered, nodding vigorously.

Eleanor looked at the most independent one of the trio. ''Meghan?''

''Yes, ma'am.''

''I promise, too, Ms. Wilson,'' Jessie said in a wobbly little voice, wiping her tears away with the back of her hand.

Before she could give in to the temptation to pull them all into her arms, Eleanor saw an older woman enter the back of the auditorium. Wearing a flowered dress that hung halfway down her calves and black low-heeled shoes, Nonnie Moore made her way slowly toward the girls. Ryan's housekeeper was favoring her left hip more than she had the last time Eleanor had seen her.

The triplets danced around Nonnie, eager to be gone, and Eleanor watched uneasily as the elderly woman led them away. All three were talking at once while Mrs. Moore nodded occasionally. Eleanor didn't doubt that the grandmotherly woman loved the girls. How could she not? But she suspected that the housekeeper didn't hear even a third of what the triplets were telling her. Which may have been why they weren't telling her anything important.

Eleanor went in search of Barbara Thomas.

"PICK YOU UP at seven?" Jacob asked Michelle the following Wednesday as they cleared off their workstation after the show.

"What?" Did Jacob have her confused with his date of the week?

"Childfair America's tonight." He'd stopped shuffling papers and was looking at her rather oddly.

"Oh. Right. I knew that," Michelle said. "Seven's fine." She'd been the one to suggest that she and Jacob emcee the charity gala that was to benefit the fight against child abuse in Los Angeles.

"See you then," Jacob said, and with one last look in her direction, left the studio.

"Yeah, see you," Michelle said to the empty room. Why was she becoming so obsessed about Jacob Ryan these days? So he had a body to die for. He'd had it all the years she'd known him and it had never bothered her before. One trip to the girls' department with him didn't change things. She was still very much married, very much in love with her husband. And Jacob was still the world's worst womanizer. She needed to get a grip. Of course a little sleep might not hurt, either. If she wasn't careful she was going to drive herself right back into the emotional mess she'd been in when Brian first disappeared.

THE RED LIGHT on her answering machine was blinking when, with Noby in her arms, she walked into her den an hour later. With trembling fingers, she reached out to activate the machine.

"You know it's just Mom," she warned the cat.

"Frank Steele here, Mrs. Colby." There was a pause, as if the detective was waiting to see if Michelle was going to pick up the phone.

"I'm on my way to a village in Yemen where your husband lived for almost a year about three years ago. No one's saying yet why he was there or, for that matter, why he left. I'll be in touch."

Noby's ears flicked when the machine clicked off, as if the sound were offensive to her. But the cat could just as easily have been reacting to the tears that were soaking her fur.

JACOB'S MIND was on his girls as he drove to Michelle's that evening. They'd auditioned for *Cinderella* two days before and had been suspiciously quiet ever since—except to tell him that they didn't get the parts. They'd obviously forgotten the flyer they'd brought home the Friday before the auditions. Not only had it listed their audition times, it had also stated it would be at least Thursday before any definite decisions were posted.

They were up to something. And Jacob was having a hell of time trying to stay two steps ahead of them. Damn Eleanor Wilson and her suspicions. She had Jacob second-guessing every move he made. If she'd just left him alone Jacob would simply have asked Allie what was up. He and the girls had always kept everything out in the open. At least *he* had. And until recently he'd thought they had, too. Now he had to try to be a mind reader.

Shelving his worries for the moment, he pulled into Michelle's driveway and honked, just as he always did when he picked her up for their occasional evening functions. Equally predictably he looked around at the run-down condition of her neighborhood, wondering why she didn't move. It couldn't be a matter of money. KOLR showed ample appreciation to both of them.

Curious when she didn't come out, Jacob turned off the ignition and headed to her front door. He'd never been any farther than her driveway and was a little startled when he saw her doormat. Printed on it in large letters was "The Colbys." And beneath that was "Brian and Michelle." The mat was as faded and frayed as the rest of the neighborhood.

Jacob knocked and then, when there was no answer, knocked again. He was getting concerned. This wasn't like Michelle. Wasn't she home? He was just about to pound on her door for a third time when he heard the lock slide open. He waited for her to open the door, ready to tease her about spending hours primping for him. The words never got past his lips. Michelle was a wreck.

CHAPTER FOUR

STUNNED, JACOB STARED at Michelle's tear-ravaged face. He was going to kill whoever had done this to her.

"I'm s-sorry. Come in," she said, stepping back to let him by her.

Jacob strode in and grasped her arms. "What happened? Do I need to call a doctor?" he asked, looking her over from head to foot.

Michelle attempted to smile as she shook her head, but the gesture was too weak to do anything except concern Jacob more. "I'm okay. Really. I just need a couple of extra minutes." Jacob might have believed her if her voice hadn't cracked on the last word, and if she hadn't still been wearing the jeans and shirt she'd had on at the station that morning. She was the one who'd insisted they dress to the nines for this evening. It had taken her several days of fresh doughnuts to talk him into pulling out his tuxedo for the occasion.

She turned away with an embarrassed toss of her head.

"What happened, Michelle?" he asked, following her into the living room. She had to turn on a light so they could see, and Jacob wondered if she'd been sitting there in the dark.

"Nothing, really. I had a phone call…" Her words trailed off. "Everything's fine. It wasn't bad news or anything. Please, have a seat. I'll be ready in a minute."

Jacob seriously doubted that.

He reached out to her again, grabbing her hand when she would have walked away from him.

"Michelle. It's okay. So we'll be a little late. Our part of the show doesn't start until after dinner, anyway. So what was this phone call?"

She looked down at their interlocked hands, up at him and then down again. He'd never seen her anything but calm and unruffled before, and the misery he glimpsed in her eyes unnerved him.

"Come on. I don't do too badly when the girls need a shoulder to cry on. Why don't you give me a try?"

Tears sprang to her eyes, but she started to smile. "You're not supposed to be this nice, Ryan. Where's your sarcastic wit when I need it?"

He reached out a thumb to wipe the tears from her cheeks. "I guess these knocked it clear out of me. What caused them?"

She looked at him for a long moment and then sat on the edge of the couch. A fluffy white cat slipped out from behind a chair and jumped into her lap. Michelle stroked it tenderly. "About a year ago I hired a private detective to find Brian."

"But I thought the government was trying to find him."

She took a deep breath. Her frustration ran so deep he could feel it across the small room. "The government didn't want to spend any more money or waste any more time looking for him. But he's never been found, Jacob. Five years ago he ordered room service, somebody ate it, and that's the last anybody's ever seen or heard of him. He's not dead. I know he's not."

Jacob wasn't so sure, but what did he know? "So you hired a detective."

She nodded, still stroking the cat. "He called a couple of weeks ago to say he'd finally found someone who might know where Brian had been taken five years ago."

"Taken? Does that mean he knows for sure that your husband was abducted?"

"No. Until today nothing was for sure."

Jacob's gut knotted. Was Brian Colby dead, after all? Was that what she was about to tell him?

"Until today?"

"There was a message from Frank Steele, the detective, when I got home from work this morning. He's on his way to a village where Brian lived for at least a year."

"Does he suspect Brian might still be there?"

Her lips started to tremble again as she shook her head. "Not for the last three years. I know the news isn't very hopeful, but don't you see?" Her eyes pleaded with Jacob to understand. "It's the first real news I've had about him since he disappeared. Now I know that he wasn't just robbed and murdered like the government said. For some reason he was living in this village for at least a year. Two years after his disappearance he was alive. I've been hoping for so long, Jacob. And when I heard from Frank today it was like touching Brian. For the first time in five years I touched him." Her last words were barely audible through her tears.

Jacob couldn't stand to see her so torn up. But he didn't know how to help her. She was holding on to hope on the basis of three-year-old information. It seemed to him that her life was slipping away while she waited around for a man who could very well never be coming back to her. She was too beautiful, too sweet, too giving and funny to waste her life loving only a memory. And yet who was he to tell her that?

He watched her bowed head for as long as he could stand it, and then he pulled her to her feet.

"Come here," he said, tugging her awkwardly toward him.

She came willingly, almost innocently, like a child seeking comfort, burrowing her face against his neck, wrapping her arms around him. Her tears stopped almost instantly, but still he held her. He kept thinking of her sitting on her couch, in the dark all alone, and he couldn't let her go.

And as the minutes passed, as the tempest inside

her calmed and she softened against him, it came to Jacob why he'd never held her before. There was no running from it, no more denying the hard truth. She was his partner. She was his buddy. But he wanted her. He wanted another man's wife.

"AND NOW, LADIES and gentlemen, I want to introduce two of L.A.'s favorites. They've appeared at countless charity functions over the years, giving their time generously to help build Los Angeles into the kind of city we all want it to be. Best known for their witty repartee that gets us all going in the morning, one of L.A.'s most beloved couples—except they claim they aren't one—Michelle Colby and Jacob Ryan."

Jacob ushered Michelle up onto the podium to the accompaniment of thundering applause, his hand burning where it touched her back. It had taken her an amazingly short time to change from the distraught woman who'd met him at the door to the elegant, self-assured woman who now walked beside him. Some fresh makeup, a few rhinestones and a backless black evening gown, and she was once again the buddy he'd always known. Or so he kept telling himself.

When he looked closely, though, he could see her tension. Her smile was forced, her bare shoulders a little too stiff.

"I think I just split the seat of my pants coming up the steps," he whispered as the applause died down. "And damned if I'm not wearing red polka-dot boxers."

Michelle glanced at him, humor replacing the strain in her eyes as she stepped up to the microphone. No one looking at her would have any idea of the heartache she was hiding.

"Good evening, ladies and gentlemen." Her husky voice flowed clear and easy. "I'm Jacob Ryan—"

"No, *I* want to be Jacob tonight," Jacob interrupted before she could falter at her mistake. "There are a lot of beautiful women here."

Laughter filled the ballroom. Michelle joined in and Jacob knew she was going to be okay.

"Yeah, on second thought, I'd probably be crushed if I had to carry your ego around," she said. "Though I wouldn't mind the paycheck."

The audience laughed again.

Jacob leaned one elbow on the podium and leered at Michelle. "It looks like you could use it to buy the other half of that dress."

Michelle's eyes promised retribution, and Jacob relaxed. Work had begun.

"We've got a great evening ahead of us, ladies and gentlemen, dancing to the sounds of Huey Michaels's band—" Jacob waited for the applause to stop "—but first we have a treat for you. As you all know we're gathered here tonight to honor the children of our city. Most of us were fortunate enough to grow up in loving homes, but many of the children living in our city today are not so fortunate, which is why we're all here—to help those children. We have hot-lines young people can call, but not enough qualified people to man them. We have buildings to use as shelters, but no way to pay the utilities. These pro-grams take money. Lots of it. And tonight the dona-tions you've contributed have already totaled more than two hundred and fifty *thousand* dollars—'' A burst of applause interrupted him. ''You've just saved some lives, folks,'' Jacob said, stepping back as the audience stood as a whole, applauding their cause.

''And now for that treat Jacob mentioned,'' Mi-chelle said, when the noise had died down.

''I know the one I'd like,'' Jacob said, as he eyed Michelle's bare shoulders.

The audience laughed, relieving some of the ten-sion in the room.

''Tonight for your entertainment we have with us eight youngsters whose hard work and ability have won them positions as 'Talent Quest' finalists. Judges will select which four will compete on national tele-vision on 'Rising Stars'…''

Jacob and Michelle took turns at the microphone, introducing the acts before they came onstage. The children sang, danced, and one little guy even did a stand-up routine. Jacob was as awed as everyone else by the talent. He just wished he hadn't glanced at Michelle during one of the acts. The longing in her eyes as she watched the children on stage unsettled him. It dawned on him that she'd probably planned to be a mother by now. And probably would have

been, if she wasn't so adamant about living in the
past. He'd thought of several different explanations
for Brian Colby's disappearance, not all of them in-
voluntary. None of them had happy endings. But
maybe the worst scenario was no ending at all.

JACOB NURSED his scotch, watching the women on
the dance floor, waiting for one to spark his interest.
There was certainly a bevy of lovelies here tonight.
Maybe that was why he was still standing on the side-
lines alone. There were too many choices.

He caught a glimpse of honey gold skin as a couple
sailed past and he looked the other way. He was glad
Michelle was having a good time. He just didn't think
her current partner needed to have his hand pressed
so intimately in the small of her back. Her bare back.
The tip of her shoulder would have done fine.

Taking another sip of his scotch, he looked around
for a partner for himself. A brunette across the room
caught his eye and smiled a come-hither smile that
men the world over could translate in a second. She
was available. He looked again. And she was beautiful. Her figure was model perfect in her shimmering
gold lamé gown. She was young enough not to have
that look that said she'd seen it all, yet old enough to
know the score. And she wanted to score. With Jacob.
He looked away.

He was sipping ice water and making small talk
with the bartender when he saw Michelle again. She
was with some guy who was so smooth-looking Jacob

wondered why her hands didn't just slip right off him. He oozed money and position and just a little too much confidence for Jacob's liking. And he was holding Michelle far too close.

Jacob set his glass down on the bar. It was time to go. Michelle might not have to get up early in the morning, but just because they didn't have to go to work tomorrow didn't mean that *he'd* be able to sleep in. He had three little terrors who would be bouncing into his room by seven in the morning. If he was lucky. If not, they'd be jumping on the end of his bed by six.

He strode onto the dance floor for the first time that night, tapped Michelle's partner on the shoulder and, when they turned, grabbed Michelle's wrist.

"It's time to go."

Michelle's partner glared at him. She didn't look too pleased, either. Neither did the five or six couples who bumped into them in the middle of the crowded dance floor.

"I've got a headache," Jacob said, wondering what in the hell he was doing creating a scene just because some man had been dancing a little more closely than necessary with Michelle. A few hours ago he'd been encouraging her to have a good time, knowing that it was the best thing for her.

"You're not feeling well?" Michelle asked solicitously.

"No." Jacob was surprised to hear himself contin-

uing the lie. Her concern was making him feel like a
heel. But he still didn't let go of her wrist.

"Just let me get my purse," Michelle said.

Jacob cursed himself every way he knew how
while he waited for Michelle to return. Being jealous
of her dance partners was ludicrous. He was way out
of line, overstepping the boundaries that governed
their friendship—the boundaries that he himself
needed if he and Michelle were going to remain partners.

MICHELLE WAS QUIET on the drive home, and Jacob
welcomed the distance their silence placed between
them. She stared out the window and he wondered if
she was thinking about Brian Colby. Was she wondering where he was or remembering a night spent
dancing in his arms? Envy welled up inside Jacob,
although he'd long passed the days when he wanted
a woman to care for him as loyally as Michelle cared
for Brian. He knew better. And as much as he wished
it could be different for Michelle, he suspected that
someday she'd know better, too.

"Mind if we stop for something to eat?" he asked,
breaking the silence that was suddenly deafening in
the darkened vehicle.

"Not at all. I'm starving. I'll even buy, since we
missed dinner on my account."

"In that case, I'll have two of everything," Jacob
said, pulling into an all-night restaurant famous for its
breakfasts.

The young, long-haired host who seated them at a cozy booth for two eyed Michelle appreciatively. She wasn't the only woman in the restaurant in evening clothes, but she was definitely the most beautiful. The young man glanced at Jacob with envy.

"You're one lucky dude," he muttered as Jacob waited for Michelle to slide into the booth. Jacob didn't bother correcting him.

"You feeling better?" Michelle asked half an hour later as they finished their breakfast.

Jacob nodded. The food had definitely helped improve his mood.

"You probably just needed something to eat," she said, smiling at him.

"Probably."

"So what'd you think of the show tonight?"

Jacob grinned at her. "Are you fishing for a chance to say, 'I told you so'?"

"Well, I did tell you it was worth our time, and I was right, wasn't I?"

"I'm not sorry we went," he said.

"After all the doughnuts I had to buy to get you to come tonight, I think I at least deserve the chance for an 'I told you so,' Ryan."

"You were absolutely correct, Ms. Colby. Our time was well spent and I'm glad you talked me into going. I had no idea how much one evening could accomplish."

"Those kids were really something, weren't they?" she asked, getting serious on him all of a sudden.

Jacob agreed that the kids had been remarkable. Remembering the yearning he'd seen on her face when she'd watched the talent show that evening, he was once again struck with how much she was cheating herself out of as the years rolled by without her.

"Did you and Brian plan to raise a family?" he asked before he could stop himself. What he needed right then was more distance, not more familiarity.

"I was six weeks pregnant when he left to go overseas."

"You were? But…" She'd said the words so softly Jacob wondered if maybe he'd misunderstood. But as he looked across the table into her pain-filled eyes, he knew he hadn't. "God, Michelle. I'm sorry."

She shrugged, looking down at her empty plate.

Jacob cradled his coffee cup in his palms. "What happened?" he asked.

"I lost the baby the day after they told me Brian was missing. It was a boy."

He could tell she was trying hard not to cry again. She looked up finally, a sad tremulous smile on her lips, and Jacob admired the hell out of her. He was amazed how she could come to work every day, be cheerful and optimistic, when her life had held so much tragedy. Until tonight, he'd had no idea how much.

"Did Brian know? About the baby, I mean?" he asked.

She looked down at her diet cola, stirring the near-empty glass with her straw, and shook her head.

"I wanted to wait until I was completely sure. It was going to be a homecoming surprise." Her words were little more than a whisper.

Silence stretched between them as her words hung in the air.

"How do you do it?" he finally asked. "How do you find so much good in this world when it treats you like it does?"

She shrugged and looked up at him. "I don't always find good. But I know it doesn't help any to focus on the bad. When I lost the baby I almost lost myself, as well. It hurt so badly I didn't have the strength to get up in the morning. I kept thinking I'd be okay when Brian came home. The loss was as much his as it was mine. He'd be as devastated by it as I was, and together, sharing that, we'd get through it. I didn't think things could get any worse. But they did."

Jacob wished he were someplace he could take her into his arms. "You mean not finding Brian?"

She shook her head. "No. I was staying with my mom and dad after the miscarriage, and one morning a couple of weeks later, the first time I'd been alone since leaving the hospital, I got a phone call. It was a government official wanting me to identify a corpse that had washed up on the shore of the Gulf of Suez near Cairo. Brian had been staying in Cairo. The body was still intact and they were certain it was Brian. When I hung up the phone I promised myself, and God, that if I was spared that—if it wasn't Brian, if only I could still hope he was alive—I would handle anything else. They brought the body back here, my dad drove me to the airport to meet the plane, I looked into the body bag, and it wasn't Brian. I'd never been so thankful in my life. I knew then that I had to get a grip on my grieving or it was going to kill me before Brian made it home. Ever since then, I just do what I have to do to get through and look for whatever good I can find to make the waiting easier.''

''I think you're a remarkable, woman, Michelle Colby,'' Jacob said softly, holding her gaze with his own.

She looked down. ''I'm not really. Sometimes I think maybe I'm just taking the easy way out, doing nothing but waiting. But I just don't know any other way. So I wait.'' She shook her head. ''Anyway, I don't even know why I'm telling you all this, except that tonight I needed a friend and you seemed different somehow, more human.''

Jacob frowned. ''More human? What have I been up to now? An alien?''

''You always seem so invincible. In all the years I've known you I've never heard you ask anyone for anything.''

''Maybe you weren't listening,'' he said lightly, reaching for his wallet as he picked up their bill.

''And maybe you weren't asking.'' She snatched the bill from his fingers. ''I said I'd pay. See if you can handle having someone do that much for you.''

Her tone was teasing, but her eyes told a different story.

Jacob drove her home, waiting until she'd waved at him from her living room window before he pulled away. Michelle might think he needed to reach out to people more. But she was wrong.

HE WALKED his baby-sitter to the end of his driveway, watched while she ran across the street to her mother's bungalow and went slowly back inside, locking up for the night. Looking in on the girls on the way to his bedroom, he tucked in a stray limb here and there. As he bent to put Jessie's teddy bear back into bed with her, he was surprised to see his daughter's big brown eyes gazing up at him. Her brow was puckered, her lower lip quivering.

Jacob sat down on her bed and lifted her onto his lap. "What is it, precious? Did you have a bad dream?"

She sniffled and shook her head. "Tomorrow's Valentine Day," she said softly. Her little voice was so forlorn Jacob had to struggle not to smile.

"Is that a problem?" he whispered back.

Her head moved against his chest as she nodded. Jacob loved the feel of her slight weight leaning on him, trusting him. Needing him.

"I forgot to tell you that me and Meggie are s'posed to bring cookies to the party."

"That's easy enough, punkin. We'll stop at the store on our way to school in the morning. Okay?"

"'Kay." She didn't sound any happier.

"Jess? Is there something else wrong?"

She sat up and studied him for a moment, then settled back against him. "Meggie says not to say," she said barely above a whisper.

While Jacob was concerned to hear that his daughters were deliberately keeping things from him, he was even more concerned about the reason for their silence. Picking Jessie up, he carried her out to the living room, reaching to flip on the light by the couch as he sat down with her on his lap.

"Okay, sport. Get this once and for all. There is never, *ever,* anything you can't tell me and there never will be—got that?" He took hold of her shoulders, turning her so that she was looking at him.

Wide-eyed, she nodded.

"I can't keep you and your sisters safe unless I know what's happening, Jess. So it's important that you guys don't keep secrets from me."

She fiddled with one of his shirt studs. "It's just that when I said me and Meggie'd bring cookies to the party, some of the kids said we always bring yucky store kinds, so I said uh-uh and they said uh-huh, 'cause we didn't have a mommy to make cookies for us to bring and I said we had you and they said daddies couldn't make cookies, so I said you could and now we're going to be bringing yucky store ones, any-way 'cause I forgot to tell you about making them," she finished in a rush.

Jacob would have loved to have a talk with each

and every kid in Jessie's class. "I'm not glad you forgot to tell me about the cookies, Jess, but I think we can solve this pretty easily. Lucky for you I don't have to work in the morning because of tonight's benefit show. So I'll make a deal with you. You put your pretty little self right back to bed, go to sleep, and I'll see about getting those cookies made. Deal?"

Jessie flung her arms around his neck and squeezed him so tightly it hurt. "Thank you, Daddy."

MICHELLE FLUFFED the pillow on the end of her couch and settled down against it—again. She couldn't sleep. Usually, when her demons drove her from her bed, she'd be out as soon as she lay down on the sofa. There was something soothing about being in the living room. There were no expectations there. But it wasn't working this time.

She turned over, closed her eyes and tried to will herself to sleep, but a restless energy hummed through her. Her traitorous mind replayed the scene that had taken place hours earlier in this very room. She could still feel Jacob's arms around her, pulling her against the solidness of his body.

She reached for the picture on the end table, gazing at Brian's likeness in the moonlight. Not that she needed the picture to remember every line of his face, every expression, every smile. She didn't need to see his laughing green eyes to imagine them gazing at her lovingly—or burning with desire the way they had the last time they'd made love.

Dear God, how could she continue just existing like this? She was young and passionate. She needed a man. And Brian had been gone for so long.

Rolling over, she hugged Brian's picture to her breast. Tonight Jacob had been warm and solid—real. He was more than just a memory. She remembered the compassion she'd seen in his eyes when she told him about the baby she'd lost. She had a feeling that underneath his irreverent facade was a deeply caring man. And a passionate one.

But none of that gave her the right to be unfaithful to her husband. She'd rather die a dried-up old maid than take the chance that Brian might come home to find that she'd given her body, her heart, to another man.

JACOB COULD THINK of a lot of things he'd rather be doing at one in the morning than looking through cookbooks. Like going to bed, for instance. And not necessarily alone.

Sugar cookies. That sounded doable. He had sugar. He looked at the picture in the book and figured he could cut out a pretty mean heart with a paring knife. Then scanned the list of ingredients, hoping he wasn't going to find something like chocolate squares or coconut. He didn't stock many baking supplies. Flour, salt, butter. Vanilla he had for when he and the girls, mostly he, cranked out homemade ice cream. And baking soda. Jacob opened his refrigerator—yes, he still had that open box of baking soda Nonnie had told him to put there when he'd forgotten to throw away the bologna before leaving on vacation last summer. He was set.

He dumped the ingredients into his biggest bowl, determined to make the best damn cookies Lomen Elementary had ever had. Maybe then his little girls could just go about living their lives like the happy kids they should be. He'd bet there weren't too many mothers who'd stay up half the night baking cookies simply because their daughters had forgotten to say they needed them. Unless of course that mother were Michelle. He had a feeling she'd stay up *all* night to bake cookies if she had to.

Not that he had any business thinking about Michelle. Nope. He was going to make life easier on himself and keep thoughts of Michelle strictly off-limits. There would be no more spurts of jealousy, no more hormonal reactions. She wasn't the type of woman a guy had a casual affair with. And casual affairs were all Jacob had.

Besides, he didn't have a chance in hell of starting an affair with Michelle, casual or otherwise, even if he chose to, which he wouldn't. Brian's hold on Michelle went much deeper than the loyalty of young love Jacob had originally thought it was. She'd made a pact with fate to hold on until Brian returned. Just hold on. She wasn't really living at all, just existing. It sounded as if she hadn't even yet begun to grieve for the baby she'd lost. She was waiting for that, too.

Jacob cracked an egg on the side of the bowl. After

what he'd witnessed and heard that evening, he didn't think Michelle was ever going to get on with life until she had her answers—one way or another. And by the sounds of things, those answers might never be found.

He spent the next few minutes picking eggshell out of his cookie dough.

CHAPTER FIVE

"Jacob, call for you on line six." Bob Chaney, their producer, poked his head into the sound room during a commercial break Friday morning.

Michelle pushed a button on the telephone and handed Jacob the receiver. He looked so different this morning than he had on Wednesday night, and she'd hoped the return to his usual uniform of sweats and T-shirt would have a grounding effect on her growing obsession with him. It hadn't.

"Of course I remember. I never forget a beautiful woman," she heard him say into the receiver. His voice, usually deep and clear, had taken on a low sexy tone.

Michelle studied the program sheet in front of her. They had three promos coming up, a telephone interview, a weather spot, sport scores to announce again and six songs to play. What did she care if Jacob was talking to a beautiful woman? It certainly wasn't anything new.

"Tonight?"

Please say no.

"How late?"

You have children to watch.

"I only stay up past my bedtime on special occasions."

He was grinning. Damn him.

"You're on. I'll pick you up at eight."

Michelle had never felt lonelier in her life.

JESSIE, ALLIE AND MEGGIE dragged in from school Friday afternoon, the oversize 49ers T-shirts they were wearing seeming to weigh them down. They walked through the kitchen, their multicolored backpacks still across their shoulders, not even stopping to take a sip from the three glasses of milk he'd set out on the table.

"Hi," Jacob said, smiling at them.

"Hi," they answered in identically unhappy voices as they continued on out of the kitchen, traipsing down the hall to their room.

Jacob looked at the untouched peanut-butter sandwiches still sitting on the table while a knot formed in his stomach. The only time Allie had ever passed up food was that time she'd reacted to her diphtheria inoculation and run a fever of 103. Enough of this mind-reading routine—he was going to trust his own judgment. Leaving the sandwiches on the table, Jacob turned and strode down the hall.

The girls were sitting on Meggie's bed, their backpacks dropped haphazardly in the middle of the floor. Jacob stood in the doorway, wishing he was a hell of a lot more sure of himself. He could hardly believe he was intimidated by three pint-size seven-year-olds.

"Who's going to tell me what's going on?" he asked glancing from one to another. They looked so small and vulnerable as they sat there huddled together. But he managed a relentless stare, anyway.

"We promised Ms. Wilson we'd do our best on everything from now on," Allie finally said solemnly.

"That doesn't sound so bad." He didn't see the problem yet.

"I have to be Cinderella, Daddy," Jessie said, looking wistfully excited and ready to cry all at once.

"You got the part?" he asked. He'd thought the triplets had either skipped the auditions or blown them.

"And we're her evil stepsisters," Allie said, pointing to herself and Meghan. Meggie's hair was loose, hiding her face. Jacob hoped she wasn't crying.

He went in and sat down on Allie's bed. "I don't get it. You guys loved acting in the Christmas play. It's all you talked about for months. And now you're upset because you got picked for the starring roles of a story you all three know by heart?" He tried not to panic as it occurred to him that his daughters weren't just his children—they were females. This was what Eleanor Wilson and, later on, Michelle had been trying tactfully to point out. That just by the nature of the beast—male versus female—there were going to be times when he missed the boat.

Allie's little chin trembled. "If I gotta tell you something, you promise you won't get mad enough to go away like Mommy did?"

"Go away?" Jacob was completely unprepared for that. He joined the girls on Meggie's bed, pulling them all into the circle of his arms. "I'm not going anywhere, ever—at least not without you three. You could lie and cheat and steal, and I'd punish the heck out of you, but I'd never leave you. Never. *I love you.*"

Three little pairs of arms wrapped themselves around Jacob, and his words of love echoed back to him in triplicate. Jacob sought the gaze of his eldest daughter by nine minutes. "We're a family, Allie, you and Meggie and Jessie and me, and nothing's going to change that. You guys are stuck with me until you're all grown-up and so sick of me you'll be begging for your own apartments."

Jacob felt an extrahard squeeze around his middle. "I'm going to live with you forever, Daddy," Jessie said.

"You can't, Jessie," Meggie said. "Not when you get married and have babies."

"Then I won't get married."

"Don't you ever want to be a mommy, Jess?" Allie asked.

"Not if I have to leave Daddy."

"That's dumb." Meggie scooted off the bed and sat on the floor by the bookcase.

"It's not dumb, is it, Daddy?" Jessie asked, climbing onto his lap.

"It is kinda dumb, Jess," Allie answered for him, playing with the fringe of his cutoff denim shorts.

"Is not," Jessie said, burrowing her head into his chest.

"Is too," Meggie said. She was leafing through *Green Eggs and Ham*.

"Is n—"

"Okay, girls. We're kind of getting off the subject here. But for the record, whether Jessie's feelings withstand the test of time or not, they aren't dumb— not if Jessie's feeling them. Now, back to *Cinderella*. What's the problem? You don't like acting anymore?"

"I do," Jessie said.

"Me, too," Meggie agreed, still thumbing through the book.

"It's the costumes, Daddy. Ms. Thomas—she's the boss of the play—says they all have to be homemade and we don't even have a sewing machine," Allie said, frowning up at him.

"And Cinderella has to have *two* costumes because of being a maid *and* going to the ball," Jessie added.

Jacob's mind was spinning as he tried to find a way to reassure his daughters and find a solution to their problem at the same time. "So we'll learn how to sew," he said, knowing that was going to be a near impossibility. A sure impossibility considering the time he had to work with.

"Even we know you can't sew, Daddy," Meghan informed him. She was no longer turning the pages of her book. Glancing down he read silently, *Would you could you?* He had a feeling Meggie hadn't stopped there by coincidence.

"So we'll find someone who can," he said, realizing he knew someone who both could and probably would. He remembered the homemade curtains at her windows, the throw pillows on her couch.

"But we can't just go take them to somebody, Daddy, 'cause we have to help," Allie said.

Jacob shifted Jessie more firmly onto his lap. "Then we'll have to find someone to come here just like Nonnie does."

"We could ask Nonnie," Jessie suggested.

"Nonnie can't *sew,* Jess," Meggie said, clearly irritated with her sister's naiveté. "Her fingers hurt her all the time and she has to look through those funny glasses just to read our papers."

"I'll find someone, girls, I promise," Jacob said before another argument flared up.

"There's more, Daddy," Jessie said timidly.

More? "Well, now's the time to lay it on me." Jacob injected an extra note of cheer into his voice. He wanted them to trust him with their troubles, which meant that one way or another he was going to have come through for them when they did.

"Ms. Thomas said to tell you we need someone to help us change during the show," Meggie said, closing her book with a snap.

"Yeah, she said we couldn't have another incibent like the one at the Christmas play where you came into the girls' changing place. The other girls and mothers didn't like it 'cause you're a boy,'' Jessie said.

Jacob figured he'd been more embarrassed than anyone else present that night. ''I'll tell you what. When I ask someone to help with the costumes I'll make sure she can be there on play night, too. How's that sound?''

Meggie's smile transformed her usually serious face. ''That sounds real good, Daddy.''

''Yeah,'' Jessie and Allie chorused.

''Laurie's coming over to baby-sit later tonight, but how about we play a game of hoops before dinner?'' Jacob asked.

''Yeah!'' All three girls scrambled up, their worlds all right again.

Jacob shook his head and wondered how much his promise was going to cost him as he followed his daughters out to the small basketball hoop he'd installed beside the garage. He knew who he had to ask to help them—someone who'd already offered her services; someone who'd looked longingly at strangers' children the other night.

It was the perfect solution. The girls would have some female companionship; they'd get their costumes made and still be safe from emotional disaster. Michelle was already married, committed elsewhere. It would be no reflection on the girls when she moved on. They'd know going in that she'd already promised her life to another family. If only Jacob could trust himself to remember the same thing.

HE WAITED until Monday to approach Michelle. He could have called her at home over the weekend, but he'd wanted to keep things as impersonal as possible. He chose his moment, the two-minute commercial break in the middle of their show. Short and simple, that was how he planned to keep things.

Leaning forward on his stool, he rested his arms on the counter in front of him. "Remember what you said the other night about me never asking for anything?" he asked, turning his head to glance at her. She looked good. Hell, she looked gorgeous.

"Yeah." The one word brought him back with a snap.

"Well, I'm about to change that." *Get a grip, Ryan.*

"Congratulations." She slid off her stool and headed for the door.

Jacob sat up and stared at her. "Where're you going?" The words came out more sharply than he intended.

She turned back with a startled look. "We only have another eighty seconds and my throat's dry. I need a drink."

"So that's your answer, then?"

She walked back to the counter. "My answer to what?" she asked, clearly perplexed.

"I just took you up on your offer to spend some time with the girls." And it was much harder than even he'd thought it would be. If she said no...

She started to smile. "You did?"

He suddenly felt pounds lighter. "Yeah, I did." He smiled back at her.

"Five, four, three, two...go!" Bob's voice piped over the speaker from the control room.

Michelle mouthed yes as Jacob started in with the weather report. It was going to be a bright sunny day in Los Angeles.

MICHELLE DIDN'T second-guess her decision to take on Jacob's girls even once, though she thought of little else all morning. Spending time with Jacob's daughters would certainly entail spending more time with him, and considering the way she'd been obsessing about him lately that might have been a problem. Except that she'd just spent the longest weekend of her life picturing Jacob in the arms of some new beauty. When she realized she was actually jealous, she'd been reminded of just why she'd never been tempted by Jacob before. His womanizing and his inability to commit himself to a long-term relationship were basic flaws that were sure to prevent her from seeing him as anything more than a friend. But mothering his children for a while was another ball game entirely. Michelle knew they were just what she needed—and suspected they might very well need *her* a little bit, too.

"So when do we start?" Michelle asked the minute they were off the air.

Jacob started gathering up the material they'd used for that morning's show. "Maybe you'd better wait until you find out what you're getting into before you commit yourself,'' he said.

Michelle's smile faded as she watched him. "You don't want my help now?" she asked. She should've expected he'd change his mind. Jacob never let himself rely on anyone.

"That's not it," he said, throwing newspapers in the trash. "But I should explain a few things first. You want to go for coffee or something?"

He wasn't meeting her eyes, and she had a pretty good idea why. She just wished it wasn't so hard for him to ask for a little help. "A diet cola would be great," she said.

They went to the deli next door to the station and ordered bagels to go along with Jacob's coffee and Michelle's cola. The girl behind the counter obviously approved of the way Jacob's T-shirt stretched across his chest. Or maybe it was the challenging tilt to his lips that fascinated her. All Michelle knew was that the girl looked at Jacob more than she did her cash register; she was flirting so obviously it was embarrassing. But though Jacob flirted right back, his response seemed somewhat mechanical. Michelle wondered if that was how he managed to keep his women from getting too close.

"Allie, Meggie and Jessie are great kids," he said after he'd emptied three packages of sugar into his coffee.

"You don't have to tell me that, Jacob. I've seen them at the company picnics the past three summers.

They have wonderful manners and they certainly seem to mind you."

"But they're also an awful lot of work. Everything has to be done in triplicate, and I mean *everything*. If one gets a hug, they all need a hug. If one asks for a drink, they're all going to want one." He glanced up, the look in his eyes warning of difficult times ahead.

Michelle thought it sounded heavenly so far. "If you're trying to scare me off, you're going to have to do a lot better than that," she told him.

He set his bagel down, uneaten. "Okay, here it is. The girls are in a school play. They need costumes, four of them, homemade by the end of April."

"Okay." Michelle liked to sew. And making costumes sounded like fun.

"They have to help."

"All right." It might take a little longer that way, but considering her lonely evenings that made it all the better.

"And they need a woman to be with them on play night to help with changing and hair and things."

"Fine."

He pushed his untouched coffee aside.

"You don't even know when play night is."

"I assumed you'd tell me, Jacob. It's not like I have a demanding social schedule." She placed her hand over his. "Relax. If you knew how much I wanted to do this, you'd be charging me for it."

He pulled his hand away from hers. "I just don't want any surprises. For either of us," he said, grabbing his cup to take a sip of coffee. "And I need to know that if you agree to this, you're not going to turn tail and run when you have three voices coming at you at once demanding three different things that all have the utmost urgency."

She couldn't hold back her smile any longer. "If only you knew how good all this sounds to me. I've got enough patience and love to go around, Jacob, trust me."

He looked startled for a moment. "I guess I do trust you or I wouldn't have asked in the first place. I just don't want the girls disappointed."

She understood his concern. "I'll never knowingly do that. You have my word on it."

He nodded. "There's one other thing… You'll be spending some time at the beach house."

"I figured as much."

"I live there."

Michelle thought she was beginning to understand. She felt like sliding under that table as it dawned on her that Jacob might have caught on to the way she'd been responding to him. How humiliating! It could ruin everything—not only their camaraderie on the air but, even worse, her chance to give a little bit of the love she had stored inside to three children who needed it almost as much as she needed to give it.

"And I'm married," she said maybe a little more forcefully than necessary. "Don't you see? It's like I told you the other night. I look for good things to make the waiting easier. Helping Allie and Jessie and

Meggie is a good thing. But I'll still be waiting, Jacob. Faithfully. Every minute of every day. Especially now that Frank is finally getting some leads.''

Jacob nodded. ''And the girls need to understand that. Right from the beginning. I don't want them to start weaving impossible dreams of 'happy ever afters' in their naive little heads.''

''You'd like me to tell them about Brian?'' Michelle didn't really want to do that. She didn't want to have to start their time together with such an unhappy story.

''I'll do it. But it wouldn't hurt for you to drop reminders now and then.''

''If you think it's necessary,'' she said.

''I know my girls. They'll have us married an hour after you're in the house.''

And they both knew how completely impossible that was.

JACOB HAD LET MICHELLE talk him into bringing the girls over for dinner that night so she could start getting to know them. He hadn't been prepared to jump into things so quickly, but she'd convinced him otherwise by detailing what was involved in sewing a gown. And she had four of them to do. He could see that she probably needed to get started as soon as possible.

''Is it time to go yet, Daddy? Is it?'' Jessie asked, bouncing up and down in front of the bathroom mirror as he tried to fix her hair.

"Almost, punkin. Where're your sisters?"

"In the bedroom. They just need hair done, too."

Working his way from the bottom up, Jacob attacked the day's worth of tangles. He never could figure out how Jessie always managed to get twice as many knots in her hair as her sisters. "They're wearing their jean skirts and Mickey tops like I asked?"

"Yep. And you're wearing jeans, too, Daddy. We all match."

He made it through one section of hair. "You need to stand still, Jess, or we'll never get there."

"She's pretty, isn't she, Daddy?" Jessie's big innocent eyes caught his in the mirror, reflecting her excitement.

He pulled gently at a tangle at the back of her neck. "Who's pretty?"

"Michelle. When we saw her last summer at the picnic she smiled at us a lot."

"Sure Michelle's pretty. That's why she's married. Brian Colby saw how pretty she was years ago and snatched her right up."

"Ouch!" Jessie's hand flew to the back of her neck, covering the spot where Jacob needed to put the brush.

"Just a little bit more, honey. We almost got it," he said, gently removing her hand. He'd thought about cutting the girls' hair shorter a time or two, but he could never bring himself to do it. He loved it long.

"Do you think she'll let us pick our own material?" Jessie asked, wincing.

Jacob worked the tangle free and moved on to the next. "I'm sure of it. What color do you want?"

"Blue! No, green!"

Jacob finally made it all the way through Jessie's hair. He pulled it up into a ponytail and had it in a scrunchie in record time, a testimony to the fact that he could do most anything when he put his mind to it.

Meggie wanted her hair in a braid, but finally allowed Jacob to stick it in a ponytail when he pointed out that he wasn't nearly as good at doing braids and it might make them late for dinner. Allie had to go to the bathroom just after he'd locked the door behind them, but finally, with fifteen minutes to spare, all three girls were buckled into the Explorer.

They chattered nonstop all the way over to Michelle's condo. There was no doubt his daughters were excited about the advent of a woman in their lives. Chalk up another point for Eleanor Wilson.

JACOB WAS HAVING DINNER with four strangers. He'd done his darnedest to initiate a couple of conversations, but when his efforts fizzled, he figured he just had to ride this one out. He didn't have a hope in hell of understanding it. Michelle had barely looked at him since he'd walked in her door. And the triplets were acting like robots from a *Miss Manners* book.

They'd been their loud bouncy selves right up until

they'd pulled into Michelle's driveway. But the minute they'd climbed out of the 4×4, they'd become polite little mice. He wondered if he could bottle up some of Michelle's air to take home with him. Only for special occasions, he amended quickly. Most of the time he welcomed the life the girls brought into his home.

Thank goodness for Michelle's cat. Noby had taken to the girls as soon as they stepped in the door, wrapping herself around their legs and earning herself three slaves for life. Even Meggie demanded her turn to hold the fluffy Persian. Noby had managed to keep things rolling until Michelle had announced that the hamburgers were ready.

"Can I have some more catsup, please?" Allie asked, her hands in her lap.

"Here you go, Allie. You need some help with that?" Michelle was responding to his daughter's needs before Jacob could reach for the bottle.

"What?" Michelle asked when she caught him staring at her in surprise.

"You called her Allie," he said, impressed.

Michelle frowned. "Isn't that what you call her?"

"It's just that people usually mix us up," Allie said in her most adult voice.

Meggie reached for a piece of bread. "It mighta been a lucky guess," she said.

Michelle grinned. "Need some help buttering that, *Meggie?*" she asked.

"Nope."

Michelle's effort with Meggie's name went unrewarded. Jacob could have told her that would happen, simply because she'd offered to help the most independent of his children, though he'd have given his right arm to hear Meggie say yes. He watched as his daughter butchered her bread, leaving more butter on the knife than anywhere else. Michelle sent him an expectant glance, her smile replaced with a frown when he didn't take over the buttering. Which would have been the worst thing Jacob could have done at the moment. It was far more important for Meggie to complete the task herself than for the bread to be edible when she was finished.

Meggie's bread ripped and balled into pieces, but she ate it, anyway. Michelle gave him a disapproving glare.

Michelle had a lot to learn.

CHAPTER SIX

"FRANK STEELE HERE, Mrs. Colby."

Michelle's heart rate doubled as she recognized the detective's raspy voice. It'd been almost a week since his last call.

"What'd you find out, Frank? Did they recognize his picture? Does anyone know where he went from there?"

"It's not that easy, ma'am. I had to rely on a translator, and according to him, your husband was never in that village. And yet everyone got real nervous every time I pulled his picture out. So I figure Brian was there all right, but for some reason they don't want me knowing that." He paused, and Michelle heard him take a long drag on a cigarette. Scooping up Noby, she sank into the nearest chair.

"So now what?"

"We'd be back to square one except that last night, on a hunch, I spread the word I was leaving in the morning. I figure there's always an odd one out, and maybe, if someone had something to say to me, I could push their hand a little. So sometime past midnight, I'm in my tent and I get this visitor. It's a young woman called Jazmin. I'd seen her watching me a couple of times in the village. Anyway, as it turns out, she speaks English. She tells me about this guy Karim, who's threatened to level the village if anyone ever speaks about the American who lived with them for so many months. She says the American looked different from the picture I showed her—he had a beard and wore his hair in a ponytail—but she'd know his eyes anywhere. She says he called himself Ahmed and that she worked as his translator while he learned Arabic.''

Michelle's chest was so tight she could barely breath. ''Did this woman say what happened to him?'' After all the years of waiting she wasn't sure she was ready for the truth.

''Only that while he'd lived in the village for about a year, he'd been gone far longer and there was nothing to be gained by my hanging around. It was obvious my questions were more painful to her than frightening. She was affected in a personal way. I'm sorry to have to say this, ma'am, but you're paying me to find out what I can—I was left with the impression that Jazmin was in love with your husband.''

Michelle didn't want to hear that.

''She didn't say anything else? Like why he was there or what he did during that year?''

''She did say that he helped a lot of the villagers, like fixing things that were broken. They were all very fond of him. She said he made them laugh a lot.''

''That sounds like Brian.'' The ache inside Michelle was almost overwhelming.

"As far as I can see we have two options left," Frank said in his emotionless tone.

"Which are?"

"Either find this Karim or give up."

"Then find Karim."

"You may be asking the impossible, ma'am. Whoever this Karim guy is, he's got enough power to scare an entire village, and it's my guess he has other such villages under his thumb. If he doesn't want to be found, he won't be."

"I don't care how long it takes, Frank. I have to know."

"I've always had a fascination with this part of the world, ma'am, so I'm willing to stick at it, as long as you're sure…"

"I'm sure, but, Frank?"

"Yeah?"

"Be careful."

"Always. I'll be in touch…"

MICHELLE PLAYED racquetball with her father late that afternoon—sort of. She lost to him so badly he didn't even tease her about it. And she was preoccupied all through dinner. She knew her parents were worried about her, but she just couldn't confide in them. Not yet. Not until she'd come to terms with the fear—the jealousy—that was threatening to rise up and engulf her.

She kept seeing Brian, her Brian, looking at some village beauty the same way he'd looked at her, smiling, laughing. Brian's laugh was contagious. And somehow, although she'd tortured herself with visions of him in endless situations—hungry, holed up in the dark with rats, locked in chains, running, hiding, suffering from amnesia—never once had she pictured him laughing.

And never once with another woman.

Michelle stopped in at a craft store on the way home from her parents and walked up and down every aisle before leaving empty-handed. She went to the grocery store and bought a basketful of things she didn't need. She didn't go near the ocean or look at the Hollywood sign. She didn't go to any of the places that reminded her of Brian—the places that usually gave her comfort.

But he followed her everywhere.

She finally pulled into her driveway some time after nine, her mind still screaming with questions. *Did he hold her? Did he touch her like he touched me?*

Carrying in her groceries, she locked up for the night. Had another woman made love to Brian? Since she had? While she'd been here missing him so badly she was only half-alive?

She avoided her bedroom. She refused to take the other woman in there....

Had Brian loved her—this unknown beauty? Had he given her his heart, as well as his body? That possibility hurt worst of all. His love was sacred to Michelle—hers alone. It had transcended thousands of miles, endured years of deprivation and loneliness. It had kept her alive during the loss of their son. But was this relationship she honored with her loyalty, her life, a sham?

Michelle twisted the solid gold ring on her left hand. Maybe she was being ridiculous. Maybe *she* was the one endangering their love by allowing doubts to intrude. If she only believed in Brian when believing was easy, then her loyalty meant nothing. Frank could be wrong. And even if he wasn't, even if the young woman had fallen in love with Brian, it didn't mean Brian had either encouraged or returned her feelings. Michelle sat down on the couch next to Noby.

Brian's picture was smiling at her from the end table. She picked it up, meeting the loving look in his eyes with her own. But he wasn't looking at her. He was gazing at some young village beauty....

Michelle reached for the phone.

"HELLO?" JACOB GRABBED the phone after the first ring so it wouldn't wake the girls. He'd learned to cherish the hour or two of quiet he got each evening almost as much as he cherished the chaos of his days.

"Hi. Am I interrupting?"

His newspaper landed on the floor beside the couch as he sat up. "Michelle? No. Of course you're not interrupting. Is something wrong?"

"Everything's fine," she said, and he wondered why she didn't sound fine. "I just wanted to get started on those costumes."

"Tonight? The girls are eager, too, but they've been in bed for more than an hour."

She laughed, self-consciously, he thought. "I didn't mean tonight, Jacob," she said, sounding more like herself. "But tomorrow would be a good time for me if the girls don't already have other plans. I could pick them up after school and take them to the fabric store. We'll need patterns and material."

The girls? As in, all three of them at once? Jacob hadn't figured on that.

"We're going in-line skating tomorrow, but I guess we can do that after dinner," he said. He couldn't let her take all three of them at once. Not on a first outing. Maybe not ever.

"You take the girls in-line skating?" she asked.

"Yeah."

"With training blades?"

"No. They haven't needed them for over a year." He was rather proud of that fact.

"Aren't they a little young for that? They could sprain an ankle or something."

"They could sprain an ankle walking in the yard."

"I just thought little kids still did roller skates, you know, with four wheels and all."

She really sounded worried. "Some do. But the girls wanted in-line skates last year for Christmas. It seemed like fun, so we all went and learned how to do it. You ever done it?"

"Yeah. I've got my own blades."

"There's a track down by Lomen Elementary. You ever been there?"

"No. I usually just stay around here."

"So why not take Allie to the fabric store after school while Jessie, Meggie and I make dinner, and then we can all eat and go skating together." Jacob was quite pleased with the plan. It left him with two-thirds of the disaster-waiting-to-happen. "The girls would love it," he added for good measure.

"Sounds good, except that I need to take all three girls with me if they're going to choose their own materials and patterns."

"So, do Allie tomorrow, and Jessie and Meggie can each have a day later in the week."

"But then we're that much further from getting started. It would really be easiest to just take them all at once."

Jacob thought of the triplets in a store—any store. "No, it wouldn't."

"What's the matter, Jacob? Are you regretting asking for my help?" She was really making this difficult.

"No. I'm just trying to prevent you from running out on us before you even get started."

"I don't understand."

He was sure she didn't. "Michelle, taking a seven-year-old into a store is a serious endeavor. You're so busy reminding the child not to touch and answering the million and one questions she comes up with that it's hard to concentrate on what you went in for. Now multiply that by three and add in the little extra ingredient of needing their opinions to complete your mission. You get the picture yet?''

''I think the fabric store will survive.''

''It's not the store I'm worried about.''

''You don't think I can handle it.''

''Their mother couldn't.''

''I'm not Ellen.''

''No, you're not. But neither do you have any idea what you're getting yourself into. Trust me on this one, okay?''

''It sounds to me like you're the one who needs to do some trusting, Jacob. We're only talking about a trip to the store here. It's not like I want to take them off for a weekend or something.''

''I know what we're talking about. Far better than you do. Believe me, partner, doing for three isn't as easy as doing for one. And doing for three at once is sometimes so chaotic nothing gets done at all.''

''I could use a little chaos in my life, Jacob. It's so dull right now I'm surprised I don't sleep right through it.''

Jacob smiled. He couldn't help it. ''Okay, lady, you're on. You take the girls. I'll make the dinner. But don't you dare come in here tomorrow night and tell me you have other plans for the next couple of months.''

''Don't worry, I won't. You might as well face it, Jacob. You're stuck with me.''

Her words rang in his mind long after he'd hung

up. She hadn't meant them the way they sounded. Logically he knew that, even if for a minute there he'd wanted them to be true more than anything he could remember wanting in a long, long time.

"HERE'S A GOOD PATTERN for you, Jess. See, she even has a little crown and everything like a real princess." Allie held the picture so her sister could get a look at it.

Jessie gazed at the picture. "Michelle, Allie found my princess dress. See?" Jessie began twirling as if dancing at a ball. "I'm a princess, see?"

Trying to keep one eye on Meggie, who was sitting at the other end of the table looking in a McCall's book, Michelle leaned over the Simplicity catalog Allie had open, catching Jessie's princess act in her peripheral vision.

"Be careful, Jessie," she warned. "There's a…" She raised her head just in time to watch Jessie knock over a display of thread. Spools rolled in every direction, under the pattern table and out into the aisles.

"Oops," Jessie said with a grin, running to catch some spools that were rolling under a row of chairs.

Thankful that the display had only been half-full, Michelle hurried to help Jessie gather up the thread before one of the employees came over and kicked them out of the store. Allie sat in her chair and watched.

"You missed one under there," she said, pointing to a round table full of fabric remnants.

Michelle reached for the spool.

"I want this dress," Meggie suddenly announced.

Michelle took a second to go look over Meggie's shoulder. Of Jacob's three children, Meggie was the hardest one to get to know. The little girl didn't seem to like Michelle much.

She'd chosen a bridal gown.

Michelle returned the last spools of thread to the rack and took Jessie's hand. "We'll come back to the patterns, girls. Let's look at some material."

Holding on to Jessie's hand, she had the other two walk in front of her as she directed them to the organza display.

"Don't touch, girls," she said as Allie and Meggie reached out to run their fingers through bolts of material along the way.

Michelle heard a thunk beside her. Jessie had her face buried in a bolt of fake fur she'd already pulled off the rack.

Michelle righted the bolt. When she turned back, the triplets were no longer in sight. She heard them, though, and followed their voices over to the organza.

"I want this one!" Jessie said, pulling at a bolt of shiny red material. "I want this one, Michelle, okay? Can I have this one?"

"You can't have that one, Jess. Everyone knows Cinderella wore a blue gown," Allie said. She grabbed the end of a bolt of royal blue organza. "You have to have *this* one."

"I want the red one," Jessie said, her bottom lip jutting out. "Cinderella wore red."

Meggie walked silently around the display of material.

"I'm telling you, Jess, Cinderella wore a blue dress. Don'tcha remember that plate we got that broke?"

Michelle wondered if she was supposed to intervene. But how could she without choosing sides?

"I want a red dress. Red's my favorite color. And Cinderella's dress was red."

Allie stomped her foot. "You have to wear the blue." Jessie's eyes were filling with tears.

Letting her instincts guide her, Michelle stepped between them. "Okay, girls, what's the problem?" She was glad Jacob wasn't here—he'd fire her on the spot.

"Cinderella has to wear blue, and Jessie wants red," Allie said. Jessie sniffled, looking to Michelle to save her from heartbreak. But clearly Allie expected Michelle to back *her* up, too.

Jessie sniffled again, and Michelle made a note to carry tissues in future. "I don't think it would hurt if, just this once, Cinderella wears a red gown to the ball," she said. "What color do you want for *your* dress, Allie? Meggie, stay over here, please," she called as the little girl began to wander off.

Allie walked around the display, studying all the colors. Jessie pulled the bolt of red fabric down, hugging it in her arms.

"I already know what I want," Meggie said, coming up to point out a bolt of white fabric. "I want this one. It's just like the one in the picture."

Allie looked at Meggie's choice. "You can't have that one. It's white. White's for brides. And Cinderella's the bride. Hey, Jess, you should have white."

"Uh-uh. I'm having red," Jess said, clutching the material against her.

Meggie pulled the bolt of white down. "I want white," she said, her voice firm.

"You're not *allowed* to have white. Anyway, purple's your favorite color. You should have purple," Allie said, grabbing the end of the bolt, trying to pull it away from her sister.

Meggie wouldn't let go. "We're each s'posed to choose our own, Al. You heard Ms. Thomas."

Michelle noticed a clerk hovering nearby.

"Meggie's right, Allie honey," Michelle said, taking the bolt of cloth. "The rule was that each of you has to help make your own costume. It'll be okay if the colors don't match the movie exactly. You know, there are actually quite a few movies about Cinderella, and the characters wear different clothes in all of them." She handed the bolt of material to Meggie before turning to Allie. "So what color do you want?" She put her arm around Allie's shoulders and led her back to the display.

Allie shrugged. "I dunno," she said, fingering the fabric.

"Well, what's *your* favorite color?" Michelle asked.

Allie shrugged again.

Michelle knelt down in front of the little girl. "This yellow's a pretty color. We could trim it with gold sequins. How does that sound?" she asked.

"I dunno."

It would be one thing if Allie was just being uncooperative because she didn't get her own way, but Michelle didn't think that was the case. It was as if Allie was lost, not sure what to do. Michelle didn't know what to do, either.

Taking Allie by the shoulders, Michelle guided her toward the front of the rack. "Let's walk around one more time and you take another look," she said. "We have to hurry because I'm going to need you to help me find the thread to match these materials and your daddy's got dinner waiting for us."

Allie's shoulders straightened. "I'm a real good thread chooser, aren't I, you guys?" she said, looking to her sisters for confirmation.

Jessie and Meggie nodded obediently.

Michelle breathed a sigh of relief. All she needed was a little time and she'd get this mothering thing down pat. She grabbed Allie and twirled her around in a hug.

WHEN SHE GOT THE URGE to hug Allie's father later that evening, Michelle's apprehensions returned. They were skating, all five of them, staying on the right side of the course to let faster skaters get by. The girls were in front, with Allie in the lead. And without the triplets knowing it, Jacob was watching them like a hawk. It was amazing how he surrounded them with a security that set them free.

He'd pulled a handkerchief from his pocket earlier to wipe Jessie's scraped knee, but sent her right off to try again. He'd sat patiently, giving Meggie all the time she needed to try to tie her own laces; after four tries she asked him for help. And then when he'd tied them for her he'd made it seem as if she hadn't really needed his help at all.

Michelle was seeing another side to the Jacob Ryan she'd thought she knew so well. A side she liked—a lot.

She glanced over at him as he skated next to her. He was wearing blue sweats that were cut off at the thigh and a white tank top. His skin was browned by years of exposure to the California sunshine, and his muscles rippled with each thrust of his leg. He was every woman's fantasy man. Or at least hers. But that didn't mean she could start hugging him—or even start wanting to. She was married to another man.

"See, I told you they were pretty good," Jacob said, unaware of the disturbing road her thoughts had taken.

Michelle watched the triplets round a corner of the track. Allie turned to say something to her sisters and Meggie and Jessie grinned.

"They're incredible, Jacob, just incredible." And

they were. This arrangement was the best thing that had happened to her in a long, long time. She wouldn't let herself screw it up.

MEGGIE WAS PLAYING POGs with her sisters a couple of nights later. They'd just finished dinner and still had a while to go before bedtime. Michelle was helping their daddy with the dishes. She'd come for dinner again. That was twice in one week.

They heard Daddy's voice saying something and then Michelle laughed. All three girls glanced up from their half-dollar-size disks on the living-room floor to gaze at the hallway leading to the kitchen.

"Michelle's nice," Jessie said.

Allie nodded. "Yeah. She smiles a lot."

Meggie had noticed that, too.

"I'm glad we got picked for the play, after all, and have to make costumes," Jessie said.

Allie turned back to the game, raising her rubber slammer and throwing it down on the stack of cardboard POGs. The entire stack flipped over, and Allie gathered up every one of them.

Allie always won all Meggie's and Jessie's POGs. But it was okay, 'cause she always gave them right back afterward.

"I didn't know Daddy would bring Michelle home to make costumes," Allie said.

Meggie wondered why her sister said things sometimes. Of course Allie didn't know. How could she?

"But he did and I'm glad," Jessie said. "Let's do

three this time." She picked up three of her remaining four POGs and put them in the center of the floor. Meggie waited for Allie to add three and then put her three on top.

"Yeah, me, too," Allie said.

Meggie knew Allie was still talking about Michelle. Meggie was secretly glad, too, but she wasn't going to say it. She was afraid to.

Jessie threw her slammer down on the stack. Two POGs flipped over. "Maybe if we're real good Michelle will want to stay and we'll be a whole family just like Katie Walters's," she said, her eyebrows all crinkly like Allie's got when something was serious.

Meggie's heart started to beat hard.

"Yeah! If we're real good I bet she will," Allie said.

They both looked at Meggie. She looked back at them. She wanted to hope for a mother. She wanted to so much. But she couldn't. Sometimes when she wished it made things go bad. Like the time she'd wished her mother would come for Christmas. She'd wished every night for days and days. And that was the year their mother forgot them altogether. Meggie'd always wondered if it was her fault, for wishing for too much.

"Meggie, it's your turn," Allie said, still looking at her. "Don't you think if we're good Michelle will want to stay and make us a whole family?" she asked as Meggie threw her slammer.

"I'll be good," Meggie said, picking up the POG she'd flipped over.

Allie took her turn, tossing her slammer onto the remaining POGs. Every one of them flipped over. "You guys wanna play again?" she asked.

"Sure," Jessie said. "How about you, Meggie?"

"Okay. Only I get to go first this time."

"IT'S EIGHT FORTY-THREE on this gorgeous Monday morning—"

"Already?" Jacob leaned toward his mike to interrupt.

Michelle wrinkled her nose at him. "But before we say goodbye, we need to tell everyone what we have planned for tomorrow…"

"I don't think Bob wants us saying stuff like that on the air."

"I'm talking about tomorrow's show, Jacob," Michelle said, grinning at him.

"Then can we talk about…you know?" Jacob asked. He'd always enjoyed baiting Michelle, but especially now that he was getting to know her better.

"I guess if talk's all you can do…"

Jacob gave her a glance promising retribution. "Psychic Alisha Shane will be joining us tomorrow morning, along with City Councilman Richard Butler, who is, I hear, thinking of running for senator," he said. He looked up from the sheet he was reading. "You think she'll have some insights into his future?"

"He's a politician, Jacob. You think he'll listen?"

Jacob burst out laughing. "That wasn't nice, Michelle."

"I know, and I'm sorry. I'll be nice to him tomorrow, I promise."

Jacob felt good about the morning's show. He'd been a little apprehensive about how their new arrangement might affect their work, maybe make their banter stale, but to the contrary, things just seemed better all around.

The "on the air" light went off in their sound booth. Michelle smiled at him. She was pleased with the show, too. But there was something more to her smile than a sharing of professional success, something warmer, something almost…intimate.

"Hey, you guys were great!" Bob Chaney barged into the room. "Your ratings have been up all week."

Jacob gathered up the papers in front of him. "That's always nice to hear," he said. Why did their producer have to pick this moment to bear his good tidings?

"It sure is," Michelle added. She seemed to be giving a lot of attention to the stack of compact disks in front of her.

Bob leaned against the door frame, crossing one leg over the other. "So tell me, what's going on between you two?"

Jacob wasn't sure who sent Bob the sharpest look, he or Michelle, but he had a feeling if looks could kill Bob would have died twice.

"Nothing," they both said at once.

"Nothing?" Bob laughed incredulously. "Tell me another one. The air's been crackling around you two for days."

"We work well together, Bob. You know that. We always have," Michelle said, as calm as always.

"I can guarantee if there was anything more than that, it *wouldn't* work," Jacob added. "You know me. I love 'em and leave 'em." It was one thing for *him* to fantasize about having a relationship with Michelle, because he knew it would never be anything more than a fantasy, but he couldn't allow anyone else to get ideas.

Bob laughed. "Come on, you two. Anyone with eyes can see that something's changed over the past week or two. What about that crack a couple of days ago, Michelle, something to do with the stuff growing inside Jacob's refrigerator? And what about you Jacob? How'd you know that Michelle does in-line skating with her hands on her hips? Now come clean, you guys. After all, I'm the one who got the two of you together, so to speak." He grinned knowingly.

Michelle stood up, her face tight with anger. "There is nothing—absolutely nothing—going on between Jacob and me besides a completely platonic friendship. I am a married woman in case you've forgotten. I resent the insinuation that I would be unfaithful to my husband."

And there you have it, folks, Jacob thought. The reminder, if he needed one, that he and Michelle were never going to share anything except his daughters. Not that he'd ever thought otherwise.

Bob straightened abruptly. ''But he's… I'm sorry, Michelle, it won't happen again.'' He looked across at Jacob with an apologetic shrug. ''Whatever the reason, thanks for the ratings.'' He let the door to the sound room close behind him.

Jacob reached for the phone. He needed a date.

CHAPTER SEVEN

MICHELLE GLANCED at the clock. Eleven-thirty. How could Jacob stay out so late when he knew they had to be at work in six and a half hours? She, for one, needed to sleep. Not that he had any idea his late hours were keeping *her* up. As far as Jacob knew, Laurie was sitting with the girls.

She picked up a magazine, leafing through a couple of pages. Although her sewing machine beckoned from across the room, she'd promised Meggie she wouldn't start sewing her sisters' dresses before Meggie's was cut out. And that wouldn't be until after they made another trip to the fabric store to buy more material. But at least Meggie'd agreed to let Michelle cut out the gown this time.

Restless, she glanced at her watch again. What was Jacob doing out this late? No, scratch that. She didn't want to know. But it wasn't as if he hadn't been out in a while. As a matter of fact, he'd been out three times that week. Not that she was counting—it wasn't any business of hers if he was off with a different woman every night—but she couldn't help it if his daughters chose to fill her in on their father's social life.

She heard a rustling sound coming from the girls' room and glanced up, wondering if one of them was awake. Maybe she'd better check.

She walked quietly down the hall toward the door she'd left open at Allie's instruction after she'd tucked the girls into bed. Slipping into the room, Michelle glanced from one bed to the next, assuring herself that all three children were accounted for. Jessie's teddy bear was on the floor. Michelle tiptoed over, picked up the bear and laid it down gently next to the sleeping child.

Crossing to Allie's bed, she saw that the little girl was lying flat on her back, still tucked in just as she'd left her. Then she moved hesitantly toward Meggie, half-afraid that Jacob's self-contained middle child would sense someone trespassing in her space and wake up.

Meggie's covers were hanging off her bed, and Michelle leaned over to rearrange them. Giving into temptation, she kissed Meggie's cheek. The child stirred and Michelle froze. But Meggie settled more deeply into her pillow, a trace of smile softening her face.

With one last longing look, Michelle returned to the living room. She threw herself down on the couch, picked up her magazine, then stared into space. She loved Jacob's girls, and yet there were times when being with them made her feel lonelier than ever. Tonight was one of them.

Would she ever have a child of her own? Would

there ever be someone who turned to her with innocent eyes and a hundred questions, trusting her to
have all the answers? Would she ever be the one a
child ran to for comfort?

Michelle didn't know. And she didn't know if she
was doing the best thing, spending so much of her
free time with someone else's children. Being on the
outside looking in. She only knew that she wouldn't
trade her time with Jacob's girls for anything. For as
long as they'd include her in their lives, she would
be there.

A car pulled into the driveway, its headlights shining through the front window before turning toward
the garage. Her heart started to beat a little faster, and
her fingers tightened around the edges of the magazine she wasn't reading. He knew she was here; he'd
have seen her car out front. So what was he thinking?
That she was keeping tabs on him? That she was taking advantage of their arrangement to invade his privacy?

Michelle forced herself to breathe normally and put
the magazine down. She was being ridiculous. She
had a perfectly legitimate reason for being here. It
would've been silly to keep the sitter when Michelle
was here, anyway, working with the girls on their
costumes. And Jacob was the one who'd told her,
when she'd moved her sewing machine into his living
room, that she could come over anytime.

She heard his key in the lock, heard him close the

door. "Michelle?" His voice sounded so formal. It was worse than she'd imagined.

She stood and slipped into the flats she'd kicked off a couple of hours before, then turned to face him. But the explanation she'd prepared died before it ever reached her lips.

Damn, damn, damn! Tongue-tied, embarrassed beyond belief and so jealous she wanted to scream at him, she tried to look anywhere but at his face—but she couldn't stop staring. His lips were swollen, and his hair, bearing the unmistakable imprint of a woman's fingers, was standing up in tufts; his eyes had that sleepy unmistakable look of a satisfied male. She recognized it from the times she'd seen it before. Right after Brian made love to her.

"Where's Laurie?" He remained in the doorway, one hand in his pocket, the other fiddling with his keys.

"The girls and I walked her home earlier. There didn't seem to be much point in having both of us here."

He nodded, looking over at the material spread out around her sewing machine, at the magazine she'd left lying open on the coffee table, anywhere but at her. "You paid her?"

"I tried, but she said she'd settle up with you later."

He slid his keys into his pocket. "You never said anything about coming over tonight. I thought you were having dinner with your parents."

Michelle shook her head. "That was Tuesday. They have a standing bridge game on Thursday nights."

He nodded again.

Michelle hated this awkwardness between them. It wasn't supposed to be this way. They were friends—partners.

"The girls went to bed right at eight o'clock, though they did try the old glass-of-water routine I used to pull with my parents," she said, walking toward him.

"Yeah, they still try it on me from time to time, too. My mistake was in falling for it the first time. That's the way it is with them. If you give in once they forever hope you'll do it again."

Michelle smiled. "I'll remember that."

She slid past him, heading for the front door.

Jacob followed her. "I'm sorry it's so late. It looks like you're only going to get a couple of hours' sleep."

She turned around, once again ready to defend her presence there, to tell him that making costumes was a time-consuming business, that she didn't want to leave things till the last minute. Again her words died on her lips. His gaze met hers for the first time since he'd walked in the door. He was rubbing the back of his neck, looking remarkably unsure of himself.

It was so unlike Jacob she froze with one hand on the doorknob. His heavy-lidded eyes were filled with all the words he wasn't saying. There was anger there, the ready defense for finding his home invaded without his prior knowledge. But she saw regret, too. For what? For keeping her out so late? Or for coming home to her straight from the arms of another woman?

She couldn't look away as he moved closer, almost hypnotized by the changing expression in his eyes. He reached out, fingering the strand of her hair that lay against one shoulder. His gaze left hers to settle on her lips.

Michelle had never been so tempted to throw herself at a man in her life. At that moment she wanted him so badly it felt like a matter of life and death. She needed to be crushed in his arms until she felt nothing but him, to be kissed until she was too breathless to think, to feel what the woman he'd been with that night had felt. She ran her tongue along the edge of her lips as he stood there, looking at her mouth, his eyes still slumberous with spent passion, but filled with intent, too.

His head came down, his lips parting. So this was what she'd come to. Was she really so desperate for a man's touch that she'd take him straight from another woman's arms? She didn't try to stop him, but her eyes filled with tears.

Jacob backed away immediately. ''Maybe you should call before you come next time,'' he said as if nothing had happened. ''That way I'll know not to stay out so late.''

If he was trying to make her feel better, he'd failed

miserably. Michelle nodded and pulled open the front door. And that was when she remembered Meggie's ruined costume.

"If it's all right with you, I need to run Meggie back to the fabric store tomorrow," she said as soon as she was safely on the porch.

"You forget something?" he asked, leaning on the frame.

Michelle shook her head, gathering her usual composure about her like a cloak. "She didn't want any help cutting out her costume. She did it herself, with her school scissors, while I was helping Jessie with hers."

Jacob grinned. "I assume it didn't turn out too well," he said.

Michelle smiled back, thinking of the mangled material in his trash can. "You could say that," she said.

Jacob shook his head, the gold highlights in his hair glinting under the porch light. "I promised the girls I'd take them to the Hard Rock Café tomorrow night. Why don't you first take Meggie to the store and then come with us, since you're making the trip over here on a Friday night? I know the place is touristy, but the girls love it."

And suddenly, in spite of everything, the evening was turning out okay. "I'd like that," Michelle said. "And by the way you might want to take some stain remover to the lipstick on your collar before you throw that shirt in the wash…"

JACOB HAD KNOWN it was a mistake to invite Michelle to spend the evening with the girls and him the minute he'd issued the invitation. She was starting to make him crave things he had no business craving—that he'd resigned himself to never having. Things like a warm body in his bed all night, rather than in his arms for a few hours. Things like laughter over breakfast and loyalty even when he was a grouch. Things like mutual respect and love. Even knowing that she considered herself a married woman, even after his spending an evening in another woman's arms, he still wanted her.

As he waited with her for a table at the Hard Rock Café the next night, he regretted the invitation again, but for a different reason. He should have foreseen the crowd of people waiting for tables.

He wouldn't have minded so much if just he and the girls had been here. While it wasn't easy keeping three energetic and excited seven-year-olds entertained, he was, after all, used to it. But with Michelle here, everything was different. He was on edge, afraid the triplets' enthusiasm was going to wear on her, expecting one of them to do something embarrassing or, worse, all three of them to do something embarrassing.

"Can I have another soda, Daddy?" Meggie asked, bringing him her empty cup.

"I want one, too, Daddy," Jessie said, bobbing up and down in front of him.

"Me, too," Allie said, taking Jessie's cup and handing it to Jacob with her own.

He glanced at Michelle. Her glass was still full, but she was smiling at the girls. Deciding not to risk the unpleasantness that could occur—in triplicate—from the word *no,* he said, "Sure," and headed back to the bar.

As he waited for the bartender he wondered what he was doing trying to avoid the inevitable. At some point the girls weren't going to be perfect angels. Hell, right this minute he was probably creating the situation that was going to ruin things. As a single father he'd discovered years ago that public rest rooms were the ultimate challenge. He couldn't very well take the girls with him into the men's room. And he sure as hell wasn't sending them anywhere on their own. That was why he never took his daughters anywhere without making sure they went to the bathroom just before they left home. But after the long wait to be seated tonight—and after two large sodas—he expected to hear, "Daddy, I have to go right *now,*" at least three times before the evening was over.

The girls all knew what they wanted to eat, and they placed their orders almost as soon as they were seated at the table. Jacob sat between Jessie and Allie trying to restrain their excited chatter. Being with the triplets had never been so exhausting.

"Look at that guitar, Michelle. Isn't it cool?"

"I like the motorcycle. Did you see the motorcycle, Michelle?"

"Daddy, what's that record hanging over there? Can I go see?"

Jacob wished he were at home. "Girls, girls, one at a time, please," he said, afraid to look at Michelle. Had she had enough yet?

"Well, can I, Daddy? Can I go see?" Meggie was halfway out of her chair.

"Meggie, sit," Jacob said. "We'll look after we're done eating."

"See that guitar, Michelle? It's Elvis Presley's," Allie said, pointing to a corner of the room.

"Yeah, and the motorcycle's his, too," Jessie said, sitting up on her knees.

Michelle's head spun as she tried to keep up with the girls.

"Are they really Elvis Presley's?" she asked Jacob.

He shrugged. "I doubt it, but you never know."

"I'm hungry, Daddy. When's our food coming?" Meggie asked fifteen minutes later, long after the girls had tired of the sights in the room.

"Soon," he said, hoping he was correct. He must have been out of his mind to have invited Michelle on an outing like this—his family was an accident waiting to happen.

Jessie grabbed the saltshaker and turned it over, spilling salt in her palm.

Jacob snatched it from her. "You know better than that, Jess," he said, brushing her hand off with his napkin.

Watching Jessie, Allie and Meggie took an interest in the condiments, too.

"I'm counting the sugars," Meggie said, pulling the dishful of packets toward her.

"What's this, Daddy?" Allie asked, shaking a bottle of steak sauce.

Jacob lunged for the steak sauce, praying the lid was on tight. "Put the sugars back, Meg. People don't want to use them after you've played with them."

Jacob was surprised that Michelle still looked so unruffled. Ellen would've insisted on leaving.

"Anyone know how to play hangman?" Michelle asked, taking a small notepad and pen from her purse.

"What's hangman?" Allie and Jessie chorused. Even Meggie looked interested.

"I think of a word—I'll make it one you guys can spell—and draw blanks like this. Then you try to fill in the blanks by guessing letters. But each time you guess wrong, I get to draw another part of a stick figure up here. If he's complete before you guess the word, then I win."

"What happens if we guess the word before he's done?" Jessie asked.

"Then we win, silly," Allie said. "Okay, let's start."

"Be nice to your sister, Al," Jacob said, relaxing just a bit. Michelle flashed him a quick smile—and the game began.

With Jacob as referee, Michelle kept the girls entertained for another fifteen minutes until their food came. And she helped dispense catsup and salt to the three plates of burgers and fries as naturally as if she'd been doing it all her life.

A second of silence fell over the table while the three children dug into their meals. Jacob figured there was something to be said for keeping their mouths full.

He'd just taken the first bite of his cheeseburger when things started to go wrong. "I have to *go*," Jessie announced, bouncing in her seat.

Jacob groaned inwardly. What now? He glanced down the hall that led to the ladies' room. He could stick his head around the door and make sure the coast was clear before he sent Jessie in, then stand guard outside until she came out. It wasn't the way he liked to do things, but it didn't look as if he had much choice. He'd just have to hope that he didn't offend some poor woman in the process.

"I'll take her," Michelle said easily.

Jessie jumped up and slid her hand into Michelle's. Jacob groaned again—audibly this time. Michelle was putting up a good front, but her food would be cold by the time she got back.

"Allie, Meggie, you go with them," he said. At least he could insure that this only happened once.

"I don't have to go," Allie said, her mouth full of hamburger.

"Me, neither," Meggie added.

Jacob gave the two his sternest look. "This is your

only chance, girls. If you have to go, you better do it now.''

"I don't," Allie said, looking toward her sister for confirmation.

"Me, neither," Meggie said again.

"I gotta go *now,*" Jessie said again, hopping up and down.

Jacob watched her head off with Michelle. Then, flagging down their waiter as he passed, he asked him to try to keep Michelle's meal warm.

Three-quarters of the way through dinner, Allie had to go to the bathroom.

"Me, too," Meggie said when she heard her sister's announcement.

Normally patient with his daughters, Jacob had to bite his tongue to keep from snapping at them. He looked across at Michelle, prepared to see the irritation or, worse, the resignation he'd come to dread seeing on Ellen's face every time one of the girls needed something she'd just done for one of the others.

Michelle was standing there grinning. "Come on, you two. You won't believe what's hanging on the wall right outside the bathroom."

Allie and Meggie jumped up, flanking Michelle as they traipsed off to the bathroom giggling excitedly. Allie was holding her hand, and Michelle was keeping Meggie within grabbing distance, as well.

Jacob stared after them, shaken by a wave of desire. More than her sexy body or silky skin, it was Michelle's obvious fondness for his girls that moved him the most. It almost made him believe he might yet find that happy-ever-after he used to dream about. Until he remembered Brian Colby.

"What's the matter, Daddy? Don't you like your french fries?" Jessie asked, putting her hand on Jacob's arm.

"Sure, sport, I like them just fine," he said, looking down at one of the females who owned his heart.

"Then why did you have such a bad look on your face? Like this." She scrunched her eyebrows together and jutted out her chin.

Jacob smiled and tweaked the end of her nose. "Just to see if you'd notice," he said.

Jessie didn't look convinced. "I love you, Daddy," she said, her small features solemn.

"And I love you, too, Jess," he said, knowing he was lucky beyond belief to have his three beautiful daughters. Somehow he was just going to have to make them be enough.

JACOB EXPECTED Michelle to leave just as soon as they got back to his place that night. But she followed him into the house, offering to make him a pot of coffee while he got the girls tucked into bed. He could tell she had something on her mind. He wondered if she was about to turn tail, after all. Allie and Jessie insisted on hugging her good-night before they'd go to bed. Meggie didn't hug her, but she smiled and thanked Michelle for the trip they'd made to the fabric store that day.

Michelle was gazing out the kitchen window when he came into the kitchen fifteen minutes later. "There's diet cola in the fridge," he said, pouring himself a cup of freshly brewed coffee.

Michelle whirled around as if she hadn't heard him come in. "Thanks," she said, and filled a glass with ice.

"The girls said to tell you good-night, again," he told her when she joined him at the table. He'd had a talk with himself while he'd waited for the girls to get into their pajamas and brush their teeth. Whatever Michelle had to say, he'd deal with it unemotionally. If she was going to leave them, so be it. He'd find another way to get the costumes made. In fact, maybe that would be for the best. Her tears the night before when he'd tried to kiss her had really thrown him for a loop. But not as much as the guilt that had plagued him for coming home to her after sleeping with another woman. He'd felt like an unfaithful husband, for God's sake. Yeah, maybe it was for the best that she call it quits before he did anything foolish—like fall in love with her.

"Can I ask you something?" Michelle said softly.

"Sure."

Her eyes were serious as she looked at him. "You seemed pretty on edge tonight, and I wondered if I've done something to upset you. Because if I have I think we should talk about it now before it becomes a problem.''

"Hell, no!'' he said, setting his cup down so forcefully the coffee splashed over the rim. "I wasn't upset with you.''

She shrugged. "Well, what then? I've never seen you so uptight before. If it bothers you having me around your girls, I can make the costumes myself at my house,'' she said.

Jacob felt as if he was surfing on a wave that was about to become an undertow. "The girls have to help, I told you that.'' He'd said the quickest thing that came to mind. Now that it seemed she wasn't leaving, he forgot all about wanting her to go. After all, who else would he get to make those costumes?

She nodded, still looking serious. "I just don't want you to think I'm trying to butt in, like when I came over last night.''

"Butt in already. It's working out okay, isn't it?'' he asked, suddenly wondering if this was a roundabout way to get out of helping him.

"That's the problem. I don't know if it's working out or not. You never tell me what you're thinking, and it's driving me nuts to keep guessing, wondering if I'm getting in your way. It wouldn't kill you to open up a little bit, you know.''

He wasn't so sure. But he didn't want her to walk out that door and never come back, either. Even if she was only in his house as a friend. He wanted her there. He'd finally admitted it. To himself at least.

He leaned forward, resting his forearms on the table, cradling his coffee cup. ''The last time Ellen and I took the girls out to dinner, we'd barely been seated when Jessie spilled her drink. They're good kids most of the time, but they're still kids. And Ellen seemed to bring out the worst in them. That night, Jessie had to use the bathroom before we'd even looked at the menus. Then when Allie started to cry because we wouldn't let her have ice cream for dinner and her sisters joined in, Ellen insisted that I take them home, get a sitter and take her—Ellen—out for a real dinner. She yelled at the girls all the way home, telling them that they didn't have the right to publicly embarrass her, that she deserved to be able to sit down and enjoy a meal at least once in a while, that she wasn't going to let them steal her life away. They were only three at the time, and I don't suppose they understood half of what she was saying, but they knew she was angry and was blaming *them*. And when I intervened, Ellen went ballistic. She claimed I always sided with the girls, and she took that out on them, as well. There was no reasoning with her. I drove as fast as I could, but the girls were all crying hysterically by the time we got home. It took me the rest of the evening to get them calmed down enough to eat a sandwich and climb into bed. I've never felt so helpless in my life. I should have seen it coming, should have been able to do something more than I was doing, but damned if I knew what it was.''

When he realized how much he'd just revealed,

Jacob clamped his mouth shut. Hell, he hadn't even known he remembered that night in such detail.

"She ought to be hung." Michelle's fierce look brought a smile to his lips.

"I gotta admit to having had that thought a time or two myself, but it was a lot more complicated than that. She was partially right. I did side with the girls a lot."

"It sounds like you may have had good reason."

"Some of the time. But Ellen wasn't a bad person. She just wasn't mother material."

"Then she shouldn't have had children." Michelle's voice was as fierce as her expression. She reminded him of a mother bear protecting her young. Except they were *his* young she was defending. It was a new experience for him, one he could probably get used to with very little effort.

"You're right of course. And she probably wouldn't have had children if I hadn't pressured her into getting pregnant. I wanted kids. A whole houseful of them."

"Didn't you two talk about raising a family before you got married? I know Brian and I did."

"Yeah, we talked. I told her how badly I wanted kids. She said okay. What we didn't talk about, until after she was pregnant, was that she wanted a baby to show off but not to care for. Her idea of parenting was as far from mine as it was possible to get. She'd been raised by a nanny. Her mother was a social butterfly who always looked immaculate, who only saw her child when she stopped home in between appointments. I'd thought that Ellen of all people would understand how hard it is to grow up with parental neglect. Instead, she thought that was the only way to raise children. She was shocked when, once she got pregnant, I refused to consider hiring a nanny. Frankly I didn't have the greatest childhood, and I was determined that my child was going to be raised by his parents, not by strangers.'' Jacob knew that ultimately the fault for his divorce—for his children's motherless state—lay with him. He'd been too unbending. He expected too much. But where his children were concerned, he wasn't going to change. And he wasn't sorry for that.

Michelle laid a hand on Jacob's forearm. ''It's not wrong to expect your wife to help raise your children.''

''No, but I was so busy listening to my own needs I never really considered hers, or at least not honestly. I kept telling Ellen that once she held her baby in her arms everything would change. I was banking on that old mother's instinct kicking in. I hired someone to help her as soon as we knew the triplets were coming, but I insisted that Ellen and I would be the primary care givers. I really thought she'd want it that way, too, once the babies came. She never did.''

''How could any one look at those three precious little girls and not love them instantly?''

''That's just it. She did love them. More than she imagined she would, I think. But their care was just

too overwhelming for her. She didn't find any satisfaction in it. She told me once that she was choking
on ABC's. She wasn't fascinated by all the simple
things that I found so exciting. When Jessie blew bubbles, it wasn't cooing to Ellen, it was drooling. When
the girls started to walk, they weren't taking first
steps, they were constantly on the brink of falling and
hurting themselves. She was repelled by dirty diapers,
and the girls' crying made her nervous. And to further
complicate matters, they kept Ellen from doing the
things she enjoyed, like shopping or playing tennis or
heading up some committee. She felt like life was
passing her by. And I couldn't agree to putting the
girls in day care so young or having a live-in care
giver. They weren't going to be shoved aside like I
was. I kept telling myself that Ellen would adjust in
time, that once the girls got a little older she'd start
enjoying them. My immediate solution was to take
her out more, but while she enjoyed that, our late
nights left her tired the next day, which meant she
had even less patience for the girls.''

Jacob fell silent, thinking back over those days,
wondering where he'd made the first mistake, looking, always looking, for the solution that would have
been right for both of them. And he came to the same
conclusion as always. Maybe they'd found it.

''All women aren't like Ellen, you know.'' Michelle's words fell softly into the late-night silence.

He thought of Jenny, his former on-air partner.
She'd said she loved him, but she needed time to

herself, too. Not just an evening without the girls, but evenings at home alone in front of the television set. Jacob had never understood why they couldn't watch television together. And she'd grown tired of having the triplets as part of the package. She'd liked the girls. She just hadn't wanted them on a full-time basis. And then there was Katie Walters's mother. What was it the triplets had heard? Something about she'd have left, too? Apparently wanting a full-time mother for his children was asking for too much. But then he always had wanted more than he should. His own mother had told him so often enough. Couldn't he see she had other children to care for besides him?

"I know," he finally said.

"So relax, partner. I think I can handle anything your girls can dish out. Trust me."

Jacob wished it was that easy.

CHAPTER EIGHT

JACOB AND MICHELLE were in the station lunch room getting their caffeine fixes when Bob Chaney handed them an envelope.

"You guys had the best ratings this week, so enjoy the promo," he said as he walked away. He'd been keeping his distance ever since Michelle had blown up at him the week before.

Michelle opened the envelope, half expecting to find a gift certificate for dinner for two at some romantic out-of-the way spot. She was surprised when she pulled out four tickets to Disneyland.

"What is it?" Jacob asked, sipping his coffee. His T-shirt was blue this morning, depicting a beautiful Colorado skyline. The color looked good on him.

"Four tickets to Disneyland. Two for you and two for me."

"Seems like he got our message. We get to take dates," Jacob said with a grin.

Michelle wondered why that didn't please her as much as it should have. "I guess. Here." She handed him the tickets.

He handed two back. "You get these."

Michelle turned back to the pop machine. "You go ahead, Jacob. Take the girls."

"Don't be ridiculous, Michelle. I'm not taking your promo."

She faced him, a can of soda in hand. "And what am I going to do with two tickets to Disneyland? Take Noby? You know I don't date, and I can't think of a single friend who would choose to spend an entire day with me, rather than with the man in her life." She smiled to take the sting out of her words. It wasn't Jacob's fault she didn't have anybody of her own to take to Disneyland. "Take the girls, Jacob. They'll love it."

"Then you'll have to come with us."

"We only have four tickets."

"So we'll buy one more. I'm not taking these tickets unless you come along with us. Think of it as research. You can get a good look at Cinderella and her evil stepsisters while we're there."

As weak as it was, she accepted the excuse. "Okay, sounds like fun. When should we go?"

"How about Saturday?"

"Saturday's fine. Around eight?"

"Why don't we pick you up at seven and have breakfast on the way. My treat. We can tell the girls tonight."

It was only later that Michelle wondered if they'd both been a little too eager to spend the day together. She was in this for the kids. Period.

"YOU GONNA SEW Jessie's other sleeve on when you finish sewing that one, Michelle?" Allie asked Wednesday night after supper. She was holding the sleeve in question.

"As soon as I trim the threads on this one," Michelle said. She took her foot off the sewing-machine pedal long enough to turn the sleeve currently under the needle. She was finding it a little difficult to maneuver the material with Jessie hanging on her arm.

"I can trim the threads for you," Allie said.

"How do you make it go so straight?" Jessie asked, leaning to get a better look.

"See that line?" Michelle asked, pointing to a plate on her machine. Jessie nodded. "I just keep the edge of the material even with it, like this."

Meggie wandered over to peer at the sewing machine.

"You get that lace measured out like I showed you, Meggie?" Michelle asked.

"Almost," Meggie replied, returning to her task.

Michelle pulled one of the pins out of the sleeve before the needle hit it.

"Here's the pin cushion," Allie said, taking the pin to put it in the cushion herself. "How about if I take all of the pins out for you?" she asked.

"What can I do? It's my sleeve," Jessie said, still holding on to Michelle.

"You can help me guide the material," Michelle said. "See, take the bottom edge, and help me keep it on the line."

"Like this?" Jessie asked. She'd let go of Michelle's arm but was having a problem getting a good hold on the material.

"Here," Michelle said, lifting her foot from the pedal again to move Jessie onto her lap. "Now we can do it together."

"And I'll do the pins, all right?" Allie asked.

"Okay, you can be the pin lady," Michelle said, trying to slow the machine down to a speed Jessie could handle. "How's the lace coming, Meggie?"

"Fine."

Jessie started to slip off Michelle's lap and tried to right herself, pushing one foot against the floor. But she missed and pushed against Michelle's foot.

The sewing machine whirred loudly as the needle sped into triple time, pulling the material out of Michelle's grasp. There was a loud cracking noise, and everything stopped.

"What happened?" Jessie and Allie asked at once.

"What was that noise?" Meggie asked, coming over to see what was going on.

Michelle leaned around Jessie to get a closer look at the sewing machine. "I think we just broke a needle."

"Uh-oh," Allie said, backing up.

Jessie scooted off Michelle's lap.

Meggie went back to cutting lace.

After Michelle removed the broken needle, she turned to the girls. Two of them of them were watching her carefully, their faces puckered with worry. Meggie was hunched over her lace.

"Hey!" Michelle smiled. "It's no big deal, you guys. Needles break all the time. That's why I have extras. Allie, bring me my sewing basket."

Meggie handed the basket to her sister, who hurried over to Michelle with it. Jessie scooted closer.

It took Michelle only a couple of moments to realize she'd left her extra needles at home.

Allie looked worried again when she heard the news. Jessie started to cry. Meggie's scissors were snipping away.

Michelle cuddled Jessie under one arm and went over to Allie, pulling her under the other. "So I guess we'll just have to take a trip to my house," she said. "You girls can come along and say hi to Noby. You remember Noby, don't you?"

Meggie stopped cutting. All three girls nodded.

"She's probably pretty lonely, so it's good to be able to take a break and go see her. Allie, why don't you run out and tell your daddy where we're going?"

Allie hurried outside to where Jacob was waxing his 4×4. Jessie hopped up and down, obviously eager to get going, her tears forgotten. Meggie went back to cutting.

"Come on, Meggie, you can finish that when we get back."

"I'm staying home with Daddy," she said, concentrating on her task.

Michelle frowned. "Don't you want to see Noby?"

"I wanna stay home with Daddy," Meggie said, neatly sidestepping Michelle's question.

Michelle walked over to the little girl. "You don't *have* to come, Meggie. I just want you to know that I'd love to have you along if you *want* to come."

"I'll stay with Daddy," Meggie said, still not looking up from her lace.

"How about if we bring you back some ice cream?" Michelle asked, determined to reach the little girl.

"Okay, if you want."

And with that, Michelle knew she had to be satisfied.

ALLIE THOUGHT Saturday was never going to come. All day Friday she kept waiting for school to be over, but it was taking forever. Every time Allie looked at the watch her daddy had bought her for Christmas, the numbers had barely changed at all. She thought maybe the battery wasn't so good anymore, but if it wasn't, then the clocks at school weren't working, either, 'cause when her teacher dismissed them for lunch, it was the exact time on Allie's watch that lunch was s'posed to be.

Lunch was hardest of all. She kept being afraid that Meggie or Jessie was going to need her for something, and then she'd blab everything and one of them would ruin it. This was one plan she was just going to have to do on her own. She could, too. And then it wouldn't matter if her sisters found out that she'd almost ruined things by wishing so hard for a mommy that it made Daddy sad, because then her wish would just come true and her sisters would be happily ever after.

She and Jessie and Meggie had been to Disneyland lots of times, and Allie knew plain and simple that five people couldn't sit together on the rides. So she was going to make sure her sisters sat with her. Then her daddy and Michelle would have to sit together and after a whole day of being next to each other they'd fall in love. Now all Allie had to do was keep her big mouth shut and not tell her sisters that Michelle was going to be their new mommy. Not yet. Not until they got back from Disneyland. Then she'd tell them. After all, she wanted them to know she was the one who got Michelle for them—just in case they ever found out she was the one who started the whole trouble in the first place. But keeping such important stuff a secret was the hardest thing she'd ever done.

FRIDAY NIGHT, Michelle dropped Noby off at her parents for the weekend, worried that her pet was getting depressed at being left alone so much. Her mom and dad seemed delighted to cat-sit, but Michelle knew, as fond as they were of Noby, it wasn't her cat they were worked up about.

She wanted to tell them not to read more into her time with Jacob and his girls than was there, to remind them that she was a married woman, that until Brian was found, one way or the other, she would remain a married woman. But she'd been telling herself the same things all week, and if she hadn't managed to curtail her own excitement at the thought of the next day, she knew she'd fail miserably with her parents.

Sometimes she wondered if she wasn't overdoing her loyalty to a man she hadn't heard from in almost five years. She wanted to put her life back on track, to have babies, to raise a family. She didn't want to grow old alone. And yet each time she thought about putting the past to rest, there was something inside her holding her to the vows that she and Brian had made. She was certain he hadn't left her by choice. And until she knew for sure he'd left her for good, she couldn't stop being married to him. There was a bond between them—forged many years ago by their young idealistic love—that refused to be broken. Michelle suspected that the reason she still felt that bond so strongly was because Brian was alive somewhere, willing her to wait for him.

And she'd wait forever if she had to, she told herself as she drove home later that evening. But she was going to do what living she could while she waited. Her mother had been right to claim that Michelle had quit reaching out to people. She'd forgotten how good it felt to help someone else, how much less time it left for worrying about her own problems. Now Jacob's girls were filling up some of the empty spaces inside her; she just had to be careful not to let their father do the same.

SHE WAS READY and waiting at seven o'clock Saturday morning when Jacob's Explorer pulled into her driveway. The triplets were buckled up in a row in the back seat, looking absolutely adorable in their identical denim overalls, red T-shirts, high-top tennis shoes and their hair up in ponytails. But it was their differences that stole Michelle's heart as she told them all good-morning and slid into the front beside Jacob.

"Michelle, guess what? We're stopping at McDonald's for breakfast on the way," Allie piped up from the middle of the back seat.

"I get to sit next to you," Jessie confided.

"At McDonald's, she means," Allie added importantly.

"Hi," Meggie said, not quite containing her smile.

"I missed you guys yesterday, you know that?" Michelle said, smiling at them. The day was perfect already, and it had only just begun.

They arrived at the Magic Kingdom just as the gates were opening. Jacob pulled into one of the few vacant parking spaces in the Thumper lot, and by the time he'd turned off the ignition the girls had unfastened their seat belts. Meggie tugged on one door handle and Jessie on the other, while Allie bounced impatiently between them.

"Come on, you guys," Allie said.

"Whoa!"

Michelle was startled by Jacob's stern tone—and

by the reaction he got. The girls froze in their seats, three pairs of dark eyes trained on their father.

"I want the rules one more time," Jacob said, turning around. "Jessie?"

"We stick together and always hold someone's hand."

"Good. And?"

"If we have to go, we tell you *before* we get in a long line."

Jacob smiled. "You got it. Meggie?"

"No running."

"Right. Allie?"

"*If* we get lost, we go to the castle and wait there."

"Right."

"But we won't, you know, Daddy. We never do."

"I know, sport, but I'm supposed to worry, anyway," he said, giving Allie's ponytail a tug. "Now let's get this show on the road."

The girls climbed out of the 4×4, not one ounce less excited, but much more contained. Michelle was impressed.

She was having trouble containing her own excitement as they entered the park and headed down Main Street. The sun was shining, glinting off the lampposts lining the street. The shops beckoned with their colorful displays of candy and stuffed renditions of every Disney character ever to have graced a motion-picture screen. And best of all was the magnificent blue-and-white castle that stood tall and proud at the end of Main Street. Michelle figured even the staunchest scrooge couldn't look at that castle and not feel, just for an instant, that dreams really did come true.

They decided, at Allie's urging, to tackle Fantasyland first and work their way around the entire park. Michelle thought the plan seemed a bit too elaborate for seven-year-olds, but by the sounds of the chatter between the girls and Jacob, doing Disneyland—all of it—was nothing new to them. She hoped *she* would be able to hold out.

The girls skipped between Jacob and her talking as fast as their little tongues could manage. Michelle wondered if they even heard each other, as none of them seemed to stay quiet long enough for a single word to reach them.

"We'll do Snow White's Scary Adventures first, Daddy, okay?" Allie asked, glancing up at her father.

"Fine, sport." Jacob nodded. Though he was watching the girls like a hawk, he looked more relaxed than Michelle had ever seen him. If she wasn't mistaken, Jacob Ryan was as affected by the magic around them as she was.

Another family brushed past, and Michelle saw the mother turn around, do a double take and then nudge her husband. Michelle smiled, not yet used to the attention the triplets attracted wherever they went. She supposed to these strangers she was the mother who completed Jacob's family unit, and she wished suddenly that it was true. She could only imagine how it would feel to be the nucleus of a family, but she figured that this day with Jacob and his children was the closest she'd come to it. It might be the closest she'd *ever* come to it. And she was going to enjoy every minute, she determined as she followed the girls toward Snow White's Scary Adventures.

"Jessie and Meggie 'n me'll go in the first car, so you guys can see us, okay, Daddy?" Allie said, pulling on the sleeve of Jacob's Lakers jersey.

Jacob smiled down at her "Yep."

She grabbed the map of the park from the back pocket of his jeans. "Where're we going next?" she asked, scanning the pages of the map as if she could read every word. "How about Pinocchio's Daring Journey? Let's do that next."

"If it's okay with your sisters," Jacob said.

Jessie and Meggie were leaning over the railing trying to see what was going on ahead of them.

"They don't care," Allie said with certainty.

He turned to Michelle. "How about you? You have any special requests? If so, you better get them in quick before Allie has the whole day planned."

Michelle grinned. "I wouldn't dare interfere with the expert," she said, happy just to be standing in line with the four of them.

The line moved forward, and Jacob urged his daughters along, leaving Michelle to bring up the rear. She found herself fixating on his snugly clad backside. She'd known Jacob for years—why was he suddenly so appealing?

"Michelle, come on!"

Allie's voice jerked Michelle out of her reverie and she hurried to catch up. She hadn't even noticed that they'd reached the front of the line.

"Okay, girls, hands inside, no standing, wait for us at the end and have fun."

Michelle was amazed that Jacob had the time to get in all his instructions as he fastened the safety bar across his girls and waved them off.

"This is ours," he said as the next automated carrier came along.

It wasn't until then that Michelle realized she would be sharing a very small space with Jacob. Her hands felt a little clammy as she slid across the seat. It got worse when Jacob sat down beside her. His hip pressed against hers and his arm brushed her breast as he reached to fasten their safety bar. Michelle shivered, horrified when her nipples tightened. She hunched her shoulders and prayed the ride would be a dark one.

Jacob leaned toward her. "You cold?" he asked as their car jerked forward.

"A little," Michelle said. Jacob grinned at her in lazy satisfaction. He had a look about him that said he knew exactly what was happening—and was pleased by it. Dear Lord, how was she going to get through the next two minutes, let alone the next several hours?

They rode on a boat through the storybook canal, went through It's a Small World twice at Jessie's request and screamed their way through the Matterhorn

Bobsleds. And through it all, whether sitting next to Jacob or not, Michelle was aware of every inch of his healthy masculine body.

"I wanna sit with Michelle," Jessie said three lines later. "I don't wanna sit with you on this one, Allie. I wanna sit with Michelle."

"That's fine with me, honey," Michelle said. She hoped she didn't sound as eager as she felt to change the seating arrangements. At this stage, the impression of Jacob's shoulder and hip must be permanently imprinted on hers, and the touch of his hand was affecting more than her concentration.

"When we're done with Peter Pan can we go to Tomorrowland?" Allie asked.

"Sure, Al, as long as no one objects," Jacob said. He smiled at Michelle over his daughter's head, and even though his sunglasses hid his eyes something told her that Jacob was just as affected by their close confines as she was.

"I'm thirsty, Daddy. Can I have money for a soda?" Meggie asked half an hour later as the five of them headed for Tomorrowland.

"I could use a drink myself," Michelle said. "I'll go with you."

She took orders from the other two girls and Jacob, then remembering Jacob's rule about hand-holding, reached for Meggie's hand and headed toward the drink line. She felt a rush of happiness when Meggie's little fingers curled around her own. There really was magic in Disney's kingdom. She'd scale Meggie's walls yet.

They stopped for lunch halfway through Tomorrowland; afterword, Michelle suggested that they do some of the ''old folks'' rides like the Monorail and the Submarine voyage. She didn't want to take any chances that their day would be ruined by upset stomachs.

The girls were good sports on the tamer attractions, but as soon as Michelle announced that they'd waited long enough for their food to settle, they were back to their daring adventures. About three-quarters of the way around the building in the line at Space Mountain was a sign that said it was a forty-five-minute wait from that point, but the girls weren't daunted.

''Please, Daddy,'' Jessie said.

''You don't mind waiting, do you?'' Allie asked Michelle at the same time.

Jacob and Michelle looked at each other over the girls' heads, passing silent messages of acquiescence before they gave in with resigned shrugs. Michelle hadn't been on Space Mountain in years, but if she remembered it correctly, it was one ride on which she wouldn't mind being paired with Jacob—for moral support. She'd always been a little bit nervous of roller coasters, and this one was in the dark.

All in all the wait wasn't so bad. There were four people to a cart, two in front and two in back, and Allie was directing traffic as usual as they approached.

Meggie walked up to the cart in front of the one Allie had picked for her and her sisters to share. "I'm riding by myself," she said.

Allie turned to Jacob. "Is that okay, Daddy?" she asked.

Jacob looked at Meggie standing resolutely in her spot. "Yeah, it's okay," he said. "You keep your hands in and hold on tight, Meg, got it?"

"Got it," she said, grinning back at them.

Allie told Jessie to take the first seat in the next cart and then climbed in beside her, leaving Michelle and Jacob together once again. The carts rolled forward, and Michelle was thrown almost into Jacob's lap with the force of the turns. They climbed and dropped, spun and swerved, but none of it was as exciting as the feel of Jacob's arm around her shoulders, as they hurtled through the darkness.

CHAPTER NINE

THE GIRLS' ENERGY seemed endless. As the day wore on, they left Tomorrowland behind to hike over to Mickey's Toontown. They traipsed through Mickey's house and had their picture taken with the host himself, visited Minnie's house, climbed onto Donald's boat and laughed at the goods for sale in the Gag Factory. Michelle was busy trying to explain a particularly zany contraption to Meggie when suddenly Jacob grabbed her arm.

"Have you seen Jessie?"

Michelle glanced around the store, searching for the little girl. "She was over there with Allie a second ago," she said, pointing to the display where Allie was standing.

Jacob crossed to Allie with Michelle and Meggie right behind him. Jessie was probably just hidden by the display.

"Al, where's Jessie?" Jacob asked.

Allie turned. "She said she was going over to where you were, Daddy."

Jacob spun around, retracing his steps. "Jessie?" he called.

"You two stay right here and don't move," Michelle said, stationing Allie and Meggie by the check-out counter before following Jacob.

The store was full of patrons, most of whom ignored them. Michelle suspected that a lost child at Disneyland wasn't all that unusual. Or that alarming, either. At least she hoped that was the case.

"I'm sure she's here someplace," she said, as much for her own sake as for Jacob's. Her stomach knotted, even though she kept telling herself she was overreacting. Jessie knew the rules. She wouldn't run off alone.

"Jessie?" Jacob called again. He was striding up and down the aisles, looking beneath racks of hanging clothes, searching every spot big enough to hold a seven-year-old. Michelle searched with him, feeling sicker by the second. What if Jessie hadn't run off by herself? What if someone had *taken* her?

Telling herself to get a grip, Michelle kept an eye firmly on Meggie and Allie. The girls stood by the counter where she'd left them, playing with a display of pencils. Michelle should take her cue from them. They didn't seem worried at all. They probably went through this all the time.

"She's not here," Jacob said from behind her.

Michelle whirled around. It was time to panic.

"I'm going to ask the clerk if she saw anything," Jacob said.

Michelle went with him, her gaze darting over the store one last time. Where could Jessie be? Would she really have disobeyed her father and wandered off her own? Michelle had a hard time believing that.

Jacob guided Meggie and Allie over to the clerk. "My daughter seems to be missing. She looks exactly like these two. You didn't happen to see her walk out of here, did you?" Michelle didn't know how he could sound so calm. Always a rock, that was Jacob. But she knew him well enough now to know he had to be a wreck on the inside.

"I'm sorry, sir. This is my first day here, and as you can see, we're really busy," the clerk said, motioning to the people in line waiting to pay for purchases.

"Are you sure you didn't see her?" Michelle asked. She couldn't believe this was happening.

The clerk shook her head. "Did you check outside? She's probably waiting for you out there." She flashed a harried smile.

Jacob ushered his family outside. They searched the immediate vicinity, but there was no sign of Jessie. Something was wrong. Very wrong. And as frightened as Michelle was, she could only imagine what this was doing to Jacob.

"Where *is* Jessie, Daddy?" Allie asked, her voice thick with tears. Michelle hugged the little girl, trying to comfort her. Jacob didn't need to contend with a hysterical child right now. She looked around Toontown. There were people everywhere. How were they ever going to find one small-for-her-age seven-year-old?

"Do you think something bad happened to Jessie?" Meggie asked quietly, her voice laced with fear. She slipped her hand into Jacob's.

"No! I don't think anything bad happened to her," Jacob said, studying the compound.

Allie and Meggie stood between the adults looking lost themselves as they gazed at the people milling all around. "Let's go back to Minnie's house. Jessie liked it best," Jacob said, heading off in that direction with Meggie in tow. Michelle gripped Allie's hand and followed him, looking at every short person she passed.

"You're hurting me," Allie said, tugging on her hand.

Michelle looked down. "I'm sorry, sweetie. How's that?" She lightened her grip.

Allie nodded and sniffled. Michelle reached into the pouch at her waist, pulled out a tissue and handed it to Allie, searching the area around them all the while. There were children everywhere, some accompanied by adults. But there was no sign of Jessie.

"Are you worried, Michelle?" Allie asked softly, staring at her father's straight back in front of them.

"She'll be fine, Al. Disneyland is one place kids are still safe without their parents."

"Daddy's worried."

"Your daddy's just concentrating on finding her, honey. I'm sure she'll turn up really soon."

Allie looked at Michelle with teary eyes. "Then

how come your voice sounds all wobbly like you're gonna cry?''

Michelle forced a smile, putting her arm around Allie to hug the little girl as they walked. ''Because I'm being silly,'' she said. ''Now come on, let's catch up to your father and Meggie.''

Jessie wasn't at Minnie's house.

And she wasn't at Donald's Boat or Chip 'n Dale's Tree Slide, either.

Jacob's lips grew thinner as the minutes passed, his stride more and more determined. Michelle was having a hard time not thinking about some demented person carrying Jessie off. Her skin grew cold as they continued to search.

''Let's head to the castle,'' Jacob said after they'd been around Toontown twice.

''She knows she's s'posed to go there if she's lost,'' Meggie said.

Michelle prayed all the way to Jiminy Cricket's bridge.

''Do you think she'll be there?'' Allie asked. Her tears had stopped, but Michelle knew they weren't far away.

''I hope so, honey. I sure hope so,'' Michelle said, guiding Allie around a slow-moving family as they made their way to Main Street.

Jacob's pace had quickened and Meggie was having a hard time keeping up.

''I'll take her if you want to go on ahead,'' Michelle called to him.

He hesitated as if he didn't want to let go of his daughter's hand. And then he nodded, handing Meggie off to Michelle before jogging away through the crowd.

"Daddy's awfully worried," Meggie said as they hurried after him.

"He's not," Allie said, sniffling again.

"He is, too, Al. He just doesn't want us to know it. He didn't even hear me when I asked him what happens if Jessie's not at the castle."

Allie digested that in silence.

"If she's not at the castle then we keep looking till we find her," Michelle said. She'd never seen so many people in her life, and every last one of them was getting in her way as she tried to maneuver the girls through the crowd. She could see the castle up ahead.

"Jessie's gonna be in big trouble," Meggie said.

Michelle hoped so. But only because that would mean she'd been found safe and sound.

Her heart was pumping so hard she found it difficult to breathe as she approached the castle. Jessie had to be there. She just had to be.

"She's not here," Jacob said as soon as he spotted them.

Michelle shuddered. Images of the horrible things that could happen to children flashed through her mind. And not only was Jessie a beautiful little girl, she was far too trusting.

"Aren't we ever going to find her?" Allie started

to sob. Michelle lifted Allie up, cradling her small body.

"Shh. We'll find Jessie, honey," she murmured in Allie's ear.

Meggie watched Allie sobbing in Michelle's arms. She looked around at all the strangers passing by. Then she tugged at the bottom of Jacob's jersey. "What are we gonna do, Daddy?" she asked, bursting into tears.

Jacob swung Meggie up, perching her on his hip. "I'll find her, girls," he said.

He didn't look as sure as he sounded. In fact, he looked a little lost himself. Michelle turned away, swallowing her tears. They had to keep searching.

"What's the problem here, folks?"

Allie and Meggie both turned to see the owner of the muffled voice. But even a life-size Goofy wasn't enough to dry their tears.

"Their sister is missing," Jacob said, tight-lipped.

"Have you checked the lost-child center?" Goofy was suddenly all business.

"I didn't know there was a lost-child center," Jacob said, glancing at Michelle. She shrugged. She hadn't known, either.

"Follow me." Goofy headed through the plaza toward the end of Main Street. "Most folks don't know about the lost-child center unless they've needed it before. Your daughter's probably there right now, ma'am, having the time of her life."

Michelle smiled tremulously, hugging Allie's small

body more securely against her as she carried the child through the crowds. Goofy turned left at the Carefree Corners gift shop with Jacob walking purposefully beside him. She could only imagine the thoughts that must be running through Jacob's head.

They reached a building with a Red Cross emblem, and Goofy held the door open for them. Jacob went in first, still carrying Meggie.

"Daddy!"

Michelle heard Jessie's happy cry before she'd even gotten inside the door. Her arms went limp with relief and she set a scrambling Allie down, allowing the little girl to rush to greet her sister.

Jacob was there already, checking Jessie over, hugging her, then checking her over again. Tears started to Michelle's eyes as she watched him, knowing he'd never forget the past forty-five minutes. Meggie and Allie finally pushed by him to take their turns hugging their sister, and then Jessie, looking at Michelle, held out her arms. And that's when Michelle's composure snapped. "Oh, baby!" she cried, a sob breaking free when she finally held the little girl in her arms. *Thank you, God. Thank you.* The words played over and over in her head.

"Where'd you go, Jessie?" Allie's voice broke into Michelle's litany, reminding her that Jessie had a whole family waiting to find out what had happened. After a final hug, Michelle moved aside.

"Yeah, what happened?" Meggie asked, her voice accusing.

The girls stood right in front of Jessie, grilling her, but Jessie took it in stride. "I saw Minnie, Al. She was right outside the door and I just went to say hi, I promise." She looked from Allie's unforgiving frown to Meggie's. "I was going to come right back. But by the time I catched up with her, I couldn't find which store we were at."

"Why didn't you go to the castle, Jess?" Jacob asked, kneeling beside Allie.

Jessie looked up at her father, her face completely serious. "I forgot."

"Jessie," Jacob said, his exasperation drawing out the one word.

"I know, Daddy, but it was okay. A nice lady was picking up trash by me, and when I cried, she helped me come here and I got to watch a cartoon on TV and then Roger Rabbit came and played with me and I met a friend, Susan, except her mommy and daddy just came and found her."

Jacob looked as if he was about to tell Jessie just how okay it was not, but Goofy stepped forward as Jessie was finishing her explanation.

"Everything all right now, folks?" he asked.

Jacob's stern look faded, replaced by a grateful smile. "Fine. Thank you very much," he said.

"And you, young lady—" Goofy put his big paws on Jessie's shoulders "—you mind your mommy and daddy and stay with them from now on, okay?"

Jessie's dark eyes grew bigger as she listened to

the life-size cartoon character. "Mmm-hmm," she said, nodding solemnly.

"Enjoy the rest of your day at the park, folks," Goofy said, holding the door open for them.

"Did you hear that, Daddy? He called Michelle my mommy," Jessie said as if, because it came from Goofy, it must mean something.

Michelle held her breath, looking anywhere but at Jacob. This was just what he'd warned her about from the very beginning. He didn't want his girls weaving impossible dreams around her. She looked at the other two triplets. Allie had an odd, almost conspiratorial grin on her face. Meggie appeared engrossed in the double-decker bus making its way down Main Street.

"Goofy doesn't know that Michelle's already married to someone else," Jacob said.

"But her husband doesn't live with her, so why can't she live with us?" Jessie demanded. Allie looked expectant and worried at the same time, and Michelle felt awful. Jacob didn't need this on top of everything else.

He frowned down at Allie and Jessie. "Look girls, I told you—"

"Can we ride that, Daddy?" Meggie interrupted, pointing to the bus.

Michelle couldn't stand there quietly anymore. Afraid that Jacob might be pushed to the point of calling off their arrangement, she gathered the three girls around her, kneeling to meet them eye to eye. "Here's the thing, girls. I can't be your real mommy, like living with you and your daddy out at the beach, 'cause I already have a house and a husband. But I don't have any kids of my own, and so I kind of thought we could borrow each other for as long as you want to.''

She was probably going to be in trouble with Jacob but, dammit, she wanted the girls to believe they could count on her even if he didn't. She'd realized when Jessie was missing just how much she'd come to care for these children. She wasn't going to desert them ever—not even if, or when, Brian came home.

Jessie's brow furrowed. ''Borrow?'' she asked.

''Yes, like a loan, except we can make it a kind of permanent borrow.''

Jacob stirred restlessly but Michelle wasn't going to let him intimidate her. He was just going to have to trust her.

''Kind of like puppies are on loan from their mommies when they go to live with people, only you won't be living with us?'' Allie asked.

Michelle smiled. ''Yep. Kind of like that. For as long as you guys want me you've got me.''

Meggie shifted, backing away from the circle a little. ''But what about when your husband comes home and you have your own kids and don't need to borrow us no more?'' Meggie was certainly her father's daughter.

''Even if Brian comes home, even if I have my own children someday, I'll still love being there if you need me. That's how love works. It doesn't run out—it just keeps growing.''

"You mean you love us?" Allie asked, frowning.

Tears welled in Michelle's eyes again. "Of course I love you guys. You're a pretty special threesome."

Allie and Jessie grinned, throwing their arms around Michelle. "I love you, too, Michelle," Jessie whispered, while at the same time, Allie left the same soft message in Michelle's other ear.

Meggie stood back, watching them, her face still solemn. Even Jacob, standing behind her grinning, was melting more than she was.

"Come here, Meggie," Michelle said, her heart breaking as she saw the little girl looking so alone.

Meggie moved forward slowly and joined in the hug. But Michelle didn't miss the fact that Meggie's small arms hugged her sisters, not Michelle.

"I WORRY ABOUT MEGGIE, sometimes," Jacob said later that evening. He and Michelle had just put the triplets to bed and were having a drink at the kitchen table before Michelle left. She was driving Jacob's Explorer home and would return with it the next morning when she came to work on the costumes.

"Because she's so independent?" Michelle asked.

Jacob shrugged. "She's always been that way. When the girls were babies, Meggie was the first one to hold her own bottle, the first one to insist on dressing herself, even the first one potty-trained. But it's more than that now. She's so withdrawn."

"I've noticed."

Hearing Michelle's hurt, Jacob said, "Believe it or not, she's more open with you than she is with most people. Meggie's teacher put her arm around Meggie a couple of months ago, and Meggie told the woman to never touch her again."

"Do you have any idea why?"

Jacob shook his head. "She's still affectionate with me and her sisters, and Nonnie gets a hug now and then. But that's as far as it goes. She doesn't seem to trust anyone else."

Michelle eyed him across the table. "Sounds like someone else I know."

Jacob drained his glass. "Maybe," he said, getting up to rinse it and set it in the dishwasher.

"I guess I should get going so I can be back here bright and early tomorrow," Michelle said, following him to the sink.

"Yeah." Jacob didn't want her to leave. He walked with her into the living room.

"It's going to be weird going home without Noby there." She picked up his car keys from the coffee table.

Jacob approached her slowly, tentatively. Something had changed between them that day. Running his fingers across her cheek, he held her startled gaze. "You don't have to go, you know."

She stared up at him. "I don't?"

Jacob shook his head, still watching her closely. He kept hearing her words to the girls that afternoon.

She'd said *if* Brian returns, not *when.* "You could sleep on the couch. It pulls out into a bed. The girls would love to wake up and find you here in the morning." He trailed his fingers down her neck.

She started to say something but looked away from him, instead. He could feel her pulse beating in her throat and knew she was feeling some of the same things he was. He just wasn't sure whether she was ready to admit it. Or what, if anything, he should do about it.

"I've even got a spare toothbrush around here somewhere. The girls have a tendency to lose theirs."

She leaned toward him, turning her face into his hand. Her lips brushed his palm.

"And I fix a mighty mean breakfast," he said. She'd reduced him to rambling. He slid his hand down her silky blond hair to her shoulder as a flame of desire threatened to burn up what little self-control he had left. He'd been imagining this for far too long.

Her eyes—filled with confusion, but not fear—met his. "You're tempting me," she said. Jacob knew she wasn't talking about his offer of breakfast. It was all the encouragement he needed.

With his thumb under her chin, he guided her face slowly upward until her lips were just beneath his. She didn't resist. She didn't turn away. Most importantly she didn't cry.

Jacob lowered his mouth and finally tasted her lips. She dropped his keys.

She was everything he'd ever fantasized—and

more. Her lips were hesitant at first, as if unused to the intimate contact, but as Jacob caressed them with his own, they slowly opened for him and his tongue met hers for the first time.

He lowered her to the floor, breaking the kiss only long enough to follow her down, before recapturing her lips. With his fingers in her hair, he held her still as his kisses grew bolder, her passion driving him on. He'd never needed a woman the way he needed her.

Michelle's hands were everywhere, gliding over his shoulders, his back, touching his face, his hair. When her fingers crept slowly down his back, sliding into the pockets of his jeans, he thought he might lose his mind.

With a groan, he spread her legs with his knee and settled himself between her thighs. She rose to meet him. "Yes," she whispered. "Please, Jacob, yes."

He yanked on the waistband of her jeans and opened them, burning with his need. She gasped and moved against him, but her sighs had changed. He slowly raised his head to stare into her beautiful face.

She wanted him…yes. But she hated herself for it. He could see it in her eyes.

His movements were jerky as he sat up, his back to her. He wasn't sure what had just happened or where they went from here.

"I'm sorry," she said from behind him.

"Yeah, me, too." His hands clenched into fists.

The rasp of her zipper was loud in the too-quiet room. "You're angry," she said.

"Maybe." He wasn't sure what he was feeling, but it wasn't good.

"I led you on."

"No, you didn't."

"I let it go too far."

He turned to face her then.

"Don't worry about it. Sex isn't the problem here, anyway."

She watched him pace to the window and back. "Then what is?"

"Your loyalty to a man who was declared dead more than a year ago. Why do you do it, Michelle? Why do you hide behind him?"

She stood, gathering his keys up off the floor. Her hands were trembling. "I wasn't all that loyal a few minutes ago. But it's just like you to call being faithful hiding, Jacob."

"Don't turn this back on me, Michelle. You're so scared of losing again, you're never going to risk loving again, either, are you? That's what this is really about."

"Loving?" She laughed incredulously as she headed for the door. "What do you know about loving, Jacob? The more the merrier? Let's see, who was it last week? Gwen, Darlene and Yvonne. Tell me that you didn't date three different women in one week and then we'll talk about loving."

Jacob clamped his jaw shut before he said something he'd regret. The woman made him madder than anyone else ever had. What did she know about his dates? He wasn't about to tell her that while each of those women fulfilled something inside him, he was looking for more than they had to give. And fool that he was, he couldn't stop looking.

"I'll see you tomorrow," she said, letting herself out.

Jacob watched through the window until she was in his Explorer and pulling out of his drive. He wondered if she'd show up in the morning.

CHAPTER TEN

"YOU DO THE SPOT on Cruise's new movie. I'll take the trial." Jacob marked the program sheet in front of him. He hadn't looked at her in days, not since the night they'd almost made love on his living room floor.

Michelle studied her copy of the day's program. "What about the seismologist, Morgon? We've got him on from seven to eight. How was he when you talked to him?"

Jacob shrugged. "He's all right. Not much of a sense of humor, but he's got some interesting stuff on earthquake survival. He said he'd bring some up-to-date predictions, and we can always open up the phone lines if we need to."

Michelle nodded then reached for a newspaper. Jacob did the same. The silence in the booth was interrupted only by the rustling of paper and the occasional sound of scissors clipping as one or the other of them found something worth mentioning on the air.

"There's a good piece here about a mountain rescue over the weekend," Michelle said.

Jacob looked over the article. "Let's do it," he

said, handing it back to her. His fingers were long
and tanned and—

"You guys ready?" Bob's voice piped into the
room from the control booth next door.

They slid their earphones into place and clicked on
their mikes. "Ready."

"Ready."

They watched the seconds tick down and waited in
silence for the on-the-air globe to light.

"Good morning! This is Jacob Ryan along with
Michelle Colby getting your day started for you, and
a great day it's going to be...."

Michelle listened to Jacob, waiting for her cue, and
sailed through the show saying all the right things at
all the right times. At least on the air she and Jacob
were still magic. He went for a coffee refill during
their first commercial break, bringing a diet cola back
for her. He set it down beside her, rather than handing
it to her. She knew she should be thankful that he was
respecting her choices, that he wasn't pressuring her
to explore the possibilities that had sprung up between
them over the weekend. But her gratitude didn't quite
cover the hurt. She missed him.

"I won't be coming over tonight," she said finally,
breaking the silence that had fallen over the booth.

"The girls can't expect you every night."

"I have a lot of mail to catch up on."

"Fine."

If Jacob saw through the flimsiness of her excuse,

he was gentlemanly enough not to mention it. Either that, or he just plain didn't care.

MICHELLE DROVE straight home after the show, shutting herself in the home she'd made with Brian, hoping to recapture the certainty she'd always felt about the love they shared. She didn't let her silent answering machine discourage her. Frank had said it might be a while before she heard from him again. She reminded Noby of that when the cat jumped up on the desk beside the answering machine, purring.

Taking the cat into the bedroom with her, Michelle changed out of the slacks and sweater she'd worn to work, then pulled on a pair of Brian's running shorts and one of his old Southern Cal sweatshirts. She dusted the tops of his shoes while she was in the closet and on a sudden impulse decided to climb into the attic for the box of college memorabilia she and Brian had packed.

Noby watched as Michelle carried in the ladder, pushed open the ceiling panel in the guest room and climbed up to retrieve the box. The cat continued to stare, unblinking, when Michelle struggled to get back down with the heavy box in her arms.

Two hours later, surrounded by pictures and ticket stubs, programs and awards, Michelle still felt torn, incomplete. She picked up a letter Brian had written her from San Francisco. She smiled when she saw his decisive handwriting and started to cry when she read the part about how much he missed her. Sitting on the living room floor, she leaned back against the couch and remembered the summer, shortly after she and Brian were married, they went there together. They'd spent three days in that city made for lovers, strolling down on the wharf, exploring Chinatown and making love in their hotel room overlooking the Golden Gate Bridge.

Noby started to meow at Michelle sometime after six that evening. She wasn't loud in her demands, but she was persistent. It was time for dinner. Michelle opened a can of tuna, emptying half of it into the cat's bowl before adding mayonnaise to the rest. She wondered what the triplets were having for dinner.

Eating her sandwich, she carried on a desultory conversation with Noby. But while Noby did her best to be captivating company, no matter how Michelle tried to deny it, she was lonely. She rinsed her few dishes, thinking of the times she and Jacob had shared the same chore at his beach house. She remembered other things they'd shared, too. Forbidden things.

She spent the rest of the evening watching videos. She had two of her wedding and at least one from every trip and major event she and Brian had shared. There was his graduation, and her graduation, their honeymoon trip to Hawaii, the time they'd rafted down the Colorado River and move-in day at their house. No matter where they were or what they were doing, one thing was obvious in every video she saw—she and Brian were very much in love.

But none of the movies, none of the letters or pictures, none of the memories stopped her from wondering as she climbed into bed that night if Jacob had missed being with her that evening anywhere near as much as she'd missed being with him.

"GOOD NIGHT, SLEEP TIGHT and don't let the bedbugs bite." Jacob leaned against the door and watched as Michelle bent to kiss Allie good-night.

"'Night, Michelle." Allie looked like the cat who'd swallowed the cream.

Jessie was next. "Sweet dreams, punkin." Michelle tucked Jessie's stuffed bear under the covers.

"I love you, Michelle."

"I love you, too." As Michelle hugged Jessie again, Jacob had to fight the feeling of contentment settling over him. The scene was one he'd imagined a hundred times when he'd been planning his future. Except for one very wrong thing. Michelle wasn't here to stay.

She sat down on the edge of Meggie's bed, one hand on each side of his daughter's small body. "Try and keep your covers on tonight, 'kay, Meg?"

Meggie nodded, her wide dark eyes set on Michelle. Michelle leaned down and whispered something in the child's ear. Jacob had no idea what, but as she got up and slipped past Jacob, Meggie snuggled into the covers with a smile on her face.

Jacob did his rounds and enjoyed the nightly ritual more than he had in a long time. He wished his girls pleasant dreams, just as he did every night, but for once the burden wasn't entirely his. Someone else was wishing with him.

He thought about the evening they'd all shared, about the costumes that were far from finished. He wasn't any expert, but he could count. Although Michelle had been working on the dresses for weeks, there was only one completed ball gown hanging in the girls' closet. Jacob had a suspicion her helpers were "helping" a little too much. And she still loved them. Amazing.

When Jacob returned to the living room, he discovered Michelle with her jacket on, her car keys in hand. "I'm going to the gym in the morning, and then Mom and I are going to a craft fair tomorrow afternoon, but I could come back on Sunday if the girls are going to be around," she said.

Jacob didn't know why he was surprised. She loved his daughters, not him. That much had become obvious in the past two weeks. He'd never thought two people could spend so much time together and yet be so far apart.

"Why don't you stay awhile tonight? It's Friday. We don't have to work in the morning, and you'd probably get three times as much done with the triplets in bed."

Michelle shook her head. "I'm teaching the girls how to sew. They're supposed to be involved in making the costumes, remember?"

"They've already helped you finish one of them.

They don't have to *help* in triplicate." He was tired of their cold war. He wanted his friend back.

"Still, they'll probably be upset if I don't wait for them."

Jacob thought of the number of interruptions Michelle had put up with that night. "Michelle, they have the attention span of seven-year-olds. They've seen it all once, which means all that's left is getting in the way. Why do you think we spent half an hour picking pins out of the carpet tonight?"

Michelle grinned. "Meggie was sorting them by color."

"Exactly." She hadn't smiled at him in weeks. "So stay already. Unless of course you're afraid to be alone with me."

He'd been teasing her. Just as he'd been doing for years. But he knew he'd made a mistake as soon as saw the frozen look on her face.

"It's just like you to bring sex into it," she said. Jacob felt as if he'd been slapped.

"What's with you, Michelle? You've been avoiding me for two weeks and now you can't even take a little teasing. Where's your sense of humor?"

"I haven't been avoiding you. I've spent more evenings here than I have in my own home. Noby's going to put herself up for adoption pretty soon."

"You *have* been avoiding me and we both know it. And to be honest, until now I've been just as happy to avoid you, too. But…"

She looked at him, her eyes pleading. "Then why

can't we just leave well enough alone? It's worked for the past couple of weeks. It can keep on working.''

He wanted to shake her. "It's not working, Michelle. I feel like I'm walking in a mine field. What happens if it explodes when we're on the air?''

"I won't let it.''

"We're going to have to face this sooner or later.''

"There's nothing to face.''

"There you go, avoiding the issue again. So I'll say it straight out. I want you, Michelle. And what's more, I think you want me, too.''

"Your ego amazes me, Ryan.''

She was driving him crazy. "There's a difference between truth and ego. You think if you pretend long enough that we're not attracted to each other it'll just go away?''

"I'd hoped.'' Her tough act was gone, leaving her vulnerable.

Jacob clasped her shoulders, caressing them with his thumbs. "Is it so awful to live again, honey?''

She stared at him for a long silent moment, and then shrugged off his hands. "I've been alive all along, Jacob,'' she said, swinging the shoulder strap of her purse onto her shoulder. "If I were already dead, I couldn't be dying of loneliness. But I'd rather do that than be unfaithful to my husband. Which is the problem in a nutshell.'' Her laugh was bitter. "Because for the first time since Brian's disappearance, I'm not sure I'm strong enough to resist.''

She was out the door before Jacob had a chance to reply. He wanted to run after her. He didn't want her going off into the night by herself, hurting. He knew what it was like to be alone and in pain. But he didn't go. He couldn't help her.

Locking up, he wondered why his life was one irony after another. He'd just been told by the woman he wanted above all others that she wanted him, too. And he was still going to bed alone.

THERE WAS A MESSAGE from Frank when Michelle got home from the gym the next morning. Sweaty and uncomfortable in her workout clothes, she listened to the message a second time.

"Frank Steele, here, Mrs. Colby. I managed to track down Jazmin's younger sister. She's been living away from the village since she was a child, but Jazmin confided in her some. According to her, Karim paved the way for Brian's acceptance into the village four years ago, and then Brian left on Karim's orders. Still nothing on Karim's whereabouts. I've put out word that I'm looking for him, but he's showing no signs of surfacing. Guys like Karim have been known to disappear for years, so you may want to reconsider my employment. I'll be in touch…"

Clicking off the machine, Michelle picked up Noby and headed for the bedroom. Her mother was going to be here in half an hour and she still had to shower. She opened her closet door and then just stood there, her tears once again soaking Noby's coat.

MICHELLE TRIED to enjoy the day with her mother, but she didn't fool either one of them. By the time Grace pulled into Michelle's driveway late that afternoon she was wearing a worried frown.

"I wish you'd let your father and me take you out to dinner, honey. Choose anywhere you'd like."

Michelle smiled and leaned across the car to hug her mother. "Thanks, Mom. Maybe next weekend."

"It bothers me to think of you all alone on your birthday. It's not right."

"It's the way I want it, Mom, honest. I'm going to spoil myself rotten, eat everything in sight, watch a couple of old movies and work on the Cinderella cross-stitch I'm doing for the girls."

Michelle knew it was her last statement that convinced her mother to go. She saw Jacob's girls as the beginning of Michelle's journey into the future. Michelle knew they were the only things getting her through the present.

She grilled herself a steak for dinner, drank a glass of wine and faced the fact that life was passing her by. Frank had said his investigation could take years, and where would she be then? Still sitting alone in her too-small home in a run-down neighborhood, too old to bear children but too young to be at peace with that fact?

She poured herself another glass of wine, swatting Noby's nose as the cat tried to share her libation. She wondered if Brian knew what day it was, if he was thinking about how she'd spend it, if he ever wondered how the years were treating her. She wondered how she'd look to him after all their time apart. Wrinkles were starting to form in the corners of her eyes— how pronounced would they be when he came home? And how long would it be before gray started to take the place of blond in her hair?

After her third glass of wine, Michelle picked up Noby and went to bed. She hadn't played the movies or stitched a single stitch. And she hadn't touched the cake her mother brought her that morning. She just wanted to go to sleep and forget that another year had passed her by.

JACOB GAVE HIS PILLOW an extra punch. The damn thing was too lumpy. He laid his head back down, willing himself to relax. He should've bought one stuffed with feathers. Cursing, Jacob threw his pillow off the bed. He'd go without.

Lying flat on his back, he stared at the ceiling. He didn't know why he'd ever thought that Michelle was easygoing. Hell, she was the most stubborn woman he'd ever met. In the week since she'd admitted to wanting him, he'd seen her outside of work exactly once. It was amazing the way they could both spend so much time in the same house and still have no contact. Jacob had been doing the voice-over for a set of commercials the past week, and knowing that, Michelle had used the time to sew the costumes. She'd worked it out like clockwork. She picked the girls up from rehearsal, took them home, gave them a snack and then sewed until Jacob came back. At which time, she hugged the girls goodbye and left.

Jacob didn't know whether to kiss her or strangle her. Either way, he knew something was going to have to give soon. She was starting to look like hell, with dark shadows under her eyes and a forced smile on her lips. And he was starting to climb the walls. He'd snapped at Jessie that evening when she'd spilled her milk at the dinner table. He'd made her cry, and he hated himself for it.

Giving up on sleep, Jacob wandered out onto the deck to cool down. He knew there was more to his wanting Michelle than just sex. He'd dealt with sexual frustration before. This was different. He didn't just ache for physical release; what he craved was a way of life. A life with Michelle. But she'd made it plain that she already had plans and they didn't include him. When was he going to accept that?

IT WAS THREE DAYS before the play was due to open, and Jacob knew that whether Michelle liked it or not she was going to have to stay late at the cottage to get the last costume done. A week ago Jacob would've been delighted at the prospect. Now, it only depressed him. Because as soon as she finished that costume she wasn't going to have any reason to come back.

He was reminded of that when the silence that fell in the cottage after his daughters went to bed was broken by the soft whir of Michelle's sewing machine. He sat back on the couch and tried not to enjoy the sense of peace—of completion—that filled his home when she was there. Michelle wasn't a part of his life, of his family. Hell, she wasn't his at all. And it was time he came to terms with that.

He knew he hadn't succeeded when, an hour later, Michelle finally stood up from her machine holding a miniature white ball gown.

"What do you think?" She rubbed the back of her neck and then one of her shoulders.

"Beautiful."

She frowned at him. "The dress, Ryan."

"Meggie'll be the most beautiful woman at the ball."

"You've got your stories mixed. Jessie's the most beautiful woman at this ball." She put the dress on a hanger.

"They're all three going to look great, Michelle. You did a wonderful job. We owe you."

She shrugged. "I enjoyed doing it." She started to tidy up.

"It's late. Just leave it," Jacob said, moving behind her.

"But..." Her protest died on her lips as Jacob started massaging her shoulders.

Her muscles were so tight he was surprised she didn't cry out at his touch. "Come here," he said, pulling her over to the couch.

He worked on her knotted muscles, gently but relentlessly until he could feel her starting to relax.

"Mmm. That feels wonderful," she said, rolling her head forward.

It felt so good to be touching her again. Her skin was soft and silky, everything he'd been dreaming about for weeks. Slowly, almost of their own accord, his fingers trailed over her collarbone. Her eyes closed as she leaned back against him.

She raised her hands and covered his, not to pull them away as he'd half expected, but to guide them down to her breasts.

He turned her slowly to face him, then lowered his lips to hers.

It had never been like this before, this need, not to consume, but to give. As her lips parted, he wrapped his arms around her, lifting her onto his lap. Her weight was a sweet agony against him as he kissed and caressed her, knowing that any second she might freeze and push him away.

"Oh, Jacob." He heard the confusion, as well as the longing, in her voice.

"It's okay, darling," he murmured, wanting her to believe that as much as he did. He'd give anything to be able to fight her battle for her, to help her bury the past once and for all.

She unbuttoned his shirt with shaking hands, sliding her fingers over his chest. Her touch was tantalizing and oh, so feminine, arousing in him a need to cherish her, to protect her, to love her. It gave him hope.

"You're so beautiful," he said, taking her face in

his hands. Her long blond hair fell over his fingers like a silken veil, and he lowered his lips to hers once again.

"Hold me." He felt her plea more than he heard it—her first sweet invitation for loving—and his arms tightened around her.

"Daddy?"

CHAPTER ELEVEN

THE SLEEPY LITTLE VOICE from the hallway registered with Jacob right about the time Michelle pushed his arms away and slid off his lap. He was sitting uncompromisingly alone on the couch when Jessie came into the room.

"What's the matter, sweetheart?" Michelle asked, scooping the little girl up.

"Had a bad dream," Jessie said, her voice wobbly. "The pumpkin turned into a dragon, 'stead of a carriage, and ate Daddy."

"Shh. It's okay. It was only a dream. Your daddy's right here." Michelle pushed Jessie's tumble of hair away from her face, then dried her tears and kissed her.

Jacob appreciated the time she gave him to recover. He'd never even considered the possibility of this type of interruption.

"I'll take her," he said at last, standing and reaching for Jessie.

The little girl wrapped her arms around his neck, laying her head against his shoulder. "Will you rock me, Daddy? Please?"

He looked at Michelle over Jessie's shoulder, trying to tell her how sorry he was, asking her to wait for him. She smiled faintly, shook her head and collected her things. The regret was back.

Holding Jessie, he watched out the window long after Michelle's taillights had disappeared. When at last his daughter's weight grew heavy with sleep, he took her back to her room. But he didn't put her to bed right away. He sat with her in the rocker, instead, the one he'd bought when Ellen had first told him they were expecting a baby. He wondered if Jessie's timing had been horrendous or a gift from the gods. She might just have saved him from making the biggest mistake of his life.

Then again, it might already be too late for that. Making love with Michelle wasn't the mistake. It was falling in love with her in the first place that would cost him.

JESSIE SNUGGLED HER FACE into Daddy's neck. He smelled good. Kind of like a mixture of him and Michelle. She could hardly remember what her bad dream was about as Daddy rocked her and rubbed her back. She counted his heartbeats for a while. One, two. One, two. Daddy's heartbeat was strong, just like he was.

She wondered if Michelle had noticed that about Daddy. She thought for a minute about what she'd seen when she'd first come down the hallway. Daddy had been holding Michelle on his lap, and at first Jessie had thought that something was wrong, that

Michelle was hurt or crying like she and Meggie and Allie sometimes did. She'd been really scared. But she knew as soon as she opened her eyes all the way that Daddy was holding Michelle different. And he was kissing her. Just like the daddies and mommies did in the movies. Jessie smiled. Now maybe Daddy wouldn't be sad and Allie wouldn't be so mean about being good all the time and Meggie wouldn't be so afraid that Daddy was going to leave them, too.

Jessie's eyes got too heavy to keep open. She would love to have Michelle for a mommy. It made her feel all warm and good inside to think about telling the kids at school that she had a mommy at home, too. Michelle always made her feel like she didn't have to worry about stuff, because it would be okay. She guessed that was what mommies were supposed to do.

She could hardly keep herself awake to think of all the good things about Michelle being their mommy. She'd bet, when they went to the grocery store, Michelle wouldn't pass by those cake-decorating things like Daddy always did. Maybe, when they had their next birthday, Michelle would even…

JACOB GAZED DOWN at his sleeping daughter. If life never gave him another thing, he had more than his share already in his three little girls. His gaze trailed over the sleeping forms of his other two daughters. When he thought of Michelle heading home to only a cat for company, he knew he was a very lucky man.

He continued to rock Jessie long after the child had fallen asleep. He should put her to bed—he needed to get some sleep—but he just wasn't ready to give up the comfort her weight brought him and walk down the hall to his empty room.

MICHELLE DROVE ALL NIGHT. She went down to Long Beach and then followed the ocean highway all the way to San Diego. She was too distraught to sleep, but too tired to think. She just couldn't go home. She couldn't face the reckoning waiting there.

She couldn't put it off forever of course. Arriving home early Tuesday morning, she had just enough time to get ready for work. And looking in the mirror to apply her makeup, she finally had to admit the truth: if it hadn't been for a seven-year-old child, she'd have broken the vows she'd made to Brian. If thoughts were as bad as deeds, if *wants* were a consideration, she was already an adulteress.

Because, in spite of everything—her love for Brian, her five years of faithful vigilance, the weeks of self-loathing—she still wanted Jacob.

God, how she wished she could hate him. She'd tried to blame him for what had happened, tried to cast herself as his victim. But she'd never knowingly lied, to herself or anyone else. She couldn't start now.

JACOB WASN'T SURE what to expect when he arrived at work Tuesday morning. He saw Michelle's car in the lot and pulled his Explorer into an empty space next to it. He wished to hell he knew what to do about their situation. Part of him just wanted to wash his hands of the whole thing. But he didn't have that option.

"Morning," he said as he pushed into the sound booth.

He passed by Michelle's stool to get to his own, sat down, picked up the day's program sheet and only then realized she hadn't said a word since he'd walked through the door. She wouldn't look at him, either.

"You okay?" he asked, wanting to kiss her and shake her at the same time.

"I didn't get much sleep last night," she said.

"Me, neither. I guess we need to talk about that, huh?" He willed her to look at him. He needed to know what was going on in that head of hers. Was she really as in love with her husband as she claimed even after all this time? Or had her loyalty to Brian become a habit? A way to keep her heart safe.

She turned her face towards him but her eyes only made it to the level of his cheek. "There's nothing to talk about," she said.

Jacob was starting to get angry. He knew she felt *something* for him. This hunger that was consuming him wasn't completely one-sided. "Michelle—"

She busied herself with the papers in front of her. "We have a show to do, Ryan."

Jacob clenched his jaw. Somebody definitely needed to shake her. "Then by all means let's do it," he said. If she wanted to pretend last night had never happened, it was fine with him.

Only it wasn't fine. With either of them. For the first time in the three years they'd been on the air together, Jacob Ryan and Michelle Colby were *not* like clockwork. They did their show, announcing everything that was required of them, interviewing the chef of a new restaurant in Beverly Hills, giving away free movie passes and KOLR T-shirts, and repeating weather reports and station call letters at all the right intervals. But there was no magic between them, no give-and-take. They followed their program sheet exactly, like a couple of robots, without a single editorial comment or burst of laughter. Jacob knew even before he saw Bob's frown as they signed off that he and Michelle had to talk whether she wanted to or not. If they couldn't fool Bob, they'd certainly never fool Allie, Jessie and Meggie.

He let her leave the station without even saying goodbye. He had a hunch the KOLR staff had sufficient grist for the gossip mill to keep their tongues wagging for the rest of the week as it was. Then, maintaining enough distance so Michelle wouldn't see him, he followed her home.

He told himself he was only doing this for the sake of their careers, but he knew, as he pulled into her driveway behind her blocking her escape, that there was a lot more to it than that. He was angry as hell, though he'd be hard put to say why, and he was worried about her.

"Go home, Jacob," she said when he met her at the front door. She looked tired enough to collapse on the spot.

"Not until we get this settled," he said, standing his ground.

"I don't want to talk about it."

"I think we need to."

She opened the front door and turned to face him, still not quite meeting his eyes. "It'd be beating our heads against a brick wall, Jacob. There's nothing we can do."

Reaching out a hand, Jacob lifted her chin until she could no longer avoid his gaze. The shame he saw reflected in her soft blue eyes was like a kick in the gut. It made something dirty out of the best thing he'd felt in his life. "We need to talk, Michelle. If for no other reason than the sake of our careers. Another show like this morning, and we'll both be out of jobs."

She nodded wordlessly, then entered the house, leaving the door open for him to follow. The first thing he saw as he trailed her to the living room was the picture of her husband she kept on the end table. He looked away, unable to face the other man's smiling countenance.

"We didn't do anything wrong."

Michelle stood by the window staring out at the sunshiny day. "I did." The words cut into him.

He walked over to her, taking her shoulders in his hands, pulling her back against him. "What I felt last night when I held you in my arms was like nothing I've ever felt before, Michelle. It was different, special.''

She jerked away from him. ''I wonder how many other women you've said that to.''

The words were ugly, but he thought he understood why she'd said them. She was punishing herself. It wasn't bad enough that she believed herself capable of infidelity. No, now she was accusing herself of betraying her husband for no more than a cheap fling.

He turned her to face him, holding her teary gaze with his own. ''None. I've never felt it. I've never said it. I'd never have believed myself capable of forgetting the presence of my three daughters down the hall, Michelle. Last night meant something.''

She gazed up at him for a long silent moment as if some part of her desperately needed to know she meant more to him than all the women she'd seen come and go in his life over the years.

And then she pulled away again, crossing to sit on the couch. ''It was still wrong, Jacob. There aren't any pretty words to excuse the fact that I was going to be unfaithful to my husband.''

''It wasn't like that, Michelle. For God's sake, Brian was declared dead more than a year ago.'' How much longer was she going to hide behind a dead man?

''And you think that's going to matter if someday when I've given myself to someone else—to you— Brian comes home to claim me? It's happened before,

Jacob. Just last year a man was found living in a remote village in Korea. He'd been declared dead, too. Instead, he'd been suffering from amnesia for fourteen years.

"The government's decision that I'm a widow doesn't prove anything, at least not to me. Brian could come walking in that door any day. And to what? To find another man in his wife's bed? And what if he got beyond that, was willing to forgive me and wanted me back? Who would have first rights? My husband or my lover? Who do I choose to hurt? Don't you see, Jacob? It's not just me or even Brian I'm thinking about. It's you, too. I can't make love with you, not knowing if someday I'll have to walk away with another man. I can't do that to you."

Jacob might have been willing to take the risk for himself, but he couldn't stand to see Michelle tearing herself up this way. Her compassion, her loyalty, were qualities he'd grown to cherish in her. That they were the same qualities that would keep them apart seemed ironic. If he fought her on this, if he won, the prize wouldn't be worth having. He'd be satisfying his own needs at the expense of hers.

"Can I ask you something? How can you be so certain he's still alive?"

"Because he didn't say goodbye."

Jacob stared at her.

Her eyes pleaded with him to understand. "I don't mean verbally. It's just something I feel. Like he's still holding on to me. I can't get rid of the feeling he's trapped in some nightmare somewhere trying every way he knows how to make it home. And I can't bear to think of him finally making it back only to find that there's nothing left for him here.''

"You're something else, you know that?" he asked. He wanted to go to her, to hold her, but he wasn't going to do that—to either of them. He reached into his pocket for his keys. "Brian Colby is one lucky man."

She stood up. "Yeah, right. He has a wife who can't seem to keep herself out of another man's arms."

"You're being too hard on yourself, Michelle. I touched you first, not the other way around."

"I could have told you to stop."

"It was late. You were tired. And being with the girls has put us into an unusually intimate situation." Making excuses for what they'd shared went against his grain, but he'd do just about anything to take that look of self-reproach off her face. "You've been alone a long time, honey, and unfortunately your husband's disappearance doesn't erase your very normal needs. Everyone has to have a little human contact now and then."

She listened to him, but judging by her unchanging expression, he didn't think she'd believed him. "It was more than 'a little human contact.' If it weren't for Jessie I would've committed adultery last night."

He'd been calling what they'd almost done something else. "You wouldn't have, you know."

"How can you say that?"

"Because I know you, honey. You'd have stopped me just like you did the first time I kissed you." He reached out, placing his hand just beneath her breast. "Something in here would have kept you loyal to the man you love."

Michelle's grateful smile hurt most of all. Jacob left her, swearing to himself that, other than his daughters, he was never going to care for another human being again. He never seemed to get it right.

SOMETHING IN HERE would have kept you loyal to the man you love. Michelle studied her reflection in the mirror as she got ready for the triplets' big night. Jacob's words had been replaying themselves over and over in her head. He'd said them to comfort her. She knew that. But he'd failed to consider one very frightening possibility. What if the man she loved wasn't Brian? The idea was unconscionable, but even more, it scared her to death.

Checking the suspenders holding up her gray pin-striped slacks, Michelle's eye was caught by a glint in the mirror. Her wedding ring. Holding out her hand, Michelle studied the wide gold band. The ring was a symbol of faith, of hope—of love. If she was going to continue being true to it, then she might just have to stop seeing Jacob Ryan, which meant that she wouldn't be seeing the triplets, either. She wondered how many times her heart had to break before it couldn't hurt anymore.

THE GIRLS WERE a cyclone of excitement when Michelle climbed into Jacob's Explorer twenty minutes later.

"Did you remember the bobby pins, Michelle? We gotta have our hair not fall down," Allie said by way of greeting.

Michelle grinned. "I got 'em right here, Al." There was nothing like children to put life in perspective.

"We get to wear makeup, Michelle! Ms. Thomas said we had to so we would show up and Daddy said it was okay!" Jessie bounced up and down as much as her seat belt would allow.

"And we get flowers after the show," Meggie added, not to be outdone by her siblings on this important occasion. "We saw them in the back. Daddy bought them for us and everything…"

"…and we all practiced our parts just like you said, didn't we, Daddy?" Allie piped up.

"Yeah, and I got almost all of them right," Jessie said before Jacob had a chance to reply.

"We didn't eat much dinner, though," Meggie said. "Daddy said we can have another dinner after the show if we want to."

"You can have it with us, Michelle, can't she, Daddy?" Jessie asked.

Jacob looked at Michelle, shrugging apologetically. "Sure, if she wants to, Jess," he said.

Michelle could think of few things she wanted more than to go home with them after the play, but she knew she couldn't risk it. It would be late. The girls would be tired. They'd be in bed before she knew it. She looked at Jacob, not used to seeing him in a suit and tie, and thought of the way such an evening would surely end.

"We'll see," she said.

Michelle was run off her feet during the next two hours, applying makeup, fixing hair and getting the girls zipped into their costumes. Several of the other mothers offered to help her, probably thinking Michelle couldn't possibly manage all three of Jacob's girls on her own, but she refused them happily. This was *her* time with the girls and she cherished every second of it.

And then the girls were called to take their places backstage, and Michelle made her way to the front of the auditorium and the seat Jacob was saving for her in the second row. Nonnie was there, too, and Michelle smiled, greeting the elderly woman just as the house lights dimmed and the curtains opened.

Jessie was the most precious Cinderella Michelle had ever seen. She remembered all her lines and instilled just the right amounts of sadness and joy into each scene. Meggie and Allie were superb in their wickedness.

"They're wonderful," Michelle whispered to Jacob.

"I know," he said, smiling with pride.

Michelle elbowed him gently. "Your ego's showing, Ryan."

He grabbed her hand, squeezed it and brought it

with his own to rest against his thigh. "So sue me," he said, not taking his eyes off the stage.

He held her hand for the rest of the play, and Michelle let him, as if by some unspoken agreement they'd both enjoy this one last evening pretending they were a family. And then they were standing to applaud as the young cast members took their final bows. The lights came up in the auditorium and it was over.

Michelle met the girls back in their dressing room. Allie and Jessie threw themselves into her arms, beside themselves with excitement.

"Did you see us, Michelle? Did you see us?"

"Of course I saw you, Jess, every second. You were wonderful. Now stand still while I get you out of this dress."

"Did you like the way my eye switched, Michelle? Did I do it good?"

"That's twitched, Allie honey, and yes, you were magnificent."

"I tried to sound real wicked," Meggie said, trying to unzip the back of her dress.

"You were terrific, Meg. You made the whole audience shudder. Here, let me get that zipper for you."

"What's shudder?" Allie wanted to know while Michelle handed them the jeans and sweatshirts they'd worn to the school.

"It's this," Michelle said, shivering and making a face as if she'd tasted something sour.

Meggie was the first one dressed and, still bouncing with excitement, stumbled into Michelle as she handed over her costume. Michelle's arms came out to steady the little girl, her breath stilling as she felt Meggie's quick hug.

''Thank you, Michelle.'' Then Meggie hopped off to urge her sisters to hurry so they could go see Jacob and get their flowers.

And just like that, Michelle knew she could no more stop seeing Jacob's children than she could cut out her heart. She owed Brian many things, but she'd made promises to Allie and Jessie and Meggie, too. Promises she meant to keep.

She led the girls out to meet Jacob, promising herself, and her husband, that she would stay away from any situations that might leave Jacob and her alone together. She could make this work. She had to make it work. She was afraid she might just curl up and die if she had to go back to the lonely existence she'd had before Jacob and his family had come into her life.

ELEANOR WILSON stood in the wings and watched the Ryan girls come out of the dressing room. They were all talking at once, excited by their performances, bouncing around the woman accompanying them. Eleanor listened unashamedly as the little girls all vied for attention. It was obvious they were happier than they'd been in a very long time. And that Mrs. Colby was just as happy to be with them. Eleanor smiled. She could rest easy now, knowing her darlings were in the right hands.

JACOB'S MESSAGE LIGHT was blinking when he got home that night. The girls had talked Michelle and him into a celebratory dinner at McDonald's before dropping Michelle off at her house, and all three of them had finally fallen asleep during the drive back to the beach. He carried them inside one by one, got them tucked into bed and poured himself a scotch and water. Then he went into the living room to play back his messages.

"Hi, Jake, honey." Jake choked on a swallow of scotch. "I'm back in L.A. staying at the Beverly Hills Maison de Maison. Call me."

He played the message a second time, listening for any nuances in her voice that might give him a clue to what she wanted. She sounded sweet as honey, just the way she'd been when they'd first met ten years before. A small part of him remembered that time with affection. Mostly he remembered everything that came afterward. Grabbing the telephone book, he turned to the hotel listings, then punched out the numbers for the Maison, wondering why he was returning the call, because for the life of him, he just couldn't think of one good reason for him to care that Ellen was back in town.

CHAPTER TWELVE

ELLEN WANTED to see him. For old times' sake, she'd said. Jacob didn't think there was anything in their old times that called for another meeting. Except, maybe, his three motherless children. They were beginning to bring Michelle into every conversation. And after the talk he'd had with Michelle the other morning, he had serious doubts that she'd be a part of their lives for very much longer. Because, despite what he'd told Michelle, there was no way they could continue to share his daughters without, sooner or later, betraying Brian Colby. The attraction between them was simply too strong.

Which left him with the same problem he'd had before. Allie, Jessie and Meggie needed a mother. Did Jacob have the right to deny them this chance? If Ellen was going to make an effort to see them, didn't he owe it to the girls to find out if she'd changed?

"...SO CALLER NUMBER NINE wins a chance at the Hawaiian Tropics all-expense-paid trip to Hawaii on Delta Airlines. The number's 555-8484. That's 555-8484...." Jacob watched Michelle snap off her mike as Bob put on the Hawaiian Tropics commercial in the other room and manned the phone lines.

A Michael Bolton tune was set for right after the commercial. They had five minutes. Now was as good a time as any. "Ellen's in town. I'm having dinner with her tonight," Jacob said, tapping his pen against the program log in front of him.

Michelle's hand froze above her mike switch. "Ellen?"

"My ex."

She looked at him, the hurt in her eyes quickly masked.

"The girls' mother," she said, as if that summed it all up.

"There was a message from her when we got home last night. She wants to see me."

"Do the girls know?"

"No."

She digested that bit of information in silence. Jacob wished he knew what she was thinking. What a crazy situation. He valued her advice, yet he could hardly ask the woman he'd fallen in love with what she thought about him seeing his ex-wife.

"I don't know what Ellen wants or what this is all about. And until I do, the girls aren't going to even know she's around. They were hurt badly by her desertion, and I'm not going to risk it happening all over again."

Michelle nodded. "Will Laurie stay with them tonight?"

"Probably. It was too late to call her last night, but she usually doesn't mind short notice. Unless you want to stay with them," he offered, responding to the look of yearning in her eyes.

"Could I?"

Jacob didn't see why it should matter. The girls already adored her. One night more or less wouldn't change that.

"Of course," he said. "You're a part of their lives for as long as you want to be, Michelle. I thought we'd established that much at least."

She smiled, the hint of tears in her eyes saying far more than words. "Thanks," she said, turning to break into the last bars of the song. "That was Michael Bolton with a cut off his new CD...."

Jacob wanted to take her away and make love to her until all the pain she'd suffered was nothing but a memory. Frustrated as hell, he called the mother of his children and confirmed plans to take her out to dinner. This time around he wouldn't expect too much. He'd learned the hard way not to expect anything from Ellen at all.

ALLIE CALLED A MEETING with her sisters that afternoon after school. Daddy had told them about Michelle coming over when they'd been eating their snack. Allie'd been worrying since Disneyland that her plan for Daddy and Michelle to be in love hadn't worked, but if Michelle was coming over not to sew or anything then it must've. Finally she was gonna get to tell the others her secret.

"Come on, Allie. Daddy said he'd take us bike riding," Meggie complained as soon as Allie shut the bedroom door behind the three of them.

"Shh. He'll hear you," Allie said, climbing onto Meggie's bed. "This is important."

"What is?" Jessie asked, climbing onto the bed beside her.

Meggie sat on her pillow. "Yeah, what?"

Allie felt all excited inside. Her sisters were going to love this.

"Daddy and Michelle are in love and Michelle's going to be our mommy."

"I already know that," Jessie said, rolling her eyes at Allie.

"How do you know?" Allie asked. She'd thought this would be a surprise.

"Because. I saw them kissing on the couch."

Meggie sat forward. "When?" she asked, her dark eyes wide.

"One time when I had a bad dream. It was the middle of the night and they were kissing on the couch."

Allie nodded, satisfied. She was actually relieved to know she was right. It was too important to make a mistake about. "Okay, so now we have to be really good tonight."

"Again?" Jessie asked, frowning. "How come?"

"Because this is a pretend time for Michelle to be

our mommy and we don't want to make her change her mind.''

"That's dumb, Al. Michelle's been around lots already.''

"Yeah, but that was just to sew and stuff. This is the first time she's coming just to be with us. It's important or Daddy would've just called Laurie like he always does.''

Meggie looked scared all of a sudden. "What if Daddy's going on a date? If Michelle's going to be our mommy she won't like that.''

Allie shook her head. "He's going to do business,'' she said. He hadn't said so, but Allie knew that people in love didn't do dates with other people.

"Is this the last time we have to be so good?'' Jessie asked, sounding resigned.

"I don't know. But maybe,'' Allie said. "Come on, let's get our tennis shoes on so we can ride our bikes. Maybe Daddy'll take us to the park.''

"I get to swing first if he does,'' Jessie said, sliding down off the bed.

"And I'm second this time,'' Meggie said, joining her sister in the doorway of their closet.

Allie came up behind them. "Those are my shoes, Jess. That's my 'nitial on the heel.''

Jessie tossed Allie her shoes. "Do you really think Michelle's going to be our mommy, Al?''

Allie noticed that Meggie was looking at her, too. She loved it when her sisters asked her important stuff. "Yep, I'm sure," Allie said, crawling into the closet to find Jessie's shoes.

ELLEN WAS AS BEAUTIFUL as ever. Jacob sat across from her at a secluded table in the restaurant at the top of the Maison de Maison, remembering how he used to tell her she was made for loving.

"So how long are you in town?" he asked.

Even her shrug was sexy. "Maybe permanently. I'm between jobs at the moment."

"Do you have any leads?"

"I've had an open-ended offer. I'm just not sure I want to stay in politics. I, uh, kind of thought I'd like to, you know, pursue something else that once mattered to me."

Her blatant look made it clear that that something was Jacob. He just wasn't sure why.

"I've grown up in the past few years, Jacob. I've learned to be a little more flexible." She smiled across at him, her dinner fork poised above her plate. She was wearing a black silk jumpsuit, and it looked as expensive as she did.

"You mean I could've worn my sweats and you still would have been seen with me?"

"I said flexible, dear, not uncouth. Besides, that suit looks good on you. It matches your eyes. You clean up very nicely, you know."

He recognized that come-hither smile. "So do you, but then you always did."

"I used to wonder sometimes if you even noticed."

What? "Of course I noticed! Our sex life was never the problem."

"Not before the babies were born."

"What's that supposed to mean?"

"Just that you lost interest in sex after we had the girls."

"That's ludicrous! I've been interested in sex since I turned twelve. It was just harder to make the time after the girls were born. But we still managed. Remember that weekend in San Diego?"

Ellen's face softened. "Yeah. It was the best, Jacob. I was amazed you'd go to all that trouble just to make me feel good. You even got the honeymoon suite. I never knew you could be such a romantic. As I recall, we didn't leave that suite all weekend."

"I never stopped finding you attractive, Ellen."

"Not even when I was as fat as an elephant?"

"Especially not then. I thought you were beautiful. And afterward, too. But with the girls waking up on three different schedules all night long, sleep had to be our priority. If you remember, I took turns getting up with them, too, and still had to be at work at five o'clock in the morning. It was all I could do to keep my eyes open some days. I thought you understood that."

"I suppose I was a little inflexible on that score. I wanted to come first all the time, not just an occasional weekend. But you could have tried harder, too, you know."

Jacob shrugged, seeing those years in a new light.

The triplets had consumed so much of his time and energy then, perhaps he'd forgotten he needed to be a husband, not just a father.

They finished dinner and Ellen was charming throughout. She didn't talk much about her life in Washington, but whatever had happened there appeared to have been good for her. She'd grown up. But she hadn't changed completely. She was still a little too interested in appearances, in material things. And other than a brief inquiry the night before, she still hadn't asked about her daughters.

"So, do you have anybody special in your life?" she asked after their waiter had cleared their dinner plates and brought their desserts.

He thought of Michelle at home with his children. "I date."

"But no one steady?"

"Not right now."

She slid her fork into a three-inch slice of chocolate mousse, a smile curving her lips. "We were very good together once, you and I," she said.

"I thought so." His dessert fork still lay on the table beside him.

"I bet we could be again."

He nodded, his forearms resting on the pristine white tablecloth. "Probably."

She stopped eating, studying him across the candlelit expanse, her expression assessing. "You know, I have to commend you, Jacob. We've been together almost two hours and you haven't mentioned the girls once.''

"I wondered if you were ever going to get around to asking about them."

She shrugged. "I guess I just wanted to see if you've changed as much as I have. In the old days, you never talked about anything else. It was always the babies this, the babies that. If one of them hadn't gotten a new tooth or learned how to drink from a straw, then someone had a runny nose.''

"They're our children, Ellen. Who else would I talk to about them?''

''Well, nobody of course, but it's nice to have adult conversation once in a while, too, you know. There were days there when I felt like little ropes of ABC's were going to wrap around my neck and strangle me to death.''

One thing hadn't changed. She still had that knack for making him feel guilty. ''I guess I should have listened to you a little more closely. Maybe a full-time nanny wouldn't have hurt.''

She smiled, looking more grateful than victorious. The old Ellen would have gloated. ''So how are they?'' she asked.

And Jacob suddenly found himself not knowing what to say. He'd love to be able to spill out all his worries to the mother of his children, to have her share them. He'd love to tell her about Ms. Wilson's warnings, about the play, about Meggie's withdrawal. But he wasn't sure she really wanted to hear them.

"Good. They're doing fine."

"They're in first grade now, aren't they? How are they doing in school? Do they like it?"

"School's good. Allie's separated from Meggie and Jessie this year."

Ellen's eyes shadowed. "Is it hard for her? She was always kind of the leader of the three, wasn't she?"

"She still is. And yes, it's been a little difficult, but for the best, I think. She's adjusting. And their grades are all pretty good. Jessie's dip every now and then, but she'll come around."

Ellen smiled. "She never was a good listener."

"She still isn't." Jacob grinned back at her.

"Remember that time she fell in Rick Morris's pool right after we'd both warned her to stay back from the water?"

Jacob wasn't likely to forget. The station manager hadn't been too pleased to have his wedding reception interrupted by a wet screaming child.

They talked about the triplets for a few more minutes and then Jacob paid the bill. He didn't want to keep Michelle out too late.

He walked Ellen to the elevator and pushed the button. "Can we do this again sometime?" she asked.

Jacob slid his hands into his pockets. "Sure."

"Soon?" She ran her tongue across her lips.

The elevator arrived. "I'll call you," he said as she disappeared inside.

IN SPITE of the relatively early hour, Michelle was asleep on the couch when Jacob let himself into his beach house forty-five minutes later. As he stood gazing at her sweet gentle face, he had to consciously restrain himself from touching her.

Slipping out of his suit jacket, he wondered if maybe it wouldn't be better for both of them if he simply joined her there. If she woke up in his arms, surely she'd forget her resistance and make love with him.

Yes, maybe that was the way to end this insanity. Maybe then he could get on with his life, have dinner with his ex-wife and actually consider the invitations she was sending out.

It might even be good for Michelle. Maybe all she needed to be free from her past was to take that first irrevocable step. Because he just didn't believe she was as in love with her husband as she claimed. If she had been, she wouldn't have responded to his kisses as she had.

He took a quiet step forward. What if he was wrong? How could he be sure she *wasn't* still in love with her husband? What if her response to Jacob was a substitute for what she couldn't have? What if Michelle hated herself afterward? Could he live with that? Was one night of passion worth losing the friendship of the woman he loved?

He leaned over her, bracing his weight on the back of the couch as he smoothed her hair away from her face. With a sigh, she turned over, flinging her arm out over the edge of the couch. Something glinted in the light from the single lamp she'd left on. Her wedding ring.

Jacob straightened and backed away. It wasn't for him to decide whether or not Michelle loved her husband or to determine what was best for her. Even if she *was* hiding behind her marriage vows, he couldn't make love to another man's wife. And as long as Michelle wore Brian Colby's ring, that was exactly what she was—another man's wife.

Jacob went down the hall to check on the girls, giving himself a couple of minutes to pull himself together before he woke Michelle. As he kissed his three sleeping daughters good-night, he promised himself he'd call Ellen first thing in the morning. They'd reached some new understandings tonight. Maybe, for the girls' sake, they'd be able to salvage some of their old love.

MICHELLE MISSED another easy shot and knew there wasn't any way she was going to win the match.

"You wanna call it quits?" she asked her father.

He picked up her towel and locker key and handed them to her. "I don't think I've ever seen you so distracted," he said.

"It's been a rough week."

He looked at his watch. "I'll bet your mother's home by now. She has a way of making almost anything look better."

Michelle stood on tiptoe to kiss her father's cheek.

"I love you, Pop."

"I love you, too, baby. Don't ever forget that."

GRACE WAS OUT BACK with a pitcher of lemonade when Michelle and her father got home.

"Everything okay?" she asked, looking from one to the other for an explanation of their early arrival.

"Everything's fine," James said, answering for both of them, but Michelle didn't miss the silent communication that passed between her parents as her father leaned down to kiss his wife. "I think I'll go fix that drip in the guest bathroom before I take my shower," he said, taking a glass of lemonade with him.

Grace poured some of the freshly squeezed fruit juice for Michelle as her daughter sat down beside her in the lounge chair. "You want to talk about it?"

"Jacob's ex-wife is in town."

"The girls' mother?" Grace asked, frowning.

Michelle nodded. "He's seen her three times in the past week."

"Is she here to stay?"

"I don't know. I haven't asked."

"Why not?"

"I figure if he wants me to know he'll tell me. It's not like I have any hold on him."

Grace nodded. "Is Jacob happy to see her?"

"He doesn't seem unhappy."

"So where does that leave you? Are you still spending time with his girls?"

"Some, and I don't know where it leaves me. Part

of the problem is I have no idea where it *should* leave me.'' As fast as she blinked them away, tears welled in Michelle's eyes. She didn't want to break down in front of her mother. Grace worried enough about her already .

A bird flew over to the patio table and perched on the pitcher of lemonade. Michelle swished it away. ''How can I want the man's children and have nothing to do with the man? I keep telling myself that a relationship with Jacob is wrong, and yet it's eating me up to think of him out with that woman.''

Grace cast her a motherly glance. ''Why do you think that is?''

''Because I'm jealous, that's why. I can't have him, but I don't want anyone else to have him, either. Doesn't make me a very nice person, does it?''

''It makes you human, honey.''

Michelle stared out at the lush green lawn wishing she were a little girl again, able to climb into her mother's lap and wait for her to make everything better.

''I'm scared, Mom.''

''I know, sweetie. It may be time for you to make some decisions.''

''I'm afraid I'm going to lose the girls, and I love them so much.'' Michelle gazed at her mother. ''I don't know when I started feeling as though they were part mine, but I do know I can't bear the thought of losing them. If their mother comes home to stay, they aren't going to need me anymore.''

"Has she been spending a lot of time with them?"

Michelle shook her head. "I don't think Jacob's even told them she's in town. Allie thinks he's out doing business when he's with Ellen."

"But she's their mother! Doesn't she want to see them?" Grace asked, her usual calm manner gone.

"I'm not sure Jacob's given her the chance. She may not want to see them for all I know, but I think that even if she did he wouldn't allow it. Not until he's sure she's not going to hurt them again."

"He'll never have that guarantee. Not from anyone."

"I know. But in Ellen's case I can see him being especially careful. After all, she deserted them once, so who's to say she wouldn't do it again? The last time, she took them to a neighbor while Jacob was at the station and drove off without a backward glance. They were too young to realize what was going on, but something like that would kill the girls now."

"If it was that bad I'm surprised he's even seeing her again."

"Apparently she's changed. But it still doesn't seem fair that she can suddenly waltz back into their lives and claim them as if she'd never left. Just because she gave birth to them doesn't make her their mother, not in the ways that count."

"No, it doesn't. But it does give her some legal rights. And the truth of the matter is, honey, if Jacob decides to get back with Ellen, if the five of them become a family again, there's not a lot you can do about that.''

Michelle's voice trembled. ''Are you saying you think I should just give up?''

''No, sweetheart.'' Grace reached across the table for Michelle's hand. ''I'm saying you need to think long and hard about what you want and what you're willing to do to get it. Answer me this. Are you in love with Jacob?''

The denial that rose automatically to Michelle's lips froze there. She couldn't lie to her mother, even if she was still trying desperately to lie to herself. ''Maybe,'' she whispered, ashamed.

''It's not wrong to love someone, Michelle.''

''It is when you're married to someone else.''

''Brian's been gone a long time, honey. You're a different woman now. It's only natural for your feelings to be different, too. If Brian had been here, you two would probably have grown together through the changes the years have brought. But apart, who knows?''

''I've always thought the love Brian and I shared was like yours and Daddy's. I thought it would last forever.''

''If Brian had been here it probably would have. Michelle, your father and I have been together more than thirty years, and yes, we've been very lucky to be able to maintain our love throughout our marriage, but a lot of that comes from growing together and coping with life's challenges as a team. Who's to say what would've happened if we'd been apart for years, dealing with life's hardships separately?''

The quiet of the afternoon settled around them. ''Are you telling me I should forget Brian and tell Jacob I love him?''

''No. Whatever decisions you make have to be ones *you* can live with. And only you can decide that. I wish with all my heart I could help you, but this time I just can't.''

Michelle leaned over, hugging her mother. ''You already have, Mom. Just by being here.''

''That's one thing you can count on, sweetie.''

''OKAY, GANG, CLIMB IN.'' Jacob stood in the school parking lot, opening the Explorer's front and rear passenger doors.

''It's my turn to sit up front, Meggie,'' Jessie said, trying to push her sister aside.

Meggie didn't budge. ''It's not, either. You sat in front on the way to school.''

''I did not. Allie did.''

''She's right, Meg. Hop in back with Allie. You're first tomorrow morning,'' Jacob said. He never forgot the seating schedule.

''How come you came and got us today, instead of the bus?'' Allie asked, climbing in beside her sister.

''Because we need to do some shopping. We're all out of bread and milk.''

''We coulda goed later. I'm hungry for my snack.''

"Me, too. What's for a snack, Daddy?" Jessie asked.

Jacob checked to make sure all seat belts were fastened and then put the Explorer into gear. "We'll stop for ice-cream cones, and we couldn't go later because I have a date tonight."

"Another one?" Allie asked.

He glanced at her in the rearview mirror. Her face looked like a disapproving schoolmarm's. "I was home with you guys last night, Al, and for the most of the weekend, too. You've never minded my dating before."

He caught the look between Allie and her sisters. "We don't mind, Daddy," she said. For an actress, she did a pretty poor job of lying.

"Is Michelle coming to stay with us?" Meggie asked.

"Michelle's having dinner with her parents tonight, punkin. Laurie's coming."

"I don't want Laurie."

Jacob pulled into the parking lot of the grocery store. "What's the matter with Laurie?" he asked, turning to face Meghan. His middle child was wearing the stone-faced expression he recognized all too well.

"I want Michelle."

Allie and Jessie exchanged worried glances. The girls knew better than to talk that way to their dad.

"I already told you that Michelle's busy tonight,

Meghan. Laurie's coming and I expect you to be good for her.''

Meggie didn't argue but she didn't agree, either. She climbed out of the Explorer silently and didn't say a word for the rest of the outing. Jacob felt as if he was walking a tightrope that was about to shred.

CHAPTER THIRTEEN

THE FEELING WAS STILL with Jacob a couple of days later when Nonnie came out to the garage to find him. He was working on Jessie's bicycle, realigning the chain that had come loose when she'd sideswiped a curb the last time she'd been riding.

The housekeeper stopped just inside the door, her face lined with concern.

"Meghan pinched her fingers in the step stool. I don't think she's broken anything, but they're bleeding and she won't let me attend to them."

Jacob dropped his screwdriver and headed toward the house. "What was she doing with the step stool?"

"Trying to reach a puzzle up on her closet shelf." Nonnie wrung her hands as she hurried beside Jacob.

"Let me guess," he said, holding the kitchen door open for her. "She didn't ask for help with that, either, did she?"

"No, Mr. Ryan. I'd have reached it for her if I'd known she wanted it."

"I know you would've, Nonnie. Don't worry about it." He headed down the hall toward the sound of running water in the girls' bathroom.

"Let me *see,* Meggie." He recognized Allie's commanding voice.

"I wanna see, Meggie. Is it bad?" Jessie asked.

Both girls stepped aside as Jacob entered the room. "Meggie hurt her hand, Daddy," Jessie said, wide-eyed.

"On your step stool," Allie supplied.

Meggie looked at him as he lowered himself to one knee beside her. Fresh tears welled in her big brown eyes. By the look of things, she'd shed more than a few before he'd gotten there.

"What's the problem, sport?" he asked, removing Meggie's hand from the water. Her little fingers were icy cold.

"I'm sorry, Daddy."

"I'm sorry, too, Meg," he said. The skin had been stripped away just below the knuckles of her index and middle fingers, and the surrounding area was already black-and-blue.

"Can you bend them?" he asked, holding up her hand.

She sniffled, but very slowly all four of her fingers bent forward into his palm.

Jacob reached into the medicine cabinet for some antiseptic cream. "No bones broken, but your hand's going to be pretty sore for a while. We'll put some ice on it as soon as we get you cleaned up."

"Okay, Daddy," Meggie said, subdued.

"Does it hurt real bad, Meggie?" Jessie asked, watching from the side of the sink.

"Not too bad."

"She's not in trouble, is she, Daddy?" Allie wanted to know.

"No, Al. She's not in trouble."

But *he* was. Ever since he'd begun going out in the evenings regularly, Meggie had begun withdrawing more and more. First from Laurie and now from Nonnie. The problem wasn't going to go away. It wasn't going to take care of itself. And he couldn't ignore it any longer. He was going to have to have a long talk with Ellen. It was time to bring her home and introduce her to her daughters.

MICHELLE WENT to the gym after work on Thursday, needing to release some of the tension building inside her. She was no closer to making any decisions about her life. How could she, in good conscience, forge ahead in a new relationship while she still believed Brian was alive? And yet she dreaded waking up each day and going in to work, afraid Jacob would tell her that he and Ellen were getting married again.

She'd just walked in the front door after an hour at the gym when the telephone rang. Ms. Wilson, the principal from the girls' school, was calling. A truck had run into a hydro pole by the school, bringing down the power lines. School had to be let out early for the day and Jacob couldn't be reached.

"I called Mr. Ryan's housekeeper, Nonnie Moore, but she's out for the day, as well. Allie suggested we give you a call," Ms. Wilson said.

Michelle thought of the traffic between her part of town and Jacob's. "I'll be there in twenty minutes, half an hour tops," she said, hanging up as soon as she'd assured herself that the principal would wait that long.

Still wearing the gray sweats she'd put on after showering at the gym, Michelle hurried out to her car. She didn't want the girls waiting around like unwanted puppies. As she drove down the 405, she tried to remember if Jacob had said anything about where he was going after work. She couldn't remember him mentioning anything. She wondered if that meant he was with Ellen; he'd stopped telling Michelle when he was going to be with his ex-wife.

The girls were in the cafeteria with a handful of other students when Michelle arrived. Allie and Jessie were sitting across a table from Meggie, their backs to the door, trying to color by the dull light filtering through the windows. Meggie was watching the door.

She leapt from her seat the second she saw Michelle.

"You really came!" she said, running over to take Michelle's hand.

Meggie's grip was like a vise, nearly cutting off the circulation in Michelle's fingers. "Of course I came," Michelle said, bending to press a quick kiss on Meggie's cheek. It was a statement of how distraught Meggie was that she allowed Michelle's kiss. She'd been limiting their tokens of affection to hugs only.

Allie and Jessie bounced out of their chairs with a flurry of goodbyes to their schoolmates, and Michelle herded the girls out to her car.

"All the lights went out, Michelle, and it was really dark," Jessie said as Michelle pulled out of the school lot. Jessie and Meggie were strapped in the back seat. The girls had told her that it was Allie's turn to ride in the front.

"It *was* a little scary," Allie said.

"And Meggie said you weren't coming to get us, even though Allie told Ms. Wilson to call you," Jessie said.

Michelle stopped at the corner and glanced back at Meggie. She was looking out her window.

"Why would you think I wouldn't come, Meg?"

Meggie shrugged, her head still turned away.

A car honked behind Michelle, and she pulled through the intersection, turned into the parking lot of a convenience store and stopped.

"I told all three of you I'd be here for as long as you needed me, Meg. Didn't you believe me?"

Meggie nodded. Allie and Jessie were watching the exchange, silent for once.

"So what's changed?"

"Maybe you didn't want us anymore." The words were so soft Michelle could barely hear them. But they hurt. A lot.

She reached back and tapped Meggie's shoulder. "What would make you think such a thing?" Michelle asked, holding Meggie's solemn gaze with her own.

"Daddy's been doing dates. A lot. And not with you."

Michelle felt a rush of fear.

"And you thought that would make a difference to the way I feel about you three?"

"You won't marry Daddy if he's doing dates with other people."

"I can't marry your daddy, anyway, Meg. I thought you understood that. I'm already married. But remember what I told you? Even if my husband comes home, even if I have other children someday, nothing's going to change the way I feel about you. And that works the same if your daddy ever gets married to somebody else. I love you guys. *Nothing's going to change that—ever.*"

"Even if we're bad?" Jessie asked.

Michelle smiled at the little girl, barely holding her tears at bay. "Even if you're bad."

Allie turned, placing her hand on Michelle's arm. "Don't you think you could love our daddy, too?"

"I think your father's a pretty special man, Allie, but I already promised to love someone else, and your daddy has the right to date anyone he wants to date."

Allie chewed her lip, pondering that.

"She's just like all the rest."

Michelle looked into the back seat. Meggie was staring out the window again.

"Who is, Meg?"

"The lady. She doesn't want to meet us, just like all the rest."

"You don't know that, Meggie."

Meg looked at Michelle, her eyes too old for her age as she nodded. "Uh-huh. That's why Daddy always has to go places to be with her without us. People say we're too much trouble, 'cause there's three of us all at once, and it's true 'cause no one ever wants us. They just want to be with Daddy."

"No, Meggie! It's not like that at all." Michelle could hardly believe what she was hearing.

"Meggie's right, Michelle," said Allie. "We heard Katie Walters's mommy say it. And even our own mommy didn't want us, and not Jennie or all of Daddy's other girlfriends, either. Besides, people always look at us when we go places and say things to Daddy like 'You sure have your hands full.'" Allie's voice grew very adultlike as she mimicked.

"Have you talked to your daddy about this?"

"He told us we're not too much trouble and it wasn't our fault Mommy didn't want to stay with us, but he has to say that, 'cause he's our daddy, doesn't he, Allie?" Jessie looked at her sister for confirmation.

Michelle had had no idea things were this bad. "Well, I can't speak for anyone else, girls, but *I* don't think you're a handful at all. I think you're a heartful. Do you know what that means?"

All three girls shook their heads, their eyes trained on her. "It means that you fill up my heart until it's full of love. And that's an awful lot of love, because my heart's been almost empty for a long time.''

Allie leaned over, hugging Michelle. "We sure wish you were our mommy."

Michelle took the girls home, and while they waited for Jacob she did everything she could to convince them they were the light of her life. But nothing could stop Meggie's words from running around and around in her head. There were some home truths Jacob Ryan was about to hear just as soon as Michelle had him to herself.

MICHELLE WAS STILL UPSET as she drove to work the next morning. Jacob had invited her to stay for dinner the night before, but she'd been too angry with him to pretend, even for the girls' sake, that nothing was wrong. So she'd gone home, instead, and gotten madder and madder. Jacob had to know what he was doing to his girls. Ms. Wilson had pointed it out to him months ago. He'd told Michelle so himself. So why did he continue to foster the triplets' belief that no one wanted them? Why was he keeping even their own mother from them?

The radio show was a nightmare. Part of her knew that her attitude was irrational, but her anger continued to fester inside her regardless. And no matter how hard she tried to banter with Jacob as usual, her words kept sounding more like nasty barbs than playful darts.

"You gonna tell me what's wrong?" Jacob asked

as soon as they'd signed off the air. Even in his baggy sweats and T-shirt, he looked pretty intimidating.

Michelle tossed the CD she'd been holding onto the counter. "Yeah, I'll tell you what's wrong. You. You're what's wrong." She had no idea where the words came from. She'd never talked to anyone like this before.

Jacob stood up so fast his stool spun. "*I'm* what's wrong? And how's that?" His voice had grown soft, deceptively soft.

Michelle stood, too, her back stiffening as she thought of her conversation with the girls. "Your daughters think they're nothing but trouble—that nobody wants them. Do you realize Meggie didn't believe I was coming to get them yesterday even after Ms. Wilson told them I was on my way? I know you're aware of their problems, Jacob, because we've talked about them. Is seeing Ellen so important to you that it's worth your daughters' emotional stability? Where are your priorities? How can you be so insensitive to their needs?" *And to mine?*

Jacob's jaw clenched, his eyes like flint. "*My* priorities are right where they need to be, right where they've always been—with my children. I may not always get it right, but I *always* put them first. And right now what my girls need is a mother. One who's willing to live with them, not just visit occasionally. And it looks like Ellen might be interested in that."

"She's so interested they don't even know she's in town?" Michelle asked, sarcastically.

"They don't know she's in town because I think it's in their best interests not to tell them yet. I'm not bringing Ellen back home until I'm certain she's here to stay. I can't risk putting them through another one of her dramatic exits."

"I'm not so sure you're sparing them anything. They're already feeling rejected."

"It would be worse if they grew to love Ellen again and then lost her. At least now they think they aren't wanted by someone who doesn't know them. And maybe my way isn't right. I've never claimed to be an expert at this. But at least *I'm* trying."

"And you think I'm not?"

He slid his hands into the pockets of his sweats. "I guess that is what I think." His eyes were as hard as a rifle barrel as he delivered his blow. "You claim to care, Michelle, but you wear your wedding band like armor, and whenever things get too much for you, you retreat to your shrine of the past. You tell the girls you love them, but you're really too frightened to risk loving anyone."

Michelle hid her trembling hands in her pockets. They were talking about more than his daughters now. "You don't understand." Her voice was barely more than a whisper.

Jacob reached for his keys and wallet. "I understand, probably better than you do," he said, going to the door of the studio. "You'd rather cling to the five-year-old image of a dead man than risk giving yourself to a flesh-and-blood one again. At least Brian can't expect too much from you, can he?''

He opened the door and walked out.

Michelle stood in the empty room, shaking, hurting so badly she could hardly think. Finally she sank onto her stool. She leaned on the counter, resting her head in her arms, and willed herself to get up and go to her car.

''You okay, Michelle?'' Bob Chaney poked his head in the door.

She swung around, embarrassed. ''Fine, just tired,'' she said, hoping the words didn't sound as unlikely to him as they did to her.

He nodded, but didn't look completely convinced. ''Well, if you ever need a shoulder I've got an extra,'' he said hesitantly.

She smiled and tried not to cry. ''Thanks. I may just take you up on that sometime,'' she said. But she knew she wouldn't. The only shoulder she wanted to lean on had just walked out on her.

JACOB CHANGED into his swim trunks and headed down to the beach the minute he got home. He plunged into the water, eager to battle the white-capped waves. This was something he understood. Nature wasn't forgiving, but at least he knew the rules. And this time, at least, he knew he could win.

He wasn't so sure with Michelle. He'd had no right to lash out at her as he had. Hell, her loyalty was one of the things he admired most about her. It was just so damn frustrating that her loyalty was all for another man, one who probably was no longer alive. But what if Brian Colby *wasn't* dead? What if Michelle fell in love again and then Brian came back into her life? What would she do? What would Jacob do in her position? He didn't have any answers. So where did he get off judging her?

He swam as far out as he dared, slicing into the waves, conquering them. And then, when his skin was numb with cold, he turned over, letting the waves carry him back toward shore. He'd been a fool to fall in love with Michelle. Knowing that she cared for him, too, was no excuse. Because it wasn't enough. And that was what had goaded him into his outburst that morning. He couldn't forgive Michelle for not loving him enough to let Brian go. She'd stood there and preached to him about the girls, telling him what he was doing wrong, not even seeing that she was the one who could make everything right. All she had to do was say goodbye to a memory. Was that too much to ask?

Jacob's feet scraped the sand and he stood, welcoming the warmth of the sun on his chest. He was doing it again. Expecting too much.

He waded onto the beach, wiping himself down with the towel he'd left lying there. The girls weren't due home for several hours yet. That meant he had time to go to Michelle and apologize, to try to salvage something of the friendship that meant more to him than she'd probably ever know.

THERE WERE TWO MESSAGES waiting for Michelle when she got home. One was from Grace, telling her that Amanda Blake had just delivered a healthy eight-pound baby girl; the other was from Frank Steele, asking her to call him. Her fingers trembled as she punched in the numbers he'd left.

"There's still no word from Karim, Mrs. Colby, but I've found some people here in Sana with information for sale. And from what I gather, I'm not sure your husband's worth the money you're spending on him."

Michelle wanted to hang up the phone. She couldn't face this. Not today. "What do you mean?"

"If you want my professional opinion I think he's probably dead, just like the government said, ma'am. Three years is a long time to hide."

"Karim's doing it, though."

There was a pause as Frank took a long drag on his ever-present cigarette.

"So let's assume that he is alive. It still doesn't look good. He lived of his own free will in that village, ma'am. From all accounts, no one was holding him hostage. No one was under any direction to watch him or detain him."

Michelle swallowed. "Go on." Her throat was so dry she almost choked.

"I've found out quite a bit more about this Karim. The man is a legend on the streets. From what I can tell, he runs some kind of elite terrorist group that works for hire. Everyone fears him and everyone has stories about the murders, the stealing, the bombings he's been involved in. I'd guess that some of it has been exaggerated, but probably not much.''

''So what does this have to do with Brian?''

''The village people believe Brian was working with him, sort of a second in command, if you will. Which would explain why Jazmin was afraid to admit she loved Brian. These people don't want to be tied to Karim any more than they have to be to stay alive. Of course some of this is speculation. Without Karim, we don't know for sure Brian's exact role in things, but I'm certainly convinced we've found enough.''

''I'm not.''

''Mrs. Colby, I love the money I'm making here, but—''

''Keep looking, Frank.''

''If you're sure....''

''I have to know...'' Michelle's voice faltered. She barely got the phone hung up before she collapsed in tears.

Her sobs were harsh and hopeless, but they didn't last long. Frank had to be mistaken. He was missing something. There was an explanation—there had to be. The villagers knew what Karim wanted them to know. If the man was so powerful he could make people see only what he wanted them to, couldn't he? Not only would Brian never be involved in bombings and murder, he'd never have willingly deserted his wife. Of that, she was absolutely certain.

She got up from her desk and went in to change

her clothes, Frank's words replaying through her mind all the while. She was looking for the hole in Frank's reasoning that would prove Brian's innocence. Brian smiled up at her from her nightstand, his face innocent, boyish and unlined. She picked up the photo and stared at it for a long time, as if the answers she was seeking were hidden there.

And maybe they were. She got out her wedding pictures and looked through them, remembering the moment when Brian had pledged his love to her, his young voice strong and clear enough to be heard in the back of the church. She remembered the feel of the cool gold band sliding up her finger as he made her his wife.

And she remembered their wedding night, Brian's tenderness, his unselfish loving, his gentleness—and again, his youth. There was just no way Brian was a willing partner in any terrorist organization. He was too intrinsically gentle to be capable of senseless violence.

But neither was this young man still capable of filling Michelle's needs. She was no longer the naive girl Brian had married. The past five years could have destroyed her, but they hadn't. Instead, they'd matured her, tempered her. And with that new maturity had come desires stronger than anything she'd ever felt for Brian. She'd come to love as deeply, as passionately, as she'd suffered.

Michelle went through the house slowly, systematically, collecting all of Brian's pictures. She cried for each one of them, for the dreams lost, and stacked them carefully in a box.

Her answering machine caught her eye as she headed toward the bedroom, and she stopped, coming back to play the recorded outgoing message. She listened one last time to Brian's youthful voice saying, "This is the Colbys…" Then she pushed the record button, cleared her throat and said, "This is Michelle. I can't come to the phone right now…"

Brian's clothes came next. She pulled his shirts off their hangers, folding them neatly, and with every one of them was a memory. She brought in another box and loaded it with his clothes, until the only thing left of Brian in the home they'd had together was the shiny gold band on her finger.

CHAPTER FOURTEEN

JACOB KNOCKED on Michelle's door, shoving his hands into the pockets of his jeans as he waited for her to answer. He knew she was home. He'd pulled his car behind hers in the driveway. Mind you, he wouldn't blame her for not wanting to see him. His words to her that morning had been more than cruel. They'd been unforgivable. But he was going to apologize, anyway, if he had to camp on her doorstep until she came out.

He was surprised when her door opened almost immediately and she pulled him inside. He could tell she'd been crying.

"Michelle, I'm—"

"Shh." She put her finger against his lips. "Dance with me?" she whispered. It was only then that Jacob noticed the soft saxophone music playing in the background.

Unsure what was happening, he looked into her eyes hoping to see a glint of humor—some indication that this was merely an elaborate joke. Instead, all he saw was desperation.

He wrapped his arms around her, pulling her up

against him, and started to sway slowly to the music. *What the hell's going on?* he wondered.

She nestled her face against his neck. *She's seeking comfort,* he decided—until he felt the flick of her tongue against his skin.

Her fingers slid to the front of his shirt and freed the buttons at the neck before skimming down his body to slide the shirt off. Her hands were torturing him, arousing him and— *Dear God.* Why was she doing this? She was worrying the hell out of him, and he wasn't sure what to do about it.

Undaunted by his lack of response, Michelle continued to caress him. Jacob knew he was going to have to stop her, make her tell him what was going on. But something held him back. There was a desperation in her touch—mirroring what he'd glimpsed in her eyes.

Still slowly dancing, he looked over her shoulder, hoping to discover some clue what was prompting her to act like this. Then it hit him. Brian's picture wasn't in its usual spot on the end table. He noticed the empty mantel above her fireplace, the empty spaces on her bookcase where her wedding pictures used to be.

And suddenly Jacob understood. Michelle wasn't making love to him, Jacob Ryan. She was using him to say goodbye to Brian Colby.

He tilted her head up, intending to reason with her. But then her lips met his and all hope for a rational discussion was lost. Her kisses were too hungry, his passion too long denied.

He pulled her T-shirt over her head, trailing his hands across her ribs and breasts before reaching behind her to unfasten the catch on her bra. And then she was back in his arms, pressing her warm full breasts against his chest.

Leaving their shirts where they'd dropped them, she took his hand and led him down the hall to her bedroom. Jacob didn't need to look to know that this room, too, was bare of reminders of her husband. He wanted to ask her if she'd had word that Brian was dead, but when he started to speak her eyes pleaded with him not to.

She released his hand, then unzipped her skirt, sliding the material over her hips to pool at her feet. *Oh, Lord, she was beautiful.* Jacob throbbed with need as he unbuttoned his jeans and stripped them off. Then, still without saying a word, she lay down on the bed and pulled him on top of her. As he lowered his head to kiss her he realized with a sense of fatality that making love to Michelle like this wasn't enough. Not for him. But what he needed was more than she had to give.

Yet he'd come too far to stop. They both had.

Driven by needs he barely understood, Jacob made love to Michelle with a single-minded passion that precluded conscious thought. He was only aware of their bodies straining together, thrusting urgently.

And when it was over, when he finally looked directly into her eyes, he wasn't surprised by the regret he saw in their soft blue depths, nor by the tears trickling down her cheeks. Damn it to hell. It shouldn't be like this. It was more than he'd ever had before—but it still fell short of what it could have been. What it should have been.

She looked up at him silently, apologetically, and stroked his face with her hand. It was then that he saw her wedding band. No matter what she'd done with Brian's pictures, in her heart she was still married to another man.

Jacob slid his body off hers and rolled onto his back. As much as he wanted to be gone, he couldn't just get up and leave her. She snuggled against him.

He held her until she was sleeping soundly, and then, as silently as they'd made love, he rose, dressed and went home to his girls.

IT WAS THE LONGEST weekend of Jacob's life. He took Ellen to a preview screening of a new Tom Cruise movie and afterward over drinks tried to get a few things settled.

"When are we going to talk about the future, Ellen?" he asked, his hands on the glass of scotch in front of him.

Her eyes lit with pleasure. "I wasn't sure you thought we had one." She slid her hand across the table to his.

"You're the mother of my children. It seems to me only natural to consider a future together." *Great,*

Ryan. Think you could sound a little more excited about it?

"You don't know how relieved I am to hear you say that. Your insistence on keeping this just between the two of us really had me worried."

He wished he could be sure he was doing the right thing. "You haven't seemed overanxious to see the girls."

"They *are* my daughters, Jacob. I may not be your ideal of a mother, but I do love them. I just didn't want to push things. You were always protective of the girls, but you've guarded them like the crown jewels since I left."

"You've had access to them."

She covered his hand with hers, lines creasing her beautiful brow. "And I knew I'd have you to answer to if I said one wrong thing. You seemed to think I would just know automatically what all the right things were. And I don't. Whoever hands out that natural mother's instinct when children are born wasn't in the delivery room when I had the triplets. No matter what I did, it always seemed to be the wrong thing. I'd make them cry or make them mad— it got to the point where I was afraid to do anything at all."

Jacob thought of Michelle's relationship with his children, her instinctive ability to provide for their needs. Looking at the woman across from him, he reminded himself that Ellen was his future. She was the one who'd borne his children. She was the one who wanted him.

"You'd probably be a lot easier around them if you'd just relax a little," he told her. "Maybe it would help if you saw them more as miniature adults than little aliens," he added with a smile. He'd been happy with Ellen once. Maybe he could be again.

She smiled back. "Perhaps. I'm certainly willing to try."

And with that, he *would* be satisfied.

ALLIE WOKE Jacob from a restless sleep at three o'clock Sunday morning, climbing into bed beside him.

"Have a bad dream, punkin?" he asked, his brain still fogged with sleep. He'd been dreaming that Michelle had told Ellen that Brian had come home.

"Uh-uh," Allie said. "I'm cold." Her teeth chattered.

Instantly awake, Jacob felt her forehead. His little leader of the pack wasn't cold at all. She was hot. Too hot.

Telling himself not to panic, Jacob settled Allie in the middle of his bed, pulled the covers up to her chin and told her to stay put.

"I don't feel so good, Daddy," she said meekly.

"I know, punkin. Can you tell me what hurts?"

"Everything hurts," she said, starting to cry.

Jacob brushed the hair back from her brow. "Shh.

Don't cry, honey. I'll make it better in a jiffy. Does your throat hurt?''

She shook her head.

"How about your tummy?''

"Uh-uh.''

"You have an earache?'' The girls had had their share of them over the years.

"Uh-uh.''

What else was there?

"Just everything hurts, huh?''

She nodded, her little mouth pursed as if she was going to cry again.

"Okay, we'll get you fixed up in no time. I'm just going to check on your sisters and then I'll be right back with something to make you feel better, okay?''

She gave him a weak smile and snuggled into his pillow. "Okay, Daddy.''

Jessie and Meggie were both sleeping soundly. Jacob laid his hand against each of their cheeks and was relieved to find that both girls were as cool as the night air could make them. With any luck, they'd stay that way.

Allie was still awake when he returned to his bedroom with the thermometer and children's Tylenol. The girls had had their share of illnesses through the years, and he'd become pretty adept at recognizing the symptoms. But other than her fever, Allie didn't seem to have any. He hoped that was good news.

She held the thermometer under her tongue, but she

squirmed under the covers the entire two minutes he made her keep it there.

"I'm itchy, Daddy," she said the minute her mouth was free.

He stared at the thermometer. She had a fever of 102 and she itched. His stomach sank as he realized what was bothering his daughter. He hoped he was wrong.

"Where does it itch, sport?" he asked.

"All over, but especially here and here," Allie whined, pushing away the covers to point to her stomach and her armpits.

After a quick inspection Jacob's suspicion was confirmed. Allie had chicken pox. And judging by the number of nasty-looking red spots on her body, she wasn't going to have an easy time of it. He went back to the bathroom and located the calamine lotion he'd bought the time Jessie had fallen into a patch of poison ivy. Resigned to a long haul ahead, he returned to his bedroom and covered Allie's skin with the soothing lotion. There was no way the other two were going to escape this unscathed.

The Tylenol took effect shortly after that and Allie fell into a restless sleep. But Jacob knew his vigil had just begun. Lying down beside her, he wondered how long it would be before Jessie and Meggie started itching, too. It was times like these that the loneliness inherent in being a single parent hit him most of all.

By four o'clock Sunday afternoon Jacob was at his wits' end. He'd spent the day catering to three cranky, itchy little girls and he was exhausted. Allie's fever had risen to 103, and by midafternoon, Jessie and Meggie had fevers, as well. He called their doctor, only to be told he was already doing all that could be done for the girls and should continue administering the analgesic. The doctor told him he'd have to keep the triplets out of school for several days until they passed the contagious stage of the disease. When Jacob asked for something to help make them more comfortable the doctor suggested cool baths and lots of tender loving care.

"I itch too much, Daddy," Jessie whined when he returned to the girls' room.

"How about a cool bath, Jess? Maybe that'll make you feel better."

Jessie sat up slowly. "Okay," she said, as if agreeing to give her favorite doll to the poor.

"Can I have some juice, Daddy? I'm thirsty," Allie said, scratching at her stomach.

"Just as soon as I get Jessie in the tub, Al. Try not to scratch so much."

Meggie wrestled with her covers. "I can't get to an itch, Daddy!" she cried. "It's back here over my shoulder."

Jacob went over to rub Meggie's back. "Dad-de-e-e, my bath," Jessie wailed from across the room.

"What about my juice, Daddy?" Allie asked hoarsely.

Jacob wished he was four people. He considered

calling Ellen but dismissed the thought almost immediately. Ellen didn't tolerate sickness very well.

But as soon as he had Jessie settled in the bath, got Allie her juice and put a fresh batch of calamine lotion on Meggie, he headed for the phone. Right or wrong didn't matter anymore. He needed help.

"I SLEPT WITH JACOB, Mom," Michelle said, telling her mother over the phone something she'd probably never have been able to say in person. But she'd needed to talk with somebody. Her guilt was eating her up.

"I expected that would happen sooner or later," Grace said, surprising her.

Michelle stopped fiddling with the phone cord. "You did?"

"You're a normal healthy adult, Michelle, and sex is a normal healthy need," Grace said, sounding like the doctor she was.

"Mother!"

"It's all part of facing the future, honey."

"Maybe. I just wish I could be sure."

"You of all people should know that life is never a sure thing, Michelle. Your feelings for Brian felt right five years ago but they don't anymore, do they?"

Michelle's eyes welled with tears. "No," she said softly. Grace was putting into words what Michelle had only just discovered for herself. Somehow Michelle had outgrown the love she and Brian had shared.

"So how did you feel when you were with Jacob? Were you thinking about Brian?"

Blushing, Michelle remembered Jacob's hands, large and sure on her body. "Not once," she said. Making love with Jacob had been better than she'd dreamed it could be. She'd spent the past two days cherishing the memory, reliving it over and over, and hating herself for it at the same time. She couldn't imagine what Jacob must think of her.

"Have you talked to Jacob since then?" Grace asked.

Michelle shook her head, then realized her mother couldn't see her. She dried her eyes. "I called him last night, you know, to talk about things—seeing as we do have to work together. The girls' baby-sitter said he was out—with Ellen." She wasn't going to cry about it again. She wasn't.

There was a long pause on the line. "You may have to accept that he's made his choice," Grace said gently.

"I know."

"I'm sorry, honey. So sorry."

"Yeah, me, too…"

Grace invited Michelle over for dinner, but Michelle declined, preferring to lick her wounds in private. She and Grace talked awhile longer, her mother telling her that Amanda Blake had found a job in a day-care center so she could support her daughter and still be with her all day. Michelle was happy for the young woman, if a bit envious, and even more pleased for the baby who was going to have a fair shake at life, after all. She was proud of the work her mother did and told her so.

She'd just hung up the phone when it rang again.

"I've been trying to get you for over half an hour." Jacob's voice was disgruntled. Michelle's heart sped up in spite of herself. The last time she'd seen him they'd… And he'd been… But the next night he'd been out with his ex-wife.

"I was talking to my mother. What's up?"

"I need your help. You've already done so much and I'm a heel to ask, but I don't know who else to call."

Michelle frowned, immediately concerned. He sounded exhausted. "What's wrong?"

"The girls have chicken pox."

"All three of them?"

"Yeah. All three. Allie started in the middle of the night, Jessie woke up with them around seven, and by noon, Meggie was down with them, too. They're all running fevers, they're itchy and cranky, and…"

"I'm on my way," Michelle said, hanging up the phone.

She fed Noby and sped out the door, a smile on her face. He needed her. Not Ellen. She reminded herself all the way out to the beach that Jacob's choice was the only logical one—she'd been around so much lately the girls would be more comfortable with her than with the mother they hadn't seen in years. But by the time she arrived at the cottage she still hadn't managed to convince herself that there wasn't something significant in Jacob's plea for help.

GOD, SHE'S BEAUTIFUL. Jacob stood in the doorway of the cottage and stared at Michelle, only then realizing just how much he'd missed her.

"Can I come in?" she asked, a shy smile curving her lips.

"Of course. Sorry," Jacob said, stepping aside. She smelled like California sunshine and fresh air. She tasted that way, too, he remembered.

"Where are they?" she asked, looking around the living room, avoiding his gaze.

"In the bedroom." He wondered if she'd been thinking about Friday afternoon as much as he had.

"Daddy?" Meggie's voice trailed weakly down the hall. Michelle looked relieved as she glanced toward the sound.

"Coming, punkin," he called back. He and Michelle headed down the hall together.

"Allie and Jessie are sleeping, but I just promised Meggie a soak in the tub. They're all three due for Tylenol again in another hour," he said softly. Even if she wouldn't look him in the eye, he was damn glad she was here.

She paused just outside the girls' bedroom door.

"Why don't you try to get some rest now, and I'll see to Meggie."

He could only think of one thing that sounded better, but he knew there was no hope of that. "If you're sure…"

She pushed him toward his room. "Go," she said, and went in to cluck over Meggie.

He heard his recalcitrant daughter's happy greeting as he shut his bedroom door behind him.

TO SAY THE NEXT twenty-four hours were grueling was an understatement. Michelle called Bob Chaney Sunday afternoon while Jacob slept and arranged to have the weekend morning announcer cover for Jacob and her until further notice. She let Bob draw his own conclusions about her presence at the triplets' sickbeds.

Jessie and Allie were both awake and fussy by the time Michelle got Meggie tucked back into bed after her bath, but they were happy to see her, too. Michelle anointed and fetched, rubbed hard-to-reach places and read stories. And as much as it bothered her to see the girls so miserable, she was delighted to be able to care for them. It felt wonderful to be needed again.

Jacob finally awoke late that evening. All three girls were asleep for the moment, Jessie in Michelle's arms.

"Want me to take her?" he whispered, walking into the bedroom.

Michelle wanted to hold the little girl forever, but her arms were numb and she needed something to drink. She nodded, feeling chilled as Jacob lifted his daughter away from her and laid Jessie gently in her bed.

He followed Michelle into the hall. "Thanks for the rest," he said.

She glanced up at him. He'd obviously had a shower—his hair was still wet. "I'm glad you could sleep," she said, wishing she could touch him.

He trailed her into the kitchen, helping himself to a cup of coffee from the warm pot on the counter. "Did the girls eat?"

She poured herself a diet cola. "Some. They wanted macaroni and cheese, but no one had much of an appetite once it was cooked."

They sat down at the table together quietly, the intimacy of their situation wrapping around them. Now was the time when mothers and fathers shared a tired but still passionate kiss. Michelle wondered why she continued to torment herself with images of things she might never have.

"I called Bob," she said. "Rhonda's covering for us."

"Hell, I forgot all about work tomorrow," Jacob said, his brow creasing. God, he looked handsome! "I suppose you're about ready to head home."

"I can stay a little while longer. They'll need Tylenol again in another half an hour, and once they're awake they're probably going to need lotion, too."

Jacob grinned. "Tell me about it," he said, and then grew serious again. "Have you checked their fevers? I forgot to tell you the thermometer's in the bathroom cabinet.''

"I found it. Allie's has dropped to 101, but Jessie's and Meggie's are both hovering around 102.''

Jacob nodded and took a sip of his coffee. ''They'll probably be a lot more comfortable once their fevers break.''

Michelle grimaced. ''I don't know. I have a feeling the itching gets worse.'' She couldn't believe how much she still wanted him. Sitting there with him, close enough to touch, was harder than she would've believed now that she knew how incredible their love-making could be. She wondered if they were ever going to talk about that afternoon, but before she could broach the subject, he drained his coffee cup and stood up.

''Let's get this done,'' he said. ''The sooner they're awake, the sooner they'll go back to sleep.''

He reached into the refrigerator for a bottle of apple juice, and Michelle took three plastic cups from the cupboard. She'd learned the last go-round that the triplets would only take their pills with apple juice. She followed Jacob down the hall a couple of minutes later, careful not to spill any of the juice she carried. Waking the girls, they gave them their Tylenol, rubbed lotion on them and had them settled back into bed, if not back asleep, within twenty minutes. Even when they weren't on the air she and Jacob worked together like naturals.

MICHELLE ENDED UP spending the night, taking a turn
in Jacob's bed—alone—while he crashed on the
couch for the couple of hours all three girls slept. And
though she fell asleep almost as soon as her head hit
his pillow, Michelle's dreams were all about the two
of them together in bed. Waking up, she was hit with
a wave of desire so strong she actually considered
asking him to come and make love to her.

But she didn't. She wasn't going to repeat her mistake. If she ever made love to Jacob again, it would
only be when she was sure Brian was out of her life—
one way or another. And it would only be when their
lovemaking included promises for the future. She'd
discovered the other day that she didn't like waking
up alone when she hadn't gone to bed that way.

The girls' fevers broke on Monday, but things
didn't get any easier. For the girls' energy came back
full force. Their complaining was louder, their requests more frequent, their need to be entertained almost constant. They'd spent so much time in bed over
the past forty-eight hours none of them wanted to
sleep.

Michelle had finally coaxed them all onto Meggie's
bed to play a game of Candyland when the telephone
rang.

"I'll get it," Jacob said, abandoning his role of
kibitzer.

Michelle wondered if it was Bob calling from the
station. Rhonda's husband, a pilot, was due to fly in
unexpectedly sometime that night, which meant that

Michelle might have to go into work in the morning—she glanced down at her watch—just a little over eight hours from now. She sure hoped not. Leaving the girls to their game, she followed Jacob out to the telephone.

"I just don't think tomorrow's a good time. They've been sick for two days, and I'm not sure we're through the worst of it," she heard him say. He was looking out the living room window. He hadn't seen her yet.

"I appreciate your concern, Ellen, but I'm not sure this is a good time for your first visit. You know how you hate sickrooms."

Ellen.

CHAPTER FIFTEEN

MICHELLE FELT THE BLOOD drain from her face. Somehow over the past twenty-four hours she'd managed to forget the other woman. Or at least she'd started to believe that Ellen wasn't a threat.

"I *do* believe you've changed. I'd just feel better if the girls weren't at their worst the first time you see them." He sounded tired.

Michelle stood frozen in the doorway.

"Okay. If you insist. But on one condition."

He's agreeing? With me right here in his home? He's going to let that woman just walk in and take my place? Michelle panicked as another though occurred to her. *Will the girls be just as willing to replace her?* Fear raced through her, making it hard to breathe.

"I don't want them given any indication this might be permanent. As far as the girls are concerned you're just in town on a visit and want to see them." He was going to give in to her. After all that woman had done to those children he was letting her come back to them.

"All right. Ten o'clock'll be fine. See you in the morning."

Jacob hung up, turned and saw Michelle. She hoped she didn't look as upset as she felt. She had to get through this, and then go home where she belonged.

"I didn't know you were there," he said, looking like a child caught with a hand in the cookie jar.

"I thought it might have been Bob." *Go home now. There's no more reason for you to stay.*

"That was Ellen," he said, watching her. She hoped it wasn't pity she saw in his eyes. The last thing she wanted was for him to feel sorry for her.

She folded her arms. "She wants to see them now?"

He nodded. That was all.

Something inside her wouldn't let her leave it alone. "And you're going to let her?" She hadn't meant to sound so accusing, but how could he do this to her? She'd just spent two days caring for those girls as if they were her own. And hadn't Friday afternoon meant anything to him? Without even talking to her, he was going to resume his relationship with that other woman?

"She's their mother, Michelle."

"She lost the right to that title when she deserted them."

"She's changed since then, grown up."

So now he's defending her. "Maybe."

"I won't ever know if I don't give her a chance."

"I thought you wanted to protect the girls." Even

she knew she was being unfair. She'd heard his conditions for the visit.

"They aren't going to know we're considering making this permanent." That was the second time she'd heard that word. *Permanent.*

Michelle felt cold all over. She welcomed the sensation, knowing from experience that numbness would follow. So Jacob and Ellen were considering making it permanent. In spite of the fact that he and Michelle had made incredible love only the other day, he was still considering a reunion with his ex-wife. Not that Michelle had any right to blame him. She might have put Brian's things away, but didn't he still have a stranglehold on her heart?

"You love her, then?" She didn't know why she was torturing herself, but she couldn't help asking.

He turned around, facing the window. "She's a beautiful woman," he said.

"So you do love her."

"I enjoy her company."

"But are you in love with her?" Michelle asked harshly, having reached the end of her tether. It was time to go home to Noby.

She was unprepared for Jacob's response. He swung around, his face taut with anger. "No! I'm not in love with her. How can I be when I'm in love with you?"

"Then why…" She couldn't finish the question. She just stood there, staring at him, filled with an equal mix of wonder and fear.

"Because my children need a mother and she's willing to try to be one for them."

"And I'm not?" *The man has just said he loves you.* She willed herself to be calm. To try to understand. "What's this been, then? A holiday?"

"You're wonderful with the kids, Michelle. We both know that. But the girls and I are a package deal."

He was only across the room from her, but she felt as if there was a world between them. "What about Friday? What was that if not trying?"

Michelle's heart sped up as she watched him move toward her. She wanted him—needed him—to hold her. But she was so afraid to love him that she was choking on her fear.

He reached out to her, but instead of taking her in his arms, he grabbed her left hand and held it up.

"And what's this? A friendship ring?" he asked. "I can't share you, Michelle. I'm not that giving a person."

Tears filled her eyes as she looked at her wedding band. She wanted to pull it off, to be free of five years of anguish. She wanted to walk into Jacob's arms unencumbered and whole. But she wasn't whole. She'd loved before with all her heart. And she was terrified to risk loving that way again.

Jacob dropped her hand and turned away.

"COME ON, YOU GUYS, hurry up." Meggie stood in the door of the bedroom she shared with her sisters,

wondering why it always took Jessie so long to tie
her tennis shoes and why Allie always had to make
it take even longer by helping. Daddy was driving
them to Michelle's for the afternoon, and Meggie was
sure she was going to die if she didn't get there soon.
She'd figured it all out in the middle of the night
when her eyes wouldn't stay closed even when she
told them to. She had to talk to Michelle.

"Hey, you guys, don't tell Michelle about
Mommy, okay?" she said as an afterthought. She
didn't want to have to ask Michelle in front of them.
Just in case.

Jessie looked up from her tennis shoe. "Why not?
She always wants to hear about everything that happens to us."

"You don't want to hurt her feelings, do ya?" Allie asked, tugging on Jessie's foot.

Meggie was glad Allie had the answer. Allie always knew what to say.

Allie finished with Jessie's shoe, and it looked kind
of loose to Meggie. It probably wasn't going to stay
tied very long, but Meggie wasn't going to say anything about it now. They had to go.

"Do you think we should bring a game or something?" Allie asked, staring at the shelves filled with
toys and puzzles and games in their closet.

"'Course not. Michelle'll have stuff," Meggie
said, afraid Allie would take forever deciding what to
bring. Meggie didn't know if Michelle had anything
to do over at her house or not, but she didn't care.

She just had to get there. There was something she had to know.

"I'm bringing the pet shop," Jessie said, pulling down the case filled with plastic miniatures.

"Okay, and I'll bring the travel desk," Allie said, lugging it from its corner in the closet.

Maybe it was a good idea for her sisters to bring stuff, 'cause then Meggie could have some time alone with Michelle. Besides, they'd decided quick. "Okay, let's go."

Jessie stood by the closet door. "Aren't you bringing anything, Meggie?" she asked.

Meggie stomped her foot. "I'll just play with yours," she said, gritting her teeth so they'd know she was getting mad and start listening to her. "Now let's *go.*" This was just as important for them as it was for her, even if they didn't know it yet.

Meggie couldn't wait to see Michelle. They'd been sick for two more days after Michelle left and then their mommy had been coming to visit, so Meggie hadn't seen Michelle in days. But Michelle had called and talked to them every evening they were sick and afterward, too. And now she'd invited them over to spend the day with her because she'd promised them she would as soon as they were better. They still itched some, but Allie was the worst and even her bumps were almost all just scabs.

Daddy turned onto Michelle's street and Meggie looked out the window. She wasn't sure she'd know which house was Michelle's because they all kind of looked alike on Michelle's street, but she found it right away. It was the one with Michelle outside on the step.

Meggie waited just until Daddy turned off the car so she wouldn't get yelled at, then she unbuckled her seat belt and scrambled out of the car. Jessie and Allie always got the first hugs, but today Meggie wanted the first one. Just for once.

"Hi, Michelle," she called, heading up the walk. She felt a little funny just running up and hugging her. What if Michelle didn't hug back? Or worse, what if she just patted Meggie on the back like Mommy did?

"Hi, sweetheart, how are you feeling?" Michelle asked. She didn't even wait for Meggie to reach her. She came down the walk and grabbed Meggie right up.

"I've missed you," she said softly, her breath tickling Meggie's neck. Michelle squeezed so hard it almost hurt, but Meggie didn't care. She was just glad that Michelle was hugging her.

"I've missed you, too," Meggie said, even though she was kind of scared to say the words. And she had more to say. Right now, before she chickened out and before she didn't have a chance with her sisters around.

"I need to tell you some stuff in private, okay?" She hoped Michelle would understand how important it was.

Michelle pulled away and looked at her kind of

funnylike, but Meggie made herself stare right back even though it made her tummy cramp up like when she ate too much candy.

Then Michelle smiled. "I'll make sure we have the time," she said—just to Meggie, even though Allie and Jessie were running up the walk toward her.

It took a long time to get alone with Michelle because Allie and Jessie had missed Michelle an awful lot, too, probably as much as Meggie had. And, anyway, Meggie was hungry and Michelle had made sloppy joes, and Meggie wanted to play with Noby, too. But finally Michelle put on a movie of Bugs Bunny cartoons and gave them all cards to sew on. And as soon as Allie and Jessie were busy, she called Meggie to help her clean up in the kitchen. Michelle sure was smart. Allie and Jessie didn't like dishes any more than Meggie did, so they'd stay right there in the living room where they didn't have to help. If she'd called Meggie to her bedroom or something, her sisters probably would've wanted to come along.

Meggie's tummy started to cramp up a little again as she dropped her sewing card, and she wished she hadn't had seconds at lunch. She followed Michelle to the kitchen and forgot the words she'd rehearsed the night before. Michelle was an adult and she didn't want to make her mad. Maybe she'd made a big mistake. Allie and Jessie laughed at something in the living room, and Meggie wished she was in there, too. The sewing cards were really neat.

Michelle turned around then and smiled—all warm

and soft, just like she had when Meggie was so sick and itchy—and lifted Meggie up onto the counter, making her as big as Michelle so her neck didn't get tired looking up. That's what was so neat about Michelle. She was always doing that stuff, like she knew what it was like being seven.

"Okay, sweetie, what's up?" Michelle asked, giving Meggie her full attention. Meggie wondered for the millionth time why God hadn't made Michelle their mommy.

Meggie thought about what Allie said about hurting Michelle's feelings. She didn't know what she'd do if she made Michelle cry.

"Mommy's here visiting us." She said it real fast to get it over.

Michelle didn't look like she was going to cry, but her eyes weren't all smiley, either.

"I know, honey," she said, surprising Meggie.

"You do?"

Michelle nodded. "Your daddy told me."

"Oh." Meggie hadn't figured on that one.

"I'll bet it was great to see her."

Meggie didn't know what she was supposed to say. If Daddy and Michelle were talking about Mommy, then Michelle might tell Daddy what Meggie said. But if she didn't talk to Michelle, she would just go on being afraid. And she'd thought since that day Michelle had come and gotten them from school that she wouldn't have to be afraid anymore.

Michelle put her hands on the counter on either

side of Meggie's legs. It made Meggie feel like Michelle was kind of holding her.

"Meggie? Isn't it great to see your mother?" Michelle asked, looking at her like Ms. Wilson did when she'd better tell the truth.

Shrugging, Meggie stared down at Michelle's hands.

"Is she nice to you?" Michelle asked.

Meggie nodded. As hard as she tried, she couldn't make herself say the words she wanted to say.

Michelle lifted her chin. "So what's the problem?"

"She likes Daddy better than us." Meggie was surprised to hear her words come out, but she felt better when they did.

"Oh, honey, I'm sure she doesn't. What makes you think that?"

Meggie had never even considered the idea that Michelle might not believe her. "She does, Michelle. Even Jessie knows it. She always sits by Daddy and talks to Daddy at the table, and she only smiles at us sometimes when we say something or when Daddy talks to us. And she mixes us up."

"What does your daddy say about it?"

Finally Meggie was getting somewhere. She stared into Michelle's eyes and talked real fast so she could get it all in. "Nothing. He prob'ly thinks we don't know. But he's in a bad mood a lot and me and Allie figure it's because he's stuck with us and maybe Mommy will go away again like she did last time and then he'll be mad at us 'cause he has to stay with us.

Allie and me talked about how we could maybe take care of ourselves 'cause I know how to make sandwiches and Allie ran the washer once when Daddy was sick, but we don't think they're allowed to let us stay alone, so I was wondering if, maybe, Mommy doesn't want us, you do.''

There, she'd said it. Meggie held her breath.

''Oh, baby, of course I want you—always.'' Michelle pulled Meggie off the counter and into her arms, just like the day Jessie got lost at Disneyland and Michelle held Allie all close. ''But don't give up on your daddy yet, okay?'' she asked. ''I think he wants you three more than anyone else in the whole world.''

Meggie laid her head on Michelle's shoulder, hugging her as tight as she could. She sure hoped Michelle was right.

IT WASN'T GOING TO WORK. Jacob looked at Ellen's smiling face on the dance floor and knew there was no way he could reconcile with her. She was having the time of her life in this swank nightclub. He'd much rather be at home with the girls. It didn't matter that they were sound asleep in their beds; he just liked having them close. Taking a sip of his drink, he raised his glass in a toast as Ellen glanced over at him. She'd had more partners among this Saturday-night crowd than he could count, and he didn't even care.

She'd tried several times to get him to dance, but he hadn't wanted to join her on the crowded floor.

Not that he minded dancing, as long as he was partnering the right woman.

And there was the crux of his problem. He couldn't marry Ellen when he was in love with another woman. Not even for his girls, though he had a feeling they weren't going to suffer overly much without their birth mother. Eventually they were going to figure out that Ellen's main interest was in him, anyway.

"It's great out there. You sure you won't change your mind and join me?" Ellen asked, sliding into her chair. She'd chosen their secluded table when they'd first arrived, and now Jacob was thankful for the privacy.

"I'm sure. Why don't you sit this one out, have a drink, catch your breath." *Why don't you sit still for a moment so I can get this over with?*

She smiled at him, leaning back in her seat. "You've always been so solicitous, Jacob. It's one of the things I missed most about you when I left for Washington."

That was his opening. "Speaking of which, have you thought any more about that job offer you've had?"

She frowned at him. "Well, I kind of thought that was a decision we might make together," she said. She was pouting, just like Jessie did when she didn't get her way.

"What you do with your career is something you're going to have to decide on your own, honey. You're the one who has to work at it."

She leaned forward, sliding her hand across the table to cover his. "There's plenty of time to make those decisions later, don't you think? I didn't plan to go right back to work if we remarried."

His eyes narrowed. "You thought you might stay home with the girls for a while? Make up for lost time?" Had he misjudged her so completely?

She sat back. "I'll spend time with them, sure. But I've already been approached about resuming my old positions on the charity boards. It seems they miss my organizational skills."

"So things would be just like they were before. You running off here and there, or frustrated with the girls because they kept you from running here and there."

"No! I'm older now, Jacob. And so are they. I'm a lot more tolerant, and they're hardly likely to need as much of my time as they did when they were three."

He drained his glass. "That's the problem, Ellen. The girls don't deserve to be tolerated—they deserve to be loved. And while I'll grant you their needs are different now that they're older, they still have needs. The next time they have a mother, it's going to be someone who'd rather carve a pumpkin than play bridge, who'd willingly give up tickets to the ballet to string popcorn for the Christmas tree—and who won't yell at them for messing up their clothes when they go skating in the park."

Ellen's face hardened, reminding him of the many

times they'd argued in the past. "You're living in the Dark Ages, Jacob. Women aren't satisfied with baking cookies and wiping noses anymore. They have careers. They have equality. They have nannies to raise their children."

Jacob thought of Michelle, his partner, who didn't hesitate to work nights to finish four beautiful little ball gowns. "And who do you think those nannies are, Ellen, if not women who find satisfaction in baking and mothering?"

Ellen's look was sincere as she leaned toward him. "They're career women, too, Jacob. They're making a living, probably the only way they know how, but at least they have the satisfaction of earning a paycheck each week. You're looking for something that just doesn't exist anymore. You want a woman of the fifties, someone from the days of 'Leave It to Beaver' and 'The Donna Reed Show.' You want someone who'll be happy to be at the beck and call of your children, run your household, still look good when you come home from work and do it all for love. You didn't have that growing up, so you think you're going to make up for that by providing it for our kids. But you're not being fair. Women aren't expected to live like that anymore."

Jacob digested Ellen's words in silence. The damnable part was a lot of what she said was true. Not all of it. He was happy to share in every bit of the work involved in caring for his home and children. But he did want a woman who would put family above everything else in her life. He did expect too much. But he couldn't seem to be satisfied with less.

"Which is exactly why I'm all done asking others to live up to my expectations," he said.

Ellen sat back in her chair. "What are you saying?"

"I don't think it's going to work between us any better the second time than it did the first, honey."

Her smile was poignant, regretful, but just a little bit relieved. "That's your last word?" she asked.

Jacob nodded. This was one thing he was sure about.

"I don't suppose I could talk you into an hour or two in my room for old times' sake, could I?"

He shook his head.

THE GIRLS WERE ASLEEP when Jacob got home an hour later. He locked up the cottage and tried not to notice the silence surrounding him. If he was destined to live the rest of his life alone, so be it.

Stealing into the triplets' bedroom, he picked up Jessie's teddy bear from the floor, tucked it back under her covers and kissed her gently on the brow. He hoped she never got too old to be his baby.

Allie was lying flat on her back, the covers up to her chin. Jacob bent to kiss her good-night, loving the strength he saw in her young face, even in sleep. A few more years, and he wasn't going to have to worry about being lonely. Allie would organize his life for him, just as she was already doing for her sisters.

Meggie's leg was hanging off the side of her bed, and Jacob slid it back beneath the covers. Some difficult times lay ahead for all of them these next few years, but he suspected they would be the hardest for Meggie. She was so determined to be independent, but after seeing her open up to Michelle, he knew she was the one who missed having a mother most of all.

But maybe he could do something about that. He kissed Meggie good-night, then left the girls and headed down the hall to his bedroom, stripping off his clothes as he went. He stepped into the shower, remembering something Ellen had said weeks before. She'd accused him of giving up too easily. She might as well have called him the coward that he was. Maybe the reason he didn't know how to be satisfied with less was that he'd never hung in there long enough to try.

There was no doubt in his mind that Michelle cared about him, especially after the afternoon he'd spent in her bed. But more importantly he was certain of her attachment to his girls. Yet as usual he'd asked too much of her. He hadn't been satisfied to have her in his life as a mother figure to his children. No, he'd expected her to want to be a wife to him, as well.

Maybe it was time to try to settle for less. If Michelle only offered him friendship, so be it. He'd be a fool not to take what he *could* get. And he'd been a fool long enough.

MEGGIE'S PLEA for acceptance haunted Michelle all weekend. The children needed her. So what was she going to do about it? She'd assured the triplets of her love many times over the past couple of months, but now, as she lay in her bed watching the sun come up on a new day, she realized she'd only been mouthing words.

Afraid of where her thoughts were taking her—of the jumble of emotions twisting her stomach into knots—she got up and showered. But as hard as she tried to concentrate on her routine, to plan the day ahead, she couldn't keep her thoughts from straying to the those three little girls who needed her, or the man who'd fathered them.

Allie, Jessie and Meggie needed a mother. She'd been telling herself there was nothing she could do about that, but she knew in her heart that there was. The girls needed someone who enjoyed being with them, who considered herself lucky to see to their needs, who loved them. They needed *her*.

Michelle had run long enough. It was time to do more than proclaim she loved the Ryans. It was time to do something about it. That thought brought on the biggest panic attack she'd ever had in her life. Right there in the shower her skin turned cold and then hot and she was afraid she was going to pass out.

But suddenly as she leaned against the shower stall telling herself to breathe, she finally faced the truth she'd been hiding from for months. It wasn't guilt or loyalty to her husband that was keeping her from loving Jacob; it was plain old fear. She was afraid—no, she was terrified—to love again, to open herself up to the possibility of the pain that went hand in hand with trusting her heart to someone else.

Turning off the water, Michelle dried herself and slipped into the first clothes she came across. Fear had robbed her of five years of her life. Looking back, she didn't know when her love for Brian had faded, to be replaced by cowardice. Her emotions had been frozen for so long she supposed she'd never know. But if she was half the woman she thought she was, her days of running were over. It was long past time to get on with her life.

THERE WAS SOMETHING different about Michelle on Monday. Jacob noticed the change as soon as he walked into the sound booth. Although she greeted him normally she looked as if she was on the verge of a grin.

At first he thought she'd heard from Brian—that her husband was finally coming home to her—and hated himself for wishing it was anything but that. He loved Michelle. He wanted her to be happy. But still, as the morning wore on and she said nothing, the relief he felt was immense. If Brian Colby was on his way home, Michelle wouldn't keep it a secret.

She didn't sit still once all morning. Her fingers fluttered through program sheets, newspapers, CDs and AP bulletins. When she reached up to punch off her mike after announcing a commercial break about an hour into the show, she knocked over her diet cola in her eagerness. Fortunately there hadn't been much in the cup.

"What is it with you?" Jacob asked, half amused, half exasperated. She reminded him of Jessie on the day before Christmas.

She glanced over at him, that grin still hovering on her lips. "Nothing," she said cheerily, picking up her cup. "Want me to warm yours? Your coffee, I mean."

Jacob slid his mug across the counter. "Sure," he said, watching her through narrowed eyes. Her cheeks were flooded with color. He wasn't used to seeing Michelle flustered. Something was definitely up. And she obviously wasn't going to tell him what until she was good and ready.

He'd planned on talking to her about Ellen after the show that morning. He was all set to lay his cards on the table, to tell Michelle she was welcome to be a member of their family free of charge, no marriage vows required. He'd thought about little else all weekend. The way he figured it, divorced people shared parenting all the time—so why couldn't he and Michelle? They'd even have the added benefit of not having the bitterness of a divorce between them.

"Here you go, all nice and hot." She breezed back into the room carrying two cups. One was filled with diet cola. The other one she set down in front of Jacob.

"Thanks," he said, pushing the mug aside. Maybe he'd better wait to have his talk with Michelle. What he had to say was important, and he wanted her to be all there for the conversation. He didn't know where she was this morning, but it definitely wasn't at KOLR. She'd just brought him someone else's coffee mug. He wondered where his Number One Dad mug had ended up.

Michelle grew more jittery as the morning wore on, but the couple of times he brought it to her attention she denied acting out of the ordinary. He segued into their last commercial, determined to pin her down to an explanation as soon as the show was over. He glanced her way, intending to tell her just that as she reached for the last CD. She wasn't wearing her wedding ring.

Jacob froze as he stared at her bare left hand, telling himself not to make too much of it, just as the commercial came to an end. He was supposed to cue in the last song of the show. He reached automatically for his mike button, still staring at Michelle's hand. He was almost afraid to look up, to look into her eyes, for fear of what might *not* be there.

"Welcome back…" She was speaking into her mike. Jacob's gaze flew to hers. *What are you doing, Michelle? Don't you know I've got the last cue in front of me?*

"…and before we leave you this morning, we have one final bit of business to take care of." Her eyes never left Jacob's as she spoke. He didn't know of any last-minute announcements.

"As you all know, from time to time Jacob and I

take personal announcements from our listeners and broadcast them on the air. I have one of those announcements this morning. Except that this one is a little different. This one is from me, and since all of you have been so loyal to the pair of us doing this show, I thought maybe you'd like to help me. With all of you behind me, I figure I stand a much better chance. So here goes. Jacob, there's no other way to say this except straight out. I want to get married.''

Jacob's heart beat rapidly, but the rest of him froze. What in hell…? She was on the air. What was she going to do—take the ninth caller? He glanced from her to the phone. It was lit up like a Christmas tree.

Michelle reached over and gently grasped his chin, turning him to face her. "To you," she said, looking directly into his eyes.

Jacob's grin spread slowly across his face as, without a word, he pulled her off her stool and into his arms. Forgetting where he was, forgetting everything but her, he crushed Michelle's lips in a kiss that held all of the promises he'd been waiting a lifetime to make.

"Does this mean yes?" Michelle asked when he lifted his head.

"Yes," he said, then realized he'd forgotten to turn off his mike. The show's producer and technician were on the other side of the glass making enthusiastic "okay" signs with thumb and forefinger and grinning hugely.

Michelle snuggled closer, reaching up to pull his

mike down in front of her mouth. "This one's for you, Jacob," she said, cuing in their last song herself.

The song was half-over before Jacob stopped kissing her long enough to hear what was playing. It wasn't Sade's latest tune, which was what their program sheets had stipulated. Instead, he heard the hauntingly beautiful "I Am Your Lady" filling the room.

He looked down at the woman in his arms, at the happy tears filling her eyes, and knew that even though they still had some things to work through, this moment of happiness had been worth the wait.

"Let's go home," he said, keeping his arm around her all the way to the parking lot.

CHAPTER SIXTEEN

"I WANT TO MAKE LOVE to you, Michelle," Jacob said the minute they were inside the beach house. He pulled her into his arms and kissed her so tenderly she was afraid she was going to start to cry.

"I love you, Jacob Ryan," she said, smiling up at him. His arms felt glorious around her, so strong and sure.

His brown eyes glistened with emotion as he held her. "And I love you. Always. Enough to let you go if you ever—"

Michelle placed two fingers against his lips. "Shh. Not now. This time I want it to be just you and me." She took his hand and started down the hall to his room.

He stopped her just outside his bedroom door, and lifted her chin to kiss her slowly, gently, almost chastely. "Are you sure?" he asked.

Her heart ached at the hesitation she saw in his eyes. She'd put him through so much, and all he'd ever wanted to do was love her. She planned to spend the next fifty years making sure he didn't regret it.

"Absolutely."

"No regrets?"

"None."

She loved the wicked grin that spread across his face, feeling giddy with freedom as he swept her up and carried her to his bed. She'd told him the complete truth. She had no regrets, only impatience.

She didn't know whose clothes came off first, only that they all came off quickly. Jacob's body was as glorious as she remembered it, and she caressed him as she'd never done before, hardly daring to believe he was hers to love.

Her body was on fire for him, her nerve endings sensitized to his every touch. His hands slid up her arms and she shivered. He stroked her breasts and she moaned.

"You like that?" he asked, smiling down at her.

"Oh, yes," she whispered.

She couldn't stop looking at him, amazed that this was really happening, that after years of imagining him with other women, she finally had him for herself. And the biggest miracle of all was that she had something that none of those other women had ever had. His love.

Their union was quick and fierce, erasing any that had come before. Their gazes locked as their bodies joined, and they stayed that way as she met each strong thrust of Jacob's hips, their eyes speaking of their love as they climaxed together in a perfect melding of body and soul.

And never once, not even for a second, did Michelle have any doubts. Loving Jacob was right, destined. He was the other half of the person she'd become, the man meant to share her life.

Jacob brushed her hair back from her face with gentle fingers, their bodies still linked. "Your eyes have gone cloudy. Having second thoughts?" he asked softly.

She shook her head. "Not one."

"You don't feel like you've just been unfaithful?"

"How could I? I'm lying in the arms of the man I love. And for the record, I didn't feel unfaithful the last time we made love."

Jacob moved away, lying on his side beside her, his head propped on his elbow. "Don't do that, Michelle."

"Do what?"

"If this relationship is going to work we've got to have total honesty between us from the very beginning. The last time we made love you were eaten up with guilt."

"Of course I was. I'd just treated you like little more than a gigolo, making love to you when I knew I wasn't free to love you. I'd made it all so cheap. But never did I feel unfaithful to the man I love."

"So what's changed? Why are you suddenly free?" he asked.

Michelle sat up, not wanting to talk about another man in the bed she planned to share with Jacob for the rest of her life.

She reached for her tank top. "Can we do this

somewhere else?'' she asked, putting on the rest of her clothes.

''How about a walk on the beach?'' Jacob asked, pulling on the shorts he'd worn to work and poking his feet into a pair of old sandals.

Jacob didn't know if it was a good sign or a bad one that Michelle wasn't willing to talk about Brian while in his bed. Now that he'd had some time to recover from the shock of her proposal, doubts were crowding in on him. Michelle had been loyal to her first husband for five long years. How could she suddenly just be over him? Unless—his skin grew cold as a thought occurred to him—unless she wasn't. It was possible that Michelle was doing this because she didn't want to lose the girls, not because she'd come to grips with her past.

''I've put my house up for sale,'' she said, her bare toes sinking into the wet sand as they walked.

''I'm glad to hear that. The area's been going down-hill for years. You shouldn't be living there alone,'' he said. But selling her house didn't mean she wasn't still wedded to Brian Colby in her heart.

''And I've arranged for a headstone to be erected in Brian's memory.'' Her fingers stole into his. Jacob threaded their fingers together, welcoming the contact as if, with possession being nine-tenths of the law, he could claim her heart merely by holding on to her.

''So you believe he's gone, then?'' he asked, choosing his words carefully. If Michelle had loved Brian anywhere near as much as Jacob loved her, he could only imagine how much it must have hurt to finally say goodbye.

She shrugged. "We may never know what happened to him. But after five years he's no longer the man I married. That's the Brian I'm burying."

He could hear the tears in her voice and stopped walking to pull her into his arms. "I'm sorry, sweetheart. I'm so sorry," he said, feeling helpless.

She didn't make a sound, but he knew she was crying. She held on to him, her hands clenching into fists against his back.

"I won't rush you if you're not ready...."

She raised her head, her teary eyes filled with conviction as she looked up at him. "I'm ready, Jacob. I've spent five years pushing away the pain, refusing to believe Brian was gone so I didn't have to mourn him. I've only just realized that I lost five years of my life. And I realized something else I'm not proud of."

Keeping his arm around her waist, he started walking again. The waves lapped their feet. "What?"

"That you were right. I was hiding behind my wedding ring so that I didn't ever have to hurt like this again."

Jacob was beginning to believe she really was ready to commit herself to him. "And what brought about that realization now?"

"Meggie."

Jacob stopped, turning to face her. "Meggie?"

"The other day when the girls came over, Meggie

was afraid that you wanted to be with Ellen and that she and her sisters were standing in your way. That if Ellen went away again, you'd be mad because she and her sisters were keeping you from going with her.''

Jacob felt sick to think that Meggie had been so worried and he hadn't even known it. And then something occurred to him.

''She was worried I'd be mad that Ellen left, not sad about her mother abandoning her again?''

Michelle bent her head and said something, but her words were too soft to be heard over the surf.

''What was that?'' Jacob asked, tilting her face up to his.

''She wanted to know if I'd take them,'' Michelle said, obviously concerned about how this news was going to affect him. But she couldn't hide the joy Meggie's request had brought her.

Jacob didn't like to think that his daughters were making plans to replace him, but he was confident enough in their love to know that their plans were only in case *he* chose to leave *them*.

He pulled Michelle back into his arms, grinning. ''She did, did she? And what did you tell her?''

''That there was no way you'd ever leave them, and that I'd always want them. It was then I realized what I'd been doing all these months.''

''And what was that?''

''Telling the girls how much I loved them while

moving aside to make room for Ellen—when I knew darn well she'd never love them as much as I do.''

Jacob's grin grew wider. "She wouldn't, huh?'' he asked, amused at Michelle's defensive tone.

"How could she? She left them. And that's when it hit me that I'd done the very same thing. I'd run home to my memories every time I was afraid of getting too close, of opening myself up to that pain all over again. Well, I'm not running anymore, Jacob. I don't want the rest of my life to slip by without a single memory to make it worth having lived. Besides, could you look Meggie in the eye and run away?''

Jacob laughed. "Nope. That's why I'm saddled with three identical little witches who have me wrapped around their little fingers.''

"Well, it's two against three now, and we're bigger than they are. You think we have a chance?''

"Nope,'' Jacob said again, sealing their fate with a kiss. He still had a niggling doubt or two, but he was certain of one thing: Michelle loved him every bit as much as he loved her.

"So, when are we going to get married?'' she asked as they headed back up the beach toward the cottage. The girls were due home from school shortly.

Jacob had been thinking about that. "I think we should wait awhile,'' he said. He couldn't get away from the fact that no matter how much Michelle loved him, there was always going to be a doubt in her heart about Brian's death. He could imagine her taking second glances every time they passed someone who re-sembled Brian Colby. But his worst fear was that Brian would return someday and that Michelle, forced to choose, would feel obligated to her first commit-ment, no matter how much she loved Jacob.

"We don't have to get married at all," she said. "I guess I did kind of pressure you into it."

Jacob stopped in his tracks and turned her to face him, surprised to see the hurt in her eyes. "What on earth are you talking about?" he asked.

"You don't sound too eager, that's all." She looked like she was going to cry again.

Jacob pulled her up into his arms. "Sweetheart, I'd marry you tonight if I had my way. It's you I'm con-cerned about. I just think we should wait until Frank Steele finishes his investigation before we say our vows. I want you to feel as unencumbered as possible. No guilt."

Michelle reached up to kiss him. "I'd feel that way if I married you right now, but we can wait until we hear from Frank again if it makes you feel better. Except…"

"Except what?" he asked, liking the flush that stole across her cheeks.

"Do we have to actually live in two houses until then?"

Jacob wasn't going to send her away even for one night. "I'll sleep on the couch," he said, wondering how many times he'd have to steal into his bedroom after the girls were asleep before he could join his wife there on a nightly basis. "Now let's go home. I think there'll be three little urchins arriving momentarily who've waited long enough to have their mother welcome them back from a hard day at school."

Michelle's face was alight with happiness as they resumed walking. She'd never looked more beautiful to Jacob then she did at that moment, anticipating his daughters' reaction to their news.

"They will be glad, won't they?" she asked, sounding nervous all of a sudden.

Jacob still didn't understand women, which meant that it was lucky he'd have four of them living under his roof. Sooner or later, with that much practice, he was bound to get it right. "Of course they'll be glad. Where've you been these past months?"

"Well, they've never had to share you before. They want a mother, but will they like your having a wife?"

"They're smart kids. They'll see the advantages. Besides, if we tell them they might have a little brother or sister someday, you'll be a shoo-in."

He felt her steps falter beside him. "I wasn't sure you'd want more children. You already have three."

"And I'd take three more in a second if they were yours," Jacob assured her, stopping for a kiss they didn't really have time for. "Speaking of which, we haven't used protection. Is there any possibility we have something to hope for?"

Michelle gave him a saucy grin that earned her

definite retribution, he decided, as soon as the triplets were down for the night. "Maybe," she said, continuing toward the cottage. Jacob saw the girls clomping up the driveway, the miniature work boots they'd talked him into buying for them too heavy for their feet. He hurried after Michelle. He was anxious to introduce his daughters to their new mother.

WORD CAME from Frank Steele two weeks later. He left a message for Michelle to call him, which she did from Jacob's house. Jacob was there with her. They were planning to take the girls swimming as soon as they got home from school.

"I've got your answers, Mrs. Colby, but I'm sorry to say the news isn't good." Michelle listened to Frank's gravelly voice, feeling again that freezing of emotion that had kept her strong during the long ordeal of Brian's disappearance. And then she glanced over at Jacob, sitting in a chair beside the couch, watching her, loving her, and she knew she was ready to hear whatever Frank had to tell her.

"You've found him?" she asked, hoping that Brian was alive. She knew now that whether he was or not would make no difference to her plans.

"He died three years ago, Mrs. Colby. I'm sorry."

"Three years ago?" she repeated. Jacob got up and crossed to her. He stood behind her and Michelle leaned against him, glad for his strength. No matter how solid her plans for the future, it was still a shock to hear that the young man she'd loved was dead.

"He'd been mistaken for a government official and taken hostage by some of Karim's men, who planned to use him as a bartering tool. When they found out their mistake they took him to the village where I'd traced him, trying to pass him off as the official they'd thought he was. They bought his cooperation with threats to the village, ma'am. After two years of negotiations, Karim agreed to trade his hostage for a couple of his men who'd been sent to prison the year before. Karim's men, and Brian, were killed when his deception was found out. If it's any consolation he was loyal to you until the end, ma'am, apparently crying out your name when he was shot."

"Thank you, Frank. Thank you." Michelle was barely aware of what she was saying as she hung up the phone.

She turned into Jacob's arms, pressed her face into his chest and cried away five years of almost unendurable anguish. She cried for the young man she'd known, the young man she'd loved with all her heart. She cried for the tragedy of his last two years, and for the love they'd shared, the love he'd carried with him to his grave. She cried for herself, for the years she'd spent waiting, while he'd still been alive trying to get home to her, and for the years she'd wasted, waiting for him to come home when he was no longer alive. And she cried in relief, glad to know that her vigil was over at last.

Looking up at the strong handsome features of her husband-to-be, she smiled through her tears.

"I think the girls are home."

EPILOGUE

"SHH. YOU'RE GONNA get us in trouble."

"But Allie, Mommy says she's our baby, too."

Meggie barely heard her sisters' whispers as she peeked over the edge of the crib in the nursery Daddy'd had built onto the side of their cottage. He and Mommy were in the kitchen, supposedly doing the dishes, but Meggie could tell by Mommy's giggles that the dishes weren't getting done as fast as they could be.

At first she'd been a little hurt that Mommy sometimes wanted to be with Daddy more than her and her sisters, and a lot hurt when Daddy paid attention to Mommy and didn't always hear everything she and her sisters said, but her parents had gotten better about not going off in that funny way where they forgot that somebody else was in the room, and besides, Mommy said Noby was hers and Allie's and Jessie's, too, and Noby slept on Meggie's bed. So now Meggie was mostly just glad that Mommy and Daddy loved each other so much. None of her and her sisters' friends had parents who smiled at each other like Daddy and Mommy did. And secretly Meggie thought that none of them had parents who smiled at their

kids as much as Mommy and Daddy either. And
Daddy and Mommy didn't go out and leave them
alone a lot, or read the paper all day or do chores all
the time they were home. Daddy still played basketball with them, and Mommy had even played, too,
until the baby made her too big.

Little Brianna made a sound and bunched her bottom up in the air. Meggie hoped that meant she was
waking up. It was her turn to pick her up and take
her to Mommy and Daddy.

"How long till you think she can play?" Jessie
whispered.

"Shh. Not for a long time, silly," Allie whispered
back.

Meggie thought Allie's whisper was just as loud as
Jessie's, but she didn't care. She hoped her sisters
would wake up the baby. Brianna had been sleeping
ever since they got home from school and Meggie'd
been waiting hours for her turn to hold her.

Meggie had never felt anything as good as holding
Brianna. Her baby sister was so warm and cuddly,
and made her feel like she was really important even
though she was only eight. Nobody knew it, but Meggie had made a promise to Brianna the first day she
was born, when Daddy had taken them to Mommy's
hospital room to see her. That was the first time Meggie had gotten to hold her, and while everyone had
been talking to Mommy, Meggie had told Brianna
she'd never have to worry about not having some-

body, because Meggie'd be her person for her whole life.

Jessie ran around to the other side of the crib, jolting it as her foot knocked into one of the legs. Brianna stirred and Meggie held her breath, hoping the baby wouldn't go back to sleep. Nobody had ever told her that babies slept so much. It was the only thing she didn't like about having a baby sister.

One of Brianna's eyes popped open and then closed again. Her little mouth yawned and Meggie had never seen anything so cute in her life. Meggie reached down, sliding her arms beneath the baby.

''Wait, Meggie, she's not awake yet,'' Allie said, her voice warning of dire outcomes if the baby was woken up.

''She is too. She opened one eye,'' Jessie said.

So, she wasn't the only one who'd seen it. That was enough for Meggie. She lifted the baby into her arms.

Allie and Jessie walked on each side of her as she carried the baby into the kitchen, and Meggie knew the best part was coming. Mommy and Daddy quit kissing and moved toward her and her sisters as they came into the room. Michelle smiled, looking at each one of them so no one felt left out, and everybody cooed over baby Brianna for a few minutes while Meggie held her and then, right before Michelle lifted Brianna up to go change her, Daddy pulled them all into their nightly group hug, just as Meggie had known he would.

"I must be the luckiest man alive to have five such beautiful girls," he said.

Meggie figured he was right.

A Father's Place

JOAN KILBY

HARLEQUIN®

TORONTO • NEW YORK • LONDON
AMSTERDAM • PARIS • SYDNEY • HAMBURG
STOCKHOLM • ATHENS • TOKYO • MILAN • MADRID
PRAGUE • WARSAW • BUDAPEST • AUCKLAND

To my mother, for
being a survivor

* * *

Dear Reader,

Twenty-five years ago my mother fought a battle with
breast cancer. She lost a breast but won her life. The
idea for *A Father's Place* arose from reflecting on how
grateful I was she survived and how different my life
might have been had she not.

Karina, the heroine of my story, lost her mother to
breast cancer at an early age. Her mother's death had
a profound effect on her life, particularly when it came
to having children of her own. Breaking down her
protective barriers takes understanding, humour and a
very special man. Daniel is a man of heart and mind
with a deep capacity for loving. This is a story about
the power of love to transcend fear and to turn
abandoned dreams into reality. This is the story of
Daniel and Karina.

A Father's Place is my first book. Writing it was
personal, compelling and fun. Seeing it published is one
of the biggest thrills of my life. I hope you enjoy it.

Joan Kilby

CHAPTER ONE

KARINA PETERSON GAZED into the grinning face of an enormous pig.

It was good, this pig. She liked its pink-and-purple paisley jowls, its corkscrew tail and impossible smile. She liked the squishy feel of the paste and the gradual smoothing of the chicken wire as she built up layers of fabric strips.

Most of all she liked the total absorption she found in its creation. While she worked, her problems didn't exist.

Dishes sat in the sink, magazines and tape cassettes cluttered the kitchen table, high-heeled shoes of various colors and styles peeked from beneath chairs and counters. Karina refused to notice or care. She had her house all to herself, that's what counted. She was through playing den mother to an endless stream of tenants.

On her right breast she bore a tiny scar where an even tinier lump of flesh had been removed. That the lump had turned out to be benign ought to have put her mind at rest, but it hadn't. She was almost thirty-two, the age at which her mother had died of breast cancer. In the coming months she would need her own space in a way she never had before.

She crouched low to work a piece of fabric around the pig's hock, wavy strands of dark hair falling around her face. Tricky getting the angle just right. She pinched and prodded...got it. Time for a coffee.

Her bare feet, dabbed with paste, made little sticking sounds on the blue-and-white linoleum as she crossed from the meals area to the kitchen. Humming to the South American salsa band on the radio, she reached for the thermos jug of coffee, her shoulders and hips moving in time to the music.

Cup, sugar, spoon...cha, cha, cha. She danced over to the fridge for the milk.

Her body stilled as she caught sight of the ''Beautiful Victoria'' calendar taped to the freezer door. Today's date stared out at her from beneath a color photo of Butchart Gardens.

Saturday, July 8. Exactly one month until her birthday.

Karina shut her eyes and concentrated on reversing the spin of the earth. It was a game she'd played often as a young teenager after Mama had died. In those days, she'd been so desperate to turn back the clock she'd have sold her soul to defy the laws of nature.

She blinked her eyes open, ever hopeful—and sighed. Tulips still tossed their red-and-yellow heads in glossy profusion under July's heading. On the wall above the stove, Felix the Clock's longest arm advanced another minute, his swinging tail blithely indifferent to the passage of time.

Karina laughed at her own foolishness and pulled the milk out of the fridge. But there was a hint of a sob in her laughter. All these years later, she was no less desperate. And the laws of nature were no less immutable. No matter how many times she tried to convince herself that with vigilance she would live to a ripe old age, she couldn't shake the haunting feeling that her mother's fate would be hers.

Turning her back on the calendar, she returned to the counter to add a splash of milk to her coffee. Then she leaned over the kitchen table to crank up the volume of the radio perched on the windowsill. The opening bars of a reggae tune pulsed from the speaker. Karina went back to her pig, gratefully letting the music block her mind to the unthinkable.

No sooner had she plunged her hands into the basin of paste than the front doorbell rang. Karina smiled at the welcome distraction.

"Come on in," she called, though most of her friends just knocked and walked in. The only answer to her summons was another trill of the door bell followed by a brisk knock.

"Darn," she muttered, and gave up the attempt to prod a misshapen lump of fabric into a sow's ear. She looked around for a hand towel and, finding none, hastily wiped her hands on her oversize Hawaiian shirt.

"Coming!" Karina strode down the hall and flung open the door, prepared to give the Fuller Brush man, or whoever it was, short shrift.

But the tall, chestnut-haired man standing on her porch wasn't a salesman. Not unless they went door-to-door these days in faded denim and creased cotton shirts. He had a lean face and clear hazel eyes. And he looked dog-tired.

"Yes?" Karina said. There was more than fatigue in the fine lines around his eyes. Worry? Frustration?

"G'day." His deep voice was tinged with an Australian accent. "I'm Daniel Bowen. I reckon you must be Karina Peterson."

"That's right. What can I do for you?" Karina absently rubbed at her fingers. They were tacky with paste and starting to stick together.

Frowning, he thrust one hand into the hip pocket of his jeans and shoved the other through his rumpled hair. "I'm Betty's cousin."

"Betty? Betty Furness?" The only Betty she knew was married to Kevin in her art department. The thought sounded a vague alarm, but she ignored it and waited for him to come to the point.

"That's right. I've just come in on a flight from Melbourne." He paused, clearly waiting for an appropriate response from her.

"How nice." All Karina could think of was Petunia's ear. It would dry crookedly if this conversation went on much longer.

He smiled, a gritted-teeth kind of smile. "Betty arranged for me to rent rooms in your house. I sent a money order to cover the first month's rent. Didn't you get it? I thought you'd be expecting me."

"Oh, *now* I remember. You're Betty's cousin!" Last spring Kevin had tried to foist some long-lost relative of his wife's on her. But when she'd had to go in for the biopsy Karina had nipped the arrangement in the bud.

"Good," Daniel said. "I'm glad we've got that settled." He glanced over his shoulder at the taxi double-parked on the narrow residential street. "I'll just pay the cabby and get my bags."

Startled, Karina reached out to stop him. "Wait! Don't do that."

His biceps tensed under her fingers and a lock of dark brown hair fell over his forehead. Frowning, he looked down at his sleeve, then back up at her face.

"Sorry." She pulled her hand away, grimacing at the

traces of paste left on his dark blue shirt. "It washes out."

"Never mind that," he said, pushing his hair back into place with lean, tanned fingers. "Is there some problem with our agreement?"

"The room isn't available anymore." She smiled apologetically. "I told Kevin that when I gave him back your money order."

Daniel's frown deepened. "I never received it. Nor was I informed the rooms were unavailable."

He pulled a folded page of airmail paper from his pocket. In the crease was a scrap of neon yellow notepaper that looked disturbingly familiar. Tucking the yellow paper into his palm, he scanned the other page.

"You *are* Karina Peterson?"

"Yes, but—"

"And this is 336 Balaclava Street?" He glanced up at the house number, which undeniably confirmed he was in the right location. "According to Betty's letter, you agreed I could use your garage for a carpentry workshop." He leaned over the porch rail to peer around the side of the house. "Access to the garage is from the alley, I take it?"

Karina almost choked. "Yes, but I'm not renting!"

Then she did what she always did when forced into a confrontation. She laughed. It was an awkward habit that frequently gave people the wrong impression. And judging from the look on Daniel Bowen's face, it had now.

"Is this a joke?" he demanded. "Because I don't think it's very funny. Natalie had a cold when we left Melbourne, and on the flight over she turned really crook. I think she's got the flu."

Natalie? Who was Natalie? Kevin hadn't mentioned anything about *two* tenants. She pulled herself together.

"I'm sorry. Of course it's not a joke. It's a misunderstanding. But the fact is, I'm no longer renting."

Daniel held the bit of bright yellow paper in front of her. "I've got your receipt right here. Informal or not, it's still a contract."

She stared in dismay at her distinctive signature—little more than a giant *K* followed by a scrawl. "This is all Kevin's fault," she muttered. "I'll kill him."

"Betty's husband? What's he got to do with it?"

She laughed again. "Kevin's such a space cadet. Great guy, fantastic artist, but he wouldn't think to take out the garbage if it was placed in his hands."

Daniel folded his arms across his chest. Dark brown hair dusted his tanned forearms and peeked from the V of his indigo shirt. "Does this have anything at all to do with me?"

"I remember Kevin asking me about the room," Karina continued. "Right after I approved his design for the RollerDome. Or was it the Frosty Freeze?" She saw Daniel's mouth tighten and hurried on. "At the time I said, 'Sure.' He gave me your money order, I gave him a receipt—well, that piece of paper from my notepad.

"Then…something came up. A personal thing. Even so, I thought about it very hard for two whole weeks. I'm telling you this so you'll know I'm not just…" She cast her eyes upward, searching for the word.

"Scatty? Harebrained?"

Her eyebrows scrunched together in a quick frown. "The word I was looking for is…*capricious.*" She wasn't precisely sure what it meant but it sounded a lot better than harebrained.

Daniel Bowen looked as though he might reel right off the porch. "Capricious. Ah. And you're not."

"Of course not. I distinctly told Kevin in March—no,

it was April, because I'd just got the results back from…
Anyway, I told him I couldn't take any new tenants just
now. I probably should have told Betty, but she was in
the hospital with complications. They just had their fifth
baby. But I guess you'd know that. The point is, I didn't
think even Kevin could mess up such a simple message.''

Daniel's eyes pressed shut, the lines of fatigue around
his mouth deepening. ''It never occurred to you to write
directly to me?''

''I suppose I should have got your address from
Kevin, but we had such a rush at work back then. One
of my artists was picked up by a rival firm and I had to
do my own job plus the extra artwork he left behind.
Then my boss got sick and I was doing his job, as well.''

''Look, Ms.…Peterson, I don't need to hear all this.
I've sold my house, shut down my business and traveled
halfway around the world on the understanding that I
had a place to live when I got here. Just tell me one
thing—have you rented to someone else?''

''No, you see—'' She broke off. He'd just said he
didn't want to hear about her problems. And she certainly didn't want to discuss her personal life with a total
stranger.

''I'm really sorry about the room. And about your
money order. Knowing Kevin, it's probably still in his
wallet. Why don't you come inside and have a cup of
coffee? You can call a hotel while I see to my pig. If I
don't get back to her soon, her ear is going to dry looking like a cow pie.''

Daniel bowed his head, gripping the bridge of his nose
between thumb and middle finger. Then he glanced up,
his face haggard but resigned. ''I guess a hotel will have
to do for now. I want to get Natalie settled quickly.

We've been thirty-six hours in transit. She needs a hot bath and a good night's sleep.''

"I'm sure your wife will be fine," Karina said reassuringly. "Any of the larger hotels will have a house doctor.''

He gave her an odd look. "Natalie isn't—''

Honk! Behind the taxi, a cherry red BMW revved its engine, impatient to get past. Daniel glanced over his shoulder and signaled with a choppy wave of his hand.

"Excuse me,'' he said, turning back to Karina. "I'll get our things and be right back.''

She watched him stride down the path to the taxi, where the object of all that protective concern waited for her man. For a fraction of a second, Karina felt a twinge of longing. It would be nice to have someone who took care of *her* with such dedication.

Then the gate banged shut and she snapped out of her reverie. Men, especially the nice ones, too often came with expectations of marriage and children. Expectations she could never fulfill. For how could she ever marry knowing she might die young, leaving behind a grieving husband and children? She'd suffered so much when Mama died, she could never inflict such a loss on a child of her own.

Carefully, she unstuck her fingers from the railing and went inside. Besides, she could take care of herself.

Daniel pushed open the wooden gate, not caring that it swung back against the metal latch with a crash. What a bloody, stupid balls-up. How dare she laugh off his problem? Or blame the mix-up on Kevin? What kind of woman was capable of turning a sick child out in the street?

Capricious didn't begin to describe Karina Peterson. Natalie lay across the back seat of the taxi, her favorite blanket tucked up to her chin. Her small oval face was pale and moist and her breath a harsh rattle through chapped lips.

"Nattie," he called softly, worriedly noting the dark circles under her eyes. He'd returned to Victoria to try to heal the ten-year-old rift with his only brother. But in doing so he'd taken an enormous risk with his daughter's happiness, uprooting her from her home and the grandmother who'd been like a mother to her. He prayed she wouldn't pay too dearly for his shot at redemption.

"Natalie," he called again, a little louder. "Come on, sweetheart, we're going inside for a bit."

Her spiky blond lashes fluttered open and a faint spark shone in her dulled eyes. "Are we at our new home?"

His heart ached at having to disappoint her. "Not exactly. We have to find a hotel for the night. We'll go inside and telephone. Come on."

He reached into the cab and pulled his daughter into his arms. Her slender legs dangled to his waist, and it amazed him, as always, how big she'd grown. He could hardly believe his baby would be starting grade one in the fall.

Daniel carried her up the steps and through the open door. To the right, a staircase climbed to the second floor. Directly in front of him ran a short hallway, at the end of which he glimpsed the kitchen.

To the left was a doorway, and he walked through it into the living room. Part of his brain registered a clutter of furniture and overdecorated walls. Intent only on Natalie's comfort, he went directly to the sofa and gently laid her down. He slipped off her shoes and adjusted the cushions under her head, then tucked her blanket around her and went back for their bags.

Leaving the suitcases in the foyer, he picked the Yellow Pages up from the hall table and returned to the sofa, his gaze lowered as he flicked through the phone book.

Natalie touched his arm and he glanced up. Her cheeks were flushed and feverish, and she was staring around the room in wonder. "Daddy, look!"

His gaze followed the direction of her finger, and he blinked in disbelief. Jet lag must be giving him hallucinations.

Suspended from the ceiling of the adjoining dining room was a flock, if that was the right word, of life-size…angels? Not angels. They didn't have wings or halos, and their entire bodies were clothed in a wild floral print. There must be half a dozen of the damn things.

Before he'd come to grips with the strange celestial beings, Natalie pointed somewhere else. "Daddy, Daddy! Look at the fairy lights! Aren't they pretty!"

He turned his head. In a recess in the wall, a piece of driftwood the size of a small tree sported tiny, winking white lights from its twisted, naked branches.

"Daddy, over there!" Natalie's finger pointed first this way, then that.

Daniel got a headache trying to follow. Brightly painted wooden marionettes danced across sage green walls. Artificial grapevines festooned the doorway into the dining room. Glass baubles and spangled ceramic masks bedecked the mahogany wall unit. On the ceiling, Japanese kites sailed across an azure sky bordered by fluffy white clouds.

"Isn't it *wonderful,* Daddy?" Natalie pulled herself up on one elbow, her illness momentarily forgotten.

"Fair boggles the mind," he replied, still gazing around the room. Maybe it was just as well he and Natalie weren't staying. What kind of bizarre imagination had created such chaotic fantasy?

Karina Peterson stepped through the arched doorway, a smile on her face and a swing in her hips. Her hands and face were newly clean, but her glossy black hair spilled from her hair clip in unruly waves. She came to a halt in the middle of the living room, talking rapidly.

"I was able to save the ear, thank goodness. Sorry about the mess. The cleaning lady doesn't come till Monday. Did you find any vacancies? There's a Sheraton just down the road. I could drop you…"

Her words trailed into silence as her huge dark eyes settled on Natalie. "A child," she said in a whisper. "I didn't know you had a child."

Karina pressed a hand to her stomach and forced herself to breathe. What a funny turn the sight of the girl had given her. Almost as though she'd seen herself at that age, home sick from school, waiting for Mama to read her a book or sing her a song in her perfect, clear soprano.

"A *sick* child," Daniel corrected her. "This is my daughter, Natalie," he added, fatherly pride creeping into his voice.

Karina kneeled on the floor beside the couch. "You poor thing," she murmured to Natalie.

Damp tendrils of fair hair stuck to the child's temples, and her pale cheeks held two bright spots of pink. Her round blue eyes glittered unhealthily.

"I've got a kite, too," Natalie confided. "Mrs. Beeton thinks it's the best flyer she's ever seen. Daddy almost didn't let me bring it because he said there are kite-eating trees here. Is that true?"

Karina suppressed a smile. At least part of the glitter in the child's eyes was due to an impish spark that was instantly endearing. "Oh, yes," she replied seriously. "You've got to be very careful. The bigger the tree, the more kites they can eat."

She pressed the back of her hand against the girl's forehead and looked at Daniel in alarm. "She's got a fever."

Daniel nodded silently. His daughter's tiny hand was cradled in his large one, and he gently stroked the backs of her fingers with his thumb. An unexpected lump formed in Karina's throat. Where was the child's mother?

"This changes everything." She reached over to the coffee table and flipped the phone book shut.

Daniel's dark eyebrows pulled together in a puzzled frown. "What do you mean?"

"I can't let you go to a hotel with a sick child. You'll have to stay here, at least for tonight."

His shoulders stiffened and his hand closed protectively around Natalie's. "Thanks, but no. You weren't expecting us."

"You can't possibly move your daughter again today." Karina looked at the girl's pinched face, and her heart ached. "She needs a hot bath and a good night's sleep."

"But—"

"You said so yourself," Karina reminded him.

"We'd be better off at a hotel. At least we could see a doctor."

"I'll call my GP. She makes house calls."

"We can't stay," Daniel said stubbornly.

"I insist." Karina wasn't sure how the tables had turned so quickly, but she did know she couldn't possibly send this poor child away.

He crossed his arms over his chest. "I refuse."

Karina shook her head. "I've heard Australian men are macho."

"Not all. Anyway, I'm from Canada originally. Victoria, actually."

"Then think about your daughter."

"*Please,* Daddy."

Daniel turned to his little girl, and Karina knew by the way his mouth softened the battle was all but over. "It's the height of tourist season," she added. "There probably isn't a vacancy anywhere in city."

He glanced back to her, his hazel eyes narrow. "That didn't seem to worry you before."

Karina smiled at Natalie and smoothed back her damp hair. "Adults can take care of themselves. Children need all the help we can give them."

IT WAS AFTER MIDNIGHT when Karina clattered up the front steps and called a laughing goodbye to her friends. She kicked her shoes off in the hall and was about to drop her handbag with a thump when she remembered Daniel and Natalie.

She laid her purse quietly on the hall table and went to the foot of the stairs. One hand resting on the banister, she paused and listened. Not a sound came from the second-floor bedrooms. They must have settled in for the night long ago.

She'd had an assortment of tenants before, but never a man and a child. It felt strange, but kind of nice, almost as though a family lived here.

But they weren't family, she reminded herself. They weren't even tenants. Tomorrow they'd be gone.

From the radio in the kitchen, the somber chords of a piano concerto drifted down the darkened hallway. A wave of melancholy swept over her. Suddenly she felt empty. Alone.

Hugging her arms around herself, she wandered into the living room and sank onto the couch. In the low light of the table lamp, she gazed at the framed portrait on the wall directly opposite.

The woman in the photograph looked back at her with dark, soulful eyes and a Mona Lisa smile. Her lustrous black hair, so much like Karina's own, fell in waves around her shoulders.

Karina felt the familiar tightening in her chest and the hollow burning sensation behind her eyes from the river of tears she had never let flow.

It still hurts so bad, Mama. Why did you have to leave me?

The silence that filled the room was her only answer. Karina sat on in the semidarkness, as always, hardening herself to the pain. She'd never completely gotten over Mama's death, and her own cancer scare had brought the grief and fear flooding back as though it were yesterday.

She still had her father, but he might as well live on Mars instead of Penticton for all the contact they had. She hadn't even told him about her lumpectomy. He hadn't been able to cope with Mama's disease, or their grief, when she'd died. Stirring up all those awful memories would only increase the distance between them.

SUMMER RAIN PATTERED at the kitchen window. Karina, up to her wrists in paste, hummed along to *Aida*. As the music gave way to the midmorning news, she heard a perfunctory knock and the sound of the door opening.

"Yoohoo, anybody home?"

Karina leaned backward to glance down the hall. "Hi,

Joanne," she called to the tall, gangly woman stepping inside. "Where are the kids?"

Joanne shed her dripping raincoat and gave her shaggy blond head a shake, spraying water like a collie dog. "You mean those changelings that inhabit my children's bodies? Mom's got them for a couple of hours."

"You're so lucky she likes to baby-sit."

Joanne tramped down the hall in her sock feet. "I know. She says she's giving me a break, but I suspect she just likes to spoil them rotten without interference."

She walked slowly around the pig, nodding her approval. "Petunia's coming right along."

"Almost finished," Karina said. "Do me a favor and retie my hair for me? It's driving me crazy."

Joanne gathered up the loose strands that had fallen out of Karina's long, thick braid. "What I wouldn't give to have hair like yours."

Karina tilted her head back so Joanne could wrap a scrunchie around the braid at the base of her neck. "Don't say that. It's such a pain."

"So call me a masochist. Got any coffee?" Joanne's gaze fell on Daniel's brown leather jacket hanging over the back of a chair. Her long, skinny body jerked in an exaggerated double take. "Karina Isabella Peterson. Do you have *company?*" She peered around the corner into the dining room as though whoever it was might be hiding behind the potted palm.

"Don't be an idiot, Jo. You know me better than that."

"I do, indeed. And it's not me who's an idiot."

Joanne took a cup from the cupboard, inspected the interior and gave it a quick rinse under the hot water tap. "Who is he? And if he's not a lover, what's he doing here?"

Karina poked at Petunia's front trotter, trying for a better cleft between the toes. "He's Betty's cousin from Australia. He arrived yesterday under the impression he'd rented rooms in my house."

"Where did he get that idea?" Joanne asked, pouring herself coffee from the jug. "Wait, don't tell me. Kevin?"

Karina nodded, rolling her eyes. She wasn't surprised Joanne had got it in one; she'd been regaling her with stories about Kevin for years. "It's partly my fault. At one point I did agree to rent him the space. Then I changed my mind and trusted Kevin to pass on the message."

"Bad move," Joanne said, spooning sugar into her coffee.

Finished with the trotter, Karina stretched her fingers around the pig's wide neck and began pressing out the bubbles in the fabric. "If Kevin wasn't one of my best artists, I'd strangle him."

"So how come you let this guy stay?" Joanne stopped stirring her coffee and turned to Karina, her blue-grey eyes alight. "Is he gorgeous?"

"Shhh! He might hear you." Karina glanced uneasily at the ceiling.

"Well, is he or isn't he?" Joanne went to the fridge and opened the door. "Hey, you've got real food in here. He *must* be gorgeous."

"Of course he's not gorgeous," Karina said. "He's just a man. Quite ordinary in fact."

It occurred to her that *ordinary* didn't accurately describe Daniel Bowen. He had a sort of quiet certainty about him, a *presence* for lack of a better word. But she couldn't put her finger on anything tangible that made him *un*-ordinary, so she let it go.

"His daughter is ill," she said to explain the bagels, cream cheese and fresh orange juice sitting in her fridge where last night there'd been only half a carton of milk and an assortment of pickles.

Joanne's narrow face reappeared around the fridge door, her eyebrows raised. "Daughter?"

"Natalie. She got sick on the flight over. That's why I let them stay the night. Besides, there are half a dozen conventions in town. Every hotel is probably booked solid."

"True." Joanne took out the milk and poured some into her coffee. "Speaking of which, I'm booking the cabin at Watch Lake for the third week of August. Want to come? Peter will be up north collecting fish samples all summer, and I could use some adult company."

Karina got to her feet and stepped back to take a critical look at her pig. "I'd love to but I can't. The corporate golf tournament is that weekend."

"I thought you didn't like golf." Joanne pushed the Saturday paper to one side and sat down at the table with her coffee.

"I don't. But I've decided I'm going to break into upper management even if I have to spend a whole weekend chasing a little ball around a golf course to do it." She took a sip of cool coffee, made a face and dumped it down the sink.

"For two years," she continued, taking up the coffee jug and giving it an experimental shake, "I've coordinated all of SignCity's art departments across the country, as well as being art director of the Victoria office. I have higher responsibilities than the chief sales executive but am I considered upper management? No. Am I adequately compensated for my efforts? No. Does my title even begin to reflect my responsibilities?"

"No!" Joanne cried and raised her cup. "The time has come. The worm will turn!"

Karina stopped to look at her, jug poised over her cup. *"Worm?"*

"Sorry," Joanne said, grinning. "I was living out my own unfulfilled fantasies for a moment. So tell me, how is playing golf going to get you into upper management?"

"All major decisions are made on the golf course," Karina explained. "I hate playing the corporate game by men's rules—all that striving for success, pretending to be tougher than tough and never, God forbid, admitting you made a mistake. But there's no challenge left where I am. My only choice, if I don't want to be trapped in middle management, is to get out there and schmooze like mad at the annual golf tourney."

"Schmooze," Joanne repeated, picking up a pen to doodle on the front page of the newspaper. "Is that in the corporate rule book?"

"On page one." Karina dropped three spoonfuls of sugar into her coffee quickly before Joanne noticed. "Picture this. I'm on the nineteenth hole—"

"Er, Karina, don't look now but there are only eighteen holes on a golf course. And don't think I didn't notice all that sugar you dumped in your coffee."

"Okay, so I'm on the *eighteenth* hole." She gripped the sugar spoon like a golf club. "I'm playing with three or four members of the board of directors. Just before I tee off—is that the correct terminology?"

"Sounds right." Joanne, busy turning a photo of the mayor into a portrait of Groucho Marx, paused to gaze at her.

"Just before I tee off, I'll say—" She arrested her swing and turned to an imaginary partner. "'By the way,

Bill, or Phil, or Whomever—if SignCity is going to expand into the Asia-Pacific market, I'll need a title that will impress. I was thinking of Grand pooh-bah. What do you say, Philbert, old buddy?''

Joanne giggled. "He'd be nuts not to go for it."

"Shh, I'm in my stride. And Phil, or Bill, will say, 'Absolutely, Karina, old thing. Of course you'll need a raise in pay. And a decent expense account.' Then…'' she raised her arms and swung ''…I'll whack the ball a mile down the fairway. And they'll slap me on the back and say, 'This woman is going places.'''

"Into the bushes to look for your ball?" Joanne suggested with a grin.

"Scoff away," Karina said, waving the sugar spoon. "I'll have that rack of suits falling all over each other in a race to upgrade my position."

Joanne's smile faded. "I've no doubt you will." She put down the pen and sipped her coffee.

Karina dropped her arms to her side with a wondering glance at her friend. Joanne was usually her biggest cheerleader. "Don't be so enthusiastic."

Joanne smiled halfheartedly. "You'll be great. You'll come across as a dingbat. Then when they least expect it, you'll dazzle 'em with your competence and knowhow. Just like you always do."

Karina stepped around Petunia and sat down at the table. "So, isn't that good?"

"Yeees…" Joanne picked up the pen again and clicked the button in and out. "But if you get an even more high-powered job, when are you going to have time to get married and have a family?"

Karina fiddled with the radio dial, eliciting a succession of blaring sound bites until she came to the station she wanted. "You know how I feel about…motherhood," she said at last. "Anyway, I wonder if it's all it's cracked up to be. Look at you—your kids drive you crazy."

"I'm also crazy about them. They're noisy, messy, completely vile little creatures but they're mine. Flesh of my flesh and all that."

"But when we were teenagers you were always going on about the career you were going to have. You weren't even interested in children."

"People change. What's wrong with that? Being a mother doesn't mean I've given up sentient life. Or that I'll never go back to teaching. At least with your job you're in an ideal position to freelance. You could have a home office and easily combine the two."

"I'd get bored working by myself. Say, do you think I should wear shorts on the golf course or one of those kicky little skirt things tennis players wear?"

Joanne rolled her eyes. "You're supposed to dazzle them with your competence, not your legs. Seriously, Karina, I just can't see you being alone all your life."

Karina jumped up and paced across to the kitchen counter. "I've got plenty of friends. Not all of them are married. I'm sure I'll find someone to sit by the fire with in my dotage."

"Friends are great, but they're not the same as having your own family," Joanne insisted. "Besides, you love kids. You practically drooled over every one of my babies. Why not have your own?"

And leave them to weep for me when I'm gone? Never.

Karina busied herself at the counter, rearranging the clutter. "Aunt Maria called the other day."

"Your mom's sister?"

"Yes. She was crying so much I could hardly make

out what she was saying. Pamela, her eldest daughter, found another lump in her breast last month.''

''Oh, dear.'' Joanne's mouth twisted sympathetically. ''Was it malignant?''

Karina nodded, sorting used twist-ties into piles by color. ''Poor Pam. She must be terrified. Aunt Maria went on and on about how every generation since my great-great-grandmother's time has been affected by breast cancer. She made it sound like every female in the family is doomed.''

''Yet *she* never got it,'' Joanne argued. ''And how good could the medical treatment have been in an Italian village in the old days?''

''Not great, probably. But the best treatment in modern-day Canada didn't save my mother. And sure Maria never got it, but she's only one out of how many?'' Karina wound a twist-tie around her finger. ''I'll be thirty-two next month, Jo.''

''Oh, Karina. You're *not* going to get breast cancer and die.''

''It happened to my mother.''

''But it won't happen to you. Not with all the information and screening techniques around these days.'' Joanne frowned at her. ''You do practise self-examination, don't you?''

''I'd be crazy not to, wouldn't I?'' She didn't mention the major effort required to work up the courage to do it every month, or the cold sweat that had broken out when she'd actually found something.

''But I very nearly didn't see my doctor about that lump last April,'' she confessed. ''I tried to convince myself it was just normal bumpy tissue. I know it's not rational, but I'm terrified I'll be the next family casualty.''

"But you *did* see your doctor. You *did* get it treated. Have you told your dad about it yet, by the way?"

Karina hung her head. "I don't want to worry him. He never got over Mama. If I even try to talk about her, he gets this frozen look on his face and changes the subject. He loved her so much when she was alive, it's as if he hates her for dying. I wouldn't ever want to put anyone I loved through that. He's still suffering."

"Still, he should be told. *You* don't talk about your mother, either," Joanne added, her husky contralto sounding even lower than usual. "I've never seen you cry over her, not even right after she died."

Karina pushed the piles of twist-ties into a drawer, where they scattered among the cutlery. Some things were too painful, too frightening to talk about, even with Joanne. Anyway, what was the point of dwelling on them? She wanted to forget. She wanted to be happy.

"I..." She swallowed. "There's nothing to say, Jo."

Joanne looked skeptical but she crossed the room and pulled Karina into a hug. "If you ever do want to talk, I'm here, okay?"

"I'm fine, really." Karina gave her a shaky smile. "But thanks. I appreciate it."

"That's okay." Joanne released her and stood back. "You know, Karina, maybe you should rent to this Aussie guy. You two might hit it off."

Karina let out an exasperated sigh tempered with a tiny smile. "You never give up, do you?"

"I'm just worried about you. You push away any man who gets too close. Look at Joel. The minute he started getting serious, you told him to take a hike."

Karina's gaze slid away from Joanne's. "I was in the middle of restructuring the art department. It was a bad time."

''That was two years ago! Who've you been out with since?''

''No one special, you know that. For me to fall in love and marry—which I can tell you right now will never happen—I'd have to find one extraordinary man.''

The sound of footsteps on the landing overhead made her pause abruptly. ''Shhh. He's coming.''

CHAPTER TWO

DANIEL QUIETLY SHUT the door to Natalie's room and paused on the landing. Voices drifted up the stairs from the kitchen. Karina and another woman. Great. How was he going to convince Karina to let them stay until they found another place to live in the middle of a gabfest?

He descended the stairs and walked down the carpeted hallway, drawn by the aroma of freshly brewed coffee. At the entrance to the meals area he paused, his way blocked by a sea of newspapers surrounding the biggest pig he'd ever seen.

The two women fell abruptly silent.

"Mornin'." His brief nod encompassed them both.

"Good morning," Karina said cheerily. "How did you sleep?"

"Well, thanks. Natalie's still sawing logs." Karina wore a sunny smile, he noted, but her eyes were unnaturally bright, as though she'd been crying. Or come close to it. "I hope I'm not interrupting."

"Not at all. Coffee's hot." Karina nodded at the thermal jug. "This is Joanne. Joanne, Daniel."

"Pleased to meet you." He walked into the kitchen under the spotlight of Joanne's avid gaze. Karina, wearing another oversize, paste-streaked shirt over black leggings, was totally rapt in pouring sugar into a royal-blue-and-white sugar bowl. Her feet were bare, her toenails painted the same fuchsia color as her shirt.

Daniel gave the sticky-looking pig a wide berth. It was oddly appealing, he had to admit, with a smile as big as its maker's. He poured himself a cup of coffee and pulled out a chair at the far side of the table. As he sat down he glimpsed Joanne throwing Karina a *look,* her big eyes widening till white surrounded the blue.

Strange woman. He rooted through the newspaper for the "Want Ad" section.

"How's Natalie?" Karina asked, glancing over her shoulder at him. Her dark brown eyes were warm and full of concern.

Daniel paused, cup to his lips. For a moment he found himself wanting to pour out all his worries over his daughter. About how she still cried for her mother. How she spent too much time playing with her imaginary friend, Mrs. Beeton. How she'd clung to her grandma when they'd left Melbourne and had to be carried, sobbing, onto the plane.

He took a sip of coffee and swallowed the hot, bitter liquid. "She's developed a rattling cough."

Karina made a *tsking* sound. "And her fever?"

"Worse."

Her mouth moved outward in a moue of sympathy. Daniel's gaze fixed on the soft curve of her lower lip, noting the gradation from pale pink at the edges to cranberry at its fullest part. Then he shook open the newspaper to the "For Rent" section and focused on the tiny print.

"Sounds like bronchitis," Joanne said cheerfully. She sat down and planted her elbows on the table. "Or maybe pneumonia."

Daniel lowered the paper in alarm. "Pneumonia?"

"Don't mind her," Karina said with a quick smile. "She's a card-carrying pessimist."

Joanne made a face at Karina. "I'm a mother." To Daniel, she explained, "I've got three kids—eight, six and two. They've been through everything, twice."

"Natalie's six, too," he said.

Karina split a bagel and popped it into the toaster. "I called my doctor. She's coming around this afternoon."

Surprised, he glanced up at her, gratitude warming his gaze. "Thank you."

With a flustered laugh she bustled off, chattering about bagels and cream cheese as though she were offering him a full-course gourmet dinner.

Joanne drained her coffee and rose from the table to carry her cup to the sink. "Well, folks, I'll leave you to it."

The toaster popped. Karina whipped out the hot bagels and juggled them to the bread board, her alarmed gaze fixed on Joanne. "Aren't you staying for breakfast?"

Daniel watched Karina over his coffee cup. She seemed surprised at Joanne's departure, and just the teeniest bit annoyed. What was going on?

"Nope," Joanne replied. "I've got to stop at the store before I pick up the kids from Mom." She turned to Daniel. "Why don't you bring Natalie over to play with my girls when she's feeling better? She'll need some company to help keep her mind off her friends back home."

Daniel set down his cup. The offer was appealing, but he hadn't missed the lightning-quick glare and counter-glare that flashed between Karina and Joanne. Joanne was probably just being friendly. But Karina obviously wanted him out of the house. Well, she had no worries on that score. He wanted to get Natalie settled as soon as possible.

"Thanks. I'll have to see where we are by then."

Joanne tossed her shaggy blond hair and laughed. "Oh, you'll still be here. I heard on the news the other day the vacancy rate's at a ten-year low."

"Thank you, Joanne." Karina all but pushed her out the door, muttering something inaudible under her breath.

Daniel watched the pair with amusement, but his smile faded as he contemplated Joanne's parting words. He had less than two months to find a place to rent before Natalie started school. Buying a house would have to wait until he'd familiarized himself with prices, schools and locations. Ten years was a long time to be away, and the city had undoubtedly changed.

He could hear Karina and Joanne talking on the front porch, their lowered voices punctuated by the occasional burst of laughter. Munching on a bagel, Daniel took a pen from the pewter beer mug on the windowsill and began to mark the ads that appeared suitable. They were discouragingly few.

Karina came back into the room. "Anything good?"

He threw down the pen. "A couple. Not much."

"Try them." She plucked the cordless phone from its holder on the wall and passed it to him.

Fifteen minutes later Daniel had been through the lot. "Gone, every last one of them." He folded the phone shut. "I'll have to wait till next week."

"Next month, you mean," Karina said, spreading cream cheese over another toasted bagel.

Daniel looked at her blankly. "Beg your pardon?"

"Most apartments are rented by the month, with possession from the first. You missed it by a week." She eyed him curiously. "Didn't you know that?"

"Obviously not." Daniel pushed himself to his feet. He would have strode across the room but the damn pig was in the way. Frustrated, he braced his hands inside the doorless frame that separated the kitchen from the meals area. "In Melbourne, you can move into a rental anytime if the place is vacant. And there are always vacancies."

Karina's eyebrows lifted. "Not here. On the first of every month, there's a mad scramble among renters to grab the few available apartments and houses. People hang out at the back of the newspaper building at 5:00 a.m. to get the paper fresh off the press."

"That's insane."

She shrugged. "That's life in Lotus Land. What made you move to Australia in the first place? If you don't mind me asking."

"My wife was Australian. We can't spend a month or more in a hotel," he muttered, his mind still on the housing situation. "I promised Natalie we'd have a real home. I'll have to contact a rental agency."

"Good idea. I'll ask around at work, too. I guess Betty and Kevin are already overcrowded," she added between bites of her bagel.

Daniel nodded. "Even if they had room, they wouldn't want a sick child coming in contact with their new baby."

"No, I guess not." Karina took a sip of coffee. "I take it your parents don't live in Victoria?"

"They used to. But when Dad retired a few years ago they moved up-island. As soon as we get settled and I get transport, I'll take Natalie for a visit. They haven't seen her since she was a baby."

"I'll bet they can't wait to get reacquainted. Any other friends or relatives you could mooch off?"

"I have a brother...." Daniel's hands stiffened around

the door frame. No way could he contact Brian after a decade of silence and immediately ask a favor.

"Well?"

"I don't know what his situation is. Whether he has room or not."

Karina frowned, looking puzzled. "Give him a call and find out."

Daniel hesitated, reluctant to admit the extent of his estrangement with his brother. "He doesn't know I'm back," he said finally. "We haven't spoken to each other for ten years."

"Ten years!" Karina looked astounded. "Why not?"

"We…had a fight." Daniel straightened, flexing his hands. He turned away from her and crossed the kitchen to look out the window into the backyard. Why on earth was he telling her this? He had a problem and he would solve it, without any sympathy from a woman he scarcely knew.

He and Brian used to be best mates. They'd been through everything together—Little League, Scouts, fishing, girls. *Girls.* That's where everything had gone wrong. But Francine was dead and Natalie was growing up. Surely Brian would forgive and forget. They were brothers, after all.

Behind him, he heard Karina leave the table and set her dishes in the sink. "What did you fight about?" she asked above the clatter of china on porcelain.

The clock over the stove ticked loudly in the ensuing silence. Daniel watched the swinging tail, the eyes flicking back and forth with each passing second.

"A woman," he said finally. "No big deal." *Damn,* that hadn't come out right.

When his inadvertent chauvinism didn't draw a blast from Karina, he turned to see her staring at a miniature silver frame on the shelf above the sink. Crammed between a vase of dried flowers and a collection of scallop shells was a photo of a good-looking man with wavy dark hair.

"My brother, Tom, and I used to fight all the time," she said. "About all sorts of trivial things. We were very jealous of each other."

Were all families the same? "Do you still fight?"

She smiled. "No, we grew out of that. We hardly see each other since he moved to Toronto, but we talk fairly often on the phone."

"This is a big house for one person," Daniel said. "Why did you stop renting?"

To his surprise, the rosy bloom drained from her cheeks and she stared at him with wide, troubled eyes. Then, just as he was about to ask what was wrong, she laughed, though her laughter sounded forced.

"I've had a string of bad tenants," she said, turning away from her brother's photo. "Everything from a lech to a loser who couldn't pay the rent. I'm fed up."

"I see." What he saw was that behind her bright and beautiful facade she was afraid. Of what, he couldn't imagine, but her problems were none of his business. He had enough of his own.

Outside in the backyard, a dog barked. Karina rushed to the door, color flooding back into her cheeks. In a flash, she was across the deck, crashing down the steps to the lawn. "Get out of my tomatoes, Piper, you crazy mutt!"

Daniel stepped onto the deck. The rain had stopped. An exuberant and very shaggy cocker spaniel was running in circles around the scrap of lawn between the deck and the garage. Karina ran after it, laughing now and panting hard.

"Gotcha," she cried, and tackled the dog. Dog and woman went rolling on the damp grass, the dog's tongue lapping furiously while Karina twisted her head to avoid the slobbery onslaught. She finally knelt on the lawn, scratching the dog on the belly and muttering to it in puppy talk.

Daniel walked slowly down the stairs, his eyes roving over the backyard. In one corner, rows of tomato plants had been staked near the back fence. Between two front plants was a hole, freshly dug. His gaze went to the fence itself. Midway along the yard was a gap in a rotted board just big enough for a small dog to squeeze through.

"Piper is the neighbor's dog, I take it," Daniel said, coming across the lawn. He dropped to a squat and scratched the dog behind the ears, chuckling at the blissful look on the spaniel's face. "Nattie would go mad over this little fella. She misses her grandma's blue heeler."

Karina flopped back on her elbows on the lawn. "Didn't she have a dog of her own?"

"No. Nattie and I have lived with her grandmother for the past three years."

Karina sat up and plucked at a blade of grass. "I don't mean to pry, but—"

Ah, the inevitable questions about his wife. Daniel rose to his feet.

Karina got up, too, Piper leaping around her legs. "I'm sorry," she said. "Forget I said anything. Please."

He gazed at her, not smiling but not angry, either. Not anything. "Natalie's mother is dead."

"I'm sorry." Karina bent to push the dog away. She glanced up at Daniel and an odd expression crossed her face. "I…I hope you give your daughter lots of hugs."

Daniel blinked. Most women gushed about how sorry they were for the poor little mite. And for him. "Yes, I do, as a matter of fact."

"Good." Her lips curved in a smile as spontaneous and pure as the sunshine that was breaking from behind the parting clouds.

Daniel drew in a breath and gestured to the wooden building behind them. "Is, ah…is that the garage?"

"What? Oh, yes."

"May I see it?"

She hesitated. "Is there any point?"

"Perhaps I'll see that it wouldn't be suitable. Then I won't mind so much not being able to use it."

Her fine, black eyebrows lifted and she laughed. "That's a novel way of looking at it. Come on, then."

Daniel stepped inside as Karina flicked a switch and strips of fluorescent lighting brightened the interior. It was swept clean and was empty—except for a bright red Triumph Spitfire parked askew in the center of the four-square orderliness.

He glanced around. Plenty of space. More than adequate light, even for night work. A wooden work bench sat along one wall, while shelves lined another. There was even a high, wooden stool tucked under the bench and a corkboard attached to the wall. He walked over to the panel box and inspected it. Three-phase power—essential for some of his tools. The garage was perfect.

He nodded at the sports car. "Yours?"

Karina grinned. "Why should men with grey hair and potbellies have all the fun?"

"Why, indeed? Looks as if someone has done carpentry here before."

She nodded. "A friend used to make futon furniture

in here." She glanced sideways at him. "Guess your plan didn't work, huh?"

"Not exactly." He started to walk out of the garage, then stopped and faced her, his hands thrust in his hip pockets. "Look, I'm in a bind. I've got wood arriving from Melbourne any day and I want to get to work. How about at least renting me the garage?"

"You're importing wood from Australia? Isn't that a little strange when we've got about a zillion trees of our own in British Columbia?"

"The wood is special. What do you say? Can I use the garage?"

She went quiet for a long time, staring at the concrete floor. Daniel waited. One less stress in his life right now would be more than welcome.

At last she lifted her head and looked at him. "Would there still be room for Sammy?"

She had to be talking about the car. He noticed for the first time the chrome salamander snaking up the center of the hood in place of the traditional ornament.

"Sammy's small. There's room for both of us."

"In that case, okay."

He breathed out. "Great. Thanks." One down, one to go. Except he wasn't sure he still wanted to press the issue of staying until he found another rental. Not after seeing how upset she'd become in the kitchen earlier.

When they walked out of the garage, Piper was back in the tomato bed, head down, dirt spraying from his flying feet. Karina hauled him away from the plants, then crouched and held the dog's face so she could glare straight into his eyes. "Bad dog. No dig."

The spaniel twisted his muzzle this way and that in an effort to escape her scolding, but he didn't look particularly contrite.

Suppressing a smile, Daniel said, "When my tools arrive I'll fix the fence for you. Unless you've got a hammer and nails—I could do it right now."

Karina got to her feet, one hand firmly gripping the dog's collar. "Right *now?*"

He nodded.

"You mean you would fix the fence right this minute if you had the tools?"

What was she getting at? "Sure. Why not?"

"For one thing," she said, "there's a little matter of procrastination."

Daniel smiled. He very nearly laughed. It'd been a long time since he'd done that with anyone but Natalie. "Oddly enough, I've never suffered from procrastination."

Karina dragged the reluctant Piper back to the hole in the fence and pushed him through. "Well, try to cultivate some, because I don't want the fence fixed."

She stuck a small piece of wood against the hole and propped it there with a brick. "It keeps him out for a while," she explained, dusting off her hands and walking back to Daniel.

He shook his head. "He just lets you think that. Why not do the job properly?"

She looked at him as though he were crazy. "Then I'd never get to play with him."

"Of course," he murmured. "Why didn't I think of that?" He paused at the bottom of the steps so she could go up ahead of him. "If you like dogs so much, why not get one of your own?"

"And deliberately install another tomato excavator in my backyard? No thanks. Besides, dogs are long-term commitments." She reached the top of the stairs and regarded him thoughtfully. "But a budgie might be good. And I could teach it to talk.''

Daniel's eyebrows rose. Conversation with Karina took more turns than a tiger snake's tail. ''Er, right,'' he replied, and added a twist of his own. ''Isn't that a lot of tomatoes for one person?''

She led the way back inside the house, talking over her shoulder. ''Mama always had a tomato patch. I'm not much of a cook but I still follow her old Italian recipe for tomato sauce every year.''

''Does your mother live in Victoria?''

For a moment, Daniel didn't think she'd heard him. Without speaking, Karina took the kettle off the stove and walked to the sink to fill it.

''No,'' she said at last, very quietly. ''Not anymore.''

He was about to ask where her mother lived now when a thin wail came from above. ''Daaaddy!''

KARINA SAT AT THE kitchen table working on the logo for a friend's business card. The doctor had come and gone after diagnosing acute bronchitis and ordering Natalie to spend the day in bed. Daniel had filled a prescription for antibiotics at the local drugstore and given Natalie the first dose. He'd also registered with House Rentals Plus by telephone, proving conclusively that procrastination wasn't part of his vocabulary.

Now he was tidying up the kitchen while Karina watched covertly. She'd reminded him the cleaning lady was coming tomorrow, but he'd just shaken his head with a disbelieving smile and rolled up his sleeves.

As tenants went, Daniel would be a good one, she thought. He was neat and clean, but she could live with that. He was quiet; perhaps a bit too quiet, but that was probably a good thing. It meant he wasn't her type and therefore not a threat. He liked dogs; that was always a good sign. And he was reliable. Anyone who cared for his daughter so diligently had to be a responsible person.

On the other hand, she wasn't looking for a roommate. She'd been perfectly honest when she'd told Daniel she'd thought about it long and hard. Her rational as well as her emotional decision had been that she needed time to herself. That hadn't changed overnight.

Interesting how many muscles were employed in the simple act of washing dishes, she mused as she watched his movements. His arms flexed, which made his shoulders strain against his sand-colored cotton shirt. His torso twisted as he stacked the dishes beside the sink, causing a contraction of his denim-clad buttocks, which in turn tensed his leg muscles right down to the calves.

"You know," Daniel said, "there are so many eyes in this house I feel like I'm being watched wherever I go. Don't you find it a bit creepy?"

Karina put her head down and concentrated on the logo. "It never occurred to me. Mind you, I regard my creatures as friends. When they talk to me, I talk back."

Daniel pulled the plug, and the water gurgled down the drain. Picking up a hand towel that had been rolled into a ball and left on the counter, he dried his hands and hung the towel neatly on the oven handle.

"This bloke is a good conversationalist, is he?" He gestured to a luridly painted plaster gargoyle attached to the wall.

Karina laughed. "A bit of a complainer, but not bad."

Daniel shook his head, then glanced at his watch. "I'd better start looking for a hotel for the night."

"You and Natalie can stay here until you find a house to rent." Karina bit her lip, surprised at her impulsive offer. Hadn't she just decided she wanted him to go?

Frown lines creased Daniel's forehead. "You don't have to do that. The doctor said Nattie could be moved."

"I know." Karina sought a valid reason to explain her change of heart. And found none. She shrugged. "I would just feel better if you stayed. For Natalie's sake."

Still he hesitated, regarding her through narrowed eyes. "Just how capricious are you?"

She laughed. "Are you afraid I'll change my mind again?"

"Frankly, yes."

"Don't worry. Two or three changes on the same subject is all my brain can handle." She got up from the table and put out her hand. "Deal?"

He looked at it so long she thought he was still making up his mind. Then he wrapped his fingers around her hand and held it. "On one condition."

"What's that?"

"I can take down those cardboard palm trees from beside my bed. When I woke up this morning I felt as if I was in a commercial for suntan lotion."

Karina smiled. Daniel Bowen was sober, dull and ordinary. A model tenant and no threat at all to her equilibrium. Imagine not liking palm trees. "It's a deal."

He pressed her hand. The warmth from his fingers felt awfully good, and for a moment she wondered if she'd made a mistake. Then she remembered the palm trees. "What are you going to do now?" she asked.

He let go of her hand. The warmth in his gaze faded and the fine lines across his brow reappeared. "Call my brother."

CHAPTER THREE

DANIEL WALKED INTO the kitchen the next morning and stopped short at the sight of Karina dressed for work. She looked like an ad for *Vogue* in her tailored suit jacket, slim black skirt and high-heeled shoes. Even her lively hair had been tamed into a smooth, dark chignon.

"Mornin'," he said, and laid an envelope stuffed with bills on the table. "Here's the rent for July—two rooms plus the garage."

Karina flashed him a smile. "Thanks. Can you wait till tonight for a receipt? I'm in a bit of a rush." She took a bite of toast and followed it quickly with a sip of coffee.

"No worries." Daniel poured himself coffee and noted the unconventional details of her outfit he'd missed at first glance; the tiny silver butterfly inserted into her hair, the rhinestone salamander that slithered up the lapel of her electric blue jacket and the dozen or so silver bangles that jingled up her arm as she lifted her cup to that splendid, curving mouth.

"Do you know anything about golf?" she asked.

He raised one eyebrow. "Golf?"

"Golf." Heels clicking on the linoleum, Karina deposited her cup in the sink and brushed the toast crumbs from her hands. "I'm entering a tournament next month and I don't have a clue how to play."

He shook his head. "I played a few times, years ago,

but never liked the game enough to bother learning properly.''

She looked disappointed for a moment, then her smile was back, full force. ''Never mind, I'll just ad-lib.''

Daniel was pretty sure you couldn't ad-lib a game like golf. But if anyone could pull it off, he'd place his bet on Karina Peterson. She seemed confident enough to brazen her way through anything.

Karina gathered up her purse and briefcase. ''Any word from your brother?''

''I left another message on his answering machine. He hasn't called back yet.''

''Why don't you just drop in on him?''

Daniel sipped at his coffee. ''He'll call today.''

''If you say so.'' She glanced at Felix the Clock. ''I'm late. See you tonight.'' She started off down the hall, still talking. ''Jenny will be here…'' Her voice trailed away.

''Who's Jenny?'' he said, forced to follow her. Didn't this woman ever stand still and talk?

''The cleaning lady,'' Karina replied, going out the door. ''She comes at ten. Help yourself to anything you want. Anything you can find, that is.'' She flashed her wide smile again and waved, keys and bangles jingling. '''Bye.''

'''Bye.'' He almost leaned forward and kissed her. Such was the force of habit, even when habit was three years dead and gone. Even when habit had been formed by another woman. A totally different kind of woman.

By the time he pulled back, clutching his coffee cup a little too tightly, Daniel was alone on the step.

He hardly ever thought of Francine anymore, except with sadness for Natalie's sake and regret that anyone should die so young. He'd tried to be a good husband. As good as a man could be who hadn't loved his wife.

Daniel tipped back his head to drain the last of his coffee. Natalie would be waking soon. Going inside, he rinsed his cup and left it on the draining board. Then he made a tray of scrambled eggs and toast to take up to his daughter.

He knocked softly and opened the door. A rustle of bedclothes told him Natalie was stirring. "Mornin', Possum. Ready for some breakfast?" He set the tray on the bedside table and handed her a glass of juice and a pill.

"Yes, thanks. I'm starving." Natalie struggled to sit up in bed. She took the juice and chewed the cherry-flavored pill with relish. "Yummy."

"Don't get too used to these tablets," Daniel warned. "They're not lollies."

The antibiotics were having a positive effect, though. Her fever had gone down and her color was healthier. Another day and she'd probably be out of bed. Then he could get on with looking for a vehicle, setting up a bank account, placing ads in the local papers—

"Daddy, is Karina coming up to see me this morning?"

"No, darlin', she already left for work."

"Oh." The single word, the downturned mouth, expressed a wealth of disappointment.

He ruffled her hair affectionately. "You must be feeling better if you're getting choosy about your visitors. Do you want me to read you a book?"

Natalie brightened. "Read the one Karina left with me last night. It has dragons and everything."

Daniel picked up the book lying on the bedside table and read to Natalie while she ate her breakfast, keeping one ear open for the sound of the telephone. He finished the book and read two more, but still Brian hadn't called. Maybe he'd got in late last night and hadn't had a chance to check his messages. By this time of the morning he was probably at work.

Daniel closed the book. "Okay, Nattie, time for that bath you were too tired for last night."

The bathroom, like every other room in the house, was bursting at the seams with Karina's personality. Makeup and jewelry were scattered over the vanity, purple and blue hydrangeas erupted from a papier-mâché vase next to the tub, and a damp towel had been flung carelessly over the wicker chair in the corner.

Somewhere in the room, a top forty radio station pumped out pop music. Karina's taste in music, he'd discovered already, was as insatiable as it was wide-ranging. There was never a moment of the day or night when the radio or CD player wasn't on.

Daniel ran the bath, then started to hunt for the radio to silence it. There weren't many places to look and he found it quickly enough, a small transistor wedged into the lower shelf of the medicine cabinet. He turned it off with a wondering shake of his head. A man couldn't hear himself think around this house.

Peace restored, he helped Natalie into the bath and lathered shampoo through her straight blond hair. How was Brian going to react to seeing him again? he wondered.

The first few years after he and Francine had married, all Daniel's attempts at communication had been re-buffed. Later, there'd been too many moves, too many changes of address to keep up with. He wasn't much of a letter writer; nor, it seemed, was Brian. It'd been easier to let things slide, thinking someday he'd return to Victoria to visit his folks and patch things up.

He'd come back once, shortly after Natalie was born, but Brian had been away. Unavoidably, his father had said, but the troubled look in his mother's eyes had told a different story. Brian still hadn't forgiven him for eloping with his fiancée; not that Daniel blamed him. Why else would he have scheduled an extended trip, business or not, the month his only brother was home from Australia?

"Okay, kiddo, rinse time." He adjusted the water temperature and sprayed Natalie's head with the nozzle attached to the tap.

But the rivalry between Brian and himself had started long before Francine. Brian had always resented the fact that Daniel made the high school honor roll year after year. And he, himself, had certainly disliked the attention Brian received as captain of the football team and ace basketball player.

Okay, so they'd been jealous of each other as teenagers and rivals in love as young men. But they were brothers. Surely that was a bond that could never be broken?

"Look, Daddy, I'm a submarine!" Natalie submerged her face, bubbles roiling around her head as her legs thrashed the shallow bathwater.

"You're one sick chook, is what you are," he said when she emerged, gasping.

"I'm not a chicken." She pushed wet hair out of her face and drew herself up with great dignity. "I'm a little lady."

"Who told you that?" he asked with a grin.

"Grandma." Her small mouth drooped. "I miss Grandma. When are we going to see her again?"

His grin faded. "It might be a while, Nattie. We'll

give her a ring tonight, let her know we arrived safely. Come on, time to come out.''

He helped her from the tub and wrapped a big, fluffy towel around her shivering body. So sweet, so fragile, her little pixie face. Her blue eyes so serious. ''You'll learn to like it here in Canada, sweetheart.''

''I guess so. But why won't Karina let us live here?''

''I don't know exactly,'' he said, rubbing her hair dry. ''I suppose she likes living alone.''

Natalie pushed the towel back from her forehead, her fair brows pulled together in confusion. ''But yesterday she had all those friends around.''

Daniel nodded, remembering the small crowd that had dropped in by ones and twos to drink coffee and yak the day away while Karina worked on her pig.

''Having friends over when you want company and having strangers living in your house are two different things.''

''We're not strangers,'' Natalie said. ''We're us.''

Daniel laughed and hugged her tightly. ''So we are, Possum, so we are.''

The telephone rang.

Daniel leaped to his feet. ''Wait here,'' he told Natalie, and thundered across the landing to the stairs. He was halfway down when he remembered the extension in his bedroom and hastily backtracked. He dived for the receiver on the eighth ring.

''Hello?''

''Goodness, you sound as if you've been running. I forgot to tell you there's a tin of tuna in one of the lower cupboards if you get hungry. And there's always peanut butter, though I'm not sure how much bread's left. Sorry about the lack of food. I'm going shopping any day now.''

"No worries." Daniel sank onto the bed. He tried to imagine Karina scheduling artwork and organizing staff and failed completely.

"If you see Piper in the yard, would you do me a favor and chase him back through the fence?" she rattled on.

"Sure." Karina's voice had a musical quality he hadn't noticed when talking to her in person. For a moment, he considered asking if she would say hello to Natalie, then dismissed the idea. He could hear the click of computer keys in the background. Karina had more important things to do than talk to a child.

"You never did tell me if you had a hammer and nails," he said.

"In the basement— Wait a minute! Don't you go locking Piper out. Someday he'll learn not to dig up my tomatoes."

"I wouldn't bet my last dollar on it," Daniel replied. "All the spaniels I've known act as though they have a 'roo loose in the top paddock."

"Pardon?"

"In other words, not too bright."

"And I thought you were a dog lover. How's Natalie?"

"Improving." He heard a faint beep on the line.

"Can you hold a sec?" Karina said. "I've got another call." A moment later, she was back. "Sorry, gotta run. The boss has a bee in his bonnet about something. See you later." She hung up.

Daniel stared at the receiver, then slowly replaced it. For two whole minutes he'd forgotten to be disappointed the call wasn't from his brother.

The bathroom, when he returned, was empty, and a trail of watery footprints led to Natalie's room. He paused outside her door. She was sitting on the floor, wrapped in a towel, talking to herself. Or, rather, talking to Mrs. Beeton.

Daniel frowned. With difficulty, he restrained himself from interrupting the one-sided conversation. When was she going to get over her friendship with the invisible Mrs. Beeton? It had begun shortly after Francine's death and it worried him. It also made him feel somehow inadequate, though he knew he did the best he could. The simple fact was, the girl needed a mother.

Maybe he should have tried harder with that single mom he'd met at Natalie's kindergarten. But he knew he needed someone for himself, as well.

Someday he'd meet the right woman. But next time around he wouldn't rush into marriage until he was sure his love would last. He wanted it all—wife, lover, friend—for himself, for Natalie and for his children yet to be born. *Their* children, whoever she might be.

Natalie glanced around, saw him and smiled. "Can I have a scratch-back, Daddy?"

"Sure thing." Daniel smiled at the word inversion, something she'd done ever since she'd learned to talk. He helped her back into her pajamas and tucked her into bed, arranging the favorite blanket just so. "Do you want me to sing you a song?"

Silence. "No, thank you, Daddy," she said in a small polite voice.

He couldn't blame her. He was tone deaf and he never remembered the words.

"When our trunks arrive we'll dig out that tape of Mommy singing your favorite songs, okay?" They'd made the recording once when Francine had gone away on a business trip, and he was grateful for Natalie's sake that she would always have her mother's voice on tape.

He'd even made several copies in case the original wore out.

She brightened a little. "Okay."

He gently scratched her back and told her a story about when he was six and Brian was eight and they'd caught tadpoles in the old gravel pit up the hill from their house.

Soon Natalie's small back rose and fell in the regular rhythm of sleep. Daniel pulled her pajama top down, tucked the covers around her neck and went downstairs.

He wandered restlessly into the living room. What now? He couldn't sit by the phone all day. The house and its inanimate inhabitants made him claustrophobic, so he went through the kitchen and out the back door.

A furry black snout poked through the crack in the fence. Now there was a problem just begging to be fixed. Karina had told him not to board up the fence, but she obviously wasn't aware of the alternatives.

Whistling, Daniel strode back into the house. In the corner of the meals area, he found the door to the basement.

KARINA STEPPED OUT of her office, and an elastic band zinged past her nose. She glanced in the direction it came from and saw a shiny bald head duck out of sight behind an office divider.

"*Kevin,*" she admonished in her best authoritarian voice. The "boys," as she called her team of artists, got a little silly sometimes, but she cast a blind eye on most of their antics because they produced good work. And they were fun.

Tiptoeing through the maze of open-plan cubicles, she leaned over Kevin's divider and cocked the elastic above his hairless head, trying very hard not to laugh. He looked up, his blue eyes twinkling innocently above a full, black beard threaded with grey.

"I was aiming at Wally, Your Honor." Kevin held his hand over his heart. "I fired in self-defense."

"Sure, and I'm Annie Oakley." She let the elastic drop to his desk, then nodded at his rendering of a storefront with a penny-farthing bicycle done in neon lighting. "This is excellent."

Kevin smiled modestly and waved a stubby hand. "I used your suggestion about putting a kid on the bike. It made all the difference." He leaned back in his chair. "You're wasted in management, Karina. You're a better artist than the rest of us put together."

Karina leaned one arm on the top of the divider and rested her chin on her hand. "I do miss the hands-on aspect of designing...."

She straightened. No point in pining over the past. "But I can do more good for the department as art director. We'd never have got the new computers and graphics packages if I hadn't convinced Ross it would boost productivity." She nodded at Kevin's sign design. "Have you shown this to sales yet?"

"I was going to take it across a little later when I meet Jackson for lunch."

Karina raised her eyebrows a fraction.

"Or...I could go right now."

"Good idea." Karina rewarded him with a brilliant smile. "Then come and see me in my office. I've got a new project I want you to start on right away."

"Okey-doke." Smiling, Kevin snapped her a salute.

Karina turned to walk away, then stopped. "By the way, Betty's cousin, Daniel, and his daughter arrived on my doorstep on the weekend, expecting to rent rooms in my house."

Kevin's smile was replaced by a puzzled frown. "I thought you weren't going to rent anymore."

"I wasn't. But it seems no one let Daniel know."

Kevin's mobile face twisted. "Uh-oh. I screwed up again, didn't I?"

"Royally. The little girl's sick, and they've got to stay at my place till they find another rental." Seeing Kevin's contrite expression, she softened. "It turned out okay in the end. But do you happen to have Daniel's money order lurking around? I imagine he'll want it back."

"Sure thing." Kevin clapped his hands down his torso as though frisking himself for the money order. Not finding it, he began pulling out drawers and peering through his overflowing in-tray. "It must be around somewhere."

"Try your wallet," Karina suggested. "How are Betty and the baby doing?"

Kevin smiled broadly. "Just fine. We'll drop in next time we're out your way. I know Betty will want to catch up with Daniel and his little girl."

"Come over next week sometime. Natalie should be better by then." She turned and started to walk away. "I'll be in Ross's office if anyone wants me."

"Okay, boss."

Karina stepped briskly along the plush carpeted hall to Ross Preston's office, straightening her shoulders a little more with every step. Ross the Boss was the only sour note about her job. Sometimes she wished she possessed a tongue sharp enough to cut him down to size.

No small job, she thought as she caught sight of him through his glass-fronted office. His burly shoulders bulged above a tilted-back chair, and his surprisingly dainty feet were crossed at the ankle and planted on the windowsill. He was talking on the phone, but at her knock he swiveled around, grinned under his bristly orange mustache and motioned almost coyly for her to enter.

"Good morning," she said pleasantly, determined not to let his penchant for innuendo spoil her good mood.

Ross hung up the phone. "Karina! Always a pleasure." He leaned back in his chair with his arms crossed behind his head, exposing transparent sweaty patches beneath the armpits of his white shirt.

Karina gritted her teeth and lowered herself into a chair. Only Ross could make the word *pleasure* sound like a perversion. "What's up?"

"This." Lowering his arms, he picked up a sheet of paper and snapped at it with a pudgy forefinger.

Karina peered across the desk. The paper was a handwritten memo from herself to Ross, requesting a spot in the corporate golf tournament. "Oh, yes. I'd like to enter this year."

Ross slumped forward, elbows on his desk, a hangdog expression on his freckled face. "Karina, Karina, Karina. You know I'd give anything for you to come to Parksville for the weekend. We could have such a great time."

Her smile stretched tautly across her face. When she got her promotion she'd never have to smile at Ross Preston again. "Yes, I'd love to get to know your wife better."

"Tina never attends these things," he said with a dismissive wave. "The sad fact is, neither can you."

Karina's smile froze. "I beg your pardon?"

Ross held his hands palms up in a gesture of helplessness. "The tournament is by invitation only."

"I thought it was open to all executives employed by the Franklin Group of Companies."

"Other corporations take part, as well. But, yes, in a manner of speaking, you're right."

"In a manner of speaking? I'm art director. I should get an invitation. Right?"

Ross squirmed in his chair, reminding Karina of a small boy hiding his dirty fingernails at the dinner table. "What's going on here?" she said. "Don't tell me only male execs get invitations."

Ross laughed a little too heartily. "That would be discriminatory."

"Exactly." She stared him down. "Since SignCity doesn't discriminate against women, why didn't I receive an invitation?"

Ross pushed back his chair and began to pace the area behind his oak desk. "The first corporate cup was held over thirty years ago. In all that time, no woman has ever been invited to attend the tournament."

Karina laughed, though she was anything but amused. "Then it's definitely time one was."

Ross stopped pacing and leaned over his desk toward her. "Franklin is big on tradition."

"SignCity moves with the times," Karina retorted, quoting from the company brochure.

Ross shook his head solemnly. "If it were just our company, I'd go to bat for you. But dozens of other firms are involved. The invitations were sent out weeks ago. Everything is all arranged."

"I can't believe this." She laughed again. "Do you know what year this is?"

"Hey, I'm a nineties kind of guy," Ross replied, assuming an earnest expression. "But the old boys on the board, well..."

Karina was stunned. "You mean no woman has *ever* gone to the tournament?"

"Alice Whitehead from the Vancouver office finagled an invitation from someone in a subsidiary firm a few years ago."

"And?"

Ross shrugged. "She went, but I don't think she had a good time. Honestly, Karina, the tournament's just a guy thing. You know, locker-room humor, sweaty socks. It wouldn't be any fun for you."

Karina rose to her feet. "This isn't about fun, Ross. It's about power and keeping women from having their fair share."

Ross smiled at her. "Now, now, Karina. Don't take it personally. Look at you, you're art director. I wouldn't have given you the job if I didn't think you could handle it."

"You didn't *give* me the job," she replied. "I *earned* it."

"And a damned fine job you're doing, too. You make me look real good upstairs. I appreciate that."

Karina muttered a hasty goodbye and left his office before she gagged. *No wonder there are so few female executives at SignCity,* she thought angrily as she walked back to her own department. *They couldn't stomach their male counterparts.*

She had nothing against men. Some of her best friends were men. It didn't mean she wanted to *be* one. Or act like one. Or think like one. The thought of becoming like Ross was enough to make her violently ill.

Maybe she should do as Joanne suggested and start her own business. But the thought of working in isolation scared her. She liked being able to walk out of her office and toss an idea around with half a dozen people. She thrived in the creative, chaotic atmosphere of the art department.

At this stage in the game, giving it all away would be tantamount to giving up. She wasn't ready to give up. If Ross thought he could brush her off this easily, he and the board had a big surprise coming.

DANIEL GOT TO HIS FEET and brushed the dirt from his knees. Gathering up Karina's tools, he stepped back from the fence to admire his handiwork. He couldn't wait to see the look on her face when she saw what he'd done.

He climbed the steps to the deck and pushed open the back door to find a young woman sloshing water around the kitchen floor with a mop.

"Who are you?" she demanded, brandishing the mop. Her anxious gaze flicked from his face to the hammer in his hand.

"Daniel Bowen." He placed the hammer on the stove top. She was more a girl than a woman, with mouse brown hair and wide brown eyes. "You must be Jenny."

"Daniel Boone?" she said skeptically.

"Bowen," he repeated. "I'm Karina's new tenant. She mentioned you were coming this morning."

"Oh." The girl looked less frightened but still suspicious. "Karina said she wasn't renting anymore."

"She made a temporary exception in our case because my daughter's sick."

"That sounds like Karina." Seemingly reassured, Jenny lowered her mop back into the bucket. "And *you* sound Australian."

Daniel went to the sink and started to wash the dirt off his hands. "I lived there for years but I was born and grew up here."

"What were you doing with the hammer?" Jenny asked, wringing out the mop.

"Fixing the hole in the fence."

She shook her head. "Karina's going to kill you."

"We'll see." Daniel picked up a towel and dried his hands. "Pretty hard yakka cleaning up around here."

Jenny leaned on her mop. "Yakka?"

"That's Australian for *work*."

She grinned and resumed mopping. "I'm 'yakkaing' my way through university. I think Karina makes a bigger mess just so I can earn a few extra bucks. She's so great."

The corners of Daniel's mouth curved slightly. "She very generously left a heap of laundry in the dining room for you to iron."

"Great," Jenny said, mopping energetically. She glanced over her shoulder at him. "Do you have anything you want done?"

"I look after myself, thanks." He paused. "Do you know of a supermarket nearby that delivers?"

"There's a Safeway on Oak Bay Avenue. I think they deliver."

"Good. Do you know what Karina likes to eat?"

"Gee, I don't know.... Wait a minute. Pasta. She loves pasta. Her mother was Italian."

"So I've heard. I gather she used to live here, too."

Jenny nodded. "A long time ago. She's dead now."

Like the turn of a kaleidoscope, the pieces that made up the puzzle of Karina Peterson rearranged themselves to form a different pattern. Why hadn't she mentioned yesterday that her mother was dead? She'd gone so quiet. Was it possible her mother's death still affected her? He had a sudden vision of Natalie mourning her mother for the rest of her life, and a chill passed over him.

"I'll let you get on with your cleaning," he said, and

took the telephone and phone book into the living room. He made a list, dictated it to the clerk at the supermarket and was assured the groceries would be delivered within a few hours.

He put down the phone, satisfied. A nice meal was the least he could do to thank Karina for taking them in. From the looks of her cupboards and her slender figure, she could do with a good feed.

DANIEL HEARD THE front door open and Karina call "Hellooo" in a singsong voice just as he picked up the upstairs extension. He punched in his brother's number anyway. He'd probably just get the answering machine again.

The phone rang. Daniel sat on his bed and immediately stood again. *Brrring…brrring….* Anchored by the cord, he tapped his foot, shifted position and tapped the other foot. By the tenth ring he was ready to give up. Then he heard his brother say, "Hello?"

Daniel swallowed hard. "Brian."

"Hello? Who is this?" Brian's voice was brisk, tinged with impatience.

Daniel took a deep breath and gripped the receiver. Okay, so he was a little disappointed Brian hadn't recognized his voice. But after all, it was ten years since they'd spoken and his accent had changed.

"Brian, it's me, Daniel." Silence. "Your brother. I left a message the other day."

Another silence. "I got the message," Brian said finally. "But frankly, I couldn't think of anything I wanted to say to you."

Head bowed, Daniel pinched the bridge of his nose. He'd expected Brian to be cool at first but he never thought he'd hear such frigid dislike from his own brother.

"I don't know what you mean." Daniel spoke lightly, deciding to ignore Brian's tone. "We've got years of news to catch up on."

"Do you think you can waltz in here after what you did to me and carry on like nothing happened?" Brian said. "Think again, *Danny boy.*"

Daniel sucked in his breath. He hated that nickname.

"I know what I did was wrong," he replied as evenly as he could. "Some might even say unforgivable. But we're brothers, and once upon a time we were friends. Can't we get together and talk things out?"

"Sounds fascinating," Brian drawled. "But I'm a busy man. I really don't know when I could get around to it."

"Pick a time," Daniel said through his teeth. "I'll be there."

"My, my, aren't we conciliatory? A bit late now, don't you think, Danny boy?"

"At least I'm making the effort!"

"You're wasting your time. I'm not interested in patching things up. As for our being friends when we were younger, whatever made you think that? So long, little brother."

"Brian, wait—!"

It was too late. Brian had hung up.

Daniel dropped the receiver with a clunk onto its cradle. He paced the room, anger and frustration building. He'd admitted he was wrong. He'd said he was sorry. What more could he do?

The sound of light footsteps on the landing made him glance up. Through the open door he saw Natalie fly past on her way downstairs in her bare feet.

"Natalie! Put your slippers on!"

No response but the receding thud of her steps on the staircase. Muttering under his breath, Daniel went to her room, found the slippers and hurried down the stairs. Dammit, he and Brian *had* been friends once upon a time.

Thinking of his brother, he almost tripped over Natalie. She was sitting on the floor in the hallway, poring over a clear plastic sheet filled with cartoon drawings and the name *Natalie* written in several different type faces.

"How many times have I told you not to go around in your bare feet?" He crouched beside her and jammed the sheepskin slippers over her toes. "Don't you know you've got bronchitis? And where did you get that? Put it back."

Natalie's bottom lip wobbled but she stuck out her jaw. "It was on the hall table," she declared, clutching the transparency to her chest. "It has to be for me. My name is all over it."

"That may be, but you wait till it's given to you."

"Aw, Daddy," the little girl wailed.

"*Natalie.*" Daniel waited impatiently until she did as she was told, then he stalked down the hall to the kitchen.

Karina stood at the kitchen counter, her hips moving in time to the music from the radio as she spread peanut butter over a slice of whole wheat bread. She glanced up as Daniel strode into the room with Natalie trailing behind.

"Hi, guys," she said with a big smile. Tossing the peanut butter knife into the sink, she took a clean one from the drawer and opened a jar of mayonnaise. Daniel watched, appalled, as she spread a large dollop of creamy white goo on top of the peanut butter. She folded it over and lifted it to her mouth.

Just before she sank her teeth into the bread, she said, "Just grabbing a quick bite before I go out. I've had the worst day imaginable. How was yours?"

CHAPTER FOUR

DANIEL GAPED AT HER. Pans of food simmered on the stove. The table was laid for three. The spicy aroma of tomatoes and garlic filled the kitchen. And Karina was snacking on peanut butter and mayonnaise.

His day just couldn't get any worse.

"Daddy made dinner 'specially for you," Natalie informed Karina as she shuffled across the floor in her slippers.

"Shhh, Nattie." Daniel drew a deep breath and mentally counted to ten. "It doesn't matter. Anyway, I made it for all of us."

Karina stopped chewing and looked around, clearly noticing for the first time the full extent of his labors. "Gosh, I'm sorry. I already made plans." She reached for the phone. "I'll call and cancel."

"Don't be silly," he said roughly, and moved the phone out of her reach. He walked over to the stove and turned off the heat under the boiling pasta.

She came to the sink and peered around his shoulder as he emptied the contents of the pot into a colander. "Fettucini," she murmured regretfully. "My favorite."

Daniel carried on with his task, forcing himself not to look at her. She couldn't have known he'd go to any trouble over dinner. It wasn't fair to take out his anger at Brian on her.

Karina took another bite of the revolting concoction

in her hand. The aroma of peanut butter reached his nostrils, splitting wide the thin skin of his control.

He turned on her. "Peanut butter and *mayonnaise?*"

She smiled up at him. "I like it."

"Peanut butter is eaten with bananas." His voice rose over the grating sound of Bjork's vocal gymnastics. "Or jam if you're a child." He knew he was getting worked up over nothing, but at this moment, he really didn't give a damn.

"Oh, that's so boring." With a laugh and a careless flip of her hand, she walked away.

Daniel slammed the pot back onto the stove. So he was boring, was he? Just because he ate decent, regular meals? Or was it because he didn't like her stupid palm trees?

Into the thickening silence, Natalie piped up proudly, "Daddy fixed the fence for you, too."

Karina stopped short and whirled to face him, bangles jangling, wisps of dark hair flying. "You did *what?*"

Daniel held her gaze. "I 'adjusted' the fence."

She gave a snort of laughter. "I asked you not to!"

"Before you get your knickers in a knot, I'd advise you to take a look at what I did."

He might as well have been speaking to the fence itself. Daniel could almost see the angry rebuttal forming on her lips. To his surprise, instead of invective came another burst of laughter.

"Why do you do that?" he said.

"What?"

"Laugh when you're feeling angry?"

She obliged him with a scowl. "Don't try to change the subject."

"It's important." He crossed to the window and snapped off the radio. His blood pressure dropped immediately. "If this is one of your little foibles, I want to know about it."

"Little foibles?" Karina repeated, eyes flashing. "You make me sound like a neurotic housewife. You're angry, too, about dinner and trying not to show it."

"Yeah, I'll admit I'm a little ticked, but I'll get over it."

Her high heels clicking over the linoleum, she strode to the table and snatched up her purse. "Thank you for making dinner," she said, her voice tightly controlled. "And it really was nice of you to try and help by fixing the fence," she added, her voice softening slightly. "But please put the broken boards back the way you found them."

Daniel folded his arms across his chest, leaned against the counter and sent her a long, hard glance. He could explain exactly what he'd done to the fence, but why should he when she'd condemned his handiwork without even seeing it?

"I'm not touching it until you've had a look. Then, if you're not happy, I'll bash a hole big enough for a bull mastiff to walk through on its hind legs."

She clamped her lips together in a fixed smile, her blouse lifting as she drew a deep breath. "Okay. I'll look at it later."

She would get over it once she'd seen the fence, Daniel assured himself as he heard the front door close. But staying here, even temporarily, was clearly a mistake. Karina was used to a freewheeling lifestyle. Natalie needed stability and regular meals.

First thing in the morning, he'd check with the rental agency to see what progress they'd made. Then he'd look in the paper again. There had to be *some*place they could call home.

Wearily he straightened and moved away from the counter. A faint, sniffling sound drew his attention to Natalie. She was huddled in the corner, very still. Her small hands were clutching the belt of her robe and she looked ready to dissolve into tears.

"Nattie, sweetheart." Closing the distance between them, he knelt down and hugged her tightly. "What's wrong?"

Natalie's small frame trembled inside the circle of his arms. She began to hiccup. "K-Karina didn't even notice I was b-better. She didn't even say h-hi to me."

"Yes, she did, sweetheart, when we first came into the room." He pressed a kiss on top of her head, overwhelmed by his child's sudden, passionate need.

"She was l-looking at *you*," Natalie wailed accusingly.

"Now, Nattie," Daniel said firmly. "Karina had a bad day. You're not feeling a hundred percent, either. Come on, let's eat. I seem to recall fettucini is your favorite, too."

To his relief, she scrubbed away her tears and put her hand in his. He rose to his feet and led her to the table. If only all their problems were so easily fixed.

"I COULD KILL THAT MAN." Karina stabbed at the lemon twist on the rim of her glass of Cinzano until it fell to the table with a watery plop.

"Ross the Boss?" Joanne asked sympathetically. She took a sip of white wine and reached for the bowl of rice crackers the waiter had just deposited on their table.

"No, Daniel."

"Whoa! Back the executioner's truck up. Didn't you call me because you were upset about what happened at work?"

"I'll get to that in a minute. It wasn't even what he did—though that was bad enough—so much as the way he looked at me."

Joanne leaned across the table, holding her string of amber beads to her chest so they wouldn't drag in her drink. "Was it…sexual?"

"No." Karina jabbed at the fallen lemon twist with her straw. What really rankled was his comment about her laughing when she was angry. If he noticed things like that after only a few days, what else would he perceive about her? "It was more like…insolent."

"Insolent?" Joanne leaned back in her chair, biting her lip. "That sounds interesting. I wouldn't have thought he was capable of insolence."

"He's capable, all right." Karina signaled to the waiter for another drink. "Maybe he had a right to be annoyed, but how was I supposed to know he'd cooked a meal? Am I expected to be home every night from now on? I'm not used to this. I've always picked tenants who fit into *my* life."

"Knowing the state of your pantry, he probably thought he was performing an act of mercy. I think it's sweet of him."

"Of course it's sweet, that's the whole problem. If he's this nice, how can I ever kick him out?"

"You should hear yourself, Karina," Joanne said, a tiny, smug smile on her face. "One minute he's insolent, the next minute he's too nice. Admit it, you're crazy about him."

Karina crossed her arms over her chest. "That's ridiculous."

"*He* obviously likes *you*," Joanne persisted. "Why else would he go to all the trouble of making dinner?"

"To feed himself and his daughter," she said, refusing to believe otherwise. "If he really liked me, he wouldn't have tampered with the fence."

Joanne waved that away. "Men just like to fix things. It gives them a reason for being."

Karina sighed and leaned forward to rest her arms on the table. "Okay, so I'm overreacting. But it's time he and I worked out some ground rules. This sort of stuff is usually sorted out before tenants move in. Daniel kind of sneaked up on me."

"Not such a bad thing in my humble opinion. How's the kid?"

Karina's expression softened. "Getting better. I heard her in her room this morning, talking to her dolls. She's got one named Mrs. Beeton she chats to just like a real person."

Joanne smiled. "They're so cute at that age." Then the waiter arrived with another Cinzano and white wine, and she sighed as she took her glass. "I'm going to regret this tomorrow, but what the hell."

Karina removed her straw from her glass, sucked on it, then jabbed it in Joanne's direction. "Your problem is, you don't get out often enough."

"That's one of my problems," Joanne corrected her. "My main problem is a husband who's gone half the year doing fieldwork. He's home now, but only for a week. If it was another woman, I could fight it. But how do you compete with fish guts?"

Karina made a face. "Is Peter still doing fish guts?"

"Gut *contents,* I should have said. Apparently it's of vital importance to the salmon fishery. Something about food species and environmental damage."

"Why don't you go with him sometime? I'd help your mom with the kids. You could have a romantic weekend on the banks of the Nechako River...."

"Up to my bazookas in freezing-cold water counting stream insects? I don't think so."

"Where's your sense of adventure? Think of moonlight on rippling water...."

"Think of the black flies."

"Wind, whispering in the pines…"

"Grizzlies raiding your food supply."

"Sunrise over the mountain peaks…"

"Working from dawn till dusk, which in the northern summer is eleven o'clock at night. No, thanks. However, if I can talk Peter into a weekend at Whistler, I might take you up on the offer."

"Anytime. I mean it."

"Thanks. Now, tell me more about Daniel."

Karina moved her glass in watery circles around the table. "I think he's chomping at the bit to get started on his carpentry business. Because Natalie's sick, he can't even go to the bank, though he seems to have a wad of Canadian cash on him."

"Carpentry, eh? Does he do renovations? I'm dying to get our bathroom fixed up."

Karina shook her head doubtfully. "I don't think it's that kind of carpentry. I'll ask him. If I ever speak to him again, that is."

"Give him a chance. Now, what has Ross the Boss been up to?"

"Wait till you hear," Karina said, and explained about the golf tournament.

"Ross is such a creep," Joanne said when Karina had finished. "Any chance he'll relent?"

"No," Karina said. "He's too concerned with his own position to stick his neck out for me. Besides, the decision really is over his fat, round head. Since there's nothing in writing saying women are excluded, I have no way to fight the powers that be. Going as a guest of someone from a sister company seems to be my best prospect so far.''

She noticed Joanne's gaze drift to the other side of the lounge. ''What are you tracking now, Jo?''

''That waiter over there with the cute buns.''

''Joanne! You're a married woman.''

''I was thinking of you, not me.''

Karina sighed. ''Give it up already.''

''Come to think of it,'' Joanne said with a sly grin, ''Daniel has a pretty nice derriere, too.''

''Forget it,'' Karina replied, laughing. ''He's on my hit list.''

SHORTLY AFTER MIDNIGHT, Karina parked Sammy on the side of the garage farthest from the workbench and went into the backyard.

She flicked on the tiny flashlight attached to her key chain and tiptoed through the damp grass to the edge of the tomato patch. Even without the faint beam of the flashlight she could see that wooden boards covered the spot where the gap used to be.

Cursing under her breath, she stepped gingerly into the soft dirt between the tomato plants to take a closer look. It shouldn't be too hard to knock out the patched section.

Aiming the tiny light at the fence, she stooped to inspect Daniel's handiwork. What she saw made her catch her breath in surprise. Slowly she smiled. Her smile grew until it broke into a peal of laughter that rang out through the balmy summer night.

On the other side of the fence, Piper woofed excitedly.

KARINA BOOTED UP her computer the next morning with a flourish of her wrists that reminded her so much of a flamenco dancer she stamped her heels in a rat-a-tat-tat. While the computer whizzed through its warmup, she punched in Joanne's telephone number.

Instead of beginning work as she usually did while on the phone, Karina swiveled back and forth in her chair, gazing absently out the window. She smiled to herself and hummed the light, jazzy tune that had been playing on the radio as she'd drifted off to sleep the night before.

"Hello? Karina?" A voice broke through her reverie. "I can hear you humming. Speak, woman."

"Hi, Jo." Karina's smile became a grin. "You wouldn't believe what he did!"

"Ross the Boss?"

"No, Daniel."

"It must be good from the sound of rapture in your voice."

"He put a *door* in the fence where Piper's hole used to be."

"A door?"

"It's got little hinges and a latch."

"Cute."

"I can open it and shut it anytime I want. I mean, face it, spaniels aren't the brightest of dogs."

"Last week you swore he was a prodigy."

"I know, but no dog can resist a hole in a fence. Or a garden full of fresh dirt."

"I take it Daniel's out of the doghouse, so to speak?"

"Oh, Jo, I feel terrible about the way I spoke to him. I seriously underestimated his respect for my feelings."

"Not to mention his powers of lateral thinking."

"I wish I could make it up to him somehow."

"Make him a special dinner. On second thought, not such a good idea. I know, take him *out* to dinner."

Karina's euphoria faded abruptly. Daniel was turning out to be not quite so ordinary as she'd thought. A date could be dangerous. "Gosh, Joanne, I don't know...."

"You could use the occasion to set those ground rules," Joanne suggested helpfully.

"Hmm. You have a point. That sort of thing should be done in a neutral atmosphere. But what about Natalie?" she said, feeling compelled to create obstacles.

"I'll baby-sit."

"Didn't you say Peter's going on another field camp soon? I'm sure you'd rather spend your last few evenings together."

"This is more important."

Karina sat up straight, pulling the cord taut. "We've been through this, Jo. Don't start matchmaking again."

"Karina, how could you think such a thing?"

In the background, a child began to wail. "No, you're not having chocolate milk on your porridge. Sorry, Karina, not you. Although, come to think of it..." Joanne's tone became faintly accusing. "Julie only started asking for chocolate milk on her cereal after you were over for breakfast two Saturdays ago."

"Gee, Joanne, gotta run...."

"Karina!"

"Yes?"

"Better give him plenty of warning."

"Naturally. Daniel's not the spontaneous type."

BUT WHEN IT CAME right down to it, Karina couldn't find quite the right moment to mention dinner to Daniel. The further they got from their standoff in the kitchen and her discovery of Daniel's handiwork, the harder it became to call the invitation either an apology or a thank-you—especially as she'd already done both.

The closer Saturday came, the more it started to seem as if she'd be asking for a date. She wasn't, of course, but he might think she was. At least until she explained. And explanations were always so embarrassing.

If only it would just sort of happen on the spur of the moment. She preferred spontaneous events, anyway. If you planned too far ahead, expectations tended to reach mythic proportions.

By the time Saturday morning rolled around she was convinced it was a disastrous idea. But when she called Joanne to cancel, Joanne wasn't home. How could any-one exist without an answering machine? Karina won-dered as she hung up the phone after another fruitless attempt to contact her friend.

Now it was Saturday evening. Dinner was over and Natalie was upstairs getting ready for bed. Karina wan-dered into the living room, where Daniel was drinking a cup of coffee and reading a book. It was a thick, hard-cover book, one she felt certain had very small print. The kind of book that gave her a headache.

Karina sank into a chair opposite and watched him from under her lashes while she flipped idly through an arts magazine. He certainly had interesting bone struc-ture with that high-bridged nose and those prominent cheekbones. She liked the way his eyebrows peaked at the corners of his eyes, then drifted away in little wings to his temples. And his mouth curved up at the corners even when he wasn't smiling. And he didn't smile very often.

Why was she finding it so difficult to ask him out for the evening? She wasn't a shy person. And it wasn't as though she had any special feelings for him.

Daniel tucked a leather bookmark in the shape of a

gum leaf between the pages and got up. "Think I'll check on Natalie."

Karina glanced at her watch. Almost seven. Joanne was due any minute. Well, whatever happened after that would certainly be spontaneous.

Even though she was waiting for it, Karina jumped when the doorbell rang. "I'll get it," she called, and hurried past Daniel into the hall. No telling what Joanne might blurt out if he opened the door.

Daniel paused, his hand on the banister. One eyebrow disappeared into a lock of chestnut hair that had fallen over his forehead. "Big date?"

Breathless, she managed a nonchalant shrug. "Just Joanne."

Karina waited until he'd climbed the stairs and disappeared into Natalie's room before she opened the door. "Where have you been?" she exclaimed to Joanne. "I've been calling all day."

Joanne entered with her usual bustle of bags and layers of extraneous clothing. "We took the kids to Sealand and then for a pizza. All ready for your big night out with Daniel?"

"Shhh. I haven't asked him."

"What do you mean you haven't asked him!"

"I just couldn't. Anyway, it's too late now. Dinner is best for talking, and we've already had dinner."

Joanne shoved both hands into her hair and pulled it into a frizz. "Karina Peterson! Peter leaves the day after tomorrow, and I left him all alone tonight just so I could baby-sit. You get right up there and speak to Daniel."

"Come on, Joanne. You know you only offered to baby-sit because you're trying to matchmake. It won't work. Anyway, I can't think of anything to say at this late hour that sounds plausible."

"*You* at a loss for words? I don't believe it. Just tell him you're going out and you want some company."

"What if he gets the wrong impression? He might think I like him."

"What a catastrophe. Go."

"It's all very well for you," Karina argued in hushed tones. "He isn't your tenant. The fence incident is all but forgotten. Best to let sleeping dogs lie."

"Sleeping dogs. Very funny. What's the big deal? You've never had a problem asking anyone to go out before. It's not as if you're asking him to *marry* you."

"Will you keep your voice down? Go home. Peter needs you."

"Daniel needs *you*. Think about it. He's all alone in a new country with only a child for company. Do you think he wants to spend another night hanging around the house? Would *you?*"

Karina opened her mouth in denial, then shut it again. "Maybe that's what's making him so tense."

Joanne put her big straw bag down on the floor beside the hall table and started to peel off her jacket. "He's tense?"

"Yes. I assumed he was fretting over his brother, but maybe he just needs to get out. He's hardly put a foot outside the yard since he got here."

"See? That's it for sure."

Karina pushed back her hair with both hands and nodded. "Okay, I'll do it."

She ran up the stairs. Just as she cleared the landing, Daniel stepped out of Natalie's room. Karina pulled up short, her nose inches from his chest.

"Daniel! Hi. You're coming out with me tonight."

He gazed down at her with a quizzical smile. "Beg your pardon?"

Karina took a small step back and tried to ignore the uncharacteristic fluttering in her stomach. "I mean, would you like to go out? Get out of the house for a while?"

"I can't leave Natalie."

"Joanne will baby-sit."

Karina squirmed. Daniel was staring at her as though wondering how to say no as kindly as possible. "I meant to take you out to dinner as a way of saying sorry for our little blowup the other night," she continued. "And to thank you for fixing the fence the way you did. But I...well...I didn't quite get around to it. Say you'll come. We need to talk."

Daniel glanced at Natalie's door and back at Karina's animated face. She was right about needing to talk. And anything would be better than another night sitting around the house, brooding. Besides, Karina had seemed a little tense this week. If she wanted an escort, maybe he ought to be a sport about it.

"Okay. What did you have in mind?"

Karina's smile lit her eyes as she twirled away to her bedroom. "Let me surprise you."

DANIEL TILTED HIS JAW and ran the electric razor over his skin as he eyed himself in the bathroom mirror. Granted, Karina's excitement was infectious, but he was surprised at how much he was looking forward to going out with her.

His hand stilled. Was this a date? Nah, he thought, moving the shaver under his chin in short, quick sweeps. It was an apology or a thank-you. Neither was necessary but women were funny that way—they always wanted to even the score. Still, an evening out with Karina could be fun. Daniel began to whistle along with the transistor radio in the bathroom cabinet.

He'd finished washing up, changed his clothes and was chatting to Joanne in the living room when he heard Karina's footsteps on the stairs. Suddenly he found it impossible to focus on what Joanne was saying about primary schools.

He twisted in his chair for a glimpse of Karina. Then she came swinging through the arched doorway and his powers of concentration deserted him completely.

Her glossy, dark hair swirled around bare shoulders, and a short, flouncy skirt swished against her thighs. She came to a halt in the middle of the room, fiddling with the clasp on a silver charm bracelet and chattering excitedly.

"This is going to be great. You won't regret going out tonight, Daniel, I promise. Darn this clasp, I really must take it to the jeweler. I hope you're wearing comfortable shoes."

Daniel rose to his feet. Karina snapped the clasp shut and glanced up. He saw surprise flicker in her eyes and instinctively reached up to adjust the scrap of bright red fabric below his jaw. "It's a bow tie."

Karina laughed, a high, musical sound. "I can see that. I love it. It's so…debonair."

Daniel grinned. The woman had taste. Turning to Joanne, he said, "I'll call in about an hour to see if Natalie's okay."

"Don't worry about a thing," Joanne replied, making little shooing motions toward the door. "She'll be fine."

Daniel held open the front door and Karina floated past on a cloud of some delicious scent that reminded him of a tropical garden. "Comfortable shoes?" he said. "Are we going bush walking?"

CHAPTER FIVE

"BALLROOM DANCING," Karina informed him as they picked their way through the ballroom of the Empress Hotel to an empty table beside the dance floor. She glanced at him as he pulled out her chair, watching closely for signs of bolting. Not everyone cared for ballroom dancing.

Across the vast, high-ceilinged room, the band was tuning up, a discordant medley of horns and strings interspersed with impromptu bars of Latin rhythms. Under the table, Karina's feet twitched eagerly in their blue satin pumps.

Daniel caught the attention of a passing waiter and ordered drinks, white wine for her and lager for himself. His gaze swung back to Karina. "Did you think I wouldn't like dancing?"

She smiled and shrugged, flicking her hair off her shoulders. "I didn't know. It seemed easier to keep you in the dark than hog-tie you and drag you here. Do you mind very much?"

"Not at all." He gave her one of his rare smiles, a tantalizing glimpse of white teeth against tanned skin.

Ground rules, she reminded herself. She was here to set ground rules. But before she could organize her thoughts, Daniel spoke again.

"You've seemed a little upset this week," he said. "I hope you're not still annoyed about the fence."

Karina laughed. "I love what you did with the fence. It's like something out of *Alice in Wonderland*." She fiddled with a coaster. "But if we're going to share living space for a while, we need to talk about arrangements and expectations."

"You don't want to be tied to meals or other domestic events," he said, leaning back in his chair. "I got the message the other night."

"It's just that my schedule is so erratic," she said quickly. "I often work late, or I go out for a meal with friends."

"You don't have to explain. I don't necessarily want to be tied to a routine, either. I cook because I enjoy it and because I want Natalie to eat properly. You'll find out when you have kids of your own someday."

Karina felt a familiar jab of annoyance. "Why does everyone assume that I'm going to have kids?"

His eyebrows rose. "Won't you? I got the impression you liked children."

"I do, but…I'm committed to my career."

"That doesn't preclude a family, surely?"

"Now you sound like Joanne." To her relief, the opening bars of a lively waltz began to filter through the ballroom, putting an end to the conversation. Karina glanced at the couples straying onto the dance floor and back to Daniel, her body already starting to move.

He rose from his seat. "Shall we?"

"Yes!" She led the way to a clear spot on the polished hardwood dance floor. Daniel caught her hand from behind, turning her to face him. He put his other arm around her waist and drew her closer.

Okay, so his face wasn't quite as ordinary as she'd thought when they'd first met. Interesting, intelligent and kind, yes. But not what you'd call handsome. Not the kind of face a woman saw in her dreams at night.

No sir, no way.

Around them people had begun to dance, but Daniel was still gazing at her, a slight frown on his face. With a stab of compunction, she realized maybe he didn't know how to dance.

"This is a waltz," she explained matter-of-factly. "You go forward one step and I go back—like so. To the side one step, and close." She moved as she spoke, pulling him along with her.

A tiny smile appeared at the corners of his mouth. She beamed back at him encouragingly. "I'm so glad you're not one of those men with a massive male ego who can't stand to be instructed by a woman. One, two, three, one, two, three… See? You're getting the hang of it already."

"I have a good teacher," he said, still smiling. They took a few more turns before he said, "Mind if I lead for a while?"

Karina nodded. She mustn't be patronizing. Men were men, after all.

Daniel raised their clasped hands a notch higher. His arm tightened around her waist. Suddenly his grip seemed both expert and possessive. He gave her the tiniest of winks.

Then he whirled her away across the dance floor.

Karina's astonished grin turned to a smile of delight as they whizzed past other couples, turning, turning to the lilting strains of "The Merry Widow."

He could dance! She laughed with pure pleasure. Boy, could he dance!

The waltz slid into a mamba. Then a cha-cha, followed by a tango. Karina had to work to keep up with Daniel as he led her in variations she'd never seen before. Through it all, the faint, enigmatic smile never left his face.

The band took a break and Karina and Daniel made their way back to the table. "Why didn't you tell me you could dance so well?" she demanded, laughing.

Daniel shrugged. "You didn't ask."

"And I thought I had you all figured out. Wait a minute," she said as he was about to sit down. "Your tie is crooked." She reached up and straightened it for him, conscious of the raspy warmth of his jaw where her knuckles brushed his skin. "That's better."

"Thanks." His eyes met hers.

She quickly took her seat. Daniel seemed different tonight, more dominating, more…physical. And his smile was positively lethal when he got around to it. If she *were* looking for a man…

"Where did you learn those moves?" she asked, striving for an offhand tone.

Daniel leaned back in his chair and crossed one ankle over his knee. "Francine and I were in the state championships three years running. Strictly amateur, of course."

"There's nothing amateur about those fancy dips and spins. I feel like a complete idiot." She held back her damp hair and fanned her neck with the makeshift ponytail.

"You're an excellent dancer. Plenty of natural rhythm." His gaze strayed to her bare shoulders. "You look warm."

Self-conscious, she let her hair fall. "Was Francine your wife?" She hoped he wouldn't think she was prying again, but she was curious about the woman.

He gave a curt nod, then glanced around the room.

"Never a waiter when you need one. I'll go get some water."

Karina watched him weave through the tables toward the bar. Darn, she'd done it again. Where did natural curiosity stop and prying begin?

Francine was probably blond like Natalie, with legs like Ginger Rogers. Karina imagined Francine and Daniel coming home after a night of dancing, laughing and talking as they climbed the stairs to their bedroom....

An icy drop of water splashed across Karina's bare arm as Daniel deposited a jug of ice water on the table in front of her. "The waiter's bringing more wine and beer in a moment," he said, and filled a glass for her.

"Thanks." She reached for her water glass and her fingers brushed against his. The touch brought her daydream flooding back, and she snatched her hand away. What had gotten into her, fantasizing like that about Daniel? Somewhere between the staircase and the bedroom the woman's hair had become dark brown like her own.

He drank deeply of his water, draining the glass. "Did you ever find someone to teach you golf?" he asked, lifting the jug to refill his glass.

Karina pushed her hair behind her ears, a few strands catching in her dangly silver earrings. "I'm not sure I'll be going to the tournament. It turns out only *male* executives are invited. Can you believe it?"

Daniel removed his jacket and leaned back in his seat, regarding her thoughtfully. "It sounded to me like you don't even play golf. Why do you want to go so badly?"

"It's not golf I want to play, but politics."

"Ah."

She took a sip of water. "You can't beat 'em if you can't join 'em."

"The question is, why do you want to?"

Karina traced swirling patterns in the film of condensation on her glass. The answer was simple. Without the prospect of a family to raise, she had nothing to mark her progress through life except rungs on the career ladder. That was enough. It had to be.

"When I started at SignCity," she said, "I was at the bottom of the pecking order. Last one hired, first one fired. I couldn't afford to be vulnerable to every economic downturn that came along, so I became the resident expert on computer graphics. That was eight years ago. These days I'm the one that does the hiring and firing."

The waiter appeared with their drinks. Daniel waited until he'd gone, then reached for his beer. "And now you want to climb even higher."

She sipped at her wine. "It's the logical next step." What else was there for her to do?

He gave her an odd look. "Somehow I never thought logic would be your guiding light."

She smiled. "Maybe I put that badly. I need a challenge or I'll stagnate." And a reliable income because she would always be on her own.

"That I can understand. Once I've mastered something, I like to move on to something new."

"In a way, I envy you, working for yourself," she said. "No one to answer to, no one stabbing you in the back, no one taking your ideas and getting the credit."

He shrugged. "I just prefer working on my own."

She shuddered. "I'd go bananas."

"Hire someone. Form your own company. There's got to be a happy medium. If you don't like what you're doing, try something else."

Karina smiled and shook her head. "I do like what

I'm doing. It's the system I can't handle. So far I've gotten ahead on my own terms, but I'm up against the big boys now. Sometimes I wonder if it's all worth it.''

''You mean,'' he said, one eyebrow lifting, ''being committed to a company that's not as committed to you?''

She made a face. He'd summed it up in a nutshell, and for once she couldn't think of a snappy comeback. ''I hate it when you do that.''

''What?'' he asked. ''Make a valid point?''

''No,'' she said, laughing. ''Shut me up so effectively.''

He smiled. ''I'm not trying to shut you up. I just can't help but notice certain inconsistencies in your life.''

Karina laughed again, unperturbed. ''That's all part of my capricious nature. Being consistent is boring.''

''No one could accuse you of that.'' He raised his glass. ''To inconsistency.''

''To surprises,'' Karina added, thinking of his prowess on the dance floor. She clinked her glass against his.

The music started up again and she was on her feet in an instant. ''How about showing me that fancy little twist in the lambada again,'' she said, pulling him onto the dance floor.

''Liked that, did you?'' he said. ''I came up with it myself.''

DANIEL CAME QUIETLY out of Natalie's room and shut the door. Moonlight streamed through the window above the stairwell, flooding the second-floor landing with silvery light. He heard Karina say good-night to Joanne and start upstairs.

She appeared before him, her blue dress looking dark

grey in the moonlight. He nodded at the door he'd just closed and put a finger to his lips. "Nattie's fast asleep."

Karina bent to slip off one shoe, then the other, and stood with them dangling from her fingers. "Thanks for coming out tonight."

"It did me good," Daniel replied. "And I enjoyed dancing with you." The faint music issuing from Karina's bedroom made him aware of the midnight quiet of the rest of the house. They were whispering so as not to wake Natalie, and it seemed to lend a clandestine air to their conversation.

"I'm glad we got everything sorted out," Karina said, but she made no move to go to her room.

"We didn't decide anything about meals."

"We can work it out tomorrow."

"There you go, procrastinating again. How about I cook enough for three and you can eat if you're here, or not, as the case may be."

"That's generous of you. I'll cook sometimes, too."

"Okay. Just give me some advance warning."

The shadows around her mouth deepened in a smile. "Why? So you can run out for a hamburger first? Believe it or not, I can cook when I put my mind to it."

He grinned. "I believe you, though millions wouldn't. I meant so I wouldn't start dinner. I'm not as easy as I look, you know."

"You're easy to get along with." She bit her lip, looking as though she wished she hadn't said that. "Did you ever get in touch with your brother?"

He pulled off the bow tie hanging loosely around his open shirt collar. "I talked to him."

"Great. Are you getting together with him soon?"

Daniel glanced away. "He's pretty busy right now."

Karina gazed at him in silence for a moment, then

crossed the landing to sit on the top step. "Come over here and tell me all about it." When he didn't move, she patted the floor beside her. "Come on. I can't stand up any longer. My feet are killing me."

He wasn't looking for sympathy, but her matter-of-fact tone was a powerful draw. For ten years he'd never confided in anyone. Suddenly he felt an overwhelming need to unburden himself.

He went and sat beside her on the step, breathing in the scent of jasmine that clung to her warm skin. With her rosy coloring and smile like sunshine, he'd always thought of her as a creature of daylight. But now, with moonlight silvering the smooth curve of her bare shoulder and shadows darkening her hair to black, she looked like a goddess of the night.

She touched his arm and the silver charms on her bracelet tinkled faintly. "What caused the feud between you and your brother?"

He leaned against the banister, half facing her. "Before I married her, Francine was Brian's fiancée."

"Oh!" Karina's eyes widened. "What happened?"

"It's a long story…."

"I'm listening."

"Brian was living in Vancouver at the time," Daniel began slowly. "I knew he was seeing someone, but we were all surprised when he announced he was engaged."

"Why surprised?" Karina stretched her legs along the step below.

His gaze dropped to her thighs, and for a moment his mind went blank. "Sorry, what did you say?"

Karina tugged her skirt lower. "Why were you surprised your brother was engaged?"

Daniel returned his gaze to her face. "Brian was always very popular with women. I expected him to play the field for years.''

She shrugged. ''He must have been in love.''

''That's the obvious conclusion....''

''But?''

''I don't know. Sometimes he acted so offhand with her. Anyway, the weekend he brought Francine home to meet my parents, I came, too. They were all sitting around the living room having a drink before dinner when I arrived.'' He paused, recalling that fateful moment he'd walked through the door.

''I took one look at Francine—'' He twirled the bow tie between his fingers, groping for words. ''Maybe it was the way *she* looked at *me,* but I knew immediately something big was going to happen. I didn't know whether it would be wonderful or terrible. Turned out it was a bit of both.''

''So it was love at first sight?''

Daniel was silent, considering how to answer. How could he describe his feelings at the time, tainted as they were with all that came after?

''I was attracted to her immediately but I tried not to show it because she was Brian's fiancée.''

''And she was attracted, too?''

''Not openly flirtatious, but she kept looking at me when no one else was watching. I tried to ignore it....''

''But...?''

''I'd barely turned twenty-two. Francine was almost two years older and light-years more sophisticated. It was just friendly banter at first. I never intended to get serious.''

He passed a hand across his forehead, wishing he could wipe the memories from his mind. At what point could he have stopped the train of events that had thrown all their lives off track? Would he do things differently now if he could? But then Natalie would never have been born. And that was unthinkable.

"That night," he continued, "Francine knocked on my door on the pretext of lending me a book we'd talked about at dinner. She was in her nightgown. I was half undressed. Brian's room was right next door but she didn't seem to care."

"What happened?"

"Nothing, really. She sat on my bed and we talked. I can't even remember what about—the book, most likely. But the thoughts going through my head should have been X-rated. I lay awake all night. The next day I took off before breakfast. I couldn't face Brian after what I'd been thinking about his fiancée."

Karina pulled her knees up and propped her elbows on them, cupping her chin in the palms of her hands. "So, how did you two eventually get together?"

"Francine came to Victoria on her own one day and looked me up. I was flattered, I can't deny it. We had lunch and walked around Beacon Hill Park till dusk, holding hands like a couple of honeymooners." He paused. "She didn't take the ferry back to Vancouver that night."

Why was he telling Karina all this? And what would she think of him when he was done? He contemplated glossing over the rest, but now he'd started he couldn't stop. If she thought worse of him for what he'd done, well, he'd just have to bear it.

"After that we saw each other every chance we could. I wanted to tell Brian about us, but Francine kept saying she should be the one to do it. Like a fool, I listened to her."

"Did she ever tell him?"

"No. Finally I couldn't stand sneaking around any-more; it made what we had seem so cheap. So I went to Brian and told him I was in love with Francine."

Daniel stared into the shadows, his cheeks burning at the memory of that humiliating scene. "He just laughed in my face. I was furious he didn't take me seriously. After that, I thought, why bother?"

"He must have been shocked when you two suddenly got married."

Daniel nodded. "Three days before their wedding was due to take place, Francine and I eloped. We sent him a telegram from Melbourne." He paused and ran a shaky hand through his hair. "Brian's never forgiven me or willingly spoken to me since."

Karina was silent. He heard only the faint rustle of her dress as she leaned her back against the wall. "I can see why he'd be angry," she said at last, then reached out to squeeze his arm. "But you mustn't feel so bad. It couldn't have been easy for you."

The understanding in her voice made him feel slightly less grim. At least Karina didn't despise him. "It wasn't. I had to choose between my brother and the woman I honestly believed to be my partner for life."

"Choices can be hard to make," she agreed quietly, tucking her hand back in her lap. "And consequences even harder to accept. 'Partner for life' has such a solid, dependable ring to it, yet it's so rarely true these days."

He nodded. "If Francine had lived, I doubt we'd be together now."

"What happened to her, Daniel? How did she die?"

"Leukemia. It happened so fast we hardly had time to adjust before she was gone. Natalie took it really hard. She was only three and couldn't understand why Mommy wasn't ever coming back."

The image of his tiny daughter's bewildered, tear-stained face floated in the darkness before him. His throat closed up and he went silent, remembering.

Then he glanced at Karina. Her head had dropped forward, her long, dark hair spilling over her bare arms and hiding her face. His hand hovered over her shoulder, not quite touching. "Karina?" he said gently. "What is it?"

She lifted her head, rubbing at the corners of her eyes with the heel of her hand. "Nothing. It's just…poor Natalie."

"I know. She's suffered so much. I worry about where she'd live if anything happened to me."

"Relatives?"

He locked his hands around one knee and shook his head. "Her grandmother in Australia is getting too old to look after a child. My parents head south every winter in their mobile home. Betty and Kevin have enough children of their own. The only person Natalie could go to is Brian. But he has to want that, too. I *have* to make peace with my brother. For Natalie's sake, as well as my own."

"Unless you were to marry again."

"I want to, when the right woman comes along."

Their eyes met for a flicker of a second before Karina looked away. Marriage, Daniel reflected, was one helluva conversation stopper.

Her face still averted, Karina began to hum softly to the faint music coming from her open bedroom door.

"Don't you ever turn that off?" he asked.

"I program it to go off long after I'm asleep." She covered a yawn with her hand and rose to her feet. "It's late."

Daniel rose, too, but he didn't want to say good-night. "One last dance?"

Karina looked up at Daniel, intending to tell him she was too tired. But the slanting crest of one high cheekbone shone in the moonlight, and the shadows made a mystery of the hollow at the base of his throat. Compelled by reasons she didn't want to examine, she nodded.

Daniel put his arm around her waist, drawing her to him. She started to pull back, but he held her firmly, nestling his chin next to her temple. Turning her face into the hollow of his neck, she breathed in his scent, cotton and warm skin with just the faintest hint of a woodsy aftershave. It seemed hard to believe that only a week ago she hadn't even known he existed.

They slow-danced around the landing, moving in small circles. Karina was aware of him in a way she hadn't been at the ballroom—the heat of his body, his thighs brushing hers, the firm pressure of his hand on her back.

"Thanks for listening," he said, his breath ruffling the hair at her temple.

She swallowed and nodded, not trusting her voice.

His hand moved on her back, and she could feel each of his fingertips like a tiny caress. Her breasts tingled against his chest; their lower bodies pressed together, moving sensuously to the music.

He was aroused. And so was she.

This was not good.

Struggling against instinct, she pulled back until her body no longer touched his. "Daniel?"

"Hmm?" His eyes were closed.

"There's another house rule I haven't mentioned."

"What is it?"

"The landlady never gets romantically involved with her tenants."

He opened his eyes and looked at her. "Why not?"

"It just doesn't work."

He stopped dancing and just held her. "Are you saying you don't like me?"

"I'm not saying that at all."

"Then what's the problem?"

"Living in the same house would be too awkward when the romance is over."

"Natalie and I are only staying here temporarily. Besides, how do you know it would end?"

"It just won't work," she insisted.

Daniel gazed back at her in silence, and now she wished for enough light to read his expression. Part of her, God help her, wanted him to override her arguments with a kiss. And more.

Instead, his fingers slipped away from her waist, brushing her bare arms as he slowly released her. "Good night, Karina."

"Good night."

Deprived of his touch, Karina fled to her room. She undressed, slipped beneath the covers and, shivering, tucked her knees up to her chest. The sheets felt cold after the warmth of Daniel's embrace.

Her bed, like her heart, was a lonely place.

CHAPTER SIX

KARINA GAZED INTO Natalie's shining eyes and gently tweaked one pink cheek. "Natalie Bowen," she said in a large and important voice, "I hereby declare you healthy as a horse, strong as an ox and fit as a fiddle."

Natalie giggled and danced in a circle around Karina's latest papier-mâché creation, a prancing unicorn clothed in swirls of green and ivory, peacock blue and crimson.

"Can I help? Please?" The little girl plunged her bare arms elbow deep into the basin of paste.

"Hang on," Karina said. "You can help, but you have to do exactly as I tell you."

"I will, I promise." Natalie pulled a dripping strip of fabric from the basin. "Where should I put this piece?"

"Here, on the back." Karina guided her hands. "Smooth it down. That's right."

Natalie's small fingers worked diligently at flattening the fabric over the wire mesh. "Why does it have so many colors? Unicorns are supposed to be white."

"White is made up of all the colors mixed together," Karina replied. "And I like colors."

"I do, too," Natalie agreed, nodding vigorously. "Once I painted all my arms red and all my legs blue with the paints Grandma gave me for my birthday."

Karina suppressed a smile and resisted the urge to ask how many arms and legs she'd had at the time. "Was your dad impressed?"

"He was not."

Karina turned at the sound of Daniel's voice. Behind his attempt at a frown she could see a smile lurking. His collarless white shirt contrasted sharply with his tan, and the lightweight suit jacket over clean, pressed blue jeans gave him a casual business air. Under one arm he carried a large portfolio.

"Daddy!" Natalie cried and launched herself at him.

"Steady on, Nat. You're as sticky as a fly on a bushranger's back." He let the portfolio slide to the floor and grasped her by the arms. With her hands well away from his jacket, he gave her a quick hug.

One arm around his daughter, he glanced over her head at Karina. "Mornin'."

"Hi." Unexpected confusion brought heat to her cheeks. Dropping her gaze, she stripped the excess paste from the piece of fabric in her hand and concentrated on shaping the unicorn's spiral horn.

When she looked up a few minutes later, Daniel was at the table, pouring cornflakes into a bowl. The portfolio was propped against the wall at his side. *A carpenter with an art portfolio?*

"Come and have breakfast, Nattie," he said. "Now that you're better, we've got things to do."

"Karina made me some toast," Natalie replied. "I don't want to go to the stupid old bank."

"Now, Natalie. There's also a house for rent I want to look at."

"She can stay with me for a few hours," Karina suggested.

Daniel's gaze collided with hers and bounced away. "Aren't you working today?"

Oh, great, Karina thought. They got a little carried away while dancing and suddenly they couldn't even look at each other. "No, this year I decided to spread my vacation out by taking a few days off here and there."

"Thanks for the offer, but I need to buy Nattie some new shoes for school while we're out." He paused. "That toast wasn't covered in peanut butter and mayonnaise, I hope."

Karina turned indignantly, then noticed his amused expression. "Specialty items are restricted to the dinner menu," she replied with a grin.

He smiled back at her, and suddenly everything was all right again. They were friends and roomies.

"What have you got in there?" she asked, nodding at the portfolio.

Daniel scooped another spoonful of cornflakes. "Have a look."

Karina wiped her hands on a towel and went to clear a spot on the table, only to find it was already clean. She ought to be paying Daniel, she thought as she laid the portfolio flat and untwisted the string that held the two halves together. She opened it up.

Sketches of fine furniture met her gaze—dining tables, bureaus, chests, desks, beds. Beside each sketch was a photograph of the finished product. Elegant and unique, the designs would suit any style of decor, from rustic to sophisticated.

She turned to Daniel, astonished. "I had no idea! Are these all your designs?"

He nodded, his mouth full of cornflakes. Then he swallowed. "Design and workmanship. Didn't I tell you I made furniture?"

"No. I thought you did kitchen cabinets or something." She glanced back at the photographs. "These are works of art! What kind of wood is that?"

"Jarrah, mostly. That's red gum," he said, reaching across the table to point out a red-hued chest of drawers. "I shipped a container containing both types a couple of months before I left Melbourne. It should arrive any day."

Karina studied the photograph of a jarrah bed frame, admiring the smooth-grained wood and flowing lines of the headboard. The corners were rounded, yet the design, like all the others, looked clean and sharp.

"Now I see why you import your own wood," she said.

Daniel nodded. "I reckoned red gum and jarrah would be unique over here, especially since it's recycled from old woolsheds and warehouses. When I locate a source of local timber I'll incorporate it into my designs."

Karina pulled out a chair and sat down, leafing through the rest of the sketches. "You must have had a good business going in Melbourne."

"Not bad. The problem was, I got too big. And the bigger I got, the less I time I had for the woodworking. I still did the designs and a lot of the finishing, but it wasn't the same as putting my hands to raw timber and turning it into fine furniture."

Karina thought of her rise through the ranks at SignCity and nodded. "I know what you mean."

Daniel pushed his bowl away and poured a cup of coffee from the jug on the table. "In a way, my decision to come back to Victoria was opportune. A chance to sell up and start fresh. I'm going to show my portfolio around a few places, see if I can drum up some business."

She gazed at him with new respect. "It takes guts to start over. I'd like to place the first order with your new company."

Daniel paused while reaching for the blue-and-white creamer. "Seriously?"

"Yes. I've wanted to replace that old oak dining table for ages but haven't seen anything I like." She glanced back to the portfolio. "Till now."

"Fine, then," he said, looking pleased. "You could pick out one of these designs or I could do something new."

"Something new," she said. "I want my table to be one of a kind."

"Like its owner."

The quiet timbre of his voice and the intent look in his eyes jolted her into remembering the need for caution. Friends and roomies they might be, but there was a definite undercurrent of something more.

She closed the portfolio, once again avoiding his eyes. "May I have some say in the design?"

He sipped his coffee. "Just tell me what you like."

She could think of several answers for that one, none of them fit for Natalie's small ears. Grinning, she risked a glance at him. "I know you're not easy, and I suspect you're not cheap, either...."

His mouth lifted in a smile, and a spark appeared in his eyes. "You're darn right I'm not cheap."

Karina laughed. Was it her imagination or was he smiling more often lately? "Name your price."

"The unicorn, or another like it," he replied. "For Natalie."

Natalie, who had been industriously layering strips of fabric onto the unicorn's back, looked up, eyes wide. "Really?"

He nodded.

Natalie gave an excited bounce. "Goody!"

"That's not a fair exchange," Karina protested. "One

of your tables is worth far more than a papier-mâché unicorn."

He shrugged. "Nevertheless, that's my price."

"Tell you what. I'll throw in a logo design and layout for business cards. You'll be needing new ones."

"Done." He held out his hand to shake on the deal.

Karina put her hand in his. This time he didn't seem to notice the bits of paste that clung to her fingers. Palms linked, fingers clasped, his eyes held hers.

Then he pulled his hand away, absently brushing at the sticky bits. "Natalie will like having something of yours when we find our own place."

Karina stepped away, curling her fingers into her palm. Why did she keep forgetting they weren't staying? And why was she getting all moony-eyed over him all of a sudden? He'd think she was an idiot, telling him they couldn't be more than friends, then blushing and starting like a schoolgirl at the sound of his voice or the touch of his hand.

"So, where's this house you're looking at?" she asked, forcing a casual tone.

"Out near the university. Sounds like a palace, but you know what real estate blurbs are like."

"Well, don't take just anything. You're welcome to stay till you find something suitable."

"Thanks," he said, and smiled at her again.

Oh, boy. "How are you getting on there, Nattie?" she said, turning to the girl. "What a good job you're doing! Let's just smooth down this lump on his back a little. We don't want your unicorn to end up looking like a camel."

The girl looked up at her with shining eyes. "Is he really going to be mine? Really truly?"

"Absolutely. Can you think of a magical name for him?"

Natalie's face scrunched up as she thought. "I know! I'll call him Merlin."

"Perfect." Karina pulled a wet strip of cloth from the basin and laid it over the unicorn's nose.

"Karina?"

She glanced across at Daniel, who was stirring sugar into his second cup of coffee. "Yes?"

"I just had a thought about your golf tournament."

She perked up. "Oh?"

"Why not go as someone's guest?"

"I can't go with anyone from SignCity," she said, her shoulders slumping. "They're all married. It wouldn't look good no matter how innocent it really was."

"Then what about an executive from another company?"

"I thought of that. I've already talked to a guy I know at Westholm Foods, but he's taking his girlfriend. Then there's Jason Doncaster from our Vancouver office. But he broke his leg water skiing, so he's out."

Daniel rocked back in his chair, frowning. "Are all the companies taking part affiliated with SignCity?"

"No," Karina said, shaping the unicorn's nostrils. "It's pretty much a free-for-all. But I don't know any male execs outside the Franklin Group of Companies."

Daniel rose and took his dishes to the sink. Then he leaned one shoulder against the frame between the rooms and gazed at her.

She glanced at him. "What?"

"Whoever you get should be someone you can trust."

Yes, Karina thought, gazing into his trustworthy hazel eyes. Technically speaking, he was CEO of his own company, small as it was. Immediately she dismissed the idea. He'd never do it; he didn't play golf, and, of course, the tournament was by invitation only, unless...

"Ideally, your escort should be a friend," Daniel continued, and she noticed he was watching her closely. "Someone with your interests at heart."

He meant *himself,* she thought with a quickening of her pulse. Nope, still no good. After what she'd said last night, asking him to go away for the weekend would send exactly the kind of mixed message she wanted to avoid.

Then another idea occurred to her. "That's it!" she exclaimed. "Daniel, you're brilliant."

His eyebrows lifted into the shock of hair that fell across his forehead. "What are you thinking?"

"What you said just now about how my escort should be a friend. I know just the person."

He pushed away from the door frame. "You do?"

"Yes. An old high school buddy of mine recently joined the Calgary office. I know he's not married, because he just got divorced. I'll give him a call first thing Monday morning."

He took a step toward her. "I meant *me.*"

"You?" Flustered, she backed away. "Remember what we talked about last night?"

"I meant I'd come just as a friend." He held her gaze. "What are you so worried about, Karina?"

"Nothing. It's just..." She laughed. "Wouldn't we be a pair, two nongolfers like us? We'd spend all our time trying to hit our way out of sand traps and I'd never get my schmoozing done. Thanks, Daniel, but I'll call my friend in Calgary."

"Maybe you're right." His smile seemed strained.

"Excuse me. I'm going to give Brian a quick call before I go out."

Daniel plodded upstairs. So what if she hadn't taken him up on his offer? He didn't even like golf. Anyway, hadn't he decided last night to back off?

Opening his address book to Brian's number, Daniel sat on the bed and dialed. He waited, tapping his foot soundlessly on the dhurrie carpet that covered most of the polished hardwood floor. With the palm trees gone and only a set of framed Balinese batiks decorating the walls, he felt more at home in the spacious, airy room.

Brian picked up the phone on the second ring. "Hello?"

"Hi, Brian. It's Daniel."

"When are you going to get the message, Danny boy? I don't want to talk to you."

"Look, I know you have a right to be angry," Daniel said quickly before Brian could hang up. "Even Karina thinks so. But your niece doesn't deserve this kind of treatment."

"Karina? Who's Karina?"

"She's the woman I'm staying with," Daniel explained impatiently. "The thing is, Natalie—"

"What is she—three, four years old?" Brian asked in a bored drawl.

Daniel's jaw clenched. "She just turned six."

"Is that so? Tell me more about Karina. She must be a very perceptive lady to take my side in the matter."

"I never said she took your side—"

"No point splitting hairs. What's she like?"

What possible difference could it make to Brian what Karina was like? Daniel thought irritably. "She's a graphic artist. Very talented. Bright, bouncy—"

"Sounds like a rubber ball." Brian's interest seemed to fade.

It was the perfect opportunity to drop the subject, but somehow, now he couldn't. "She's nothing like a rubber ball," he said. "She's got beautiful eyes. And hair like a cloud at midnight." *A cloud at midnight? Where the hell had that come from?*

"You sound completely besotted, Danny boy." Amusement tinged Brian's voice. "Had her in the sack yet?"

"She's my landlady," Daniel snapped. "And a friend. That's all."

"Steady on, Sir Lancelot. I wouldn't dream of tarnishing the lady's honor. Look, I've got to run. Call me again next week. I might have a minute or two to spare."

Daniel slammed down the phone, but not before he heard his brother's derisive chuckle. Now Brian was playing games with him. Daniel was tempted to call him back and tell him what a jerk he was.

But knowing Brian, that was exactly what his brother wanted him to do; lose his temper, making it Daniel's fault their feud remained an open, festering sore. Well, Daniel had no intention of becoming a martyr to his brother's nasty disposition.

Then he remembered Natalie and he dropped his head into his hands. He would call again and again if necessary.

Not only for Natalie, though. For himself, as well, to right the wrong he'd done. Somewhere inside the supercilious bastard he'd helped create was his brother. Somehow Daniel had to reach him. Then maybe he'd find that small piece of himself that had been missing all these years.

He rose slowly and went downstairs, his footsteps

heavy on the carpeted staircase, an almost physical pain in his chest from the mixture of anger and guilt he felt toward his brother. In the doorway to the meals area he paused and jerked his head at Natalie. "Come on, Nattie. Sooner we go, sooner it's done."

"But, Daddy…"

"Now!" he barked, and turned on his heel. Meekly Natalie ran after him.

Seconds later Karina heard the front door slam. Fury welled up in her, a protective instinct for that blameless child and her agonized father. Something would have to be done about that brother of his.

She reached for the phone book on the kitchen table and started flipping through it. Abruptly she pushed it away, appalled at herself. What she was contemplating was interference on a grand scale.

Not interference, she argued with herself, *helping.*

He won't like it, a little voice in her head warned.

It's for his own good.

He'll be angry, and rightly so.

The end justifies the means.

That's what the Nazis said.

"Oh, be quiet," she muttered and opened the white pages.

There were three Brian Bowens in the book. The first lived across the Gorge in Esquimalt, home to the navy and most of the industry in the area. Intuition told her that wasn't Daniel's brother. She dialed number two and waited while the phone rang.

"Hello," she said when a man answered. "This may sound a little strange, but do you have a brother named Daniel?"

"May I ask who's calling?"

Those few words were enough to answer her question.

In spite of Daniel's slight Australian accent, the two men sounded almost identical.

"I'm sorry. You don't know me. I'm Karina Peterson."

"Ah, Karina," he replied more warmly. "The woman Daniel's living with."

"The woman Daniel and his daughter are renting rooms from," she replied. She was wrong. Daniel's voice was a little deeper, Brian's a little smoother. But still pleasant.

He chuckled. "I stand corrected. To what do I owe the pleasure of your call?"

"Daniel's told me so much about you," Karina said, improvising as she went. "I know he's longing to see you again after all this time away, but it's been difficult with Natalie sick. I wondered if you'd like to come for dinner one night. Say, this Saturday?"

"Saturday? Let me check my diary."

Karina twined the cord around her finger, waiting. He'd sounded a little surprised but not antagonistic. Maybe Daniel had blown things out of proportion. It was easy to do with siblings.

"Saturday would be fine," Brian said, coming back on the line. "I hope Natalie is better. It's been so disappointing not being able to catch up with them yet. I've been very busy at work lately."

"What do you do?" Karina asked politely.

"I'm sales manager for a British car dealership."

"Really? I've got a '78 Triumph Spitfire."

"Is that so? A great little sports car, the Spitfire. Of course, we deal mostly with Rolls-Royce and Bentley, but if you ever need parts, I'm sure I could help out."

"Super."

"My pleasure. Till Saturday, then."

"Till Saturday. About seven."

Karina gave him her address and replaced the receiver, pleased with herself. Brian seemed perfectly charming and genuinely interested in getting together with Daniel. Surely it must all be an unfortunate misunderstanding.

CHAPTER SEVEN

"YOU DID WHAT!" Daniel shook his head in disbelief. Either he was losing his hearing or Karina had lost her mind.

"I invited your brother to dinner." Karina carried on calmly painting her toenails a bright copper color. "I thought you'd be pleased."

Daniel threw down his portfolio and the bundle of documents he'd collected at the bank and various government offices. Maybe he ought to be pleased but he wasn't. His only brother would barely talk to him, let alone agree to meet, yet he'd come running at the drop of a hat for Karina. Why?

He pushed aside the stirring of jealousy that sprang out of nowhere. It was absurd not to want Brian and Karina to meet, yet...

"You should have asked me first."

"Would you have said yes?"

"No."

"I don't understand you, Daniel. Brian seemed anxious to see you. Does it really matter that you weren't the one to make the arrangement?"

"That's not it at all."

"Then don't look a gift horse in the mouth." She stretched her leg and waggled her toes to dry the polish.

She *didn't* understand, Daniel realized. If Brian had

accepted so readily, he must have an ulterior motive. But she probably wouldn't believe him if he told her so.

"Do you realize you've done exactly what you didn't like me doing when I fixed your fence?" he demanded.

Her cheeks colored but she said, "Look how well that turned out. This will, too, you'll see. I thought I'd invite Joanne to even out the numbers. And, of course, Betty and Kevin. Is that okay with you?"

Daniel pushed a hand through his hair. She really thought she was helping him. "Sure, why not. The rest of you ought to be able to hold up the flagging conversation."

"Great. How did the house check out? Any good?"

"Wonderful. If you overlook the Hell's Angels living in the basement and the early Depression decor. Joanne was right, pickings are mighty slim."

He gathered up his papers to take them upstairs. "By the way, I talked to Betty earlier. She's going to be in town tomorrow with the kids. She said they'd all drop over after Kevin gets off work."

"Great. I haven't seen the baby since he was born."

Daniel turned to go, then paused. "Oh, and, Karina?"

"Yes?"

"Thanks, I guess."

She smiled. "My pleasure."

KARINA KICKED OFF her shoes and dropped her bag on the hall table. The faint whine of the power saw told her Daniel was in the garage, working. And since there was no sight or sound of Natalie, she assumed the little girl was out there, too.

Karina ran up the stairs. Betty and Kevin and their brood would be here any minute. She had just enough time to change out of her work clothes.

Sure enough, the doorbell rang as she was pulling on a pair of beige linen shorts. Quickly she buttoned up a fitted sleeveless shirt in dark purple and ran down the stairs to open the door.

"Hi, Betty! Kevin! And let's see…" she took a big breath "…Ryan, Gillian, Matthew, Cara and baby Alex. Come in! It's so good to see you all again."

The family trooped into the house, filling the foyer and spilling down the hallway.

"It's great to see you, Karina," Betty said, holding the baby carrier close to her chest. "Sorry to descend en masse, but the kids just had to meet their new cousin."

"Well, of course they did." Karina peeked through the folds of the blanket at the baby's tiny, pink face. "What a cutie! He's got your red, curly hair, Betty. And your ears, Kevin."

Kevin grinned and shook his head. "Poor kid. We'll have to get 'em fixed."

"Daniel and Natalie are out in the garage," Karina said, then turned to the jumble of kids who ranged in height from midthigh to neck-bending adolescence. "I can't believe how big you've all grown. Too big for soft drinks and chips, I'll bet."

Amid a loud chorus of nos, Karina laughingly led the way to the kitchen, trailing children like ducklings. As she entered, the back door opened and Daniel stepped inside. He saw his cousin and her family and his face creased in a wide smile.

"Betty. Great to see you." He hugged her, then broke away to grip Kevin's hand. "G'day, Kev. You've got a lot to answer for, mate."

Kevin rubbed the top of his head and chuckled. "You look like you're surviving, at any rate. How are you? It's been a long time."

"Too long. This is Nat—" Daniel glanced around. "Hang about, where's Natalie? She was right behind me a second ago." He retraced his steps and opened the door wider to reveal his daughter holding a toy koala by one paw.

He bent down and Karina heard him whisper, "It's okay, Possum. There aren't as many as it looks."

Natalie took his hand and shyly came forward. Daniel ran through the children's names for her, looking to Betty for confirmation.

"Pretty good," his cousin said, "considering Ryan was the only one born before you left for Australia."

"That's right. He was what, two or three when I left?"

"I was pregnant with Gilly, so he would have just turned three." Betty extended a small, blunt-fingered hand to Natalie. "Come here, honey, and show me your koala."

Natalie proudly brought forth the brown-and-grey stuffed toy. "His name is Blinky Bill."

"He's beautiful. And now you've got lots of cousins to play with, as well."

Kevin poked the tubby koala in the stomach with his forefinger. "Don't let this little guy eat them, though, eh? He looks like he's got an appetite."

Natalie giggled. "He only eats gum leaves."

"Speaking of food, we were about to get you kids something to eat and drink," Karina said. "Natalie, can you get the chips from the pantry?"

Natalie nodded and did as she was asked. Karina got out the soft drinks and poured the chips into a wooden salad bowl. Then she shooed all the children onto the deck. "Off you go and get acquainted."

Daniel, meanwhile, had popped the tops on a quartet of beers for the adults and handed them around.

"Brian's coming over for dinner on Saturday," Karina said to Kevin and Betty. "Will you two be able to make it?"

Kevin turned to Betty. "Isn't that the day your mother's coming in from Winnipeg?"

"*Moosejaw,*" Betty said, rolling her big green eyes. "She lives in Moosejaw."

"Moosejaw? When did she move there?"

Betty turned to Karina. "Honestly, I don't know how you put up with him at work. But he's right about my mother arriving that day. I'm sorry. I would have liked to see Brian."

Ignoring the glasses Karina had set out, Kevin took a swig of beer straight from the can. "Yeah. He hasn't been out to our place for what—?" He turned to Betty. "A couple of months?"

Betty nodded. "About that." Sounds of discontent emerged from the bundle of blankets at her feet, and the car carrier began to rock. She unclicked the straps and scooped up her baby. "Are you hungry again already, little one?"

Lifting one corner of her blouse, she positioned the baby and began to nurse. "Have you seen Brian yet, Daniel?"

Daniel took a long sip of beer. "Not yet."

"I was a little surprised you wrote to me instead of him when you were looking for a place to rent," she said. "Or are you two still not talking?"

"We're talking. Just not very nicely."

"Too bad," Kevin said. "The guy's a riot. Last Christmas he dressed up as Santa and handed out presents to the kids."

Daniel raised his eyebrows. "*Brian* did that?"

"He's great with the kids," Betty said enthusiastically. "Teases them unmercifully, and they adore him."

Kevin laughed. "The older kids caught on right away who was under the red suit and teased him about his paunch. I've noticed he's been working on it since."

"At least he didn't lose the Santa Claus outfit like someone else I know," Betty said with a pointed glance at her husband.

Karina laughed. "Oh, Kevin. Only you could lose a Santa costume."

"It's around somewhere," Kevin replied, pulling on his bushy mustache. "Which reminds me…" He dug his wallet out of his back pocket. "Here's your money order, Danny. Sorry about the mix-up."

"No worries." Daniel accepted the dog-eared slip of paper with a grin. "Glad to see you didn't absentmindedly cash it."

"You'll have to come out to the farm for Christmas, Daniel," Betty said. "The kids'll have a ball together."

"Sounds good. Are you still on that acreage out on the Saanich Peninsula?"

Kevin nodded. "With the falling-down farmhouse and the barn in constant need of repair. Still handy with a hammer and nails, Danny?" he added with a grin. "We've been saving up a few jobs, just waiting for you to come home."

Daniel smiled. "I'd be glad to give you a hand."

"You don't know what you're getting yourself into," Betty said, laughing. "But you're welcome to visit whenever you want." She took the baby off her breast and raised it to her shoulder where it promptly issued a loud burp.

Her beer growing warm in her hand, Karina leaned

against the counter and watched the three of them laughing and talking. Daniel's pleasure in seeing Betty and Kevin was obviously reciprocated. Soon he'd be reunited with his brother and he'd be part of a large, happy family.

Unlike hers. With Tom in Toronto and her father in Penticton, cards and telephone calls formed the only tenuous links. If only Mama hadn't died, they might not have drifted so far apart.

The sound of the back door opening made her glance around. Natalie entered, bearing an empty chip bowl. "That was fast," Karina said.

Natalie set the bowl on the counter and gazed shyly at Betty. "Can I see the baby?"

"Of course. We'll let your daddy hold him, then you can get a good look. Say hello to cousin Daniel and Natalie, Alex," Betty cooed to her baby as she handed him to Daniel.

Daniel took the infant and nestled him in the crook of his arm. The sleeves of his faded denim shirt were rolled up to the elbows, and the baby looked tiny, pink and fragile against his strong, tanned forearm. A tender look crept into his eyes, and he smiled gently as he touched the baby's nose with the tip of a callused forefinger.

Little Alex's rosebud mouth lifted in a smile. Natalie laughed delightedly. "Oh, Daddy, can I have a baby brother?"

"Maybe someday, Possum."

She stroked the baby's tiny, curled fist. "When?"

Daniel laughed and shook his head. "Someday. I promise."

And he would keep that promise, Karina thought. Any lingering ideas she might have had about getting involved with Daniel were banished. The man was a natural father. He deserved a family.

Daniel glanced up at her. "Do you want a go, Karina?"

"Me? Oh, yes." She reached for Alex, and her bare arm brushed Daniel's as she slid her hand beneath the tiny bundle.

"Don't be nervous," he said, his breath warm on her cheek.

"I've held lots of babies." But she was trembling by the time they'd completed the delicate transfer of the baby from one pair of arms to the other.

She held Alex upright, close to her face, her fingers splayed behind his head for support. "Hello, Alexander the Great. How's my guy?"

She gazed into Alex's tiny, perfect face and breathed in the soft scent of talcum, mother's milk and new baby. Bittersweet longing stabbed through her. Then he smiled at her, and such a rush of pleasure filled her heart that she laughed softly.

"Amazing what power you little nippers have," she murmured, and stroked his satiny cheek.

She felt Daniel's gaze on her and glanced up to see him leaning back in his chair, watching her intently.

"He's absolutely beautiful, Betty," she said, and handed Alex carefully into the other woman's arms. Then she turned to the others and added brightly, "Is anybody else hungry? Since it's my night to cook, what do you say we order pizza?"

KARINA HUNG the spare leash Piper's owners had given her on its hook by the back door. She stepped inside the kitchen, exchanging the fresh morning air and the chirping of birds for the aroma of freshly brewed coffee and the sound of Daniel and Natalie laughing. Their happy voices made her smile even though she didn't know what the joke was.

"Hi, Nattie," she said. "You're looking better every day. I see you've got a peanut-butter smile. Is it as good as Vegemite?"

Natalie giggled. "It's messier. Can I play with Piper after I wash up?"

"I don't see why not. We'll just knock on his door and ask him, shall we?" She brushed a hand lightly across the girl's head, the smile lingering on her face as she watched Natalie run off.

She glanced over at Daniel. "Hi."

His eyes seemed to be waiting for hers. "Mornin'. I thought you'd gone to work."

"No, I got up early and took Piper for a walk in the park," she said, pouring herself a coffee. "Since there's a lull at the office, I thought I'd take another day off."

"Good. I'm going to work on the design of your table after breakfast. You can put in your two cents' worth if you like."

Karina smiled and reached for the sugar. "I'd love to."

Daniel eased his long legs out from behind the table and carried his dishes to the counter, where she stood stirring her coffee. Then she felt his hand in her hair and glanced up, startled.

"You've got enough twigs in here to build a bird's nest," he said, pulling one out. "Looks like Piper took *you* for a walk."

She gave a husky laugh and ducked away from him, brushing at her hair with her hand. "A bowl. I need a bowl," she muttered and stooped to rummage in the bottom cupboard.

"Joanne called," he said, going to the coffeepot and pouring himself another cup. "She said to tell you she'll bring a dessert tomorrow."

"Great. I was hoping she would." Karina straightened, clutching a cereal bowl in her hands. "Are you sure you're okay with this dinner thing?"

"No worries."

"No worries," she repeated. "What does that mean exactly? That *you're* not worried or that *I* shouldn't worry about you?"

"Both." He crossed to the fridge and took out the carton of milk. "By the way," he added, pouring some in his coffee, "is it true you put chocolate milk on your cereal?"

"Joanne has *such* a big mouth." Karina stalked to the fridge, pulled open the door and gestured inside. "Do you see any chocolate milk in here?"

"No, but then, I did the shopping last week." He handed her the carton.

"It's not as if I make a habit of it," she said grumpily, flooding her cornflakes. Then she smiled. "It's not bad, though, once you get used to it."

He laughed out loud. "Just don't show Natalie that particular culinary delight if you don't mind. I'm going out to the garage to get started. Will you be long?"

"Just as long as it takes to down a bowl of cereal."

He was still laughing as he went out the door. She made a face at his back. Such a nice laugh for such an irritating man.

It was the fastest bowl of cornflakes she'd ever eaten.

THE GARAGE WASN'T all hers anymore, Karina thought, walking through the door into Daniel's workshop.

At the bench, Daniel leaned over a sheet of drafting

paper illuminated by a goosenecked lamp. Spread around him were the tools of his trade: rulers and pencils, compass and calculator. Farther down were vises and hammers, nails and sandpaper. The mentholated scent of gumwood shavings mingled with the odors of glue and linseed oil.

He'd taken over her garage and her life with his tools and his way of fixing things she never admitted were broken because then she'd have to deal with them. She ought to mind, but somehow she didn't.

She joined him at the bench, conscious of the snug fit of his faded blue jeans and the way his cotton shirt stretched across his shoulders. "Very professional rendering," she said, examining his sketches of the top and side view of a dining table.

He nodded without looking at her. "I studied architecture for a while."

"Really?" she said, glancing at him with raised eyebrows. "Why did you quit?"

"I moved to Australia."

"Oh." *Francine.* Her gaze slid back to the drawing.

"I probably would have quit anyway," he said, leaning an elbow on the bench and gazing up at her. "I found I got more satisfaction from creating the wooden models of my designs than I did from working with pen and paper."

Again Karina felt a spark of kinship. "I know what you mean. It's a good feeling to see the tangible results of your ideas. I hardly ever get that from my work anymore. Maybe that's why I do so much *papier-mâché.*"

His gaze drifted from her eyes to her mouth and back again. Disconcerted, she glanced back to the drawing on the workbench. "The table looks very long."

"Eight feet. It's a little wider than usual, too, but I

measured your dining room and it should fit nicely. Since you like to entertain, I reckoned you'd want a table you can bring a crowd to.''

She smiled. ''However did you guess?''

He grinned and tapped his temple with the end of a pencil. ''I have amazing powers of deduction. What do you think of the corners?''

''I like them,'' she said, tracing the elongated octagon with her finger. ''They're different.''

''I plan to use some jarrah beams salvaged from an old woolshed in Western Australia. They'll give your table great character.''

''Sounds wonderful. I can't wait to see it finished.''

Daniel straightened away from the bench and his bare forearm brushed hers. Somehow she'd edged closer to him without noticing.

''About these legs...'' she said, forcing her attention back to the table. ''I like them, but I wonder if they could be angled like this...?'' She picked up a pencil and lightly sketched over Daniel's drawing.

''That would look good,'' he admitted. ''But there might be a problem with stability. You can't have too great an inward angle. How about this instead...?'' He took the pencil out of her hand, and with broad, sure strokes, sketched an alternate design.

Karina watched, fascinated by his hands. His fingers carried the odd scar from nicks that had healed. Lean but muscular and tanned by the Australian sun to a light reddish brown. Even more interesting than their appearance was the way they moved, as though they were capable and clever. Which, of course, they were.

''Yes!'' she said, turning to him when he'd done. ''I love it.''

His clear hazel eyes reflected her pleasure as he gazed

back at her, silent and smiling. She thought briefly about auras and wondered why she'd never believed in them before. What else could explain the thickening of the air around them, the sensation that she could feel him even though they weren't touching?

Then his eyes grew intent, his mouth lost its curve and she knew with a breathless sense of the inevitable that he was about to kiss her. She had a split second to retreat…but she didn't.

Slowly Daniel bent his head, closing the space between them. Their lips touched for the very first time.

"Daniel," she murmured against his mouth, her heart pounding. "We agreed not to get involved."

"Shhh. Don't talk."

He cupped his hands around her jaw, his callused fingertips caressing the soft hollow behind her ears. All her objections faded in the immediacy of lips against lips, breath mingled with breath.

Her arms slid around his waist, and his shirt felt smooth and warm beneath her fingers. She inhaled his clean, male scent. Her lips parted, and she tasted him in a warm, moist fusion of tongues.

Then the thing she'd longed for practically all of her life finally happened.

Time stopped.

Just like that. No movement, no space. Only a warm glow that started in her heart and spread to every reach of her soul. A glow that had no beginning and no end.

A glow reflected in Daniel's heated gaze when she finally broke away, drawing in air on a long gasp.

That first breath, like the tick of the second hand on Felix the Clock, moved her back into the present. Into a world that kept spinning, no matter how much she wanted it to stay still. Into a fragment of time that couldn't last, no matter how much her heart yearned for it.

"Daniel." It was agony to move apart from him.

"Don't run away," he murmured. "It was only a kiss." With his fingertips, he lightly touched her lips.

A sensual shudder ran through her and she heard his own sharp intake of breath. Only a kiss, indeed.

She drew back another step. Just because he kissed her didn't mean he wanted to marry her. But the path they were treading like eggshells could only lead to a dead end. For Daniel's sake, as well as her own, she couldn't let this go any further.

"I wonder what Natalie's up to," she said, edging farther away. "We should check on her."

"She'll be all right for a minute."

"I've got a lot to do today," she said, avoiding his eyes. "I'm thinking of setting up a study in that extra room in the basement. I used to rent it out but I could use it myself if I installed a computer with a modem and a fax machine." She took a deep breath, aware she was talking too much, too fast.

Daniel stepped closer and put his arms around her waist. He held her loosely, his chin resting on her head. "What are you so afraid of, Karina? Tell me."

She shook her head mutely against his chest, barely breathing. The comfort of his embrace was almost as seductive as his kiss. She longed to tell him of the pain in her heart, but nothing anyone could do, not even Daniel, could ever make things right again.

She pushed him away for the second time, avoiding his questioning gaze. "Please. I've got to go."

CHAPTER EIGHT

KARINA SWUNG DOWN the hall toward the kitchen, humming softly to the music in her head. At the doorway, she paused. Daniel was standing in front of the fridge studying the calendar, unaware of her presence. His hair, damp from the shower, was slicked back off his forehead. His freshly shaven jaw looked shiny and tanned.

She fingered the tiny salamander brooch that curled up the lapel of her dress. They'd hardly spoken since yesterday's encounter in the garage. Would he be as nervous as she felt?

Surely not. It was only one little kiss between friends. A spur-of-the-moment thing. Hadn't she been wishing Daniel was more spontaneous?

But friends had no business kissing like that. Their relationship had to return to a strictly platonic level, *immediately.*

The thing to do was act as though nothing had happened. So, head high, a deliberate swing in her step, Karina sauntered into the room.

"Good morning!" She crossed to the table, leaned over and flipped on the radio. Dixieland jazz filled the sunny room.

"Mornin'." Daniel's smile was both genuine and uncomplicated as he nodded at the radio. "Bill Bix I like."

Karina let out a silent sigh of relief. Daniel was a

mature individual. He wouldn't let a little thing like a kiss ruin a good relationship.

"You're very intent on that calendar," she said, helping herself to coffee. "Something important coming up?"

"I'm registering Natalie for school at Oak Bay Primary the week after next. We've got an appointment to meet her teacher."

"Oh? Have you found a house?" She wasn't sure if she was pleased he'd be nearby or disappointed he'd be leaving.

"Not yet, but I've decided to concentrate my search on this area. I like the older houses and established gardens. Being near the water is nice, too."

"I still remember my first day of school," Karina said, stirring in sugar and milk. "For some reason I thought I'd learn to read and write that first day. After all the excitement of getting new pencils and erasers, I was terribly disappointed."

Daniel chuckled. "I'll warn Natalie not to expect too much." He glanced back at the calendar. "That's an interesting hieroglyph marking August eighth. Does the date have some special significance?"

For a moment, Karina had trouble breathing. She dropped a fourth spoonful of sugar in her cup and stirred so hard the coffee slopped over the side. "Oh, that," she said, trying to sound casual. "It's just my birthday."

A drying lock of hair fell across his forehead as he turned his head to glance at her. "Your birthday? Are you having a party?"

"No." Karina popped a piece of rye bread into the toaster and reached for a knife from the drawer. She stared at her distorted reflection in the shiny chrome surface of the toaster, willing him to drop the subject. Any second now, he'd ask why not.

Questions and concern; she couldn't handle it. She hadn't wanted to rent in the first place. Why hadn't she stuck to her guns? Her thoughts had become so confused lately. She felt all the old grief of her mother's death, as well as fear of what was in store. Plus something new. A sort of regret. But for what?

"You don't sound very excited about it."

Karina forced herself to look at him and immediately wished she hadn't. His hazel eyes seemed to burn right through her. With a shrug, she glanced away. "It's just another day."

Daniel circled around her, his gaze piercing the curtain of hair that fell across her face. "I've only known you a few weeks, but somehow that doesn't sound like you. I'd have thought you'd have a huge party with lots of people and loud music. Dancing, decorations—the works."

Abruptly she pushed past him to the fridge. "Where'd you get that idea?" she said, searching for the cherry jam.

He gave a short laugh. "I can't imagine. You're like an open book…in a foreign language. So what *are* you going to do?"

Her toast popped. Karina pulled it out. "I haven't decided yet." She glanced sideways to see him studying her, a puzzled expression on his face.

"Trying to choose between a party or a night on the town?" he said. "Between a restaurant and a take-away?"

"*Out,*" she corrected, seizing the chance to change the subject.

"I beg your pardon?"

"It's called take*out* here, not take-away." She loaded her toast onto a plate, picked up her coffee and went to the table. Daniel wasn't stupid. Surely he could see she didn't want to talk about her birthday.

"Whatever." He pulled out a chair and sat down opposite her, still gazing at her. "The lingo will come back quickly. Already I almost feel as though I never left."

"Are you staying in Canada permanently, then?"

"That's the plan. But…well, we'll have to see." Daniel picked an orange out of the fruit bowl and began to peel it.

"You mean, see if your business gets off the ground?"

His gaze dropped to the orange in his hand. "I was thinking of Natalie. She's born and bred an Aussie. And she really misses her grandmother."

"That would be hard. And I can imagine how her grandmother must feel. But kids are resilient. Natalie will be happy wherever you are."

Daniel's face clouded. A continuous circle of peel dangled from his long fingers as he methodically went round and round the orange.

"Something wrong?" Karina asked.

"No." Then he sighed. "Yes, there is. It's Natalie…. She still hasn't got over losing her mother."

"Daniel—" In spite of her resolution to keep her distance, Karina reached out and touched his arm. The breath swelled in her throat until the words had to be pushed out. "She never will."

He went still, his gaze rising to meet hers. The long strand of orange peel broke free under its own weight and dropped, unheeded, to the floor. "What do you mean?"

Karina forced herself to go on. "She'll learn to live with the pain, but she'll never really get over it."

"Never?"

"Never."

Brassy, breezy, Dixieland jazz filled the silence between them.

Daniel bent to pick up the orange peel. "This is firsthand knowledge, isn't it?"

She nodded. "My mother died of breast cancer when I was thirteen." Her toast sat cooling on her plate, her appetite vanished.

"I'm sorry," he said softly. "You were right on the brink, so to speak. Your mother must have been quite young when it happened."

Karina heard the *thump-whoosh* of her heart. Felt the blood burning through her veins. "She was thirty-two."

He paused for the space of a heartbeat. "How old are you going to be next month?"

"Thirty-two." It was barely a whisper.

"I see." He was silent for a bit. "Is your father still alive?"

"He retired to Penticton a couple of years ago." Rolling her shoulders to relax them, she added, "Funny, eh? Most older people come to Victoria to retire."

"I guess you don't see him very often, then."

"Even before he left, I never saw much of him."

"Why not?"

She shrugged. "I don't know."

Daniel gazed at her intently. "Yes, you do."

Karina picked up her slice of toast and immediately put it down again. "He never really got over Mama's death. All through my high school years, he was so distant, like he was on another planet. I think—" Her voice broke.

Daniel gently pressed her hand. "Go on."

She swallowed hard. "I think I remind him too much of *her*. It seems to hurt him to be around me. So..." she drew a shaky breath "...mostly I leave him alone."

"Damn." Daniel rose and crossed the room to gaze out the window above the stove.

Slowly the breath seeped from Karina's bursting lungs. Thank God he hadn't tried to comfort her. She might have broken down completely.

"Every year on my birthday," Daniel said, still inspecting the backyard, "I make a point of doing something I've never done before. It's like a resolution to always go forward in life. Experience new things."

"Is that why you pull up stakes so easily?"

He spun around and looked at her. "Leaving Melbourne wasn't easy. I had my business, my friends. Natalie had her grandmother. But it doesn't hurt to try something difficult now and then if you've got a good reason for doing it."

Karina picked up her toast and took a bite. Getting through this birthday was going to be one of the hardest things she'd ever done, but it wasn't as if she had a choice. "So what kinds of things do you do on your birthday?" she asked.

"Last year I went rock climbing. The year before that I went on an archaeology dig with the university. I've been to a roller derby and a lecture by a nuclear physicist. It doesn't have to be exciting or daring. Just different. Something that lets you know you're alive and kicking."

Karina smiled. How could she ever have thought this man dull and boring? "I like the sound of that."

"You should try it." He leaned against the counter and crossed one leg in front of the other. "Since I'm something of an expert on the birthday adventure, I could help you plan.''

''You could?''

He nodded. ''I'd even go along if you want.''

''You would?'' She wasn't sure how she felt about that. It all sounded a little *too* appealing.

''I guarantee you won't regret it,'' he said. ''Another party or another restaurant meal will always come along, but who knows when you'll get the nerve to go bungee-jumping again?''

Karina burst out laughing. ''Bungee-jumping! No way! Even I'm not *that* crazy.''

''What then?''

''Mmm, let's see.'' Karina looked to the ceiling for inspiration. ''Chocolate pasta?''

''There's no such thing!''

She laughed at his expression. ''Yes, there is, but I'll settle for dinner in Rome.''

''Will Joanne baby-sit?''

''Of course. Hey, I know! How about dressing up as clowns and performing on the Johnson Street bridge at rush hour?''

He gave her the look he sometimes gave Natalie when she asked for something totally outrageous. ''Choose that and you're on your own, darlin'.''

''I was afraid of that,'' she said, shaking her head. ''No staying power.''

Karina's laughter lapsed into a smile, her gaze resting warmly on Daniel. This could work. They might actually become friends now that they were over yesterday's foolishness. Daniel would be a good friend to have. He seemed to know the exact degree of pragmatic cheerfulness required to lift her spirits.

But even as she gazed at him, the friendly sparkle in

his eyes turned to a darker gleam. Maybe things weren't quite as free and easy between her and Daniel as she'd hoped. She didn't want him to care for her. It was bad enough she couldn't be in the same room as him without being aware of every move he made.

"Maybe this isn't such a good idea, Daniel. I won't be very good company on my birthday this year."

Daniel pushed himself away from the counter and crossed the room to stand in front of her. Gently, he lifted her chin, his eyes grave and kind, the flame of desire banked. "You're not going to spend your birthday alone."

Karina gazed at him mutely, overwhelmed by emotions she couldn't begin to name. Sometimes she felt so *right* with him, as though life would go on forever in a haze of domestic bliss. Other times, like now, he touched her too deeply, and all her demons rose up to haunt her. She couldn't bear to ever hurt him.

The doorbell rang.

"I wonder who that could be?" she said, and started to pull away.

Daniel grabbed her by the shoulders and held her fast. "Promise me you'll at least think about it."

"I…yes, okay, I'll think about it."

He let her go and she hurried down the hall. If only he knew—she thought of little else *but* her coming birthday. Still, as she reached for the door handle, she made up her mind to try to think about something fun instead. Something she could do with Natalie to ease the girl's loneliness.

DANIEL CAME DOWN the stairs, glancing at his watch for the tenth time in the past half hour. So Brian was fifteen minutes late. No big deal.

He paused in the hall, listening to the muffled sounds of laughter that meant Karina and Joanne were still closeted in the kitchen. Karina had insisted on cooking dinner on the grounds that Daniel should be free to concentrate on his brother. He'd agreed in the end, but after experiencing several of Karina's ''dinners,'' Daniel was grateful Joanne was there to lend a hand.

In the living room, Natalie was leaning over the back of the sofa, her small rump waving in the air as she craned her head at the bay window watching for her uncle. Her hair had been fashioned into two sleek French braids, thanks to Karina, and she wore her favorite summer dress of pink pineapples on a black background.

''Feet off the sofa, young lady.'' Daniel caught her by the waist and swung her to the ground.

''It's him!'' Natalie exclaimed just as she was pulled away. ''He's here!''

Daniel glanced out the window. A silver Jaguar had pulled up at the front gate and a stocky, fair-haired man was getting out. Daniel wiped damp palms against his denim-clad thighs.

A week ago he would have flung open the door and gone to meet his brother, but the phone calls of the past two weeks had taught him caution. Suddenly he was glad Karina was there to back him up. She was so good at talking to people she would surely put them both at ease and smooth over any unpleasantness with her unfailing good humor.

Natalie showed none of her father's reservations. She ran to the door and yanked it open. But when Brian stepped onto the porch, her excitement dissolved into shyness, and she ducked behind Daniel's legs.

Face-to-face with the brother he hadn't seen in ten years, Daniel was made forcibly aware of the passage of time. Brian's blond hair had turned to gray at the temples, and faint but permanent lines creased his forehead.

A profound sense of loss came crashing down on him. They'd missed out on so much—all the milestones of each other's adult lives, the successes, the setbacks, the hopes, the dreams....

Unable to speak for the constriction in his throat, Daniel stepped forward, hand outstretched. Brian merely gazed coolly back at him.

Daniel froze in midstride, his hand dropping awkwardly to his side. "Come in." He turned and led the way to the living room.

The doors to the dining room slid open. Karina and Joanne came through on a wave of laughter and the aroma of chicken and exotic spices. Karina's smiling face registered surprise, then pleasure at the sight of their guest.

"You must be Brian," she said in her lilting, laughing voice. "I'm Karina and this is Joanne." She turned to Daniel. "Why didn't you tell me he'd arrived?"

Before Daniel could speak, Brian extended his hand, a huge smile creasing his face. "Old Danny boy forgot his manners for a moment. I guess we'll forgive him for that." Laughing now, Brian put his arm around Daniel's shoulder in a parody of brotherly love.

Daniel stared at him, speechless.

"Pleased to meet you, Joanne," Brian continued without a pause. "And Karina! Danny's description of you didn't begin to do you justice."

Karina's surprised gaze flicked to Daniel. He smiled and gave a little shrug. Then he frowned as Brian reclaimed her attention with a prolonged handshake that seemed to involve all four of their hands and a great deal of smiling.

Brian drew Natalie into the circle, crouching down to gently tug on one braid. "So this is my long-lost niece, Natalie. My, my, you're a grown-up girl already." He reached inside his jacket pocket and pulled out a small, brightly wrapped parcel. "Here's a little start on all those birthdays and Christmases I've missed."

With a squeal of delight, Natalie tore open the wrapping and uncovered a small box containing a bracelet of shiny red and blue stones. She slipped it on her wrist and gazed at her uncle with adoring eyes. Karina and Joanne looked down at the pair with soppy smiles.

Daniel wanted to punch his brother's face in.

"WINE FOR EVERYONE?" Karina asked a few minutes later as she entered the living room with glasses clutched in one hand and a bottle of Italian white in the other.

Brian and Joanne were together on the sofa, while Daniel had taken one of the wing chairs. Karina thought Daniel's expression seemed a little strained, but she put the thought aside and perched on the edge of the other chair.

Amid a chorus of assent, Natalie's small voice piped up. "I can't have wine. I'm just a kid!"

Everyone laughed. "Will orange pop do, Miss Bowen?" Karina asked.

Natalie nodded graciously. "Yes, thank you. I can get it myself." She ran off to the kitchen.

Daniel looked pleased at his daughter's polite little speech. Brian gave him a wink. "Well, Danny boy, at least you've managed to instill manners into your child. You must have done something right."

"Natalie's a beautiful child," Karina said quickly. "She's a credit to Daniel."

Daniel's irritated gaze left his brother, and he flashed

her a smile of thanks. Joanne's interested glance flicked from brother to brother.

Karina set the wine bottle on the coffee table and attempted to extricate the glasses from between her fingers, laughing as they stuck to her skin and clinked dangerously. Daniel started from his seat to help, but Brian, who was closer, leaped to her rescue first.

One by one, Brian removed the glasses and set them on the coffee table. His unblemished fingers lingered under the tips of hers. "What lovely hands you have."

Karina felt her cheeks glow. After hours spent scrubbing away ink stains and shaping and polishing her nails, it was nice to have her efforts noticed. She glanced at Daniel, wondering if he'd seen the improvement, too. But Daniel's frowning gaze was fixed on the wine bottle as he drove the corkscrew into the cork with a force that seemed excessive.

"It's a wonder Natalie has any manners at all," Brian said, grinning. "You should have seen Danny as a teenager. He'd say the rudest words imaginable at Sunday dinner just to shock our grandmother."

Daniel glanced up. "*Brian.*" His voice carried a distinct warning.

Karina's nerves prickled. Brian only smiled and lounged against the sofa, one arm resting along the back. Daniel sat on the edge of his seat, his jaw tight, his gaze fixed on his brother's lazy smile.

Ignoring him, Brian carried on with his story. "Danny would put this look on his face like butter wouldn't melt in his mouth, turn to Granny and say, 'Pass the effing potatoes, please.' But when he came to *that word* he'd drop his voice so only she could hear."

Brian laughed, and Karina and Joanne chuckled along with him. "My little brother was so-o-o bad." He leaned across and punched Daniel playfully on the arm. "Eh, Danny boy?"

"If you say so," Daniel replied quietly.

Karina's laughter slowed. Joanne covered her smile with her hand. Brian's eyes danced. A tense silence fell over the room.

Karina forced a bright smile. "You sound positively angelic compared to what *my* brother used to get up to," she said to Daniel. "I can't even repeat some of the things he did. Have you got that bottle open?"

"What? Oh, yes." Unwrapping white-knuckled fingers from around the neck of the bottle, he transferred it to his other hand and reached for a glass. He filled it halfway with a deep gold Frascati and passed it to Joanne.

"Brian," Daniel said without looking at his brother, "I'm sure Karina and Joanne aren't interested in hearing us talk about the good old days all evening." He poured another glass and passed it to Karina.

She reached for the drink and was shocked to see his eyes opaque with anger and the curving lines of his mouth flattened with pain. Sure, Brian was teasing him, but all brothers did that. Nobody thought the worse of Daniel for his boyhood pranks.

"I didn't come here to quarrel, Danny," Brian said. "And I certainly didn't intend to embarrass you in front of your friends." He held out his hand. "Forgive me?"

Daniel gazed silently at his brother but made no move to take his hand. Karina held her breath. *Why wouldn't he shake?*

Slowly, Daniel reached out. Karina started to laugh in relief. She broke off with a gasp as Daniel placed a glass of wine in Brian's outstretched palm.

"Cheers," Daniel said. He filled his own glass and raised it in a mocking salute.

Brian's eyes widened. His mouth fell open. He threw his head back and laughed. "Oh, he's a sly one. A real rogue."

"What's a rogue?" inquired a small voice at Karina's elbow.

"Oh, Natalie! You startled me." Karina had forgotten the little girl, she'd been so quiet until now. "Did you get your pop?"

"Yes, thanks. What's a rogue?"

"Oh, it's just a sort of…scoundrel." Karina could see by Natalie's puzzled expression this word was no better. "Like a bad guy but in a joking kind of way."

Natalie shook her head, obviously confused. "Daddy's not a bad guy. Why would Uncle Brian say that?"

"He didn't, not really. Oh, Nattie, it's hard to explain. Why don't you ask your dad about it later?"

She knew this was a cop-out, but how could she explain adult innuendo to the child when she herself didn't fully understand what was going on between Daniel and his brother?

Natalie skipped off to her father, and Daniel pulled her onto his lap. Joanne began telling a funny story about something her youngest child had said to the mailman.

Karina sipped her wine and studied the brothers. Brian was handsomer by conventional standards and wore expensive clothes, but she found Daniel's casual good looks more attractive. If only he would lighten up. He had a sense of humor. Why didn't he use it?

"Don't you agree, Karina?" Brian said, appealing to her.

She sat up. "I'm sorry, what did you say?"

"I said, you can't beat British-built cars for engineering excellence."

She smiled. "I don't know. My Sammy's a little temperamental. But he's also a lot of fun, so I live with the repairs."

"How about you, Daniel?" Brian turned to his brother. "In the market for a new car? I could get you a good deal." He winked at Karina.

"Thanks, Brian." Daniel spoke stiffly. "I've already bought a small pickup to use for work."

"Not that secondhand Japanese job parked out front?" Brian said, laughing.

Daniel glowered.

"I was driving past your showroom the other day," Karina interjected quickly. "I presume Bowen's British Autos on Blanshard is yours?"

Brian nodded. "Drop in next time you're going by."

"Thanks, I may do that. I noticed you could use a new sign out front."

"Watch out, Brian," Joanne warned him with a smile. "You're about to be wheeled in for an overhaul. I've seen Karina go into a restaurant for a meal and convince the owner to completely revamp the exterior of his building, including a brand new neon sign by SignCity. Which vastly improved the place, of course."

"Is business so slow that you have to go looking for it, Karina?" Daniel asked.

She flashed him a smile, pleased he'd relaxed enough to join the conversation. "Not at all. It's just that wherever I go, design ideas pop into my head and I blurt them out. Our sales department doesn't know whether to make me an honorary member or shut me down for unfair competition."

"Daniel told me you were a graphic artist," Brian

said, leaning forward. "I didn't know you designed signs."

"That's right." She sat back in her chair and crossed her legs. "SignCity Neon is the biggest neon sign company in the country. And the best, if I do say so myself."

"I don't doubt it. But neon doesn't quite fit the Rolls-Royce image."

"Don't be too sure. Neon can be very classy if you do it right. Picture this...." Gesturing with her hands, she began telling Brian her ideas for his sign. Vaguely she noticed Joanne murmur something to Daniel and the two of them leave the room.

When she had finished, Brian pursed his lips. "What you're describing doesn't sound bad. Not bad at all."

"Excuse me, Karina," Daniel interrupted, poking his head through the doorway. "Joanne wants to know where you've hidden the cinnamon."

"Goodness, are you in the kitchen again?" She turned apologetically to Brian. "I promised I'd take care of dinner, and here I am yakking away...."

Daniel cast a quick glance at his brother. "It's all right."

Karina jumped to her feet and pulled Daniel into the living room. "No, it's not. I need to prove I can concoct something other than peanut butter and mayonnaise."

She left the room to the sound of Brian's laughing voice followed by Daniel's sardonic murmur, and mentally patted herself on the back for getting Daniel together with his brother at last.

In the kitchen, she found Joanne forking through the couscous while Natalie kneeled on a chair and industriously grated carrots all over the table.

Karina rooted through the spice jars in the cupboard

next to the stove for the cinnamon. "Sorry about that, Jo. I got carried away talking shop."

"I noticed." Joanne glanced up. "He's nice, isn't he?"

Karina's gaze flicked to Natalie before answering. "Yes," she said cautiously. "I mean, what's not to like?"

"Exactly. On the other hand, siblings' relationships are like marriages. Outsiders never know all that goes on below the surface."

"True, I guess. Here's the cinnamon." She lifted the lid on the Moroccan chicken and tipped the spoon to her lips. "You were right, it needs a dash more.

"What I don't understand," she added, "is why You Know Who is so uptight." Karina glanced at Natalie again, but the girl was engrossed in scraping up bits of carrot from the far reaches of the table. "What's His Name seems so genuinely amiable. To hear You Know Who talk, you'd think he hated his guts."

"Are you talking about Daddy and Uncle Brian?" Natalie asked suddenly.

Karina rolled her eyes at Joanne, then glanced back at Natalie. "Yes." She didn't believe in lying to children, but neither did she think further explanation would serve any useful purpose. "Wow, what a lot of carrots you've grated. How about sprinkling them in the salad for me?"

"Okay," Natalie said cheerfully, and scooped up the pile with both hands.

Joanne dipped a spoon into the chicken and tasted the sauce. "Perfect." She dropped the spoon in the sink and turned to Karina with a grin. "It's showtime."

As soon as Daniel was certain Karina was out of hearing, he set his glass down hard on the table and faced his brother. "What the hell are you playing at, Brian?"

"Why, Danny, whatever do you mean?" His blue eyes widened.

"I mean, what's all this 'forgive me' crap? Every time I've called you, you've been cold and distant, if not downright offensive. Now suddenly you're slapping me on the back like the best of buddies. And don't give me that innocent expression. It's as calculated as the rest of your act."

Brian shook his head sadly. "Danny boy, I was just trying to be friendly. We've had our differences in the past, but we're still brothers."

Daniel took a deep breath and counted to ten. Was it remotely possible Brian had had a complete change of heart and sincerely wanted to be friends? He doubted it very much.

"Besides," Brian continued, "I didn't want to embarrass you in front of your lady friend by playing the nasty big brother."

"She's *not* my lady friend." Daniel got to his feet and paced the short distance to the stereo system. He flipped through the CDs without seeing them. "And why did you tell them it was me who said that to Grandma?"

"What's the matter, Danny boy? Afraid of tarnishing your image? Come on, it was just a little joke. You could have told them the truth."

Daniel threw him a look that could have withered the entire north Queensland rain forest. And should have devastated Brian, too, except he was so damn cocky.

"Well, maybe you're right. It would have looked a tad petty." Brian put his hands behind his head and leaned back on the couch. "Made a good story, though, didn't it? Put you in the limelight."

"You're the one who always wanted to be in the lime-light." Daniel slid the CD drawer shut and strode over to Brian. "Why did you really come here tonight? I'd hoped it was to see me and Natalie, but now I wonder if you didn't come just to meet Karina."

"You do me an injustice, little brother," Brian replied. "Though I must admit, when I heard Karina's voice on the telephone I was curious to see what such an enchanting-sounding creature looked like."

A chill went down Daniel's spine. "Forget it, Brian. Karina's not for you."

"Why not? You've taken great pains to assure me you're not interested—though I suspect that's a case of protesting too much."

"How would you know? You haven't seen me in years."

"You forget," Brian said quietly. "I've seen you in love before."

Daniel went still. What he'd felt for Francine hadn't been love. But how could he say so to the man who'd lost his future wife to Daniel's passing fancy?

"I'm not in love with Karina." The words seemed to stick in his throat.

"I'd hardly blame you if you were," Brian said. "She's a beauty, all right."

Daniel bit back his anger at Brian's casual remarks. He felt protective of Karina, though he knew she wouldn't thank him for it. He felt possessive of her, although he had no right to be.

"She isn't interested in getting involved with any-one," he said. "She's devoted to her career."

Brian laughed. "Hey, little brother, just because you struck out doesn't mean the rest of the team has to stay on the bench."

Daniel's hands clenched impotently around thin air. "I'm warning you, Brian, stay away from—"

KARINA CAME DOWN the hall to the living room to call Daniel and Brian for dinner, but the sound of their voices slowed her steps. Though their words were indistinct, there was no doubt they were arguing. It must be about Francine. Quickly, she retraced her steps partway, then, loudly humming a fragment of *The Barber of Seville,* she carried on without pause through the passageway into the living room.

"—Karina!" Daniel finished furiously.

"Karina!" Brian exclaimed with hearty gladness as his gaze swept over Daniel's shoulder to meet hers.

Brian's brow was so smooth and his smile so broad, she could have sworn she'd been mistaken in thinking she'd heard his voice raised in anger only a moment ago.

Or had it been Daniel's voice?

Daniel swiveled to face her. Karina felt a jolt of anguish at the tense, unhappy expression in his eyes. Maybe this little dinner party hadn't been such a good idea. Maybe it would have been better if they'd thrashed things out on their own, without the added strain of having to be polite around her and Joanne. Not to mention Natalie.

"Dinner's ready," she said, and slid open the heavy, paneled doors that connected the living and dining rooms.

The table, painstakingly set that afternoon by Natalie, gleamed with Karina's royal-blue-and-white china and Mama's handblown Italian wineglasses. Overhead, the papier-mâché ladies circled. Wildly colorful and flagrantly impossible, they stirred gently in the light air caused by Joanne's energetic bustling to and fro from the kitchen with dishes of fragrant, spiced chicken and steaming couscous.

Brian's jaw dropped when he saw them, and Natalie giggled at her uncle's astonished expression. "They're flying spaghetti pickers, Uncle Brian," the little girl explained. "Karina made them."

Brian shook his head wonderingly. *"Spaghetti pickers?"*

Karina grinned. "I made them for a friend to hang in her Italian restaurant. The venture folded before it even opened, so here they fly, forever searching for the elusive spaghetti bushes."

"Elusive or mythical?" Daniel said, an edge to his voice.

"It's just a joke," Karina replied, wondering at his mood. He seemed brittle and unhappy despite Brian's friendly overtures. "Sit down, everyone, please."

She was half afraid there'd be a scuffle for seats, but to her relief it was settled quickly, with Daniel at her side and Brian directly across from her. Joanne sat across from Daniel, and Natalie took pride of place at the head of the table.

Joanne raised her glass when they were all seated. "I propose a toast to Daniel's first big contract in his new business."

Karina glanced at Daniel, startled. Surely one dining table didn't constitute a big contract.

"I haven't had a chance to tell you," he said to her. "I dropped into a home-furnishings shop in Oak Bay Village the other day with my portfolio. They called back this afternoon saying they'd take as many pieces as I can produce."

"That's wonderful. You're on your way." It *was*

wonderful. And childish of her to feel disappointed because he'd told Joanne first.

Then she noticed Natalie squirming in her chair and looking hungrily at the untouched food. "What are we waiting for?" she said. "Let's eat."

Brian was the perfect dinner guest, Karina thought afterward as she laid her knife and fork across her empty plate. He'd kept Natalie in stitches with his teasing, likewise Joanne with his friendly banter. To herself, he'd been charmingly attentive. Maybe he was a trifle too sure of himself, but that was easy to forgive.

Daniel alone had been on edge throughout dinner, constantly alert to Brian's every word and expression. Yet even with Daniel...no, *especially* with Daniel, Brian had been nothing but warm and friendly.

"Kar-ina!" Joanne called to her from across the table. She glanced up. "Sorry?"

"Brian was just saying how much he likes to golf. Maybe he can give you some pointers."

Karina sat up and looked at Brian. "You're a golfer!" Beside her, she sensed a surge in Daniel's tension level.

"I play most weekends," Brian replied. "Are you interested in the game?"

"It's a long story...." Karina proceeded to relate the tale of her career aspirations and how they hinged on attending the corporate tournament.

"My dear Karina," Brian said expansively when she'd finished. "I'm attending that tournament myself. I'd be delighted if you'd come as my guest. What do you say?"

"I'd love—!" She caught herself. How was Daniel going to take this? Would he feel slighted that she'd go with his brother and not him? Surely he'd realize she was only doing it for her job and not because she wanted to be with Brian.

Quelling her excitement, she turned to Daniel. ''What do you think?''

CHAPTER NINE

"WONDERFUL," Daniel assured Karina, hoping his smile didn't looked as strained as it felt. *Wonderful?* It couldn't be worse if she'd announced her intention of touring hell with Lucifer as her personal guide.

He glanced across the table and caught the flash of triumph in his brother's eyes. A second later, Brian's expression changed to one of benevolent goodwill as he gazed at Karina.

Rage coursed through Daniel out of all proportion to the circumstances. He *was* glad Karina had got her wish. But why did it have to be Brian who'd granted it?

He felt Karina's fingers, soft as eiderdown, on the back of his hand. He turned toward her, expecting to see the same troubled expression that had clouded her dark eyes all evening whenever she'd looked at him.

But, no, she was smiling gently. With a nod, she indicated his daughter, who was drooped sleepily over her half-eaten dinner.

Daniel rose. "Come on, Possum. Time for bed."

"I'm not tired," Natalie protested, yawning. But she allowed him to sweep her into his arms, and she snuggled her head against his shoulder.

"Say good night, Natalie."

"Good night, Natalie." She giggled drowsily.

"Good night," Karina and Brian said together.

"Good night, Natalie," Joanne said. "Don't forget Julie's birthday party next week. It's dress-up."

Daniel paused in the doorway. "Dress-up?"

"Don't look so worried," Karina said with a laugh. "I love doing costumes. Fairy princesses are my specialty."

Daniel nodded his thanks and carried Natalie upstairs. Karina was so good to them, he thought, ashamed of his fit of jealousy. And she always managed to make it seem as though they were doing *her* a favor.

Karina rose and began to clear the table, conscious all the while of Brian watching her. She waited until Joanne had taken a load to the kitchen, then turned to him with a puzzled smile. "What?"

He spread his hands in a gesture of helpless admiration and silently returned her smile. *Uh-oh,* she thought. This golf weekend could get sticky if she didn't do a little preliminary groundwork.

"It's really nice of you to take me to the tournament, Brian," she said, gathering up the cutlery. "I'd like to do something for you in return."

Brian shook his head. He rose and began helping her stack the dishes. "Don't even think of it. It'll be my pleasure."

"No, I mean it. I'm going to design a new sign for your dealership. No obligation—take it or leave it. But if you decide to take it, I'll knock the design costs off the project."

"That's very generous, Karina, but truly, it's not in the least necessary."

Karina gave him a big smile. "Oh, but it is. You see, before tonight I considered hanging out at the local Chamber of Commerce to nab an unsuspecting golfer.

This is so much better. A stranger might get the wrong idea about the weekend...if you know what I mean.''

Brian's eyes twinkled. "I know what you mean. Men can be such *animals*."

Karina laughed. Everything was going to be all right, after all.

Brian moved around the table, picking up plates as he went. When he reached the spot where she stood piling cutlery into an empty casserole dish, he rested the plates on the table, his shoulder almost touching hers.

"I'll be the perfect big brother," he said. "I'll teach you golf and fend off inconvenient admirers. Did I mention I was on the fencing team at university?" He picked up a butter knife and made a minilunge past her ear. *"En garde."*

Laughing, she leaned backward and brandished a salad fork. "Just don't stab my boss until he's put my promotion in writing."

Behind her, Daniel cleared his throat.

Karina spun around. "Daniel! You startled me."

"Always remember to watch your back," he said, and strolled over to inspect the small collection of books lining the top shelf of the wall unit.

Brian uttered an amused grunt. She glanced back to see him gazing intently at Daniel. His brow was furrowed, but his mouth turned up at the corners, the tip of his forefinger pressed against his lips as though to prevent an incipient smile from broadening.

"I think I'll make coffee," she said. "Then we can have some of Joanne's cake. Triple chocolate delight, guaranteed to give you a coronary before you're fifty. No, stay right there," she added quickly when both brothers started to come to her assistance. "I'll bring it into the living room."

"Whew!" she exclaimed as she strode into the kitchen. "This is the weirdest evening."

Joanne looked up from the sink, where she was rinsing plates. "What's going on now? Are they duking it out in the living room?"

"Not yet, but I wouldn't be surprised if they ended up in the proverbial parking lot before the evening's over. I hope your chocolate cake will mellow them out."

"It'll weigh them down if nothing else. They won't be able to move quickly enough to damage each other."

Karina and Joanne looked at each other and laughed.

"I thought Daniel was going to pop Brian one when he invited you to the tournament," Joanne said.

Karina scraped off the side plates and handed them to Joanne. "Something deep and dark is simmering beneath the surface, that's for sure."

"Passion!" Joanne said in a theatrical whisper, her eyes widening.

"Revenge!" Karina whispered back, creeping up on Joanne with arms raised and fingers dramatically outstretched. Abruptly she lowered her hands. "Hang on. Brian's the one who should be seeking revenge, not Daniel."

"Oh, right." Joanne went back to stacking dishes. "He must have been pretty ticked when Daniel ran off with his fiancée."

Karina nodded as she poured ground coffee into the filter. "Who wouldn't be? But from what Daniel said, he and Francine weren't happy for very long."

She crumpled the empty coffee package and threw it into the garbage. Then she paused, kettle in hand, and listened. "It's awfully quiet out there."

Joanne straightened. "With kids, that's usually a sign of trouble."

"But they're two grown men."

"Yeah," Joanne agreed. "They'll work it out amicably."

Karina looked at Joanne. Joanne looked at Karina. "We'd better get out there," they said in unison.

Karina gathered up the dessert tray and, with Joanne hard on her heels, hurried back to the living room. To her surprise, the emotional temperature, far from approaching boiling point, was positively subzero.

Brian sat sideways on the sofa with the newspaper spread out in front of him. Daniel stood at the bookcase, thumbing through an ancient volume of Dostoyevsky left behind by one of her tenants. The brothers had their backs to each other, and the air between them was thick with animosity.

"Who's for cake and coffee?" Karina asked cheerily, creating a determined clatter with plates and cups.

The cake worked for a little while. Appreciative sounds issued from every mouth. But as the cake disappeared, so did all semblance of conversation. *Isn't this pleasant,* Karina thought, pressing her fork onto her plate to pick up the crumbs.

The emotional roller coaster they'd been riding since Brian had walked through the door had ground to a halt, yards from the finish. She had no more chatter, no more smiles, and from the look on Joanne's tired face, even her endless stream of quips had dried up. The silence of the brothers reigned supreme.

At last Joanne put aside her plate and stood. "I'd better go, Kar. If I'm not back by midnight, the baby-sitter will turn into a pumpkin and my kids will turn into mice." She went into the hall to retrieve her purse and coat. "On second thought, maybe that's not such a bad idea. I could put them in a cage and just give them a little food and water occasionally.''

Karina managed a chuckle, more out of loyalty than genuine humor. ''Thanks for all the help, Jo.''

''No problem.'' Joanne turned in the doorway. ''Nice to meet you, Brian. See you again, Daniel. No, don't anyone get up. 'Bye.''

Karina saw Joanne out. When she returned, Daniel was gathering up the coffee cups. ''Don't worry about those,'' she said.

With a shrug, he picked them up anyway and headed for the kitchen.

Brian rose. ''It was a wonderful dinner, Karina. I'm so glad to have met you.'' He moved toward the front door and took his jacket off the hook on the foyer wall.

''You're not going without saying goodbye to Daniel, are you?''

Brian shrugged, an eerie echo of Daniel's gesture minutes before. ''I don't think Danny's in the mood for family reunions tonight. You say goodbye for me. Please.'' He took both her hands in his and squeezed them lightly. ''I'll be in touch. Okay?''

Karina nodded helplessly. ''Okay.''

When he'd gone, she stalked down the hall toward the kitchen, her fury at Daniel growing with every step. She pushed open the door. He wasn't there. She went to the dining room. Not there, either. He couldn't have gone upstairs without her seeing him. The garage, then.

Sure enough, the back door was ajar, and from the deck she could see a solitary light burning in the low building at the back of the yard.

He was at the bench working on a drawing when she banged open the door. A muscle in his jaw jumped, but he didn't look up. In the glow of the gooseneck lamp, his profile looked as inflexible as the lengths of scarred red wood that had arrived that morning and lay stacked against the wall.

"Couldn't you even say good-night to your brother?" she said, storming into the room. "You finally get together and you treat him like some sort of...of... pariah."

Daniel's head jerked up, and he straightened away from the bench. The thin metal ruler he held between his hands bent under pressure. "Don't waste your time fretting over Brian, Karina. This evening was a farce from start to finish. The big-brother act is all for show."

Karina laughed compulsively and began to pace back and forth across the garage, hugging her arms around her waist to ward off the chill night air. "How can you say that? He was perfectly charming. He was great with Natalie, and *she* obviously adored him. He tried to make friends with you and you snubbed him."

Daniel slapped the flat side of the ruler on the bench. "He set out to make you like him and he succeeded. He wants you to think *I'm* the one who's being unreasonable. And it worked—I can see it in your face."

Karina stopped short and stared incredulously at him. "Daniel Bowen, I think you're jealous!"

His eyes sparked, green lights glinting among the amber. For a split second she saw something else there, as well, something primal and dangerous she'd never imagined could be part of Daniel.

He flung the ruler onto the bench, where it landed with a tinny clatter. Body rigid, hands clenched, he moved toward her. Rooted to the spot, she waited, electrified.

He didn't stop until the tips of his shoes nudged the toes of hers. With his face scant inches away, the memory of yesterday's kiss hung in the air between them.

Air charged with a chemistry they could neither acknowledge nor deny.

"My brother has nothing I want," he said, his voice low and harsh. "Nothing." He spun on his heel and disappeared out the door into the night.

KARINA SAT AT the kitchen table trying to concentrate on Daniel's business cards instead of wondering if he was avoiding her. He'd been back from visiting his parents in Campbell River for two days now and she'd hardly seen or spoken to him. Of course, that could also be because *she* was avoiding *him*.

She'd been wrong to interfere, she could see that now. Well, from now on she'd butt out. Daniel was perfectly capable of sorting out his own problems. First he had to *acknowledge* them, but that wasn't her responsibility, either.

She was so absorbed in her thoughts she didn't notice he'd entered the room until he sat down at the table opposite her and the faint, woodsy scent of his aftershave made her look up.

"Hi," she said, and wondered what was coming.

"I owe you an apology," he began stiffly. "I ruined your dinner party."

"It's not me you should be apologizing to."

Daniel's expression hardened. "I'll be damned if I'll apologize to Brian."

Karina put down the pen she'd been using and chose another from her set, one with a finer point. "You just apologized to me for a far less serious reason."

She began to rule a narrow border around Daniel's company name, Bowen's Fine Furniture. "Are you going to feud for another ten years?"

Daniel tossed down the spoon he'd been playing with. "I don't want to talk about it."

She shrugged as though she didn't care, but she was disappointed in him. "It's your life. I'm sorry I interfered. It won't happen again."

"Look, just because I won't apologize doesn't mean I'm giving up on Brian. I'm going to drop in on him after he gets home from work. Maybe without an audience, he and I can cut through the BS and work out our differences."

There was hope for him yet, Karina thought. She chose a favorite shade of rich, red-brown for the border on his card. "I'm sure you can."

His brow cleared. "I need to ask you a favor."

She lifted her head, giving him her full attention. "What can I do?"

"Look after Natalie for a few hours. I'd rather not take her to Brian's with me."

"No problem. I'll take her grocery shopping, then we'll make dinner. It'll be fun."

"She's not used to eating late," he said, the frown reappearing. "Six o'clock is her usual dinnertime. She should be in bed by seven-thirty. No junk food or she'll be bouncing off the walls."

Karina lay down her pen and stretched her cramped fingers. "*Relax*. I can handle it." She spun the card around to show him what she'd done. "What do you think?"

He gazed at it a moment, then glanced at her. "It's good. I like it." He pulled it closer and studied it further. "I really like it. How did you know what a woolshed looks like?"

"You can find almost anything on the Internet."

"Is that so? Anyway, getting back to Natalie—she's

meeting her teacher tomorrow. I want her to be well rested.''

Karina smiled indulgently. Daniel was behaving like a typical nervous parent overprotecting his offspring. ''She'll be fine,'' she assured him. ''Don't worry about a thing.''

''Look, Natalie, a fabric store.'' Karina tugged on the girl's hand to slow her headlong race down the sidewalk. ''Let's pop in here for a minute. We can get some material to make you a costume for Julie's party.''

Natalie bounced up and down in front of a large display of fabric rolls. ''Goody! I want to be a fairy princess.'' Then her little face puckered. ''Shouldn't we get the groceries first? Daddy always says we have to do our work before we get a treat.''

Karina laughed and waved her hand, silver bangles jangling merrily. ''That's an admirable sentiment and you should stick to that rule—most of the time. But making a fairy princess costume is very complicated. We have to decide all sorts of things, like whether your wand should be silver or gold, or if there should be sequins on the bodice or tiny pearls. How could we make important decisions if the ice cream was melting in the back of the car?''

''Gee, I guess we couldn't, but...'' Natalie had that glazed look Karina sometimes noticed on Daniel's face when she was trying to convince him of something.

''We've got plenty of time,'' Karina assured her. ''Don't worry about a thing.''

Daniel glanced at his watch with growing impatience. Six-thirty. He'd been sitting on this park bench across the road from Brian's apartment building for more than an hour.

He hoped Karina wouldn't wait dinner for him. And that she'd get Natalie to bed on time if he wasn't back. Maybe he should give her a call to remind her.

Rising, he walked a dozen paces in either direction along Dallas Road. Expensive homes and apartment buildings lined the scenic drive along the waterfront but there wasn't a phone booth in sight.

He resumed his seat on the bench and leaned back, eyes closed. Thoughts of Karina drifted through his head, the scent of her perfume mingling in his memory with the smell of sawdust. It wasn't the fight over Brian that occupied his mind, but the kiss they'd shared.

How they'd connected. Tighter than a dovetail, hotter than an arc light. He could still feel the softness of her hair as it drifted like heavy silk between his fingers. Could still see the troubled look in her eyes as she'd pulled away from him.

He might have bought her story about not wanting to get involved with a tenant if he wasn't so certain there was more to it than that. For instance, why didn't she have a boyfriend? A woman who looked like she did, who was as smart and funny and warmhearted as she was, ought to at least have a boyfriend.

Unless she was getting over one. But if so, why wasn't she all droopy and depressed?

Maybe it had to do with her coming birthday. The fact that her mother had been thirty-two when she'd died obviously held significance for Karina. Was *she* afraid of dying? So afraid she wouldn't let herself fall in love? Surely not. Karina *was* a bit capricious, but that didn't make her totally irrational.

Women could be funny about birthdays, but he didn't

think that usually happened until they hit forty or fifty. As though a few wrinkles or grey hairs mattered. As far as he was concerned, the older a woman got, the more interesting she became. More confident, more at ease with herself. More beautiful.

Was it possible for Karina to become more beautiful than she already was? Now there was an interesting conundrum....

Daniel sat upright with a jerk. A silver Jag had just pulled into the curb in front of the apartment building across the road. Shielding his face from the sun, he watched Brian get out of the car and go through the glass doors into the lobby.

He waited another ten minutes to give Brian time to settle in, then he crossed the road and found his brother's name on the directory. His hand hovered over the intercom button. What if Brian refused to let him in? No point taking a chance.

Daniel waited until a couple came out engrossed in conversation and slipped in through the open door.

Up the elevator, down the wide, carpeted hall he went, glancing at the numbered doors until he found Brian's apartment. He knocked. No answer. Shifting his feet impatiently, he lifted his hand to knock again.

The door swung open. Brian held a tumbler of dark amber liquid in his hand, and his eyebrows lifted in faint surprise. Daniel braced himself for harsh words.

Brian gave him the once-over, his lips pursed thoughtfully. Then he turned and walked back into the apartment. "Like a Scotch, Danny?"

"Thanks, I would." Daniel followed Brian inside.

At a side table in the living room, Brian dropped ice into another tumbler and poured out a healthy swig of Scotch. Daniel glanced around, surprised by the art deco furnishings and abstract paintings that adorned walls of deep Chinese red. Somehow he'd expected a lot of chrome and black leather furniture. But then again, most of his ideas about Brian were ten years out of date.

"Nice place," he commented as Brian handed him his drink. A triple, by the look of it.

"I like it. Bottoms up."

Daniel raised his glass in a brief salute and took a sip. The scotch, smooth and expensive, slid down his throat and warmed his empty stomach.

"Have a seat." Brian lowered himself into a chair and gestured to the sofa opposite. "We got off on the wrong foot, didn't we, Danny?"

Daniel sank onto the scallop-backed sofa that was covered in a dark paisley not unlike Karina's pig. "Maybe I was a little hotheaded—" He stopped, studying Brian's bland, good-natured face suspiciously. Was this some kind of trap? He wasn't going to give anything away until he knew where Brian was headed with this.

Brian leaned forward, his hands spread in a gesture of reconciliation. "I was out of line with those stories about the old days. I'm sorry, Dan, I really am."

"Why did you do it?" Daniel asked, still wary.

"I guess I was getting back at you for…Francine. We never really had it out over her." Frowning at his drink, Brian swirled the glass and set the ice tinkling.

Daniel gave a short laugh. "You mean it would have been better if we'd settled the matter with a fistfight? We still could."

Brian shook his head. "Not a chance. I've got twenty pounds on you, but they're pounds of lard, not muscle. No, I'd rather just put the past to rest. Let bygones be bygones. What do you say, Danny boy?"

"Sounds good to me." He was so pleased, he managed to ignore the hated nickname. Pleased but cautious. Feeling like Charlie Brown wondering if Lucy would whip the football out of reach before he could kick it, Daniel put out his hand to shake on it.

Brian took his hand and gripped it hard. A smile spread across his ruddy face. "I've been waiting for this moment for a long time."

Daniel grinned back. "I have, too."

Slowly, Daniel released his brother's hand, still hardly daring to believe in the change that had come over Brian. But there was no one else around to impress or mislead with a false show of brotherly love. He had to be sincere. Unless he had some hidden agenda....

Daniel dismissed that thought. Brian had simply had second thoughts about his hard-line approach. Hadn't he, himself, come here today prepared to bend a little? *Take Brian's gesture of peace at face value,* he told himself. *All that matters is that we're friends again.*

Daniel leaned forward, his drink cupped between his hands. "I drove up to see Mom and Dad this week. They're doing really well. Dad catches chinook salmon by the boatload, and Mom's busy canning them—when she's not planning their next trip, that is. They're going to Arizona in November—"

"I know." Brian rose abruptly and went to the side table. "I saw them last month. Before that, in March. In fact, I've seen them hundreds of times in the past ten years."

"Of course." Daniel sipped his scotch, chastened. "Mom asked me how we were getting along. She and Dad will be happy to hear we're on speaking terms again. Maybe next time we could go up together."

Brian glanced at him. "Freshen your drink?"

"I'm fine." Daniel watched his brother load his crystal tumbler with more ice while studiously ignoring Daniel's remarks. Was Brian afraid of losing face? Or showing too much emotion? Maybe it was better not to rush things. They couldn't just wipe out a decade of estrangement in an hour.

But they could chip away at it.

"Say, Brian, how about a little game of one-on-one someday? There's a high school with an outdoor basketball court not far from Karina's."

Brian set down the ice tongs and picked up the decanter. "Now there's an idea," he said, flashing a grin sideways at Daniel. "I haven't whupped you in ages."

Daniel felt the sting but he grinned back. "You always did run circles around me on the court, you old bastard."

Brian laughed. "That's because you never practiced." He poured the Scotch. There was a faint cracking sound as the warm liquid hit the ice.

Daniel shrugged. "I'm into sports more now—tennis, swimming, basketball. Keeps me in shape." He didn't bother to add he'd taken them up once Brian was no longer around to make him feel inadequate. "I guess I've changed."

Brian's smile faded as he subjected Daniel to silent scrutiny. "You've changed, all right, Danny boy," he said, a catch in his voice. "You're a grown man. A father. Damn lucky son of a bitch if you ask me." He turned away, placing the decanter unsteadily on the table.

Daniel stared back, guilt gnawing at his gut. If he hadn't taken Francine away from Brian, his brother might be the one with the child. The thought of not having Natalie pulled at Daniel's heart, fierce and sharp. If Brian felt a fraction of that...

He rose and put a hand on his brother's shoulder. "It's not too late, Brian. You're only, what…thirty-six? Plenty of time to marry and have kids."

Brian shrugged his hand away. "I'm getting old, Danny boy, set in my ways. But maybe…" He turned to Daniel, a spark in his pale blue eyes. "Do you believe in love at first sight?"

Karina's image flashed into his mind. "No," he said a little too quickly.

"Then you *have* changed," Brian said, eyeing him curiously. "Wasn't that how you and…Francine got together?"

Daniel hesitated. His reaction to Francine had been more like lust at first sight. But was there any point in adding insult to injury by giving Brian an accurate picture of the past? Every time his brother said her name he sounded as if he were in pain.

"Yeah, it was pretty much instantaneous." *A flash in the pan.* "I'm sorry about the way things turned out, Brian. Really sorry."

Brian gazed at him for a long moment, nodding slowly. "I'm not surprised you took to her right away. Francine was one hot babe. Although what she ever saw in *you* that *I* didn't have, I never could figure." Tilting his head back, he took a large swig of Scotch.

Daniel gripped his glass hard. He wouldn't ruin their truce by taking offense. To be fair, he'd wondered the same thing at the time. Brian had been the golden-haired boy in high school, and university had only enhanced his reputation. As captain of the basketball team and a track star, he'd attracted the prettiest and most popular girls in the school.

All that was ancient history. "So, what about that spin around the courts?" Daniel said. "Saturday morning?"

Brian's eyebrows rose. "Didn't Karina tell you? She and I are going golfing Saturday morning." He came forward and slapped Daniel on the shoulder. "You don't mind, do you, Danny, old boy? You did say she wasn't a girlfriend."

Daniel stared at him. Karina had refused to get involved with him, yet she'd made a date with his brother. It was only golf, he told himself. Not even something Karina liked to do.

"Mind?" Daniel replied, almost choking on the word. "Why should I mind?"

"I thought maybe you had designs on her yourself," Brian said, his gaze fixed on Daniel's face. "I wouldn't want to poach in your territory. Tell me to back off and I will."

What could he say? Whatever *his* feelings might be, Karina had let him know loud and clear that she wasn't interested in a romantic relationship. If the same applied to Brian, his brother would find out for himself. There was nothing to gain by staking a claim on Karina. And a hell of a lot to lose.

"We're just friends," he said at last. "Go for it."

CHAPTER TEN

"TURN AROUND, Natalie, so I can see your wings properly."

From her perch on top of the coffee table, Natalie obediently spun on her tiptoes, spreading her arms in glee. Excitement dabbed her cheeks with pink, and her blue eyes sparkled. She looked like a tiny doll on top of a music box, and it made Karina laugh to see her so happy.

"Daddy's going to be so surprised!" Natalie chattered excitedly. "He's never seen me be a fairy princess before."

Karina laughed. "He'll be thrilled. You look absolutely beautiful. Whoops, your right wing is slipping. Hang on while I sew it back into place."

Natalie stood as still as a six-year-old fairy can stand, jiggling slightly in her nearly new, pink satin ballet slippers. The slippers were a real score, Karina thought as she made tiny, neat stitches through the silver gauze wing. They'd found them in a thrift shop next to the fabric store, along with the star for the top of the fairy wand.

"Are you liking it here in Canada, Natalie?" Karina asked through a mouthful of pins.

Natalie judiciously tipped her head to one side. "It's okay. I like your house." She turned her head and Karina could see her pixie face in profile. "I like *you.*"

Her heart swelled until it felt too big for her chest. "Thanks," she managed to say casually. "I like you, too."

"And Daddy?"

Her response was a little slower in coming, but she replied, "Sure, I like your daddy, too."

"Good. 'Cause I asked him when I could have another mommy and he said when we both fell in love with the same person. I told him I wanted it to be you."

Karina almost choked. "What did he say?" She wasn't sure she wanted to know the answer, but to be forewarned was to be forearmed.

"He said you didn't want to fall in love." Natalie's round, blue eyes shone with curiosity. "Why not? Don't you want to wear a pretty white dress and have flowers in your hair and live happily ever after?"

"Gee, Natalie, all that sounds great, but there's more to marriage than the wedding day. Things don't always work out the way you expect or hope." Letting Daniel kiss her was even more irresponsible than she'd thought, Karina realized. Natalie could get hurt, too.

"If you change your mind, can I be a flower girl and wear my fairy costume?"

"Mmm," Karina murmured noncommittally, suppressing a smile. She jabbed the needle into a thick knot of fabric at the base of the wing and pushed hard.

Natalie's tummy growled. Karina winced as her conscience and the needle pricked her at the same time. They never had got around to grocery shopping. That tin of tuna was probably still in the cupboard, but it was a bit late to make a casserole now.

She tied off the knot and got to her feet. "Hey, Natalie, ever tried tuna-and-peanut-butter sandwiches?"

Natalie made a most unfairylike face. "Yuck!"

"Maybe you're right. Have another corn chip."

The little girl plunged her hand into the bag of chips on the coffee table. "Daddy never lets me eat snacks before dinner," she said, munching happily.

Karina's conscience gave another twinge. She'd promised to have dinner ready, and here it was... She glanced at the clock on the stereo.

Oh, no. Twenty minutes to eight.

"Come on, Nattie. We'd better put away this stuff and get you something decent to eat."

Spilling crumbs down her sequined bodice, Natalie crammed a last handful of chips into her mouth. "Mrs. Beeton wants Daddy to get married again, too," she confided.

Karina began picking scraps of fabric off the floor. "Ah, Mrs. Beeton. We'll have to make her a special dress for the wedding. Whenever that is," she added hastily. She'd forgotten for the moment there wasn't actually going to be a wedding.

"Mrs. Beeton doesn't need a dress," Natalie replied. "She wears heavenly rain-mints."

"Heavenly raiment?" In her surprise, Karina dropped a spool of thread and it rolled away under the sofa.

Natalie nodded. "Anyway, it doesn't matter what she wears, because no one can see her except me."

Karina got down on her hands and knees to retrieve the thread. "Isn't Mrs. Beeton a doll? I heard you talking to her in your room."

Natalie sighed with the exasperation of an intelligent child confronted with an unbelievably thickheaded adult. "Mrs. Beeton is an *angel*. Can I move now?"

"Whoa! Hold on there, Nattie. Mrs. Beeton is an *angel?*"

The girl nodded. "After Mommy died, Mrs. Beeton came down from heaven to look after me."

Stunned, Karina fell silent. The child's eyes were not alight with fantasy now. They were sober, pragmatic and tinged with a sadness that seemed far too great for her six years.

Karina searched Natalie's solemn little face, wishing she could say something to ease the child's pain. Wishing she could comfort her, let her know she wasn't alone in her suffering. But the thought of opening her own badly healed wound by telling Natalie about Mama made her heart recoil.

"Your daddy looks after you," she whispered at last, ashamed of her weakness. Though her words were true, they denied the gut-wrenching need the child had for her mother.

Natalie nodded, her mouth drooping at the corners. She turned her wand disconsolately in her fingers. Karina gazed at her sorrowfully. If only she could wave that magic wand and wish Natalie's mother back into existence. Why couldn't she say something, anything, that would help Natalie understand and accept her mother's death?

But how could she? She had little understanding and no acceptance in her own heart.

"You know what, Nattie," she said with a gentle smile. "Whenever I feel sad, I sing a silly song. It really works. Listen." She began to sing, "'Way down south where bananas grow, a bee stepped on an elephant's toe....'"

To her relief, a tiny smile appeared on Natalie's face.

"'The elephant cried with tears in his eyes...'"

Natalie's smile widened at Karina's exaggerated actions and grimaces. Encouraged, Karina got to her feet and grasped the girl's hands, spinning her around in a circle.

"'Pick on someone your own darn size!'"

Brandishing her wand, the girl marched up and down while Karina belted out the chorus.

"'Boom, boom, ain't it great to be crazy? Giddy and foolish all day long. Boom, boom, ain't it great to be cra-zy!'"

Natalie collapsed in a heap of giggles. Laughing along with her, Karina gathered her into a big hug and swung her around and around.

All at once she noticed they weren't alone.

DANIEL STARED AT Karina and Natalie, his troubles with Brian banished by shock. The living room looked as though a cyclone had hit. Snippets of muslin and satin were strewn everywhere, and drifts of the frothy material extended into the dining room. Scattered sequins winked up from the dark blue carpet along with bits of thread, bent coat hangers and lengths of ribbon and lace.

His gaze swept back to Natalie, taking in her flushed cheeks and wings knocked awry. And Karina. She might well look guilty, he thought, his mouth tightening. Natalie should have been in bed half an hour ago.

"Daddy!" Natalie leaped off the table and ran to his arms. "Look at the beautiful costume Karina made me." She pulled away again and capered around, springing on and off the coffee table like a baby goat.

"Get off the coffee table, Natalie."

"Karina said I could."

"*Get off the coffee table.*" He turned to Karina. "I didn't think I'd be this late," he said stiffly. "I hope you went ahead and had dinner without me."

"Er…" Karina's voice trailed away.

From the corner of his eye he saw her kick a corn-chip bag beneath the table.

"We haven't had dinner yet," Natalie chirped. "Do *you* like tuna-and-peanut-butter sandwiches, Daddy?"

Daniel grimaced in disbelief. "No dinner?" He looked at his watch. "You've been eating something, though, haven't you, Nattie?" He caught the girl as she swung by and stooped to inspect the yellow crumbs that dusted the front of her costume.

"Corn chips!" Natalie whirled out of his grasp. "'Way down south where bananas grow...'"

"I'm really sorry," Karina said quickly, sweeping fabric scraps off the floor and into her arms. "We got carried away. I'll make her a sandwich or something."

"'A bee stepped on an elephant's toe...'" Natalie sang blithely on, waving her magic wand.

"A sandwich?" Daniel repeated. "Surely you can do better than that with the groceries you bought?"

"'The elephant cried with tears in his eyes...'"

"Shh, Nattie," Karina said. "Not now. Your daddy's upset."

Instead of placating him, Karina's conspiratorial whisper fueled his anger. First, she hadn't told him about her golf game with Brian. Now she was siding with his daughter against him, making *him* look like the bad guy. Deep down, he knew he was judging too harshly, but at this moment, he was pretty much fed up with Karina Peterson.

"*I said,* what about the groceries?"

Karina shifted her glance back to him uneasily. "We didn't make it to the store on time."

Daniel squeezed his eyes shut and saw red. "What do you mean, you didn't—"

"'Pick on someone your own darn size!'"

"Natalie!" he bellowed. "Get upstairs and into your pajamas right this instant."

Natalie stopped singing abruptly, a stricken look on her face. She ran past him out of the room and up the stairs.

He turned to Karina. "You promised me you'd look after my daughter. That meant giving her dinner and tucking her into bed, not singing goddamn nursery rhymes till all hours of the night."

Karina let out an inappropriate burst of laughter. "I said I was sorry."

"I'm glad you think this is funny, because I don't. Sorry doesn't change a thing."

"Lighten up, Daniel," she said, not sounding sorry anymore. "It's not the end of the world if she doesn't eat on time for one night. She was having a ball till you came in doing your irate-father act."

"I've got a right to be angry. She was having a ball, all right. Bouncing off the walls. I *told* you that would happen if she didn't have a proper dinner."

Suddenly Natalie barreled back down the stairs, her pajama top only half buttoned. She pushed past Daniel and flung herself in front of Karina. "Don't yell at Karina. She's my friend and I love her."

"Oh, for Pete's sake!" He reached for his daughter, but she dodged away.

Dropping to her knees, Karina gathered Natalie into her arms. "Your father has a right to be angry, honey. I screwed up."

Fuming, Daniel watched impotently as Karina soothed Natalie. He couldn't help but notice the tenderness on Karina's face and his child's adoring response. And why shouldn't she be adoring? Karina had brought laughter and fun into her life. *And mine,* he thought, cursing himself for his misplaced anger. Did a missed meal really matter so much?

"Come on, Natalie," Karina said. "I'll make you some French toast."

"I'll do it." Daniel's voice was rough with emotion as he reached for Natalie's hand. He'd intended his words to be conciliatory, but Natalie burrowed deeper into Karina's arms.

Karina glared at him over Natalie's small blond head. "For heaven's sake, what difference does it make who feeds her?"

At that, the sobbing child wriggled free. "I'm not hungry!" Pushing away from both of them, she dashed out of the room and up the stairs. A second later, her door slammed shut.

Karina, her cheeks flushed and her mouth set in a grim line, silently began to gather up more scraps of muslin and lace.

Weary of it all, Daniel rubbed the back of his neck. "It's my fault for expecting too much. You couldn't know how important it is for a small child to get regular meals and plenty of rest. How could you? You're not a mother."

To his astonishment, Karina, who'd held up to his angry onslaught like a soldier, suddenly slumped as though he'd hit her. Tears welled in her eyes, spilled over and coursed down her cheeks.

"Daniel Bowen, you're an absolute pig!" Dropping the armload of fabric, she pushed past him and ran from the room.

Daniel stared after her in shocked silence. Overhead, her door slammed and he flinched. Now what had he done?

His stomach growled with hunger and his brother's

Scotch curdled his insides like acid, but he walked straight through the kitchen and out the back door. *Tuna-and-peanut-butter sandwiches, for crying out loud.*

He entered the garage, giving the hood of Karina's red sports car a frustrated thump with his fist as he went past.

Pieces of her dining room table were propped against the wall waiting to be put together. He ignored them and crossed to a steamer trunk tucked beneath the work bench. Lifting the heavy lid, he reached in and pulled out a large box wrapped in felt. He placed the box on the bench and threw back the wrapper.

Daniel ran his fingers over the smooth, black-brown ebony wood, admiring the way the lamp's beam brought out glints of auburn from deep within the grain. It reminded him of Karina's hair.

Once or twice he'd caught a glimpse of her dresser through her open bedroom door. Invariably, a pile of bracelets and necklaces spilled out of a pitifully inadequate pink container. A jewelry box, he'd decided, would make the perfect birthday gift.

He swung a leg over the high wooden stool and scooted it closer to the bench. Reaching for a fresh sheet of sandpaper, he started to rub the long edge of the piece of wood that was to become the lid. It was painstaking work, making small items, and he rarely did it. He wasn't entirely sure why he was doing it now.

Letting Natalie get close to Karina had been a mistake. Though how he could have prevented it, living in the same house, he didn't know. In hindsight, it was no wonder she'd bonded so quickly; Karina was a natural with children.

Soon his fingers and the lid were covered with fine dark dust. He prided himself on being a good communicator but he'd failed miserably tonight, letting his rivalry with Brian get the better of him. Images from the night of the dinner party came back with agonizing clarity. Karina's voice saying, *"Brian is perfectly charming,"* Karina's smiling eyes gazing into his brother's…

She'd said she didn't want to get involved with anyone. Maybe what she'd really meant was she didn't want to get involved with *him.* She was so kindhearted she might have merely wanted to save his pride.

Brian could give her something she needed. Daniel didn't think for a second she would deliberately use anyone, but common interests often led to stronger emotions. And if there was an attraction there to begin with…

The thought of Brian and Karina together made him grip the sandpaper hard between his fingers. Thousands of tiny grains of silica bit into his skin.

Pushing the thought from his head, he rasped at the hard black wood as if he could reduce his feeling of déjà vu to dust along with the rough edges of the jewelry box. That his brother was infatuated with Karina wasn't hard to understand—Daniel was equally infatuated.

But were his feelings for her strong enough to justify tampering with Brian's happiness *again?* He wanted her, there was no doubt about that. He liked her enormously, no question there, either, despite what had happened tonight. He admired her, respected her….

Was that love?

The thought of competing with Brian over a woman was unpalatable. He'd lived with the consequences of winning once before and it hadn't been worth the prize. But, then, the prize hadn't been Karina.

Daniel slid off the stool and paced the length of the garage to the open door. Looking out and up, he could see the light in her bedroom window. As he watched, her silhouette appeared behind the drawn curtains. His breath caught in his throat as she raised her arms and drew her dress over her head.

He turned away, his heart pounding.

KARINA LEANED AGAINST the door she'd just slammed shut. Eyes closed, she took in great gulps of air, forcing her tears under control. Tears couldn't make Daniel take back his words or change the truth of them.

It *was* true: she wasn't a mother. How could she know what a child needed, really? Oh, she was very good at playing with children; she'd had plenty of experience with Joanne's kids. She knew what they liked, how they thought. Sometimes she suspected that was because she was still a bit of a kid herself.

But her feelings toward Natalie were different. Something in the little girl struck a chord so deep it sometimes seemed as though she were reliving her own childhood. So much life and laughter, fun and silliness. Karina smiled at the memory of Natalie standing on the coffee table, singing at the top of her lungs.

Nattie was good at drawing and artwork, too. Daniel deserved a lot of credit for encouraging the girl's creative energy to bloom and grow. She'd never seen such an imaginative child—

Karina pushed away from the door. Should she speak to Daniel about Mrs. Beeton? Did she have the right? After tonight, he might not want her to have anything to do with Natalie.

No, surely he wouldn't be so unkind. But maybe he wasn't worried about Mrs. Beeton. *Was* it a worry? Or was it perfectly natural?

Karina remembered how she'd sunk into a fantasy

world for a while after Mama died. A world where Mama magically reappeared and they were all happy again. Of course, she'd known all the time it couldn't really happen. How much of what Natalie pretended did she think was real? Did it matter?

Karina wandered restlessly over to her dresser and halfheartedly tried to tidy her jewelry box. She might not be able to solve the problem of Mrs. Beeton, but she could, she *must* deal with her own behavior. She rarely lost confidence in her abilities, but tonight she had.

When Daniel had reminded her of the importance of giving Natalie dinner on time, she'd thought he was just being overprotective. But what if he'd seen something lacking in her? Something that made her incapable of handling the mundane but essential aspects of child care, like proper food and rest. He'd worried but he'd trusted her anyway.

And she'd let him down.

Karina jammed the lid on the jewelry box and pushed it away, its contents still jumbled, like her thoughts. She reached for a folding pewter frame, half hidden behind a ceramic oil lamp.

Her mother and father on their wedding day. Her mother smiled out of the photo, darkly beautiful in heavy ivory satin. She held a bouquet of deep red roses the color of her lips and the fainter bloom on her cheeks.

Mama, I'm a failure.

The idea came out of nowhere. Caught by surprise, hot tears pricked the backs of her eyes. With a sharp intake of breath, she blinked them away, but she couldn't stem the agonized thoughts that crowded her mind.

Yes, Mama, you heard me right. I was only half grown when you died. You never finished teaching me. Look at me now. I can't cook, I can't clean. I can't even take care of one little girl.

Sometimes she felt as if she'd never grown up. Never *would* grow up. A chunk of her life was missing, the part where she was supposed to follow her mother's footsteps into womanhood. Instead, she'd made the journey with no one to guide her, blindly muddling through the long years from thirteen to thirty-two.

But you run a whole art department, a voice in her head protested. *You're one of the best graphic artists around. You know the business like nobody else. Not only that, but everyone likes you. People give their best for you.*

Karina pushed the voice away. None of that was enough if she wasn't capable of committing herself to a man and bearing his children.

She folded her arms around her waist and hugged herself hard. For a little while today she'd been able to pretend Natalie was her own daughter. It had been such a good feeling, so full of joy. So *right.* Like the way she'd felt in Daniel's arms.

Two fat tears squeezed out of her tightly clenched eyes and rolled down her cheeks. It frightened her how good the two of them made her feel—Natalie greeting her with a hug and a kiss, the sound of Daniel's power saw making a man's place in her home. For the first time in what seemed like forever, she felt part of a family. She'd never realized until now how deeply lonely she was. Or how big the gaping hole in her life that friends and work just couldn't fill.

Sadly she folded shut the wedding photo and replaced it on the dresser, then crossed to the window to peer through the sheers. Cool night air curled through the small space at the bottom of the window where she'd wedged it open with a hairbrush.

The light was still on in the garage. Daniel was out there now. Karina pulled down the blind and turned away.

A multicolored silk shawl with a long crimson fringe lay draped over the back of a chair. She wrapped it around herself, breathing in the scent of gardenia that was more memory than fragrance. And thought of the last time she'd seen her mother wearing it.

It was after Mama had been diagnosed but before all the really bad stuff started. They'd sat at the table in the meals area one sunny winter afternoon drinking cup after cup of milky tea and going over old photos. Mama was writing dates and names on the back.

She'd started by telling Karina about her childhood in Italy and ended up recounting every funny thing she could remember Karina doing as a child. Some of it had sounded pretty stupid, but Mama had laughed and laughed.

Karina spun on her heel and paced. She should stop remembering now. She felt the warning tightness in her chest, the pricking behind the eyes. She tried to think of something else, but the memories wouldn't disappear. Her mother's image, dark eyes alight and teasing, wouldn't fade....

Desperate, Karina reached for the radio beside her bed and turned up the volume. The ringing tones of a steel band blasted out at her. But even that wasn't enough to escape her thoughts. Forcing her mouth into a soundless O, she blew. Nothing happened.

Heart pounding, she licked her dry lips and blew again, her hands over her ears to shut out the sound of her mother's laughing, loving voice.

A thin, cracked whistle squeaked past her lips. With a rush of relief, she gasped for another breath. Tunelessly at first, then louder, more melodic, she blew until she was whistling in time with the music. Blanking her mind from taboo thoughts of warmth and love and happiness.

Slowly Karina began to breathe normally again. Now she could feel the Caribbean beat right inside her chest, drowning out the pathetic thumping of her heart.

Safe inside the cocoon of music, she flung off the shawl and pulled her dress over her head. Then she crawled into bed to lie curled on her side, arms tucked into her chest, eyes squeezed shut against the darkness.

CHAPTER ELEVEN

ON THE CLIFF TOP golf course at Gonzales Point, Karina paused to admire the view. Across the Strait of Juan de Fuca, the Olympic Mountains soared, their white peaks etched against the clear blue sky.

With an effort, she dragged her gaze back to the small white ball on the tee in front of her. Planting her feet firmly, she adjusted her grip and waggled the club experimentally.

"Keep your arms loose," Brian coached. He'd already teed off at the men's platform, and his ball had gone zinging out of sight down the fairway. "Now, raise the club, ready to swing."

Karina dutifully did as he said. Club poised on high, she peered down the fairway, trying to remember everything he'd told her about wrists, elbows, knees.

"Ready?" he said. "Swing!"

She swung the club downward. *Whack!* The golf ball soared into the air, sailed down the fairway....

And landed thirty feet away.

"It's okay," Brian assured her as he jogged out to retrieve the ball. "Happens to everyone. Now if this were a *real* game, you wouldn't get another chance unless your co-workers are so chauvinistic they'd offer the little lady another turn."

"I doubt it," Karina replied. "Not that I'd take it even

if they did. I've got to compete fair and square or I'll lose all credibility.''

Brian replaced the ball on the tee. "This time, keep your eyes on the ball as your club connects with it. Think of it as your boss's head if that helps.''

Karina laughed. Her smile faded as she realized whose head she'd like to be whacking a couple of hundred yards down the fairway. She wasn't trying to make Daniel jealous, but he might have looked a *little* put out when Brian had come to pick her up.

Instead he'd nonchalantly poured Brian a coffee and said how nice it was for Karina to have an expert teach her the game. He'd even come to the door to see them off, cheerfully bidding her to have a good time.

Focusing on the ball at her feet, Karina adjusted her grip. It had been almost as though Daniel were officially handing her over to his brother, for heaven's sake. He'd kissed her once and regretted it. Well, that was fine. More than fine, it was great.

"Karina?''

Shaking the hair out of her eyes, she glanced over her shoulder at Brian. From his quizzical expression she realized she must have been glaring at the ball for some time.

"Sorry.'' She swung her club back, high above her head. Nobody kissed *her* and regretted it. Down came the swing and—*thwack!*—the ball went flying.

"Fantastic!'' Brian gazed down the fairway, one hand shading his eyes. "I can't even see it. You're going to knock 'em dead at the tournament.''

Karina turned to grin at him. She was actually having fun. Brian tended to be a little condescending, but for the most part he was good company, and he certainly knew golf.

Swinging her club over her shoulder, she joined him for the walk to find their balls. With his caddy trailing behind him, Brian looked every inch the serious golfer from his white cleated shoes to the pale blue polo shirt that perfectly matched his eyes.

He laid his hand lightly on her shoulder, and a faint echo of the attraction she felt for Daniel prevented her from ducking away.

"I hope you don't really believe what you said about everyone competing fair and square," he said.

She glanced sideways at him and was surprised to see he was serious. His hand began to feel heavy on her shoulder. "I said *I* would compete fairly. I'm not naive enough to think everyone does."

"Good," he replied with a nod. "Like Daniel said, you've got to watch your back. Just when you think people are playing by the rules, wham, somebody sneaks up from behind and sticks a knife into you."

Karina frowned at the note of bitterness in his voice. He wasn't talking about golf, or even business. He was talking about Daniel and what had happened with Francine. But she was *not* going to interfere again, so she just said, "Sometimes circumstances overwhelm even the best of us."

Brian directed his gaze ahead. "People create their own circumstances centered around personal gain. You can't trust anyone."

This was too much. She bent to tie a shoelace that didn't need tying, and when she straightened, her shoulder was free.

"I disagree," she said. "How people treat you is a reflection of how *you* treat *them*. And if you're too busy watching your back, you can't go forward, let alone mend fences."

He cast her a faintly sardonic smile, then continued up the fairway. "In high school," he went on as smoothly as if he weren't changing the subject, "I was good at sports but Daniel was always the popular one with the girls."

An image flashed through Karina's mind of Daniel as a lanky teenager casually leaning against a row of lockers, hands in his back pockets as he smiled his slow smile at some sweet, young thing. She nodded. Yes, she could see that.

Brian cast her a brief, assessing glance. "Sometimes it seemed as though he had all the prettiest girls eating out of his hand. He was always the smart one, you see. Girls like that."

"Come on, Brian," Karina protested. "You're an attractive man. You must have had plenty of girlfriends." It seemed to her the two brothers should have complemented each other rather than compete, but she had enough experience with her own brother to know that siblings didn't always see things logically.

Brian smiled, charming and modest. "You're sweet to say so. But I was involved in so many sports I didn't have as much time as he did to cultivate a social life."

"Did you resent Daniel for that?" Karina asked, wondering where all this was leading. She glanced ahead for her golf ball and thought she could see it lurking at the edge of the fairway a hundred yards or so away.

Again the tiny smile. "How could I help it? But we were friends, too. So I hid it as best I could." Brian looked up at the sky and sighed. "When I met Francine, it was love at first sight. I'd gone away to Vancouver to attend university and I was glad Danny had decided to stay in Victoria. You see…"

Karina glanced at his troubled expression. "Go on."

"I was afraid she'd take one look at Danny and leave me for him." Brian suddenly strode off to the right. "Here's your ball. A nine iron would be best for this shot."

Karina hurried to catch up. "Thanks," she said, taking the club from him. "Which way is the green?"

Brian pointed her in the right direction and she hit the ball, less successfully this time. She was more interested in hearing Brian's version of the story than in improving her handicap. But Brian fell silent as they walked over to his ball. There, he took his time sorting through his clubs and testing his swing. At last he raised his club and, with a short, sharp smack, sent the ball up and onto the green.

They walked off again in search of Karina's ball. "Daniel told me he met Francine at your parents' house," she said, unable to contain her curiosity any longer.

"That's right. I brought her home to meet the family once we were officially engaged. I was so happy she'd actually accepted me." A frown appeared on his brow. "I don't know if I've ever been quite that happy again."

Karina's ball rested a scant inch inside a sand trap. Brian pulled a club out of his golf bag, but instead of handing it to her, he gripped it hard with both hands.

"Even the prospect of running into Danny didn't faze me. But the moment he walked into the living room and I saw him look at Francine, I knew he was going to make a play for her."

"That must have been dreadful!" Karina exclaimed. "I can't believe Daniel could be so insensitive." Whose story came closer to the truth, she wondered, Daniel's or Brian's?

Brian's mouth twisted into a grimace. "Sorry if I've

destroyed any illusions you may have had about him. I'd hoped he'd changed over the years, but when we met at your house, well…he was just as antagonistic toward me as ever.''

That was certainly true. ''Francine obviously wasn't worth your heartache if she could fall in love with someone else so easily.''

''That's what I tried to tell myself. But Danny can charm the birds out of the trees when he puts his mind to it.''

His gaze became assessing again. Karina shifted uncomfortably. He was probably trying to figure out just how charmed she was herself.

''He's a nice guy,'' she said. Feeling a flush creep up her neck, she bent her head and nudged at the ball with her toe.

''Ah, ah, ah,'' Brian remonstrated gently. ''Play it where it lies.'' He handed her the club. ''Try to give it some lift.''

Karina nodded, swung, hit the ball and managed to bury it deeper in the sand. ''Shoot.''

Brian came round behind her. ''May I?'' he murmured. Before she could answer, he'd reached around her waist and clasped his hands over hers.

His breath tickled the back of her ear and his heavy aftershave clogged her nostrils, making it difficult to breathe. Brian swung their arms back and up. She felt awkward and claustrophobic, as though trapped in someone else's body. She gave up trying to concentrate on the game and simply let him make the swing, resisting the impulse to wriggle free the moment the club made contact with the ball.

''Wonderful,'' Brian said, still holding her in his arms for the follow-through.

Karina kept her eyes on the ball, though it had long since stopped moving. Gently she tried to pull away, but his grip tightened and he turned her in his arms to face him. His eyes were very blue and filled with an admiration she suspected had nothing to do with her golfing ability.

Before she had a chance to draw back, he was kissing her, his lips cool and moist. Time didn't stop; it didn't even slow down. It was simply unendurable. Struggling, she raised her hands and pushed on his chest to create a space between them.

"Ah, ah, ah," she said, waggling a finger under his nose. "We agreed this was a business arrangement."

Brian released her with an expression of regret. "Is it because of Daniel?"

"No." She spoke too quickly, then cursed herself for sounding unconvincing.

"Because I thought perhaps you and he…" Brian's gaze probed relentlessly.

"No," she repeated, impatient now with his prying. "We're just friends."

In silence, they walked the rest of the way to the putting green. Brian's ball rested halfway between the hole and the edge of the closely trimmed circle of grass.

Karina watched Brian line up his shot. He took an experimental swing to one side of the ball, then raised his arms for the final stroke. Something about his attitude toward Daniel didn't quite mesh with the facts.

"So, Brian, do you still hate Daniel?"

Strangled sounds of a colorful nature issued from Brian's mouth as his ball zipped past the flag a foot wide of the mark. His naturally florid complexion turned a darker shade of red.

"Karina," he said, coming up to her and putting a

hand on her arm, "I don't hate Daniel. He's my *brother*."

"But you said—"

"I said I *resented* him. A very different thing from hate. Very different."

"Maybe I overstated the case."

"Besides, that was all in the past," Brian declared, giving her arm a little squeeze. "Now I want nothing more than to regain Daniel's trust."

Karina's eyes narrowed slightly. Brian seemed just a little too earnest. And surely it was Daniel who needed to regain his brother's trust? "Why didn't you try to get in touch with him all those years?"

Brian shrugged. "At first I was too angry. Later, when I'd cooled down, he, or I, made one move too many and we lost contact. I could have got his address from my parents, but I guess I was just too proud."

Karina nodded. That tallied with Daniel's story.

She turned away, feeling suddenly weary. Lately she was spending too much time at the office trying to stay out of Daniel's way. The early mornings and late nights were catching up with her.

Raising her arms in a prolonged stretch, she gazed upward, tracking a soaring bald eagle across the blue bowl of the sky. Abruptly she dropped her arms, pin-pricks of excitement making goose bumps on her bare skin.

She knew how she wanted to celebrate her birthday.

KARINA ROCKED BACK in her office chair, enjoying the look of surprise on Ross Preston's face. It made him resemble a startled hedgehog.

"You're going to the golf tournament?" he exclaimed, jumping to his feet. With nowhere to pace in her cluttered office, he quickly sat down again, causing the guest chair to creak in protest. "But that's imposs—I mean, how did you manage that?" His small eyes narrowed to slits.

Karina waved her hand airily. "A friend of mine happens to be going and invited me along as his guest. *And* he's giving me golf lessons so I'll be able to keep up with you boys."

"Well, that's just fine, Karina. Just fine." Ross pushed a pudgy hand through his porcupine hair and got to his feet. "May the best man—ha, ha, *person*—win."

Karina smiled graciously and accepted his insincere good wishes with a mocking lift of her eyebrows.

She already has, Ross, she already has.

Karina's sense of victory lasted only until Ross ambled out of her office. Then she sank into her computer chair, oddly deflated. She was losing her appetite for the battle. Or maybe the battle didn't seem worth the effort anymore.

Just then, a frizzy blond head peered around the door. Karina spun away from the computer. "Joanne! What are you doing here?"

"Taking you to lunch." Joanne dropped into the guest chair Ross had just vacated. "Am I exhausted! I've been shopping all morning for Julie's party. Hats, streamers, balloons, paper plates, napkins… You wouldn't believe the junk. Of course, Julie wants everything decorated with pictures of some cartoon superbimbo that looks like a cross between Barbie and Attila the Hun."

She burrowed in a large plastic bag and brought out a package of colorful paper plates. "Look at that. I swear it's Pamela Anderson on steroids. Karina, you made a wise decision not to have children. They bleed you dry."

Karina managed a tight smile. "It's worth it to see them happy, isn't it?"

Joanne shoved the plates back into the bag. "Yeah. Don't mind me. I'm just complaining, as usual." Then she glanced at Karina in surprise. "Don't tell me you're coming around to the idea of having kids?"

Karina turned back to the computer screen. "Of course not." She positioned the mouse on the curving line of a hot air balloon, clicked and pulled. Instantly the balloon grew a bulge in its side.

"Darn," she muttered. "Now it's turned into a pumpkin." She pulled the line of the balloon back in with the mouse, adjusting it until it looked just right.

Joanne leaned over to look at the screen. "What's this, a sign for a sporting goods store?"

Karina shook her head. "It's an invitation to my birthday celebration."

Joanne sat up in her chair. "You're having a party after all! Oh, Karina, I'm so glad. What a fabulous idea. I'll make you a cake and some appetizers—"

"Slow down, Jo." Karina saved the image on the screen and turned to her friend. "I'm not having a real party. Not one with people and cakes and things, anyway. It's Daniel's idea of a birthday celebration."

"Daniel? Does this mean you two are back on speaking terms? From what you said about your costume-making session with Natalie, it sounded like things were pretty tense around your house."

"They are. The funny thing is, I don't think it's just about keeping Natalie up too late without her dinner."

"I'll bet he's annoyed that you're playing golf with Brian," Joanne said. "And that just proves how much he likes you."

Karina shook her head. "When Brian came to pick

me up, Daniel acted like he couldn't care less. Now, he— Oh, never mind. I don't know what's going on these days."

Joanne shrugged. "Then don't worry about it. Tell me more about this birthday celebration."

"Daniel's idea is for me to do something on my birthday I've never done before. You know, keep life interesting."

"Your life isn't interesting? Tell me another one."

"It is, but… I've been having a problem dealing with this particular birthday because, well, you know…." Karina pushed a hand through her hair. "Anyway, I thought of something I've always wanted to do—hot air ballooning."

"Ballooning! Fantastic!" Joanne stretched out her long legs, and her parcels fell over like dominoes.

"In a way it'll be a gift for my mother, as well. She had a fear of flying. Maybe she'll look down on me from wherever she is and see it isn't so bad after all."

"You'll have a great time," Joanne said, propping up her bags again. "I've always wanted to go ballooning myself."

Karina scrolled through the list of type faces until she found the one she wanted, and began to type in the invitation. "Good, because you're coming. The balloon can hold four people besides the operator—you, me, Daniel and Natalie."

"I'd love to. But wouldn't it be more fun if I took care of Natalie, and you and Daniel went alone?"

"No, it would not," Karina said firmly. "Quit it, Joanne. Daniel and I are just friends."

"But he kissed you. He wouldn't have kissed you if he wasn't interested."

Karina groaned. Why had she ever told Joanne about

that day in the garage? "Well, he's been avoiding me ever since. And that's fine by me, because anything else is just too complicated."

Joanne shook her head. "*Life* is complicated, Karina. Get used to it. Now, how about lunch? You can tell me all about your golf date with Brian."

Karina shut down the computer and reached for her purse. "It wasn't a *date*."

Ignoring her, Joanne carried on with her flight of fantasy. "You'll have the two of them fighting over you before it's over, see if you don't."

"The last thing I want is for Daniel and Brian to fight over me."

"But it's so exciting."

"*Joanne…*"

"THE WINGS AREN'T sparkly enough," Karina said, gazing critically at her handiwork. Julie's party was less than an hour away and she wanted Natalie's costume to be perfect.

Daniel lowered the newspaper with a rustle and gave the wings a cursory glance. "They look fine to me," he said, and went back to perusing the Want Ads.

"Yes, but you're no expert on fairy princesses. We've established that."

Karina reached for the tube of glue. She and Daniel had achieved a shaky truce on the subject of costume design, with Daniel agreeing to give Karina free rein as long as Natalie didn't miss any more meals in the process.

Which was okay by her, Karina thought, daubing more glue on the wings. From now on she would stick to what she knew best. "Where's Natalie?" she asked, glancing at Felix the Clock.

"Brushing her teeth." Daniel folded the paper neatly and laid it aside with a stifled yawn. "Not a single house for rent in Oak Bay this month. And I even hung out at the *Victoria Times* building at dawn with the rest of the desperadoes."

"Gee, that's too bad." She cast him a sympathetic glance.

He was silent a moment. "Karina?"

"Mmm?" she replied, tapping the end of a vial to sprinkle flecks of gold glitter randomly over the gauze.

"There's something I've been meaning to ask you."

Karina looked up, mildly surprised. Daniel didn't usually preface his speech with pointless remarks. "What is it?"

He leaned forward, elbows on the table, and rubbed his thumb around the rim of his coffee cup. "Why didn't you tell me you were going out with Brian last Saturday?"

She blinked. So Joanne was right. The golf date *had* bothered him. Laying the vial of glitter on the table, she searched his eyes for a clue to his state of mind.

At that moment a shriek came from the second floor. Daniel jumped to his feet. "Natalie!"

Karina ran after him as he raced up the stairs. Natalie banged open the door of the bathroom, her fairy skirts billowing, her blue eyes wide.

Daniel gripped her by the shoulders, halting her headlong flight. "Nattie, what is it?"

"I'm sorry," she wailed. "All I did was flush some tissues, then I was going to go pee, but the water came *out* of the toilet instead of going down." She burst into tears. "I didn't mean to!"

"It's not your fault, Nattie," Karina said. She stood on her tiptoes in the bathroom doorway and leaned across the spreading water to pull a towel off the rack and throw it onto the floor.

"Stay out of the way, Nattie," Daniel ordered. "I'll see if I can fix it."

"But, Daddy," Natalie cried, her legs writhing together. "I need to go!"

"Just hang on."

Karina skated the towel over the floor with her feet, soaking up the water. "Hand me another towel," she said as Daniel appeared in the doorway. "I *did* tell you."

"What?" He passed her a towel. "Oh, you mean Brian. Have you got a plunger? Or a plumber's snake?"

"The plunger's behind the toilet but we won't need it. This has happened before. Don't worry, I can fix it." She shuffled over to the vanity and pulled a wrench from the bottom shelf.

Before she could use it, Daniel picked up the plunger and went to work on the toilet. "It's not that I mind you seeing him," he continued. "You're a—"

"I told you, I know how to fix this," she interrupted, alarmed at the ripples in the full toilet bowl caused by Daniel's energetic plunging. "It happens all the time."

"—free agent," Daniel concluded, clearly not listening. "Damn, something must be stuck down there."

"Free agent?"

"Yes. You have a perfect right to see whomever you please. In fact, Brian is probably just your type—outgoing, interested in art.…"

Free agent? How could that be when her heart was hopelessly bound to Daniel's? "What makes you think something's going on between Brian and me?" she demanded. "And how dare you presume to know what kind of man is my *type?*"

"Did you say you have a snake?"

"Just exactly what's bothering you?"

"Da-addy," Natalie wailed. "I need to go *badly*."

Karina glanced at Natalie, hopping about the landing, and bit back a smile. She didn't quite fit the image of a delicate fairy flitting from tulip to columbine, but she was the cutest little improbable being Karina'd ever seen.

"I know, sweetheart," Daniel said to his daughter through clenched teeth. "I'm working on it as fast as I can."

He glanced up at Karina, a streak of dust smeared across the bridge of his nose and down his cheek. "You want to know what's bothering me? I think you didn't tell me because you assumed I couldn't take it. You thought I'd be jealous."

Impatiently Karina shook her head. "He called me at work on Thursday. That night I went out for dinner with some of the guys from the department and didn't get home till late. But on Friday night I mentioned our golf date to you. I'm absolutely positive I did. Well, practically positive."

"You don't have to explain," Daniel muttered, and thrust down hard on the plunger.

Water poured over the rim of the toilet onto the floor. Karina leaped back onto the sodden towels. "Would you let me get in there for a second? If you didn't want an explanation, then why bring it up?"

"Da-addy!"

"Hold on, honey," Karina said, reaching out to give Natalie's head a quick caress. "When your daddy's finished messing around, I'll have this fixed in a jiffy."

Daniel straightened abruptly. "Maybe one of your neighbors has a snake."

She jammed her hands onto her hips and glared at

him. *"You're not listening to me!* We don't need a snake! And I wasn't trying to hide anything."

The instant the words were out of her mouth, she wondered if they were really true. Maybe subconsciously she *had* avoided the subject for fear the news would deepen the rift between Daniel and his brother. She saw Daniel's mouth tighten and knew he'd seen her uncertainty. *Damn.*

An agonized moan from Natalie galvanized her into action. Shouldering Daniel aside, she hefted the wrench in her right hand. "Excuse me."

"You can't fix it with *that.*"

Ignoring him, Karina crouched down and tapped out the rhythm of an old tune on the pipe. "'Shave and a haircut, two bits—'"

"That won't work," Daniel said scornfully. "You need to get down past the *S* bend and unblock it."

"Trust me," she replied. "I know this toilet like…like I know this toilet."

"I'm telling you—" He broke off as the standing water in the porcelain bowl let out a loud gurgle and swirled down the pipe. He stared at her incredulously. "How did you do that?"

"I told you, this has happened before. I hit upon the solution—if you'll pardon the pun—quite by accident. Works every time. It must be the specific vibrations set up by that tune."

Daniel rolled his eyes. "It's a fluke, is what it is. You should get a plumber in to find out what's causing the blockage."

"I just fixed it!"

"Yes, but for how long?" His mouth twisted sarcastically. "Oh, I forgot. You're not into long-term solutions."

"Ouch. Is that the thanks I get—"

"Da-addy!" Natalie cried, hunched over in distress. "Can I go now?"

"Of course, Nattie," Karina said. "We'll get out of here right away." She pushed Daniel out of the bathroom before her, scooping up wet towels as she went.

Shutting the door behind her, she smiled at the sound of tiny staccato footsteps followed by a tinkle and an audible sigh of relief. Karina gave herself a mental pat on the back, partially vindicated for her shortcomings as a surrogate mom.

Downstairs Daniel went to the kitchen sink to wash his hands. "I'm still going to call a plumber," he said to her. "You can't leave a thing like that for long or you'll end up with real problems."

"But—"

"I'll pay for half the bill."

"It's not the money." She opened the door to the basement and heaved the towels in a long arc down the stairs to land neatly in the laundry basket at the bottom.

Daniel's eyebrows disappeared into the lock of hair that fell over his forehead. "You're unbelievable, you know that? A real nutcase."

"I am not a nutcase. I'm capricious, remember?" Karina joined him at the sink and rubbed soap over her hands. "And, Daniel, you've simply got to stop being so paranoid about Brian. I did not intentionally keep my golf date a secret."

Daniel dried his hands with brooding thoroughness. Finally he sighed. "All right. I guess I knew that, deep down. You're not deceptive and you have nothing to hide. Do me a favor and forget what I said."

Karina stared at him. Two minutes ago he'd mistrusted and maligned her. But she accepted the towel he held out to her and began to dry her hands. Maybe it would be better to forget his accusations. "You never did tell me how your visit to Brian went. Are you two any closer to sorting things out?"

Daniel leaned against the counter. "We're getting there. We talked about Francine and—" He paused abruptly. "Brian didn't come right out and say all was forgiven but he's willing to let bygones be bygones."

Karina started to throw the towel on the counter, thought better of it, and hung it neatly on the stove handle. "That's great. So, why don't you look happy?"

He shook his head, frowning. "Brian doesn't forgive and forget that easily. Once, when we were kids, I accidentally broke a model car of his. He held a grudge for years."

"So? What's that got to do with now?"

Daniel pushed away from the counter. "I just can't get it out of my head that he's got a hidden agenda."

Meaning *her?* She wasn't stepping into that one for all the noodles in China. "I'll forget everything you said in the bathroom on one condition."

"What's that?"

"*You* forget about calling a plumber."

Daniel turned to face her, hands on his hips. "What kind of condition is that? There's no connection between the toilet and your relationship with Brian."

Karina raised an eyebrow. "The connection is between the toilet and your *interpretation* of my relationship with Brian."

"But— Oh, all right. We'll let it go at that—*for now*. Just tell me one thing. What do you have against plumbers?"

"Nothing. But if the toilet is fixed properly, my technique might not work the next time it floods."

His eyes widened. "Karina," he said in a strangled voice. "That doesn't make a particle of sense."

She would have tried to explain it to him, but her eye caught the movement of Felix's longest hand as it ticked from one minute to the next. "The party!"

She ran off down the hall. "Hurry up, Natalie. It's almost time to go," she yelled from the bottom of the stairs. "Do you need any help?"

"I'm all right," Natalie yelled back. "Are my wings done?"

"They're almost dry. Come on down when you're ready and I'll pin them on."

"Okay."

Karina hurried back into the kitchen. Daniel's arms were crossed over his chest, and disapproval glared like neon from his eyes. She straightened her shoulders. "Now what?"

"I've spent the best years of my life trying to get that girl not to yell through the house."

"Oops." She tried hard not to laugh and very nearly succeeded.

A resigned expression came over his face. "Never a dull moment," he muttered, rubbing the back of his neck. "When does she have to be there?"

"Twenty minutes. I'll drive her over."

"Thanks, but there's no need."

"I know the way."

"You've done so much already." *Too* much, his expression implied, but she saw the smile that lurked behind the frown.

"I know," Natalie piped up from the doorway. "I'll fly over."

Daniel laughed. "Okay, Tinkerbell. Get your wings

on.'' He glanced at Karina. "Come on. Let's get our fairy princess to the ball.''

Karina led the way down the hall. "And we'll let bygones be bygones?''

"Okay by me.'' Opening the front door, he smiled his slow smile at her.

He had more than one way of shutting her up, Karina reflected as she sailed through the door after Natalie. And that smile was particularly effective.

CHAPTER TWELVE

THE ALARM CLOCK radio clicked on and an old Beatles tune dragged Karina from a deep slumber. Blinking the sleep from her eyes, she noted the pale light of dawn, the birds chirping....

Oh, no. Pain wrapped around her like a blanket, and dread weighted her limbs to the bed. It was the morning of her thirty-second birthday.

"Go forward in life," Daniel had said. She thought of the vow she'd made last night to be more consistent with her breast exams. Well, this was the right time of her cycle to check. And the doctor had drummed into her the importance of learning the feel of healthy tissue.

She raised one arm behind her head and cautiously reached for the underarm. As her fingers moved over her skin, gently pressing in concentric circles, her heart began to palpitate.

What if she found another lump? What if this time it was malignant?

She could still remember the day Mama had been given the final prognosis. Could still see Mama's hollow, frightened eyes when she'd looked at Karina knowing she wouldn't live to see her daughter grow up.

She finished checking the first breast and went on to the second, trying not to think of the long, pain-filled months during which they'd watched Mama's laughter fade and the music in her die.

A cold sweat had dampened her forehead by the time she lowered her arms in relief. Nothing, thank God. It was over for another month.

But she still had to get through the day. Karina hugged both arms around herself and rolled over, burying her face in the pillow. The logical side of her brain scolded her for being a ninny. The child in her cried out for comfort that would never come. If only she could slip into a dreamless sleep and wake up next year....

Humming to block out her thoughts, she shut her eyes and pulled the quilt tighter around her shoulders. She'd fallen into a light doze when she became aware of a persistent tune in her head—*Up, up "and awaaay..."*

Her eyes snapped open. Today she was riding in a hot air balloon.

Throwing back the covers, she rose and went to the window to open the blind. The sheer curtains lifted in a light breeze that carried the scent of the deep red roses beneath her window. The sound of robins chirping in the old maple out front filled her with an unexpected sense of well-being.

It was a good day to be alive.

She dressed quickly and quietly, wondering at the silence in the room next to hers. Then she remembered Daniel saying he would let Natalie sleep in as long as possible. She'd been so excited about the balloon ride she'd stayed awake long past her bedtime the night before.

Karina crept past Natalie's room. Through the half-open door she caught sight of the little girl's sleeping figure sprawled across the bed. One bare ankle peeked out from beneath the covers.

Our fairy princess.

He hadn't really meant it, of course. At least not the

way it sounded. But just for a moment, Karina wished it was true.

She lingered on the landing, gazing wistfully at Natalie's tousled blond head. The girl's mouth curved suddenly in a smile that was so like Daniel's it made her heart skip a beat.

Nattie stirred and Karina turned to run lightly down the stairs, pausing at the bottom to glance down the hallway. Daniel was at the kitchen sink, filling the kettle. Quietly she went into the living room and stood in front of her mother's portrait.

Ageless, timeless, Eleanora Rossellini Peterson shone like a rare pearl amid the eclectic bric-a-brac Karina had collected over the years.

Karina's lips moved silently, as if in prayer. *God bless you, Mama. I love you. I'll try to be strong today, for your sake.*

Eleanora's midnight-dark eyes gazed back at her, her faint smile as silent as an enigma.

Karina sighed and walked down the hall to the kitchen.

Daniel looked up from pouring ground coffee into the filter. "Mornin'," he said. "Sleep well?"

"Wonderful."

"You sure?" he persisted, his eyes searching her face.

"Yes!" She smiled to reassure him. Crossing the room, she pushed back the curtains at the window over the table. The crystals hanging from the curtain rod began to swing, and rainbows danced over the walls.

She switched on the radio and music blared from the speakers. Glancing over her shoulder, she caught Daniel's eye and quickly tuned to a station that played classical music. "How's that?"

"Fine," he said. "It's not that I don't like music, you

understand. It's just that I like to hear my own thoughts occasionally.''

Which was exactly what she *didn't* want, though he wasn't to know that. But she turned the volume a little lower.

Natalie ran into the room, face shining and hair already brushed. ''I'm ready. I even made my bed. Can we go now?''

''Not so fast, Possum. We need to eat first.'' Daniel smiled and caught Karina's eye, as if to share his enjoyment of his daughter's excitement.

Karina smiled back, her heart contracting with bittersweet pleasure. ''How about scrambled eggs?'' she suggested, knowing they were Natalie's favorite.

So they breakfasted on scrambled eggs and toast in the sunny, homey kitchen where not even Daniel could entirely eliminate the clutter. Karina and Daniel ate in the comfortable silence that came from knowing each other well enough not to always have to talk while Natalie chattered excitedly about the coming day.

When they were done, Natalie ran back upstairs to brush her teeth. Karina carried the dishes to the sink and started to rinse out the cups.

''Leave that,'' Daniel said, glancing at his watch. ''We can clean up later.''

Karina did a double take, splashing water across the counter. ''Don't look now but you just used the *L* word.''

''Beg your pardon?''

''Later,'' she explained with a laugh. ''My bad habits must be rubbing off on you.''

He chuckled. ''And here I was congratulating myself that I'd passed on my fetish for neatness. Look at you, doing the dishes.''

Karina groaned and dried her hands on a towel. "Caught in the act of cleaning. My reputation will be ruined."

Daniel gazed down at her, laughter in his eyes. "I promise I won't tell a soul."

"Thanks." She paused. "And, Daniel?"

"Yes?"

"I also want to say thanks in advance for today. I have the feeling you've gone to a lot of trouble."

He shrugged. "This is your day. I want to make it as special as possible."

"Why?" She felt her cheeks flush and instantly regretted asking. It sounded as if she were fishing for some sort of declaration of affection.

Daniel leaned an elbow on the door frame. "You took Nattie and me in when you didn't want to, and I'm grateful. Helping you through today is a way of showing my appreciation."

"Oh." Friendly but basically impersonal. That's what she wanted. Wasn't it?

"Too bad Joanne couldn't come with us today," she said, turning away.

"Did she tell you why?"

Karina glanced back at him, surprised by the faint sharpness in his tone. "She has to take her mother to the dentist. Mrs. Simpson doesn't drive."

"Oh. That's all right, then." With another glance at his watch, he straightened away from the frame. "We'd better get going."

"Okay." She cast him a last, puzzled glance, then ran upstairs to finish getting ready. When she came back down a few minutes later, Daniel and Natalie were waiting for her on the front steps. She grabbed her jacket off its hook in the foyer, slung her purse over her shoulder and slipped into a pair of flat shoes.

"Shall we take Sammy?" she asked, coming out and locking the door. "It'd be a bit of a squash, but we could put the top down."

"I'll drive," Daniel said, ushering her down the path to his newly washed white pickup. "You don't know where we're going."

"You could give me directions."

"And spoil the fun? A birthday adventure is supposed to be like life itself—you never know what's going to happen next."

"You do," she argued as she climbed into the cab of the truck behind Natalie and buckled herself into place on the burgundy vinyl bench seat.

Daniel went around to the other side and got in. "On my birthday, you can call the shots. Fair enough?"

Karina didn't answer. The thought of spending birthdays together was far too appealing for a relationship that was supposed to be temporary.

DANIEL DROVE NORTH out of the city, and soon they were climbing the winding road through dense forest to the Malahat mountain pass. As they neared the summit, the trees thinned to granite outcroppings topped with spindly firs and Karina caught glimpses of blue water far below. Under the steady hum of the truck engine, Natalie's enthusiastic chatter gradually faded, and soon she was fast asleep.

Karina glanced down at the small blond head leaning against her shoulder with a weight so slight she hardly felt it. "How did it go at the school the other day?" she said to Daniel. "Was Natalie okay?"

Daniel shifted down to second as they came to a steep

section of the road. "She took it in her stride like she does everything. I don't know why I worry so much."

"Just wait till she starts going out with boys."

Daniel scowled and gripped the wheel with both hands. "She wouldn't dare."

Karina laughed. "I can just see you, demanding to know their intentions."

"I wouldn't have to ask. I *know* what a teenage boy's intentions are."

"Oh?" she teased. "And what might those be?"

He glanced over at her, his gaze traveling from her tank top down her snug-fitting jeans to her bare ankles. "Roughly the same as any healthy adult male's."

Karina turned to look out the window to hide her blush. Yet she couldn't disguise from herself the way her body tingled where his eyes had lingered. She focused on the scenery flashing by and emptied her mind of futile yearnings.

After a long moment of silence, Daniel startled her out of her thoughts. "All right, out with it."

"Pardon?" She shifted in her seat, propping up Natalie's head when it started to slip down her arm.

"I can always tell when something's brewing in that convoluted brain of yours," he said. "But I can't always tell what it is."

"I suppose I should be grateful for small mercies." Buying time, Karina reached forward to examine the carved wooden tiki hanging from the rearview mirror and realized it was the source of the faintly spicy aroma that permeated the cab. "What a wonderful scent."

"Sandalwood," he replied. "It makes a change from eucalyptus. So…?"

"It's Natalie," she said, seizing on a topic that had

in fact been bothering her. "Do you know about Mrs. Beeton?"

Daniel frowned. "What about her?"

"Does it worry you that Natalie spends so much time with an imaginary friend?"

"Of course it does."

"I didn't realize till the other night who Mrs. Beeton was," Karina went on. "I'd always thought she was one of Natalie's dolls. Strange, isn't it? We think it's all right for a child to talk to dolls or stuffed toys but not a being created from their imagination. Why is that?"

"Maybe because it makes us realize there's something lacking in their lives that we can't provide." He glanced across at her, openly concerned. "The hell of it is, there's nothing I can do about it other than give Natalie as much love and attention as I can. And as many opportunities to play with other kids as possible."

"You're a wonderful father, there's no question of that."

Daniel just nodded but she could tell by the way his tanned cheeks reddened slightly he was pleased she thought so.

"Even so," he said, "there are times when I don't know if I'm doing the right thing or not."

"I imagine most parents feel that way." She held a hand out the open window and let the cool, moist wind buffet her fingers. "Not that I'm an expert or anything."

They crested the summit, and Daniel slowed to allow the car in front to pull off into a view point. He glanced at her, his expression softening. "You know how to act with kids. You're natural and you like them. They pick up on that."

Karina glowed, unable to speak.

He flashed her a quirky smile and accelerated. "Don't

you dare say anything nice to me in return or we'll have to call an official meeting of the mutual admiration society."

She laughed, then checked on Natalie. The child was still sleeping soundly, her breath coming soft and regular through her partly open mouth.

"It seems to me she misses her mother more than any friends," Karina said, lowering her voice anyway.

Daniel let out a heavy breath. "I know. But I can't give Francine back to her and I'm damned if I'm going to marry just to provide my daughter with a mother."

"What was Francine like?" she asked, quickly adding, "if it doesn't bother you to talk about her, that is."

They had started down the long descent through thickening stands of evergreens. Daniel took a moment to shift gears before answering. "What do you want to know?"

"I suppose Natalie got her blond hair from her?" The question was merely a conversation opener, for Karina had seen the small, framed photograph of Francine on Natalie's bedside table.

"Yes," he said. "And her blue eyes. She's got my mouth, though, I think."

Karina's gaze traced the wayward, curving lines of his expressive mouth and the tiny creases in the corners that hinted at the humor lying below the surface. "Yes, she does."

"Francine was beautiful in a Nordic sort of way," Daniel told her. "Into sports of all kinds. That's how she and Brian met, at a tennis match."

A faint crease appeared between his eyebrows. Was he thinking about Brian and the golf tournament? For the first time she realized just how difficult their situation might be for him.

"What did she do for a living?"

"She was a political reporter for the *Melbourne Age*. She was very good, if somewhat obsessive. When she wanted something, nothing stood in her way."

"Like a fiancé?"

He glanced sharply at her. "Maybe."

"You must miss her very much."

He didn't reply.

Karina stared straight ahead. "Sorry," she muttered. "That was a stupid question."

Daniel remained silent for a long time. The road flattened, and the forest thinned to pastureland as they entered the farming delta of the Cowichan River. Karina fished in her purse for her sunglasses and put them on.

"I'm sorry she died," he said at last. "I miss her for Natalie's sake."

Was that all? Behind her dark glasses, Karina's eyebrows lifted. He'd implied it hadn't been a good marriage, but hadn't he sacrificed his relationship with his brother for the woman? She shouldn't press him, but for some reason she had to know. "Only for Natalie?"

Daniel's fingers gripped the steering wheel until his knuckles whitened. "I didn't love her. For a while I thought I did. God knows, I *tried* to love her. But once the initial infatuation wore off there was nothing there. Nothing at all."

Objections to what must have been years of loveless marriage swirled through Karina's head. "You didn't have to *stay* married."

His mouth twisted bitterly. "It sounds stupid in retrospect, but at the time I felt I had to stick it out if only to give some meaning to what I'd done to Brian. By the time I realized how totally unsuited Francine and I were, she was pregnant. I couldn't leave her then."

"No, of course not."

"After Natalie was born things got better for a while, but that didn't last. I asked for a divorce and custody of Natalie, who was almost three."

"What did Francine say?"

Daniel scowled. "She was actually considering it. I couldn't believe she'd be willing to let Natalie go. I'd have stayed married rather than lose my child."

His anger faded suddenly, leaving him pale beneath his tan. "As it turned out, she didn't live long enough to choose."

He fell silent, mouth stretched tight. He may not have loved Francine, Karina thought, but he'd cared about her.

"Oh, Daniel, I'm so sorry." Karina reached across the sleeping child and put her hand on his shoulder. "At least Natalie still has you."

Daniel frowned, looking unconvinced.

"What I mean is," she explained, "Natalie is lucky to have a father who shows his love in a dozen different ways every day. A father who…" her voice fell to a whisper "…who lets her grieve."

Daniel glanced up sharply. He geared down as they approached the town of Duncan. "What do you mean? Didn't your father allow you to mourn your mother? I know there was a problem, but…"

She gazed out the window at rows of fast-food outlets and car lots. *Please, don't let him ask about her father,* she prayed.

"It helps to talk about it."

She waited, expecting more and dreading it.

Just then Natalie lifted her head, blinked her eyes open and stretched tall in her seat to look out the front window. "Are we there yet?"

Daniel patted her knee. "Nearly, sweetheart. Just a little longer."

He stopped at a red light and consulted a sheet of notepaper covered with handwritten directions. The light changed and he made a left, driving across town and out the other side. Another turning took them down a narrow country road past well-kept farms with black-and-white cattle grazing in lush, green pastures.

Twenty minutes later, they turned into a gravel drive and pulled up in front of a portable office. In the field beyond, a trio of hot air balloons sprouted like multi-colored mushrooms.

They signed a waiver in the office, then followed the pilot, a short, grizzled man named Frank, across the field to where a bright yellow balloon tugged at its tether, as if it, too, wanted to be up and away on this fine summer morning.

Natalie skipped ahead, beside herself with delight. Karina felt like skipping, too, but forced herself to walk sedately at Daniel's side. She glanced up at his animated face and was struck by a feeling of intense liking for this man.

He'd arranged this day for her at a time when his own personal life was tainted with unhappiness. Yet he looked anything but unhappy now. Just seeing his eager grin sent an extra thrill of excitement through her.

Smiling down at her, Daniel laced his fingers through hers. His touch combined the unknown and the longed-for, giving her excitement a physical edge. She tensed, ready to pull away. Then she saw the uncomplicated gladness in his eyes and squeezed his hand instead.

She gave a little shrug. "Today isn't like other days."

He nodded and she knew he understood.

"Your daughter's a lively little scamp," Frank said

over his shoulder to Karina. "Hope we can keep her inside the basket."

Karina glanced uncertainly at Daniel. He just smiled and shrugged. She opened her mouth to explain that Natalie wasn't her daughter, but it was already too late. They'd reached the balloon and Frank was setting the wooden steps in place so they could climb aboard. With an odd mixture of pride and guilty pleasure she took Natalie's hand to help her up the stairs.

Then she forgot everything else in the excitement of takeoff. Frank cranked up the gas jets, inflating the balloon until it strained at the ropes binding it to the earth. One by one he released the lines. Smooth as an elevator, the balloon lifted skyward and the earth dropped away.

Karina's stomach leaped skyward, too, with a thrilling sensation of lightness and butterflies. She laughed with sheer delight. "It feels like we're really flying."

Once aloft, Frank turned off the gas jets, and the sudden quiet was deafening. They floated in eerie silence over farms and lakes and silver, winking rivers that wound through field and wood. To the north and west, mountains rose from the valley floor, cloaked in dark green.

Karina gazed over the side, enraptured. The fresh air swirled around her head, loosening tendrils of hair from her braid. "This is so beautiful! Natalie, look!"

She turned to beckon the girl. But Natalie had overcome her usual initial shyness and engaged the bemused pilot in a game. Karina laughed as the child clicked her heels together and pleaded with the Great Oz to take her back to Kansas.

Daniel shook his head and leaned his elbows on the edge of the wicker basket beside Karina. "Poor man," he murmured. "He doesn't know what he's in for."

"I think he's enjoying himself," Karina said, watching the pair.

"Look," Daniel said, and raised his arm over her shoulder to point to a clearing in the middle of some woods. Karina gazed in the direction he was indicating and saw a doe grazing peacefully, a fawn close by her side.

"She looks so tiny. How high are we?" Karina pressed a hand to the sudden flutter in her stomach that had more to do with the warmth of Daniel's bare arm brushing her cheek than the altitude.

"Frank said we'd get to about five hundred feet." Daniel withdrew his arm and gazed at her, so close his hazel eyes resolved into forest green flecks embedded in amber. "Your mother would have been proud of you today."

At the reminder of her mother, an ache rose in her heart. She glanced at Daniel, who'd resumed his survey of the scene below. His high, straight nose and slanting jaw were sharply delineated against the deep blue of the sky. A thick lock of chestnut hair strayed over his forehead.

The ache in her heart intensified. But for the grace of God...

"Yes, she would have been proud," Karina agreed quietly. "She never had time to overcome her fear of flying." She was silent for a moment. "I guess we all have something we just can't face. Something we have to simply forget."

"You can't forget your mother," he said softly. "You told me so yourself. All the music in the world, all the laughter and people and parties won't make you forget."

Karina didn't reply. He was right. But she was frozen

in the past, unable to grieve, unable to go forward. "You don't know what it's like."

Daniel put one hand over hers where it rested on the edge of the basket, and with the other brushed away a wisp of dark hair that had blown across her cheek. "Tell me about your mother. I have a feeling I would have liked her very much."

Karina smiled. "Everybody liked Mama. She was fun and funny. She was always laughing. And she loved to sing. The house was always filled with music."

"Sounds like someone else I know," Daniel murmured.

Gripped with remembrance, Karina hardly heard him. "She grew tomatoes and garlic and...oh, all sorts of herbs. She'd make mountains of pasta and invite half the neighborhood for dinner. She was always busy—sewing, painting, she could do anything."

"Did she work?"

Karina nodded. "She was a nurse before she had my brother and me. She didn't go back to work afterward because she wanted to stay home with us." Karina chuckled. "She called me her *bambina*. I used to hate it when she used the term in front of my friends."

Her smile faded. What she wouldn't give to hear Mama's dear voice murmur *bambina* to her just one more time.

Daniel's thumb stroked soft circles over the back of her hand. "What else?"

Karina shrugged. "She wanted to have lots of children, but for some reason she never had any more after me." She paused. "Sometimes I think she should never have had any at all."

Daniel shook his head. "She sounds like a wonderful

mother. Better to have a short time with someone like that than no time at all.''

''But don't you see?'' Karina protested, turning to face him. ''If I hadn't been born, Mama wouldn't have suffered at having to leave me. I wouldn't have suffered when she died.''

''Nor would you have laughed and sang and done all the other things that have given you such happy memories.''

She fell silent. Did the good really outweigh the bad? This birthday forced her to confront her greatest fears, her deepest sorrows, and yet... Wasn't she also having a wonderful time with Daniel and Natalie, doing something new and exciting?

''There's a difference between sorrow and fear,'' Daniel explained. ''One makes you stronger and gives you greater understanding. The other limits your ability to grow.''

Karina gazed into the fathomless blue sky. The way he put it seemed so clear, but when she tried to apply the concept to herself, her mind stumbled. Grief and fear of loving had been linked in her heart for so long the chains seemed indestructible.

Behind her, Frank cleared his throat, breaking the silence. ''You folks want some brunch?'' he asked, nodding to a large picnic basket wedged in a corner.

''Goody!'' Natalie cried at once. ''I'm starving.''

''Me, too,'' Karina said, glad of the diversion. With Natalie's help, she delved into the basket and pulled out a plastic container. ''Cold barbecued salmon,'' she announced, lifting the lid. ''Whew! I was afraid for a minute the 'new and different' would include roasted grasshoppers.''

"They're at the bottom of the basket," Daniel replied straight-faced. "Right next to the fried ants."

She made a face and tossed a plastic wineglass at his head. "Catch."

With a swift movement, Daniel reached high, his fingers closing around the stem just before the glass went over the side. He looked at her and just shook his head.

"Sorry." She suppressed a giggle. "I'm used to eating on the fly, but this is ridiculous."

Daniel uncorked a bottle of champagne and filled their glasses. The bubbles spilled over the top and ran down Karina's fingers. Laughing, she quickly sipped at the froth, glancing at Daniel over her raised glass.

Maybe it was the altitude, or the sparkling wine, or maybe it was the look in Daniel's eyes… Suddenly Karina felt light-headed and quivery, as if she were on top of the world. What she felt for Daniel was far more than liking, she realized on a shock wave of exhilaration.

She was in love with him.

Her moment of pure happiness lasted all of two seconds.

Then, an old hand at blanking out unwanted thoughts, Karina began to whistle under her breath. She turned back to the picnic basket and feverishly unpacked the rest of the containers and plates and cutlery.

Later. She'd worry about her feelings for Daniel later. Today she was going to enjoy herself if it killed her.

CHAPTER THIRTEEN

DANIEL GLANCED OVER at Karina as he cruised down the tree-lined street toward her house. She looked tired but contented, which was exactly how he felt. He'd had her all to himself, more or less, for one perfect day. As he watched her, she glanced up at him and her mouth curved in an oddly shy smile.

He smiled back and resisted the urge to reach over and stroke her cheek.

Natalie had fallen asleep again, this time with her head lying across Karina's lap. But as he pulled in to the curb and cut the engine, she sat up, rubbing her eyes.

"I wonder what Joanne's doing here," Karina said, nodding at the familiar blue Volvo parked ahead of them.

"Probably came to give you a birthday present," Daniel suggested.

"Maybe Julie's here, too," Natalie said excitedly, and scrambled across Karina.

"I doubt it," Daniel said, but she was already out the door. Then he remembered Joanne would have things to take inside, and tossed his keys after his daughter. "Here. You can get Joanne to open the front door."

He was wondering how he could distract Karina for a few minutes when he felt her hand on his arm.

"Daniel?"

"Yes?" God, but she looked beautiful, her cheeks flushed, her eyes dark and sparkling.

She cleared her throat and turned slightly pinker. "I know of another birthday custom. I didn't invent it but it's a good one."

His gaze drifted down to her mouth. "What is it?"

"The birthday kiss."

To Daniel, it seemed the entire day had been leading to this moment. One by one, Karina's barriers had fallen. All the small moments of contact lovers took for granted had been allowed him today—his hand on her shoulder as he pointed out the sights, his lips at her ear as he teased her over the roar of the balloon, his thigh brushing hers as they contemplated the world from five hundred feet in the air.

With each glance, each touch, his awareness of her had grown until it was like a second skin surrounding him, making him ultrasensitive to every nuance of expression, every smile of delight, every laughing light in her eyes.

As he gazed at her now, the cab of the truck seemed to shrink around them, enclosing a space that belonged to them alone. He leaned toward her, his heart thundering.

Just before he kissed her, the thought of Brian flashed through his mind. A moment of guilt, an instant of unconcern, a fleeting sense of bridges being burned. Then Daniel pressed his lips against Karina's and thought was no longer an option.

Her mouth was warm and deliciously soft, tasting of champagne and strawberry shortcake. He heard her moan softly and twined his fingers in her hair, drawing her closer. Beneath his palm, her cheek felt like warm satin. His elbow brushed her breast, and the sudden swelling in his groin made him urgently aware of how much he wanted her.

Her own urgency as she wound her arms around his neck surprised as much as it pleased him. He had no illusions she would surrender unconditionally, but at least she was acknowledging her desire. With all the pent-up longing of the past weeks raging inside him, he parted her lips with his tongue.

"Daniel," she gasped, blissful seconds later. "I'm sorry. I shouldn't have. We mustn't."

"I know," he murmured. And kissed her again.

Dimly he heard a dog barking in the distance, the tinkle of an ice-cream truck and the sound of children's voices in the street. All he felt was Karina's hand slipping inside the collar of his shirt to lightly caress his shoulder.

Gradually, one child's voice separated itself from the rest. It was calling to them through the open window on the passenger side of the truck. "Daddy! Karina!"

His mind glazed with confusion, Daniel slowly disengaged himself from Karina. His daughter was beside the car, trying to tell them something.

"What is it, Natalie?" he said, leaning across Karina. "What's wrong?"

"Karina's brother is on the phone from Toronto. He wants to say happy birthday." Natalie glanced with bright, curious eyes from him to Karina. "Were you guys *kissing?*"

Daniel groaned.

Karina touched his lips lightly with her fingertips and smiled. "I'd better go talk to Tom," she said, and climbed out of the truck.

Daniel watched her run up the steps, then glanced back at Natalie. Covering his lap with one arm, he rubbed the other hand across the back of his neck and patiently began to explain.

Karina smiled to herself as she went through the door. She'd give anything to know what Daniel was telling the girl, but she wasn't about to stick around and find out.

She met Joanne coming down the hall, making weather talk with her brother on the cordless phone. Sultry and warm in Toronto from the sounds of it. Here, too, she thought, lifting her blouse away from her chest.

"Good time?" Joanne mouthed as she handed over the phone.

Smiling, Karina nodded. "Hi, Tom!" she said into the receiver.

Joanne lifted one eyebrow. "Your lipstick's smudged," she whispered into Karina's ear before drifting back to the kitchen.

Karina dabbed at her mouth in the hall mirror as Tom wished her happy birthday. Goodness, she looked wild—hair everywhere and blouse rumpled. Joanne was wrong, though. Her lipstick wasn't smudged, it was kissed right off.

She chatted to Tom, telling him about her day and asking after his wife and kids, pleased to hear they'd be coming west for Christmas this year. As she said goodbye and hung up, her mind leaped ahead. Maybe she could convince her father to join them.

Natalie skipped through the door and past her, down the hall toward the kitchen. Daniel lingered in the foyer, casting a glance into the darkened living room.

"Everything okay with Natalie?" she asked. She followed the direction of his gaze. "I wonder why the curtains are drawn at this time of day." She started into the living room.

"We probably just forgot to open them this morning.'' He took her by the elbow and steered her back into the hall. ''I explained to Natalie about birthday kisses. She wants one, too.''

''I'd be delighted.'' She moved a step ahead of him and half turned out of his reach. All this talk of kisses while his warm hand cupped her bare elbow was too distracting. ''I'd like to take you both out for dinner by way of thanks.''

He shook his head and smiled his slow grin. ''You already thanked me.''

Her gaze ricocheted away from his. ''O-kay.'' One more second of that devastating smile and she'd be prostrate with gratitude.

''The next item on your agenda is a long, hot bubble bath,'' he said, guiding her toward the staircase. ''Don't worry about dinner. Everything's being taken care of.''

Karina nodded and fled up the stairs.

She was too keyed up to lie in a bath, so she opted for a shower instead. As she lathered scented shower gel over her body, she thought how grateful she was to Daniel for turning her birthday from a requiem into a celebration. Her fears had been, if not buried, at least put into perspective. Telling him about Mama hadn't been nearly as hard as she'd expected.

In fact, it had felt good to talk about Mama.

Happily humming along to the radio in the medicine cabinet, she stepped out of the shower, splashing drops of water on the floor.

One thing was certain, she realized more soberly as she reached for a towel—she couldn't kiss him again. She was playing with fire, as careless of the consequences as a child. But she wasn't a child. In spite of her implicit promise this morning to suspend barriers, in spite of the birthday kiss, she had to draw back. It was only fair to Daniel—and Natalie.

She brushed her teeth, blow-dried her hair into glossy, dark waves and reached for her robe in its usual spot on the back of the bathroom door. *Darn.* Too late, she remembered throwing it into the laundry the night before.

Wrapped in a royal blue towel, she peeked cautiously out the door. Silly to worry. It was only two steps to her bedroom. No doubt Daniel was downstairs with Joanne, plotting the next instalment of her birthday surprise.

She'd taken only one of the two steps when Daniel's door opened and he stepped out of his room onto the landing. He stopped short, looking as surprised as she felt. A few weeks ago she would have simply breezed past. Now her pulse roared into overdrive and she stood rooted to the spot, clutching the towel.

His gaze strayed to her bare shoulders and points south before he brought it abruptly back to her face. "Done in the bathroom?" he said at last.

"I…yes. It's all yours." Heat crept up her chest into her neck and face. This time Daniel's gaze went to the flushed tops of her breasts where they swelled above the towel, and stayed there.

He took a deep breath and plowed a hand through his hair. "Get dressed," he said. "I'll just have a quick shave and meet you downstairs."

"What should I wear?"

"Anything. You look good in anything." His gaze lingered on the towel.

Karina managed a light laugh. "I should know better than to ask a man for his opinion on clothes. Are we going out somewhere? Fancy? Casual?"

"Dressy," he said firmly. "Wear something dressy." Then he turned on his heel and beat a hasty retreat.

Dressy. Karina went to her room and flicked through her wardrobe. *Aha.* She reached to the back and brought forth a hanger barely weighted down by the slim slip of black fabric draped over it. Perfect.

DANIEL WAS CHECKING last-minute arrangements with Joanne when Karina sauntered into the kitchen. He glanced at her and his mouth dried up in midsentence. Below his freshly shaven jaw the pulse in his neck began to beat faster.

"What?" Karina glanced down at the thin-strapped dress that clung to every curve of her body. "Not dressy enough?"

"It's fine." He cleared his throat. "You look fine."

"What he means," Joanne said, bustling from fridge to stove with something on a baking tray, "is you look sensational."

"Too right!" Natalie chimed in. "You look super!"

Daniel continued to stare at Karina, trying to pinpoint exactly when she'd started having this paralyzing effect on him.

Karina peered around him at Joanne. "Looks like we're eating in. What can I do to help?"

"Nothing," Daniel said quickly. He glanced at his watch, then at Joanne. "I think it's time."

Karina glanced from him to Joanne. "Time for what?"

"Time for...a drink," Daniel said. "Some champagne?"

"Maybe a mineral water to start. I'm parched."

Karina started to reach for the fridge handle, but Daniel whisked the bottle out and quickly shut the door before she could help herself. He and Joanne had worked so hard he didn't want the surprise blown at the last minute.

"What's going on?" Karina asked, laughing. "You two are acting very suspiciously." She turned to Natalie. "What's in the fridge they don't want me to see?"

Behind Karina's back, Daniel held a finger to his lips and cast a warning glance at his daughter.

"Nothing," Natalie said, her round blue eyes the picture of childhood innocence.

Daniel released his breath. "We just want you to relax on your birthday," he said, and handed Karina the glass of fizzing water. "Take a seat in the living room. The food won't be long."

"All right." She glanced once more at each of them and started back down the hall.

Daniel waited until she was almost to the door. Then, motioning to Joanne and Natalie to follow, he led the way on tiptoe into the dining room. They took their place behind a lacquered Japanese screen and waited.

Karina stepped into the living room through the other door and flicked on the light.

Smiling faces popped up from behind the couch, the chairs, and poured out of the dining room toward Karina with a chorus of, "Surprise! Surprise!"

Karina jumped. Her water spilled. She burst into laughter, her hand on her heart. "Kevin…Betty…and the baby, too! Hi, Doug, Carol—" She didn't get another word out. Everyone was trying to hug her at once.

Daniel stood at the edge of the crowd and watched, taking pleasure in Karina's delight. Then her gaze scanned the room and came to rest on him and Joanne. She narrowed her eyes at Joanne and mouthed the word "You!"

Beside him, Joanne shook her head.

Karina's gaze shifted to Daniel. He just grinned. Karina's answering smile took his breath away. Had she always smiled at him like that?

He started to move toward her, but as Karina attempted to meet him she was cut off by another friend wishing her happy birthday. Never mind, he thought, they had all night.

Daniel sipped his drink. Karina was laughing and talking at the center of a small crowd of her friends. Her body swayed lithely as she illustrated her golf swing, only to double over with laughter at her own amateurish efforts.

He couldn't get over the way she looked in that black clingy dress with the midthigh hemline. He'd suggested dressy and she'd come up with knock-down-drag-out sexy. Hell, when he thought about it, she always looked sexy, even in those oversize shirts she wore when working on her papier-mâché.

Joanne tugged on his sleeve. "Can you give me a hand getting the rest of the food to the table?"

"Sure." He followed her back to the kitchen and went to the fridge. "That was a close call earlier." He started handing plates out to Joanne.

"No kidding. Everyone went overboard bringing food, and the cake takes up almost a whole shelf on its own."

"Mississippi mud cake," he said, sneaking a dab of chocolate icing. "She'll think she's died and gone to heaven." Joanne glanced sharply at him and he winced. "Sorry, bad choice of words."

"Was she all right today?" Joanne placed the last plate on the counter. She reached for a packet of blue tortilla chips and emptied it into a bowl.

Daniel nodded and began loading hors d'oeuvres onto

a platter. "We were so busy she didn't have time to think about being sad. She told me about her mother. Sounds like she was quite a lady."

"She told you about her mother?" Joanne's hands stilled, her eyebrows rising.

"Nothing heavy," he replied. "Just how she liked to sing and cook pasta for the neighborhood."

"Still, that's a breakthrough. She never talks about her mother. Not even with me." Joanne crumpled the empty chip bag and tossed it into the trash. With a wink and a smile, she added, "I'd say that's pretty significant."

Daniel nodded calmly, but inside pride and pleasure coursed through his veins. Karina had trusted him with memories she'd never shared with anyone else. With a jaunty step he followed Joanne to the dining room, three heavily laden plates on one arm and two more on the other.

Engulfed by party guests drawn by the sight of food, Daniel set the platters on the already overburdened table. Maybe there was a chance for him and Karina. He'd never have thought she'd be the type he'd want to marry, but now he couldn't imagine marrying anyone else.

Her mother had died young, he reminded himself. As much as he knew the odds of it happening to Karina were slim, it was still a possibility. Francine's death had been hard enough, and he hadn't even been in love with her. Karina's death would be too awful to contemplate. Natalie loved her, too, and so did—

Damn it all, who invited Brian?

His brother stood next to Karina at the table, speaking into her ear. She laughed and met his gaze. Daniel did a slow burn.

He'd left the guest list up to Joanne, never dreaming

she'd invite Brian. In hindsight, he could see how it might have seemed reasonable—Karina had played golf with Brian, and they were going to the tournament together. For the first time in his life, Daniel wished he'd taken up golf. If he'd been the jock in the family, this never would have happened.

Brian picked up a prawn, dipped it in cocktail sauce and fed it to Karina with his fingers. The bile that churned in Daniel's gut rose in his throat.

Then Brian spotted him. "Danny boy!"

"Hello, Brian." Daniel noted his brother's flushed cheeks and loud voice. Brian had had a few drinks already.

"I've got a bone to pick with you," Brian scolded, draping his arm over Karina's shoulder. "Karina missed a golf lesson to go ballooning with you."

"It's her birthday, Bri," Daniel said, forcing a smile. "There's more to life than golf."

Why wasn't she moving away from Brian's arm? Daniel looked directly at her, but her gaze was innocent and smiling. Either she had no objection to Brian's attention or she didn't think it worth making a fuss about.

"Sacrilege!" Brian rejoined with mock horror. He smiled at Karina and squeezed her shoulder. "Golf is like life, eh, Karina? You have to play to win. I'm not sure Danny understands that."

Karina smiled. "You'd be surprised what Daniel understands." She winked at Daniel and slipped out from beneath Brian's arm.

Daniel followed her with his eyes as she was caught up in another group of people. He walked over to Brian and forced himself to act civilized. "It's nice to see her in such good spirits."

"She's fantastic!" Brian said, shaking his head. "Everything a man could want in a woman." He clapped Daniel on the back. "You made up for past sins when you introduced me to Karina, Danny boy."

"Karina introduced herself, if you recall," Daniel said between his teeth. "Are you serious about her?"

Brian nodded, still gazing at Karina. Then he glanced at Daniel, his blue eyes intense. "Wouldn't you be?"

"We're not talking about me."

"Good Lord, Danny, quit glowering at me. In a minute you'll be asking me my intentions. Lighten up. The lady is a fox and I'm the hunter."

"She's not into marriage."

"Oh, I think if she had the right offer, she'd be into anything," Brian replied with a nudge and a wink.

Daniel gripped his glass almost to breaking point. Surely any jury would consider Brian's comment justification for fratricide. "You haven't got a clue what she's really like."

Brian laid a hand on Daniel's sleeve, his expression sobering. "I was only joking, Danny. She's a wonderful person and I don't mean the slightest disrespect. Any man would be damned lucky to land her." With a smile, he smoothed back his hair and straightened his tie. "And tonight, I feel lucky."

"What makes you think she's interested in you?" Daniel sipped at his wine, half dreading the answer.

"Who knows what women think, Danny boy? But I'll tell you one thing, she kisses like a goddess."

The wine turned to vinegar in Daniel's mouth. "Things have progressed that far between you, have they?" He forced himself to speak casually, but he felt as if his fingernails were being ripped out one by one.

Brian smiled modestly. "I guess I shouldn't be kissing

and telling but, hey, you're my only brother. Who else can I confide in?''

''Maybe she's got someone else in her life.'' *Like me.* But he knew a moment of doubt. Should he warn Brian he wasn't the only one Karina was kissing? Was he doomed to face divided loyalties every time he fell in love?

Brian looked at him thoughtfully. ''She says not.''

CHAPTER FOURTEEN

DANIEL GLANCED AT his watch. It was long past midnight and the party was still going strong. *Karina* was still going strong. He'd put Natalie to bed hours ago, right after the birthday cake. He wished he could escape the noise and crowd himself, but he'd promised Karina he'd see her through her birthday.

He'd hardly had a chance to speak to her all night. Every time he'd tried, someone else had joined the conversation or taken her away to dance. Still, he was glad she was having a good time. It meant she wasn't brooding over her mother. Or herself.

Then she looked at him across the room. Her eyes seemed to hold a special warmth just for him. He smiled at her, willing her to break away from her friends and come to him. To his pleasure, she excused herself and did just that.

"Are you enjoying yourself, Daniel?" She touched him lightly on the chest. "I didn't think you liked parties."

Beneath his shirt, his skin burned where her fingertips rested. "Dinner parties are more my thing. Most of the time," he added, thinking of the last one he'd attended.

She laughed. "I'm glad to see you're on better terms with Brian."

"We're…working things out." He paused, wondering

exactly how she felt about his brother. "Brian really likes you, Karina."

Her mouth slanted upward. "Good. I like him, too."

Salt in a wound couldn't have burned more fiercely. Daniel forced a smile. "He's always been popular with the ladies."

Karina tilted her head to one side and studied him. "Funny, that's what he said about you."

"He's dreaming. Or rewriting history again. Brian was always the most popular guy in the most popular group in high school. At university, too, or so I understand."

"And you? Surely *you're* not going to tell me you couldn't get a date?"

"I wouldn't say that," he replied, wondering at the inflection in her voice. "I usually had a girlfriend, but only one at a time. Crowds of any sort have never been my thing."

"They don't seem to bother your brother." Her gaze settled on Brian as he held forth in the center of a little gathering. From the expressions of humorous anticipation on the faces of his audience, he was telling a joke.

"He has a way with people." Dammit, why did they have to spend these moments together talking about his brother? Everything she said seemed to confirm that Brian was more her style.

But he had things in common with her, as well, Daniel thought. As much as she liked to party, she also loved her home, children, creative pursuits. The odds weren't stacked overwhelmingly in Brian's favor.

He glanced sideways at Karina. She was still moving to the music. "Care to dance?"

She flashed him a brilliant smile. "I thought you'd never ask."

They danced through three tracks before a slow song came on and he could finally take her in his arms. When Karina leaned into him and released a sigh that pressed the warm, sweet weight of her breasts against his chest, he knew he could have danced all night just for this moment.

"How are you doing?" he murmured into the damp, jasmine-scented tendrils of hair that curled around her temple.

The arm she'd twined around his neck tightened in a hug. "Wonderful, thanks to you." She lifted her head, her eyes lit with a smile. "You've worn me out today, Daniel Bowen. Not many men can say that."

"Worn out, my eye," he replied, entranced by the feel of her heart beating against his breast. "That engine of yours will purr for hours yet."

The room was darkened, lit only by a table lamp and the winking fairy lights. A few other couples were on the floor, but Daniel was aware only of Karina, her scent, her warmth, her softness as he held her in his arms. Pressed together, they moved in sensual rhythm to the slow, bluesy music.

Then he felt a hand on his shoulder.

"May I cut in?"

Daniel dragged his gaze from Karina's to see Brian standing behind him. Instinctively he tightened his hold on her. "Sorry, mate, this dance is mine."

"The next one, then." This time Brian's words were directed at Karina. She gave Daniel a questioning glance.

He wanted to say, "No, you're mine. Not just for this dance or the next one, but forever." But Karina was no more his possession than she was Brian's. "Whatever you want."

Karina hesitated, then nodded at Brian.

Brian melted into the crowd. Daniel pulled Karina back into his embrace and pressed his cheek against her temple. But the warm awareness that had built between them was shattered. At the end of the dance he released her and watched painfully as she went from his arms to his brother's.

AT LAST the party was over. The house was quiet and the landing dark when Daniel climbed the stairs. Karina had gone up half an hour ago. He'd heard the shower running and killed time clearing dishes until the bathroom was free.

There was no light under her door when he went into the bathroom to brush his teeth. She must have been worn out after all, he thought as he stepped into the shower a minute later. Too tired to do anything but sleep.

He finished his shower quickly. Wrapped in a towel, he slipped out of the bathroom and started across the landing.

He paused. A yellow glow that hadn't been there before shone from beneath Karina's door.

He listened. Not a sound penetrated the silence. What could she be doing? He pressed his ear to her door. Nothing.

He knocked. He heard a faint gasp, then a deeper silence, as though she were holding her breath.

"Karina?"

"What is it?" Her voice was low and strained.

"Are you all right?"

No answer.

"Karina, I'm coming in." He waited a moment to give her a chance to put on a robe if necessary. Then, with only a brief thought for his own unsuitable attire, he opened the door.

She was huddled on the bed, wrapped in a colorful silk shawl. Her eyes were huge and dark, her face pale and drawn in the light of the ceramic oil lamp on the bedside table. As he entered, she turned the framed photo she was holding facedown.

Wordlessly he crossed the room and sat on the bed beside her. Any sexual thoughts he'd entertained about entering Karina's private chamber vanished when he saw the heartache in her eyes.

Without hesitation he put his arms around her and pressed her head to his shoulder. She lay passively yet tense, as though afraid of falling apart. Daniel stroked her back but found no response. How could he break through the brambled walls of grief that had grown around her over the years?

"Talk to me, Karina," he said softly. "Tell me what troubles you the most."

She was silent for a long time. Finally she said, "I can't cry for my mother. I've never been able to cry for her. The pain builds inside me till I'm ready to explode but no tears come."

"You've never cried?" He could hardly believe someone as passionate about life as Karina would be able to stop the grief.

She shook her head and he felt the dry heat of her cheek on his bare chest.

"The day she…" Her voice faltered. "The day Mama died, my father told me we had to be brave, that Mama wouldn't want us to weep for her."

Daniel stifled an oath and searched for some understanding of the man who'd been so insensitive to his daughter's pain. "He must have been hurting very badly himself. He probably didn't know how to deal with his own grief, much less yours."

Karina drew away from him a little, her face cast down. "It was a long time ago. It doesn't matter anymore."

Daniel stroked back a strand of ebony hair and tucked it behind her ear so he could see her face better. His other arm gently tightened around her shoulders in case she had any thoughts of ending the conversation.

"It *does* matter," he said. "If you're still hurting, it matters very much. I'm sure if your father knew, he'd be appalled at what you're going through because of him."

"Oh, Daniel, it was so awful," she said with a shudder, her voice cracked and pained. "If only we could have talked about her, maybe we could have helped each other. Instead, he locked himself away in his grief and left me alone to deal with mine."

Daniel thought of Natalie's sorrow and confusion after Francine's death, and of the tears he would first encourage, then dry, night after night. "Children need help to deal with grief."

"I guess Dad didn't know that. He destroyed every family photo that included her. He gave away all her belongings. He wouldn't talk about her. He wouldn't even let me say her name. I had nothing left of her. It was as though my mother never existed." Karina broke off, hiccuping.

"What about your brother? Couldn't you talk to him?"

"Tom was almost as bad as my father. He went all stoical and silent, although I knew he was just as miserable as I was. He was sixteen. Said he wasn't a little boy to be blubbering for his mommy."

Daniel held her tightly, rocking her as he would have Natalie. "It's okay, love." He stroked her hair, pressing soft kisses against her temple. "It's okay to cry. You *need* to cry to heal." He pulled her even closer, as though he could insulate her from pain with his own body.

The warmth and caring in his voice penetrated deep into Karina's swollen, aching heart. She felt the tears clogging her throat, burning her eyes.

"Let it go, Karina," Daniel murmured. "Let it go."

She could hold on no longer. A painful, racking sob tore through her chest and her control broke at last. Great burning tears rolled down her scalded cheeks. The oil lamp flared and hissed. She sobbed, gasped for breath and felt Daniel's arms tighten around her. She pressed her face against his chest, soaking his skin with almost two decades' worth of tears.

Anguish washed over her, building and breaking like waves on a rocky reef as she wept in his arms. Her own arms struggled out from between them and went around his waist to hold him as tightly as he held her. Daniel stroked her hair and back, whispering meaningless phrases that bespoke comfort and safety and, above all, the assurance that she wasn't alone. That someone cared for her. Someone who loved her unconditionally.

She cried and cried until she didn't have a single tear left to shed. As her sobbing slowly ebbed, the tightness in her chest eased. She heaved a last great sigh and went still against his chest, breathing softly. She never wanted to move again.

For a very long time she lay nestled against Daniel, absorbing his warmth, taking comfort from his strong arms and gentle hands. Today he'd taken her out of herself with his adventures and his companionship. Tonight he'd forced her deep into her pain and pulled her through to the other side, whole and intact. She felt bonded to him in a way she never had to anyone else.

Finally a cramp in her leg forced her to move. She pulled away a little, smiling sheepishly at Daniel as she twisted her ankle this way and that.

His eyes searched her tearstained face. "Are you okay?"

She nodded, knowing he wasn't talking about her leg.

Daniel reached for a tissue from the box beside her bed and dabbed at her eyes. "At least you've got the portrait in the living room," he said. "How did that survive your father's purges?"

"It belonged to my aunt Maria, Mama's sister. She gave it to me much later. It was taken when Mama was eighteen, before she was married."

Daniel reached for another tissue and handed it to her. "Blow."

Dutifully, Karina blew her nose and threw the wadded tissue in the wastebasket. "I've also got their wedding photo," she said, reaching over to the table to show him.

She watched him study the photo of her mother and father. Their youthful faces were alive with love and happiness, blissfully unaware of what was to come.

"I snuck it out of my parents' room when Mama was still in the hospital," she told him. "I had no idea my father was going to destroy the rest of them. I just wanted something to have beside my bed at night. For seven years I hid it in my dresser and only took it out when I was alone."

Daniel replaced the photo on the table and tilted her head up until she met his gaze. "My poor darlin'."

Her bruised and battered heart swelled with the warmth in his eyes and voice. His thumb trailed down her wet cheeks, wiping away the last traces of moisture.

Slowly his lips descended to hers, touched, withdrew and touched again with the utmost gentleness. Drawing her close once more, he pressed his chin against her forehead.

Karina sighed softly. He was too good a person to lead on. She should move apart from him, now, before anything happened. Even as the thought entered her mind, he slipped his hands beneath the shawl, gently massaging the tension from her shoulders. His hands moved down her back, the callused tips of his fingers circling each vertebra. Karina breathed a sigh of deep relaxation. Nothing else could possibly feel so good.

But no sooner had she relaxed than tension returned in a tingling awareness of his touch. His hands framed her sides now, and his wrists brushed the edges of her breasts as his fingers kneaded her back muscles. With each nudge of her breasts, waves of exquisitely subtle desire pulsed through her, and she gripped his waist tighter.

She lifted her face, felt the roughness of his unshaven chin on her forehead and smelled the clean, woodsy scent of his skin. Then somehow her gaze was all tangled up in his and she couldn't seem to breathe.

He dipped his head, their noses bumped and warmth rose from her skin and mingled with his. She wanted to laugh, she wanted to cry. Beneath her lips, she felt one side of his face stretch in a smile.

"Karina." He spoke her name as though it were a phrase of music. "Let me love you."

It took all her strength, but she forced herself to pull back. "Daniel, I'm sorry, we can't do this."

"Are you worried about protection?" he murmured. "I've got condoms somewhere. Hang on." He started to get up.

"No, it's not that. There are some in my bedside table."

He tilted her head, forcing her to gaze directly into his eyes. "Then what?"

Oh, how she wanted him. Needed him. "They're not one-hundred-percent foolproof. I...I don't want to take a chance on getting pregnant."

He stroked her cheek with the back of one finger. "Nothing's one-hundred percent, darlin', except abstinence. I'd rather wait awhile, too, before having children. But maybe you don't realize how I feel about you."

"Oh, Daniel..." His gentle warmth brought back the aching need in her heart. It wasn't just her body that craved him but her soul, as well. Surely just this once she could allow herself the love she longed for. And longed to give to Daniel.

Leaning away from him, she opened the drawer of her bedside table and searched around until she found a condom. She turned the plastic packet over in her hand, inspecting it. "I hope these things don't have use-by dates."

Daniel chuckled softly. "I don't think so."

She hesitated a moment, then placed the packet in his palm.

Closing his fingers around it, Daniel looked into her eyes. "Are you sure?"

With a tremulous smile, she nodded.

"If you were to get pregnant, I'd be there for you," he said, still serious. "I'd welcome a baby. Our baby."

His words sparked a longing so deep she could hardly bear it. Pressing a finger to his lips, she whispered, "Just love me tonight, Daniel. That's all I ask."

His eyes shut briefly. Then he bent his head and his

lips met hers. Born neither of yearning nor passion, the kiss was a pact of love, warm and giving, wholehearted yet sensual.

She trembled, hardly daring to breathe as he drew back to kiss the tip of her nose before slipping the shawl from her shoulders. From beneath lowered lashes, she saw his gaze drop to her breasts and heard his almost inaudible sigh.

Then his eyes lifted to hers once more. He slipped one thin strap of her nightdress over her shoulder. Then the other. The slippery material slid down, catching on the fullness of her breasts. Her breath shortened, her heart pounded against her chest.

Lowering his head, he pressed his lips to her breast. Her skin burned at every tiny kiss laid on each soft mound. Trailing behind his lips came his fingertips, sending out shimmers of sensation like the ripples of moonlight on water. His touch lingered on the tiny scar on her right breast, and he raised his head in mute enquiry.

"It's nothing," she murmured. Trembling, she arched her neck. Her nightie slid farther down, exposing the dark brown tip of her nipple.

Cupping her breast in his hand, Daniel guided it to his mouth. She heard him groan deep in his throat as his lips closed over the hardening peak. Tremors of desire shot straight to the tingling warmth between her legs, inflaming her.

I love you. I love you. I love you. Over and over, the words formed in her brain. Words she didn't dare speak aloud.

She ran her hands over Daniel's chest, wanting to know every ripple of muscle, every rib, every inch of tanned, supple skin. When she encountered damp terry towel, she pushed at it impatiently.

He stood, pulling her up with him. Satin slithered across her heated skin as her nightgown slipped all the way to her waist and clung precariously to her hips. Daniel's towel fell away, leaving him naked. In the candlelight, his lean body glowed, shadowed by ridges of muscle and bone.

Then he pulled her close, and she gasped softly as her breasts touched his bare chest. He pressed his hips into hers, letting her feel the strength of his desire. And all the while his mouth clung and tasted, his hands moved and touched as though he would never get enough.

She could feel his erection hard against her belly and wriggled closer, wrapping one leg around his to press herself against his thigh.

His breathing was ragged now, his eyes glazed with need. With a groan he pushed up her nightdress and cupped her buttocks. Overbalancing, they fell on the bed, tangled in each other's limbs.

She shifted, her legs parting around his. Mindless with need, she bit her lip at the effort of controlling the primal urge to rock her hips upward and take him inside herself. "Daniel," she murmured. "Now. Please!"

His eyes fixed on hers, he ripped open the condom packet and, with a trembling hand, sheathed himself. A strangled groan emerged from his throat as he surged into her, filling her with a sweet, hard heat. She thrust upward, pulling him deep inside.

Daniel blanketed her in fiery love, his face animated by desire, his eyes penetrating her soul. His body moved with hers in a fit so perfect they might have been dovetailed by a master craftsman.

Deep in the moment she didn't think about tomorrow.

Filled with the love she'd longed for she didn't fear losing it. Daniel took her spinning through the distant reaches of time and space, the pain in her heart left far behind, a universe away.

Calling out his name, she arched upward. Explosions of neon-splashed ecstasy fused her body and soul in formless pleasure. Daniel plunged into her again and again, until at last his body shook with a final convulsive shudder.

"Karina," he whispered, and lowered his spent body onto hers.

When conscious thought returned, she was still wrapped in Daniel's embrace, his body a welcome weight on hers. She breathed in the musky scent of their lovemaking, savoring the intimacy of limb on limb, skin on skin.

With his face buried in her hair, she stroked her fingernails lightly down his back and up his sides. The skin over his ribs shivered at her touch and he wriggled his hips, setting off an aftershock that rippled through her body.

"Mmm, Daniel… Ohh!"

Daniel peered up at her, hair falling over his eyes as he smiled cheekily. He moved his hips again. Her eyes started to close as another pulse of lingering bliss washed over her. Just before her lids fluttered shut she saw his expression change to adoration and wonder.

At last she lay still, replete and exhausted, her limbs heavy. Daniel eased his weight off her and rolled them over onto their sides, still inside her. Her eyes halfclosed, Karina smiled dreamily, savoring recent memory.

Daniel traced the outline of her lips with the tip of his

finger. "You look like the cat who swallowed the canary," he said, and laughed softly.

Her smile widened. "When you guarantee a girl a good time on her birthday, you really come through."

Daniel grinned and leaned forward to touch her lips with his. "Satisfaction or your money back. Don't forget to tell all your friends."

"Not a chance. I want you all to myself."

"Darlin', I'm yours."

Caught up in the banter, she'd spoken without thinking. He'd spoken lightly, matching her tone. Then she saw something flicker deep in his clear, hazel eyes.

"I want you all to myself, too," he said. This time he wasn't joking.

"I, uh…" She didn't know what to say. She was fine when everything was lighthearted, but how did she deal with this? One expectation led to another.

Her damp skin cooling rapidly, Karina wriggled under the covers, bringing the duvet up to her nose. "No problem," she said, taking refuge in further teasing. "Just knock aside the dozens of men beating a path to my door."

Daniel crooked one finger around the edge of the quilt and pulled it down far enough to plant a kiss on her lips. "Including Brian?"

Karina just laughed. Then her laughter faded as she realized she had to put this night in perspective, for both their sakes. "Seriously, Daniel, today was really special and I want to thank you, but—"

"I was that good, was I?"

The teasing light was back in his eyes, and for that she was grateful. "I meant about taking my mind off things."

"Nothing like sex to take your mind off your troubles.'' His expression sobering, he brushed a strand of damp hair off her face. ''Does this mean you've come to terms with your grief over your mother?''

The image of Mama, smiling and serene, came into her mind. Karina knew with a startled certainty the crippling sorrow had, if not disappeared, at least greatly diminished.

''I'll probably never get over it completely, but having you with me, being able to cry…yes, it helped. You wouldn't believe how much.''

''I'm glad. Maybe marriage won't seem such an awful fate to you anymore.''

She went still in his arms. ''Marriage?''

He smiled. ''I know you've heard of it.''

She rolled out of his arms, put her legs over the side of the bed and reached for her shawl. How could she not have seen he wouldn't be content with one night of lovemaking, or even a brief affair? Wrapping herself in her shawl, she rose, putting distance between them while she searched her mind for plausible reasons to put an end to this conversation. Any reason would do—except the real one.

She laughed, hoping it sounded casual. ''I'm not ready for marriage. If I get my promotion, as I expect I will, I'll be traveling a lot, spending more time at the office.'' Somehow that didn't sound as appealing as it once had. ''How could I take care of a family?''

He propped himself up on one elbow. ''Karina, I work at home. Natalie is going to school soon. It's not an issue.''

Karina began to pace. He hadn't come right out and asked her to marry him, but there was no mistaking his intent. ''As a wife, I'm not a good bet, Daniel. You've seen what kind of housekeeper I am—''

"Karina, if you don't love me, just say so."

His quiet words tore at her heart. She stopped pacing and faced him. "You want a family. Natalie wants a baby brother or sister. I want you both to have all the things you want."

"I want *you,* Karina."

He sounded so certain, she knew a moment of doubt. What if she was wrong to deny them a future together? Then she closed her mind to the thought.

"Aren't we getting ahead of ourselves with all this talk about babies and marriage?" she pleaded. "Let's just enjoy this night together and worry about tomorrow when it comes."

He was silent for a long moment, his expression sober. Then, slowly, he nodded. She crossed to the bed and let the shawl fall away from her breasts.

His gaze remained on her face. "I want more than tonight with you, Karina."

Instead of answering, she reached into the drawer and dangled another condom in front of him, letting her smile speak for her.

He sighed. Then a humorous light appeared in his eyes and he reached for her. "But for now, I'll take what I can get."

She grinned and straddled his thighs. "Spoken like a true pragmatist."

His hands slid down her back, urging her higher. "Being a romantic isn't doing me much good at the moment. But tomorrow—"

Karina laid a finger across his mouth. "Shh." She moved her hips against his and felt him swell beneath her. "Do you like that?"

Daniel's eyes closed. "You're absolutely ruthless."

She brushed the silky fringe of the shawl across his

chest, watching his nipples rise and harden in its wake. Then she stretched her arms forward over his head, enclosing the two of them in a glowing silken tent.

She bent her head and kissed him, her mouth warm and giving. She didn't want to think about tomorrow. Or the tomorrow after that. She just wanted to let him know without words that she loved him with her whole being, this minute and forever. Even if they couldn't have forever.

"Daniel," she whispered against his lips just to hear the sound of his name. She began to move against him more insistently, enticing him into slow, seductive lovemaking.

Much later, through a pleasure-hazed exhaustion, she was dimly aware of Daniel drawing the duvet over them. Just before she sank into sleep she felt him press a kiss, soft, warm and infinitely tender, on her temple.

THE CREAK OF the floorboards on the landing woke Karina sometime in the darkness before dawn. She opened her eyes a crack to see a small figure with tousled blond hair and dinosaur pajamas stumble into the room and crawl into bed on her side.

"Daddy, are you in here?"

Natalie's eyes were half shut, and it was clear she was more asleep than awake. Karina grunted softly as small hands and elbows dug into her stomach.

"*Mommy?*" Natalie's sleepy voice took on a bewildered note. "Mommy, is that you?"

The hope and rising expectation in the little girl's query tore at Karina's heart. On the other side of the bed, Daniel flicked on the table lamp. Squinting against the light, Natalie awakened fully and recognized Karina.

Her startled expression was swiftly followed by one of crushing disappointment.

"What are you doing out of bed, Nattie?" Daniel said, rising on one elbow.

"Shhh, Daniel," Karina said quickly. Natalie looked ready to burst into tears.

"I had a sad dream," Natalie said, her voice quavering. "I dreamed Mommy was back. And then I thought…" She broke off, gazing uncertainly at Karina. "But it wasn't—" Two big tears broke free and rolled down her cheeks.

Daniel started to get up. Karina stopped him with a hand on his chest. "I'll take her back to bed." She rose and wrapped herself in her shawl. Placing an arm around Natalie's slender shoulders, she led her out of the room.

Karina tucked Natalie back into bed and pulled the coverlet up under her chin. She stroked wisps of hair back from the girl's forehead. "You miss your mommy, don't you, sweetheart?"

Natalie nodded, swallowing. "It's worser when I dream. I forget she's not here, but when I wake up…she…she's always gone." Her thin voice trailed off as more tears snaked down her cheeks. "I'm sorry," she said with a sniff.

"Don't be sorry, darling. And don't ever be afraid to cry. Someday it won't hurt quite as much and you'll be able to think about your mother without crying. You see—"

She paused, unsure whether to burden the child with her own grief. Then she thought of how alone she'd felt before Daniel had been there for her. Understanding and caring could never be a burden, she decided.

Taking Natalie's hand in hers, she soothed, "You see, Nattie, my mother died, too, when I was young. Not as young as you, but pretty young. It's very hard to live without your mommy. I...I still hurt inside.''

Natalie's tears slowed and she gazed solemnly at Karina. ''You do?''

Karina nodded. ''I think part of me will always hurt when I think of her, but I also remember the good things. Things that make me smile.''

''Like what?''

''Oh, like when she used to let me play dress-up with her old clothes. And every year I helped her pick tomatoes and make a special sauce with them. But I think my happiest memory is of her singing to me.''

''Mommy used to sing to me, too,'' Natalie confided with a tremulous smile. ''She knew lots of funny songs that made me laugh. Like you.''

''There you go. Hold on to those beautiful memories, darling. And don't forget you've got a daddy who loves you very much and...and you've got Mrs. Beeton to take care of you.'' It was a poor second and Karina knew it, but she also knew the child needed to take comfort where she could.

Natalie's eyes widened. ''Mrs. Beeton's gone.''

''Gone?''

Natalie nodded. ''She had to go help another little girl who needs her.''

''Don't you need her anymore?'' Was Daniel aware of this new development? she wondered. He'd be so pleased.

''No, 'cause I've got you now.'' She snuggled under the covers.

Speechless, Karina contemplated the enormity of her responsibility. She had neither the heart to deny, nor the courage to confirm, Natalie's casual but confident assertion.

The girl's long lashes fluttered sleepily. "K'rina?"

"Yes?" she said faintly.

"Would you sing me a song?"

Karina swallowed. "Of course." She drew a deep breath and softly, she began to sing, "'Hush little baby, don't say a word....'"

She could barely get the words out past the lump in her throat. Her heart was so painfully swollen with love and grief for this poor motherless child she was afraid she'd break down before the song was over.

Natalie fell asleep within seconds but Karina sang on, the tears rolling down her cheeks as she mourned the mother she'd loved and lost.

Daniel was asleep when Karina crept back to bed in the grey light of early morning. His face was smooth and at peace. A tiny smile curled the corners of his beautiful mouth. She lay for a long time just watching him and loving him....

And knowing she could never marry him.

The responsibility was too great and the potential for tragedy too awful. Seeing Natalie's trusting face in the lamplight had brought home how theoretical her fears had been until now. The child was a live human being, not some hypothetical baby. Natalie was already fragile and vulnerable from losing her mother. How would she ever recover if she lost another?

CHAPTER FIFTEEN

KARINA TOSSED AND TURNED for hours until finally giving up all hope of sleep. She slipped out from beneath the covers and dressed quickly and quietly, casting a last longing glance at Daniel. If only they could make love just one more time, she thought, her heart quietly breaking. But it would be wrong.

She went downstairs and moved mechanically around the kitchen, flipping on the radio, making coffee. While the coffee brewed, she went down to the basement, and a few minutes later, climbed the stairs dragging a roll of chicken wire behind her. When her inner self was in turmoil, nothing was as soothing as the feel of paste or as distracting as creating a new papier-mâché creature.

With little conscious thought she molded the wire into a stout body with four spindly legs. What she would create this morning she wasn't certain, but she knew it wouldn't be beautiful or elegant. Sure enough, before long she'd fashioned a short, thick neck with a long, upturned snout.

Karina stood back, eyeing the mass of chicken wire critically. Yes, she thought grimly, a warthog was exactly what she felt like. A warthog who'd had no sleep and had precious little happiness to look forward to.

She sipped at a cup of coffee and with one hand pinched the top of the head into small, pointy ears. Thoughts of Daniel crept into her mind as she worked but she cast them aside, focusing all her attention on the beast in front of her.

She couldn't help glancing at Felix the Clock every now and then, wondering when Daniel would wake up and what he'd think when he saw she wasn't beside him.

That was how she knew it was exactly 8:37 when the telephone rang. Absently wiping a hand down her shirt, she picked up the receiver with two fingers and clicked it on. "Hello?"

"Good morning," said a pleasant female voice. "Is this Mrs. Bowen?"

Karina hesitated, startled by the unexpected temptation to lay claim to that title. "Er, no. May I ask who's calling?"

"My name is Diana Wallace. Is Mr. Bowen in?"

"He's not available right now. Can I take a message?"

"Certainly. I'm from House Rentals Plus. Mr. Bowen asked us to locate a house for him. I'm pleased to say we have one that will suit his needs perfectly. It's just two blocks from the primary school he mentioned and it has a huge garage."

"Sounds perfect," Karina replied dully.

"It's available from the first of September," Diana Wallace went on. "But there's a good possibility the present tenants might vacate earlier."

"I…I'll let him know," Karina said, and copied down the address. "Thanks for calling."

She clicked the phone off but made no move to hang it up. *Daniel would be leaving.* She shivered, cold all over.

It's for the best, she told herself, rubbing her arms to bring some warmth back into them. He would have had to leave anyway. At least now she'd know he and Natalie had a home to go to.

Daniel entered the kitchen to see Karina standing by the window, the telephone hanging from her hand as she stared into nothingness. In the middle of the floor was the biggest, ugliest-looking pig he'd ever seen. Petunia had been positively dainty by comparison.

Sneaking up behind her, he snaked an arm around her waist and planted a kiss on the back of her neck, bared by the ponytail that hung halfway down her back.

"Mornin', darlin'. You're up early."

To his surprise, she backed away from his embrace without meeting his gaze. "Everything okay?" he asked. He was eager to touch her, to kiss her, to drag her back upstairs to her bed. Or his. He wasn't fussy.

"Fine." She slanted him the briefest of glances before slipping the phone back into its slot on the wall. Silently she tipped some powder from a bag into the basin on the table, added water and began to mix up a fresh batch of paste.

Daniel frowned, perturbed by her withdrawal. "Was Nattie upset about finding us in bed together?"

Karina shook her head. "She was too troubled by her dream to notice. I think she thought you were helping me with a nightmare."

He gave a short laugh. "I'm a bit of an expert on nightmares."

"I can imagine." The paste prepared, Karina began to cut strips of cloth from a piece of dark plaid spread flat on the table.

"A little subdued for your taste, isn't it?" He fingered the cotton fabric, his gaze never leaving her averted face.

"It suits my mood."

Why should her mood be so dark after the night

they'd spent together? He placed a hand on her cheek and gently brought her face around to his. "My kisses are renowned for their mood-lifting qualities," he said, smiling.

She ducked away again before he could claim her lips. Her fixed smile disappeared as she gazed over his shoulder. Worry, sorrow, fear—and something else that he couldn't decipher—shifted across her face.

Daniel crossed his arms over his chest, tired of the cat-and-mouse game. "Okay, Karina, what's wrong?"

She shrugged. "There's a message for you from Diana Wallace at House Rentals Plus. She's got a house for you."

He pushed a hand through his hair. "I'd almost given up on them."

Karina dipped a piece of fabric into the paste and laid it over the warthog's back. "She said the house is perfect for you and that you can move in at the beginning of the month."

He moved toward the phone. "I'll ring her back and tell her I don't need it anymore."

Karina stepped in front of him, blocking the way to the telephone. For the first time since he'd entered the kitchen, she looked him directly in the eye.

"I think you should take it."

The skin on the back of his neck prickled. "I don't want it."

Karina rested a hand on the chicken-wire frame, her fingers closing around the open mesh. "It's close to Natalie's school."

"I can drive her."

"It's got a big garage for your exclusive use."

"I'm all set up here."

"I want you to go."

He stared at her in disbelief. "Why?"

"I just do. Don't ask me any more."

She meant it. Through his mind-numbing pain, he saw that Karina was on the verge of tears. He wanted to reach for her but didn't. She was suffering, but he was suffering, too. The time for comforting was past. It was time for some answers.

"I—" Her voice cracked and she cleared her throat. "I'll give you a good reference."

Daniel's head snapped up. "Reference! Forget the reference. Forget the damn house! Just tell me what's going on. Why are you acting this way?"

She turned back to the basin and picked out another strip of fabric, squeezing off the excess paste with trembling fingers. "I just don't see how we can go on living in the same house when...when..."

Coming up behind her, he gripped her shoulders. She shuddered at his touch. Her reaction gave him a sick feeling in his stomach but he couldn't bring himself to let her go.

"Karina, I love you. I want to marry you."

Her head went back, eyes closed. Tears squeezed beneath her lids. "I can't marry you, Daniel. I'm sorry."

"Dammit, Karina, do you love me or not?"

"Love has nothing to do with it."

"The hell it doesn't." His fingers dug into her shoulders as he turned her to face him. "What's the real reason you won't marry me? Is it Brian?"

"Brian?" she repeated. "What does Brian have to do with you and me?"

He shrugged, an attempt at nonchalance he didn't feel. "You and he are...close."

"Daniel, for once and for all, I feel nothing for your brother beyond friendship."

"You kissed him."

She wrenched herself away. "For your information, *he* kissed me. There's absolutely no reason for you to be jealous of him."

"Then why are you turning me down?" His hand crashed onto the table, shaking the basin of paste. "I'm not some young fool you can make love to, then cast off like last year's fashion. Tell me the truth!"

Natalie skipped into the kitchen, oblivious of the tension. "Can I help?" she said, spying the new papier-mâché animal. "Can I, please?"

Karina turned away to lean against the kitchen counter but not before Daniel saw more tears spring to her eyes. He grabbed his daughter's arm as she went by and turned her back toward the hall.

"Have you made your bed this morning?" he asked, knowing she rarely did such a thing without prompting. "No? Then off you go upstairs. When you've done that *and* have your hair brushed, you can see if Karina needs help."

Grumbling, Natalie ran up the stairs. Daniel stalked back to find Karina still leaning over the counter, her forehead resting against the cupboard. He jammed his hands in his back pockets to avoid touching her and made an effort to sound reasonable.

"Why won't you marry me? You've begun to grieve for your mother. That's a sign of healing—"

"It's not that simple, Daniel," she interrupted, a sob in her voice. "I've got a family history of breast cancer."

"I know. And I'll do everything I can to give you whatever emotional or material support you need. But I don't see that as a reason not to marry. Karina, *look at me*."

She turned, her fear and frustration plain on her face. "Don't you see, if I were to—" she swallowed hard "—*die* and leave you and Natalie and...maybe another little one, I could never forgive myself."

"Where is it written you're going to die? You're too smart to let anything like a lump get by you."

"But it almost did!" she cried. "Last spring I found one in my right breast. That's why I changed my mind about renting."

The scar on her breast. His heart seemed to stop beating. "Oh God, Karina. You mean..."

Eyes wide, she reached out a hand. "No, it's all right. It was benign. But it could just as easily have been malignant."

Relief turned his knees to water and he leaned against the counter. "Okay. But even if it had been malignant, that still doesn't mean you'd have succumbed to an early grave."

Karina went to the coffee jug and fumbled the lid open. From clear across the room he could see her hands shake as she poured herself a cup. "You don't know what you're talking about."

"Then tell me."

The pain in her tear-filled eyes when she looked at him almost made him wish he hadn't asked.

"My grandmother died of breast cancer in her thirties. As did my great-aunt and God knows how many others on my mother's side. It's in my genes."

"That still doesn't mean you're doomed. Treatment has advanced since your mother's day."

She threw up her hands. "Oh, don't be so damned *rational*. Think of Natalie if you can't understand for yourself. I know I could never take her mother's place, nor would I want to, but if we were to marry, she'd get attached to me.''

''She's already attached.''

Karina's eyes pressed shut. ''I know. I love her, Daniel. I love her so much I don't want to cause her a single moment of pain. How do you think she'd feel losing another mother? How many Mrs. Beetons do you think she can conjure up?''

Daniel's fists clenched inside his pockets and he turned away. This time he didn't have any answers. He gazed at the molded chicken wire, so frustrated he wanted to kick it. ''What is this thing anyway?''

''A warthog.''

He stared at it with loathing. They could have been making love right now, or planning their future. Instead she'd deserted his bed—okay, *her* bed—to make a damn warthog.

He tried another tack. ''Your mother must have known the odds of getting breast cancer were pretty high, yet she still had you.''

Karina set her cup down on the counter so hard the murky brown liquid spilled over the side. ''That's what makes her actions so irresponsible. She knew it was in her family, but she had me anyway. And then she *left* me.''

''Is that the trouble? You haven't forgiven your mother for dying?''

''Don't be ridiculous. She didn't *want* to die. How could I blame her?''

She dropped her face in her hands, shoulders heaving as she fought for control. When she looked up, her eyes seemed to plead for understanding. ''I would *never* knowingly inflict that kind of suffering on a child. Daniel, do you understand? *I will never have children.*''

She really meant it. Daniel read the agonizing truth in her eyes and the strength of her determination in every line of her slim, rigid body. He'd never known the joy that children brought until Natalie had come along. But like a blind man suddenly gifted with sight, once he'd found out what he'd been missing, the prospect of someday having more children had become as expected and as necessary as the rising sun.

His heart breaking, he said, "I want a family, Karina. With you. Think of it, our babies…"

"Don't!" she cried, her voice raw with pain. "I'd give anything if I could be part of it. But I can't."

He grasped her by the arms, desperate to make her see reason. "Yes, you can, if you only want to. You've told me the worst. I'm willing to take a chance."

"Well, I'm not." Her eyes blazed up at him. "I couldn't inflict that suffering on you, either. Not after seeing what my father went through."

"Karina," he pleaded. "Talk to your doctor. Assess the probabilities, discuss the options.…"

"I *have* talked to my doctor. Endlessly. If it were simply a rational decision I'd say yes right now. But it's not, and I can't." Tears streamed down her face. "I never wanted to hurt you, Daniel. I…I hope you find what you're looking for. I hope Natalie will be happy. I hope…"

Daniel pulled her into his arms, and this time she didn't resist. With all his heart and soul he wished he could erase her anguish. And his. It hurt knowing his love, deep and strong as it was, still wasn't enough to overcome her fears. But she'd made her decision long before she'd even met him. The sooner he accepted the fact her path would never converge with his, the better. For all of them, he thought, remembering Natalie.

"I'd better pack my bags," he said, drawing back.

She clutched his arms, gazing up at him in alarm. "Where will you go? The house isn't available for two more weeks."

"I'll find some place to stay, don't worry."

"Daniel, I'm so sorry." Fresh tears started from her eyes.

"Shh, love." He dropped his head and his lips met hers with all the love and tenderness he could place in one brief kiss. He tasted the salt of her tears and the bittersweet nectar of love gone awry. He could hardly bear to look into her eyes as he lifted his mouth from hers.

"Goodbye, Karina, my love." His fingers trailed down her wet cheek and lingered a moment at the edge of her lips. "Goodbye."

"FOR CRYING OUT LOUD, Karina, do you know what time it is?" Joanne hung on to the doorjamb with one hand and clutched her head with the other. Her purple dressing gown hung open over a Snoopy nightshirt.

"I thought you were always up early with the kids." Karina edged past Joanne into the house. From the living room came the sound of Yogi Bear's voice entreating Boo Boo to steal a picnic basket.

"*They* let me sleep in on Sunday mornings, unlike some people I know."

"Sorry. Can I make some coffee?"

Joanne sighed. "Sure, why not. Just let me wash the sleep out of my eyes so I can see you while we're talking."

Karina went through to the kitchen and put on the kettle. The fridge bristled with colorful children's drawings, and small handprints in plaster decorated the walls.

A family kitchen. Marbles underfoot, crayons on the counter, sticky patches on the backs of the chairs. Nothing had ever seemed so desirable. Or so impossibly remote.

Joanne reappeared a few minutes later wearing a faded tracksuit, her hair brushed and damp around the temples. She went to the sink, filled a glass of water and popped a couple of painkillers.

"You really danced up a storm at the party last night, Jo. Feeling frisky, were you?" Karina turned away from the counter, a cup of instant coffee in each hand.

"Feeling good," Joanne said with a sudden smile. "I didn't get a chance to tell you. Peter got a promotion! From now on he'll manage projects from the office instead of doing the fieldwork. He'll still have to go away sometimes, but for much shorter periods."

"That's wonderful," Karina said, brightening at her friend's good fortune. She handed Joanne a cup. "You must be so happy."

"You bet. We've been waiting for this for so long. Next time I go to a party, I'll be dancing with my husband."

Karina removed a toy truck from a stool and sat down at the breakfast bar. "I don't know how you two have survived as a couple with all the time you've spent apart."

Joanne shrugged. "It's been hard at times, but…we love each other. You can get through a lot of tough stuff that way." She hoisted herself onto another stool and looked expectantly at Karina. "So, what's up?"

Karina reached for the cream and sugar. She'd come here because she wanted to be with someone rather than mope alone. And because she couldn't bear to be around

Daniel after all they'd said to each other. Now she realized she badly needed to talk.

"I...I had a fight with Daniel."

Joanne's eyebrows shot up as she reached for her coffee. "What? Are you kidding me?"

"I wish I were."

"When I left last night you two were wrapped tighter than wisteria around a trellis. What happened? Was it Brian?"

Karina frowned. "What is this obsession with Brian? He had nothing to do with our disagreement. It started long after the party was over."

Joanne sipped at the black steaming liquid and squinted over the cup at her. "So, you and Daniel stayed up after the party was over. That sounds cozy. What's that old saying, 'Make love not war'?"

Karina fiddled with the lid to the sugar bowl, spinning it around until Joanne slapped her hand away.

"Honestly, you're as bad as the kids." Sudden comprehension lit her face. "You slept with him, didn't you?"

Karina heaved a resigned sigh. "Yes."

"Fantastic!" Bug-eyed, Joanne ogled her. "Was it?"

"Yes." Karina was annoyed to feel herself flush. "For God's sake, Joanne, quit looking at me like I swallowed a baby bird or something."

"But it's so exciting," Joanne gushed, undeterred. "This is a first since Joel, isn't it? That's what, two years?"

Karina nodded, but there was really no comparison. What she'd had with Joel went nowhere near as deep as her relationship with Daniel.

"So how did you go from loving to fighting?" Joanne asked. "Usually it happens the other way around."

Karina hooked her feet around a rung of the stool and leaned an elbow on the counter. "It all started when he asked me to marry him."

"Holy cromoly, Karina. What did you say?"

Karina frowned. "*No,* of course."

"Oh, of course." Joanne rolled her eyes. "The greatest man you've ever met in your entire life asks you to marry him and you just naturally say no."

"Greatest man I've ever met?"

"Well, isn't he?"

Karina shrugged. "Okay, so what if he is? That's not the point. I made a promise to myself never to get married."

Joanne leaned forward, incredulous. "So break it. No one else would hold you to such a silly promise. Think about it, Karina. He's creative, he's intelligent, he's got a sense of humor, he's sensitive without being a wuss, he's good in the kitchen, he's good with kids, he's good with his hands, he's good in bed, *and*—" she finished on a triumphant gasp "—he loves you. What more do you want?"

There was nothing left to ask for, Karina thought, except infinite patience. And even that might not be enough.

"It doesn't matter what I want, Jo. I can't seem to come to grips with this fear I have of dying young and leaving the ones I love behind. I know my feelings aren't entirely rational but..." She paused, searching for words. With a sigh, she gave up. "It's hard to explain."

"Try," Joanne prodded.

Karina clutched her head with both hands and struggled to overcome her confusion. "Well, for instance, last night Natalie had a nightmare and came into my room looking for Daniel. She was half asleep and for a moment she thought I was her mother.''

Tears filled Karina's eyes at the memory. "Jo, you should have seen the look on her face when she realized *again* that her mother wasn't ever coming back. It brought home to me how much responsibility goes with having children.''

"Responsibility? Well, of course," Joanne said, frowning slightly. "But the most important thing is to simply love them.''

"You have to be alive to love them," Karina argued, rubbing her thumb around the rim of her cup. "If you can't guarantee you'll be around to see them grow up, then you shouldn't have them.''

"Karina! I can't believe anybody so smart can be so dumb. No one can guarantee their children that. All anyone can do is care for them as best they can.''

Karina burst into tears. "That's exactly what I'm trying to do!" When she'd told Joanne all that had passed between her and Daniel, she wiped a hand across her eyes. "I've turned into such a baby, Jo. I don't cry. I never cry. Suddenly I'm crying every half hour.''

Joanne got off her stool and pulled her into a hug. "Everything will turn out all right in the end, you'll see.''

"I don't see how it can." She snuffled into the piece of paper towel Joanne had handed her in lieu of a tissue.

"It will. And don't worry about crying. No one can be strong all the time. It's not healthy.''

Karina nodded, thinking about her father and how his outer strength hid an inability to adapt and accept. Maybe it was time to stop protecting him with her complicity. It wasn't too late for them to reestablish a relationship. She'd grown up some. Maybe *she* could help *him* now.

"Give yourself time," Joanne said. "You've been fretting over this for so many years you can't expect to rid yourself of all your worries in a single night."

"Daniel seems to think I should be able to."

Joanne squeezed her hand. "You caught him at a bad time. Don't forget, you'd just turned down his marriage proposal."

"I can't expect him to wait for me indefinitely." With a sigh, she got to her feet. "I'd better go. Thanks, Joanne," she said, hugging her friend. "I'll see you later."

Joanne followed her to the front door. "What are you going to do now?"

Karina turned on the step. A breeze caught a length of her hair, blowing it across her face. "I'm not sure," she said, brushing the hair out of her eyes. "I guess the first thing I need to do is get home before Daniel leaves. I didn't even say goodbye to Natalie."

"You two will work it out," Joanne assured her.

Karina couldn't answer that. Whatever lay between her and Daniel was complicated by what she felt for Natalie—a fierce, protective desire that nothing she did should ever hurt the child.

Talking things over with Joanne had made her feel better, but nothing was resolved in her mind. She didn't feel any closer to being able to say yes to Daniel than she had before.

She started down the steps, then turned back to Joanne. "I'm really glad for you. About Peter's job, I mean."

"Thanks. Me, too. Take care." Joanne waved once more and closed the door.

Karina steered Sammy toward home. By the time she pulled up in front of her house, she was eager to see Daniel. One thing had changed, she realized as she ran up the steps. She desperately wanted to try to work things out. Maybe with his help, she could overcome her fears.

CHAPTER SIXTEEN

THE FRONT DOOR was locked. Frowning, Karina rattled the knob. She was sure she hadn't locked it when she'd fled to Joanne's. She scrabbled in her purse for the key and quickly opened the door.

All was quiet. To her frazzled nerves, the silence seemed to scream out loud. Daniel never could remember to leave the radio on when he went out so there'd be music to greet her on her return.

She pushed the door shut harder than necessary just to break the stifling hush. With hurried steps she went from room to room, searching in vain for some trace of Daniel and Natalie. Surely they couldn't have packed up and left already?

She ran up the stairs, calling his name. The tinny sound of the transistor in the bathroom seemed to mock her as she hurried across the landing.

Without knocking, she flung open Daniel's door. Her anxious gaze whisked from corner to corner. Her heart sank. The room was empty of all his belongings.

It was only when she retreated to her own room that she found the note pinned to her pillow.

DANIEL LAY ON the hotel bed and gazed glumly at the bland, characterless walls with their color-coordinated pieces of pseudoart. A week in this cold, impersonal hotel had been more than enough to show him how lackluster his life was without Karina. He never thought he'd see the day when he'd miss her weird and wonderful creature collection.

He glanced at Natalie, asleep in the other bed, clutching her doll to her chest like a lifeline, and tried to count his blessings. The current tenants of the house he'd rented had moved out early. He'd picked up the key this afternoon, and tomorrow he and Nattie could move in. The house was just as perfect as described. Except for the fact that Karina wouldn't be there.

For the thousandth time, he pondered the note he'd left and wondered if it was too impersonal. Maybe if he'd been more forceful. Maybe if he'd pleaded. Maybe if he hadn't been so worried about Natalie, he would have said the right words to convince Karina to take a chance on him, on them, on life itself.

He'd hoped she would ignore his note and come looking for him. But she hadn't even called. God, how he missed her. Her laughter, the tapping of her high heels, her endless commotion, and yes, even her ever-present music.

Wearily Daniel rolled off the bed to turn down the neutral brown bedspread and slide beneath the cold, starched sheets. On top of everything else, he'd forgotten to give Karina her birthday present.

KARINA STARED forlornly at her TV dinner. Her appetite had disappeared with Daniel, along with everything else worthwhile in life.

The house echoed with emptiness. In vain she listened for the sound of Daniel's rich, accented voice as he calmly countered her outrageous comments with maddening logic. Or Natalie's happy laughter as she played her endless games of make-believe.

Gone was the smell of good cooking, the fragrance of the eucalypt sawdust that clung to Daniel's clothes and the scent of childhood in Nattie's newly washed hair.

All gone.

Pushing the tray aside, she got up and wandered onto the deck. Looking at the garage made her think of all the tools and wood still sitting out there. He'd have to come back for them, but he'd probably do it while she was at work. He didn't want to see her again, he'd said as much in his note.

She'd read the note so many times it was little more than a rag, yet she knew it by heart. "Dear Karina," he'd written, "Natalie and I will be gone by the time you get back. I don't fully understand your feelings, but I respect your wishes. I won't try to see you again. If you change your mind about us, call me. Otherwise I think it's best we have no further contact. Thank you for everything. Natalie sends her love. Daniel."

Straightforward, unemotional and definitely final. Well, what had she expected? A torrid declaration of undying love and a desperate plea for one more chance? He wasn't the type to beg, and she wouldn't respect him if he did. Yet her heart ached for the smallest sign of the warmth and affection she'd come to associate with him.

On a separate piece of paper he'd written the name and address of their hotel. Several times she'd picked up the telephone only to slam it back into its cradle. He obviously didn't have enough faith in a future together to keep trying. Or maybe he simply didn't love her enough. In which case, why prolong the agony?

Leaning over the balcony, Karina noted apathetically that the tomatoes were ripe and badly needed to be picked. Behind the fence she spotted a wriggling black shape between the cracks in the boards. Piper saw her, too, and let out an encouraging yip.

"Okay, Piper," she called. "I'm coming."

She picked up a long-handled woven basket from the deck, donned her gardening gloves and clumped down the steps to the backyard. Life went on.

A short time later she knelt back on her heels and wiped a sun-warmed arm over her damp brow. Piper danced around her, kicking up bits of dirt and snuffling at her heels.

"Piper, you cheeky mutt! Bring back that tomato right now."

He paid no attention at all. Laughing around the tomato gripped in his slobbery mouth, the dog ran off, ears and tail flying like flags.

Karina ignored him and turned her attention back to the tomatoes. They were all that tomatoes should be—ripe, red and firm. She breathed in the tangy scent the plants gave off as she moved among them. Inevitably her thoughts turned to her mother.

She plucked a large, red globe and smiled at the memory of Mama surrounded by mountains of tomatoes, chopping the ripe fruit, stirring the big pot of pasta sauce. The air would be redolent with garlic and herbs, the counter lined with glass sealing jars. She'd taught Karina the secret family recipe, explaining how it had been handed down from her mother and her grandmother before that.

Who would *she* pass things on to? Karina wondered with a painful quickening of her heart. At least she was there to remember her mother. Who would remember *her* when she was gone?

The thought nagged at her as she climbed the stairs with her load of tomatoes and set the basket on the counter. Going to the shelf beside the fridge, she pulled out an old and tattered volume from her sparse collection of cookbooks.

The book bulged with loose pages, recipe cards and half-torn pockets filled with newspaper clippings of long-forgotten summer favorites. There were yellowed scraps of paper in cramped Italian script, so faded she could hardly read them. She'd have to go through it all someday and sort things out.

She flipped to the section that contained her mother's recipes, handwritten in Mama's elegant slanting script. Her mother had given her the book just before she died. Who would she leave it to when she was gone? Her brother? Joanne?

With *La Traviata* playing in the background, Karina went to work preparing the jars and measuring the herbs that went into the sauce. It wasn't any fun this time, she thought dismally. It was supposed to be a family ritual, not a solitary ordeal.

She ladled the steaming red sauce into the sealing jars, screwed on the lids and put them in the pressure cooker to boil. She'd been counting on Natalie to keep her company, she realized, and wondered if she would even bother growing tomatoes next year.

Felix's white-gloved hands pointed to midnight when she finally took the last jar from the pressure cooker. They were lined up two deep on the counter, gleaming dark red in the low light of the range hood. Karina sank onto a chair, staring blankly at them, the dying strains of Violetta's final aria drifting through her head.

She sat on in the semidarkness, her head resting on her hand, and drifted off....

A door slammed in the breeze from the open window. She awoke with a start. Her elbow flew out, knocking the recipe book off the table. It crashed to the floor in a scattered heap of pages and papers. Karina bent to gather the bits and pieces together.

What in the world—?

She reached for one of the overflowing pockets. What was a photo doing in with the recipes?

She pulled it out and crossed to the counter, where the light was better. The photo had been taken here in the kitchen one sunlit day—years ago, judging by those old green curtains. A row of sauce-filled sealer jars lined the counter, just as they did now. And a woman who looked exactly like her smiled down at a young girl with long, curling dark hair.

Mama. And she was the girl.

Tears filled her eyes. Aunt Maria must have taken the photo. Yes, she'd come out from Toronto that summer.

Karina breathed in on a sigh, and the scent of tomatoes and herbs filled her nostrils. They permeated the kitchen, just as they had then, and the smell brought that day forward with crystal clarity. There'd been a bowl of roses on the table. And a canary singing. Funny, she'd forgotten about Tweety Pie.

Karina peered closer at the photo. Yes, and there were the dangly beaded earrings she'd given her mother for her birthday that year.

A shiver ran over her shoulders and skittered along her arms, making her go cold all over. Mama's thirty-second birthday. Six months after this photo was taken she was dead.

It was hard to believe that someone so vibrant and alive could have died so young, she thought, lightly touching the photo. Behind Mama's smiling face, tragedy lurked.

In the dark, silent kitchen, memories quietly flowed

back into Karina's mind. Memories she thought she'd buried forever.

Mama, sending her to the basement for more sealing jars. The light was dim down there and she didn't like the spiders that hung in the corners. The jars were dusty but she gathered as many as she could carry. Then she was standing on the top step, trying to reach around the armful of jars for the knob....

And she heard something she wasn't meant to.

Mama, her beautiful voice troubled, telling Maria about a lump in her right breast. Aunt Maria begging her to see a doctor, take some tests. Mama's voice fearful but evasive, promising nothing, reminding Maria of the suffering their mother had gone through. And all for nothing in the end....

But wait, the visits to the doctor, the biopsy...all that hadn't started until *October* of that year. She remembered because Mama hadn't been able to finish her costume for a Halloween party; she'd been too upset by her first appointment with the specialist.

Karina doubled over, struck by a squeezing pain behind her breastbone. Her hand closed around the photo, crumpling it. *Mama knew.* Not just that she was predisposed to cancer, but that she *had* it. And she hadn't gone for treatment until it was too late.

Karina tried to breathe, tried to whistle, but her throat was dry. *Mama might have lived.* Why hadn't she gone to see a doctor in time? If not for herself, then for her family. How could she have let them down?

Anger forced air into Karina's lungs, but she no longer had the urge to block out her thoughts. They were too powerful and too insistent not to vent. Hardly knowing what she was doing, she jumped up, grasped the wooden spoon and smashed it down on the counter.

"Mama!" she shouted. "How could you have done that to us!"

Her angry cry rang through the dark and silent house. All those years, all that pain and grief. Wasted. No wonder she'd never been able to cry. She was too furious with her mother for dying.

Karina had allowed herself nothing. *Nothing.* All because of Mama. No husband, no children, no future.

No Daniel.

Once again she raised the spoon. And with a slashing blow, broadsided the row of sealing jars.

Damn you, Mama! Damn you to hell!

Glass shattered against glass. Heavy jars slid over the counter to smash on the floor. Red splashed the blue-and-white linoleum and spattered the cream-colored wall.

She hit out again. And again. Every blow was a blow against her mother. For all the moments in her life, large and small, when she'd needed Mama to be there—her first date, graduation night.... And for all the times Karina had called out for her in the night and she hadn't come.

"*Ma-a-mma!*" she called out now into the emptiness.

All the jars lay smashed on the floor, tomato sauce bleeding between shards of glass, dripping from the walls. Karina dropped the wooden spoon from her cramped hand. Gasping, she sank to her knees. Her hair fell around her face as she bowed her head and wept. Pain racked her body and she rocked back and forth on her heels, hugging herself.

Mama hadn't had to die. She *should not* have died.

She was going to die like her mother.

Karina stopped rocking, still clutching her sides.

No. She was not her mother, no matter how much

alike they were. She was her own person. One who could learn from her mother's mistakes. Mama's death need not have happened. But that thought, which a moment ago had caused her anger and despair, now filled her with hope for the future. If the future brought cancer, she would face it. Defeat it. *She would not die.*

Rising to her feet, she made a new promise to herself—a promise to survive. A fierce, exultant joy swept through her. She would marry Daniel, be a mother to Natalie and, God willing, bear Daniel's children.

Her mother had looked so proud of her in the photo. Well, she would give her something to be proud about.

The photo. What had she done with it?

Frantically she glanced around the room and spied the photo on the floor where she'd thrown it, one corner steeped in tomato sauce. She snatched it up, sponged the sauce away with a towel and hugged the unexpected treasure to her chest.

Poor Mama. Maybe she'd been angry, too.

Karina sat again, her eyes closing as images of her mother filled her mind. Here in the kitchen where so many memories of Mama dwelled, she felt her mother's presence all around her. A wave of love washed over her, refreshing her parched heart with the living memory of a mother's love, flooding her soul with joy and serenity.

Soon another pulse of love wove in with the first, like a second melody. It was her love for Daniel. More vibrant, more compelling, but just as pure and strong and filled with the promise of a future.

Karina let the waves of love and joy ripple and flow through her like a symphony. Her heart healed and swelled to contain the expanding love she held inside, for Mama, for Daniel, for Natalie.

Thank you, Mama.

Tears of forgiveness and gratitude streamed down her face. Mama might not have had time to teach her all the ways of a woman, but she'd given her the greatest gift a mother could give a child—life itself.

Mama had had a passion for living and a talent for loving. Surely the greatest tribute Karina could pay her would be to pass those qualities on to her own children. To give of herself to those she held dearest.

Karina pushed herself out of her chair. She had to talk to Daniel. Squinting at the number of his hotel she'd tacked to the corkboard, she picked up the phone and began to punch in the numbers. Then she glanced at Felix.

Shoot. It was 2:00 a.m.

Slowly she replaced the receiver. She might not be a mother yet, but at least she knew better than to wake a child in the middle of the night.

Never mind. Tomorrow would soon be here.

"NOT SO MUCH JAM on your crumpet, Nattie," Daniel chided. "And sit up straight."

Though it was barely 7:00 a.m., they were already in the hotel coffee shop having breakfast.

"Gee, Daddy," Natalie complained, "why are you so grumpy today?"

"I'm not grump—" He broke off, catching sight of his reflection in the window. His face was set in a disagreeable frown, and he was hunched over his plate like an old bear.

Well, who wouldn't be grumpy? Today the woman he loved was going away for the weekend with his brother.

He forced a strained smile onto his face. "Sorry, Possum, I haven't been sleeping very well lately. I guess I am a bit grumpy.''

"You're *very* grumpy," she declared. Then, in a small voice, she added, "I haven't been sleeping well, either."

Daniel grunted sympathetically and buttered a slice of toast for which he had no appetite. "Did you have another nightmare last night?"

Natalie nodded sadly. "I miss Karina. And Mrs. Beeton won't come back."

"Don't worry, Nattie," he said, trying to put some animation into his voice. "I called Grandma last night and she said she'll come and visit us soon."

"Oh."

Daniel reached across and felt her forehead. Natalie should have been over the moon at the prospect of a visit from her grandmother. Maybe she was coming down with something. And he thought he recognized the symptoms—Karina withdrawal.

"We're going to move into our new house today," he said, making another attempt to cheer her up.

"I don't want to move to a new house," Natalie wailed. "I never even got to say goodbye to Karina. She was going to show me how to crochet an elephant."

This struck Daniel as bizarre, even for Karina. "An elephant? Wouldn't that take an awful lot of wool?"

"Not a *real* elephant." Natalie's mouth crooked up in a tiny smile. "A *toy* elephant."

"Oh, I see," he said with a chuckle. He reached for his coffee and sipped pensively, his smile fading.

"Why did we have to leave, Daddy?"

They'd been over this at least a dozen times in the past week. Nothing he said, no reason he could give, satisfied the little girl. Or himself, for that matter. If only Karina hadn't been so stubborn.

"I told you, sweetheart, Karina wanted us to go."

Natalie looked crestfallen. "Doesn't she like us anymore?"

"Of course she does," Daniel said, mentally kicking himself for his thoughtless words. "She loves us. She definitely loves you, and I'm practically positive she loves me."

"Did you ask her nicely if we could stay?"

"I asked her to marry me."

Natalie's face brightened. "Goody!"

Good God, now why had he gone and said that? "Don't get excited, Nattie. She said no. That's why we're at this hotel instead of Karina's house."

"But, Daddy," Natalie persisted, trying to puzzle things out. "If she loves us, why won't she marry us?"

Daniel picked up his toast, searching his mind for an answer that would make sense to the child. And to him.

"It's complicated. You see, sweetheart, her mother died when she was young." He wasn't sure he should be talking about this to Natalie, but he knew she needed answers just as much as he did.

"I know. She told me."

"She did?" He was surprised at that.

Natalie nodded. "After I had the nightmare. She told me someday it wouldn't hurt so much to think about Mommy. She told me to think about the good things instead. But you know what, Daddy?"

"What?"

"It already doesn't hurt quite so much. Not after Karina told me about *her* mommy." Natalie smiled bravely and tears swam in her eyes. "I wish we still lived with her."

With all his heart, Daniel wished the same thing. He took a bite of his toast and chewed mechanically.

"Daddy?" Natalie fixed worried eyes upon him.

"Yes?"

"Karina won't get sick and die, will she?"

The toast turned to cardboard in his mouth. "Did she say that?"

"No. But I loved Mommy and she died. I just thought…" Her small voice trailed away as she gazed at him, fearful yet trusting.

"Sweetheart, Mommy didn't die because you loved her."

"I know, but…"

Daniel rubbed the back of his neck with one hand. He couldn't tell her about Karina's fears; the child would be terrified. Besides, even though he understood why Karina felt the way she did, he refused to accept the possibility she might be right.

"Nobody knows exactly how long they have, Possum," he said, taking his daughter's hand and squeezing it. "But *I* believe Karina will live to be a very old, very nutty lady who makes papier-mâché unicorns from her rocking chair."

Natalie giggled. "I could help her reach the high parts."

Daniel smiled at the thought, then sobered. "Problem is, Nattie, we won't be around. For reasons of her own, she doesn't want to have babies. But she knows I want more children. She also knows you want a baby brother or sister and she doesn't want us to be disappointed."

Natalie sniffed, and pushed her crumpet around her plate. "I'd rather have Karina than a baby brother."

Daniel froze with his toast halfway to his mouth. "What did you say?"

"I said I'd rather have Karina than a baby brother."

His hand dropped to the table. How could he have

been so stupid? The way out of their misery was blindingly simple. Yes, he wanted more children. And not having them would leave a huge gap in his life. But that was nothing compared to the black hole that threatened his universe when he contemplated a future without Karina.

"Do you really mean that?" he demanded.

Natalie nodded, on the verge of tears again.

Daniel tossed the piece of uneaten toast on his plate. Karina might be as stubborn as a mule, but he was the biggest jackass that ever lived. He didn't deserve to have her if he wasn't willing to take her as she was. With or without children. If he truly loved her, he should be with her now, helping her continue the fight against whatever fears she had yet to confront.

She would still be worried about Natalie, but somehow he would have to convince her she needed their love as much as they needed hers. That the gain would outweigh the risk.

He started to get up, then stopped. Before he could ask for Karina's future, he had to resolve the past with Brian. She might not have feelings for his brother, but Brian had implied more than once that *he* had feelings for *her*. Daniel was fed up with trying to atone for Francine, but keeping secrets was what had damaged his relationship with Brian in the first place. He wasn't going to add to the hostilities by repeating that mistake. For good or ill, it was time to come clean about his love for Karina.

"Come on, Nattie," Daniel said, pushing his chair back. "We've got to go, right now."

"Back to Karina's house?" the girl asked eagerly, her crumpet forgotten on her plate.

"No. To Uncle Brian's." He pulled some bills from his wallet and tucked them under a saucer. "Let's go."

"Don't forget," he said to Natalie a short time later as they rode the elevator to Brian's floor, "what I have to say to Uncle Brian is serious and private. I want you to stay in the living room and—"

"I know, watch TV while you talk in the kitchen." Her face took on a mischievous expression. "Don't worry, I won't hear a thing. I'll turn the TV up really loud."

Daniel rolled his eyes and cuffed her lightly on the shoulder. Control of the TV's volume was a continuing battle of wits with Natalie and he'd just lost a round.

But that was the least of his worries.

"So, DANNY BOY, what's up?" Brian lounged against the gleaming white kitchen counter, coffee mug in hand, and glanced pointedly at his watch. "I have to pick up Karina in an hour."

Daniel fought down the surge of irritation his brother invariably provoked in him. "It's Karina I want to talk to you about."

Brian's eyes narrowed over the rim of his mug. "What about her?"

Daniel leaned over the central cooking island and planted his hands on either side of the pristine chopping block. "I'm in love with her. And I believe she loves me."

"In love, you say. Big step, Danny boy." Brian thoughtfully smoothed the crease line of his front-pleated pants.

Ignoring Brian's mocking tone, Daniel continued, "I wanted to tell you how I felt about her in person, rather than have you find out the hard way."

Brian glanced at him sharply. "Like last time, you mean, when you sent a telegram from Australia saying you'd married my fiancée?"

Daniel shoved a hand through his hair and felt the sudden dampness around his temples. "I tried to tell you about Francine and me but you wouldn't listen."

"I might have believed it was serious if *she'd* said something. Right until the end, she never once let on she was leaving me." His voice threatened to break on the last two words.

"She meant to, I know," Daniel replied, trying to make amends for what never should have happened. "But everything was so chaotic those last few days before we left."

The skin around Brian's mouth tightened. "Thank you, brother. That informative little twist of the knife opened up the wound nicely. To be rejected is bad enough, but to be forgotten, as well…"

Daniel wiped his hand, damp with perspiration, on his jeans. "The point is," he persisted, "Karina and I have things we need to work out. I'd rather you didn't go away with her this weekend."

Brian, about to take a sip of coffee, set his mug back on the counter and laughed. "You think Karina would give up her golf tournament even if I agreed to do as you ask? Think again, Danny boy."

Daniel pressed two fingers to the bridge of his nose and closed his eyes. "Look, Brian," he said, glancing up. "You're my brother. I want to be friends with you. But I also want Karina."

Brian's laughter faded, to be replaced by the familiar derisive hostility. "And you think you should be able to have anything you want."

"No. Yes. In this case, yes." Daniel straightened and glanced away.

Brian tossed the dregs of his coffee down the sink. "Are you telling me you and Karina are getting married?"

If only he *could* say that. Daniel stalked across the white-tiled floor and halted in front of the breakfast table with its view of the ocean.

"I want to marry her, yes." The bald statement didn't begin to convey the extent of his love for her. Or his need to protect her and to make her the mother of his child. But Brian wouldn't be interested in all that.

"I take it she said no?" Amusement tinged his brother's voice.

Daniel nodded sharply, his gaze fixed on a bobbing scrap of white sail rounding the breakwater. "So far."

Brian chortled. "She obviously prefers me, Danny boy. Why don't you bow out now and save yourself some heartbreak?"

Daniel spun around. "Because I *love*—" He broke off, shocked at the triumphant gleam in Brian's eyes. Triumphant not because he thought he'd won, but because Daniel was suffering.

"I thought you were in love with her, too," Daniel said slowly, starting toward his brother. "But you don't care about her at all, do you?"

Brian shrugged. "Did I ever mention the word *love?*"

Daniel halted, boxing Brian in against the counter. "You orchestrated your whole involvement just to get revenge on me." Sick with anger, he jabbed his fingers at his brother's chest. "Didn't you?"

Brian raised an arm as if to defend himself—or was it to strike out at him? "What if I did? I'm going with her this weekend whether you like it or not. You're going to know how it feels to lose the woman you love to your brother. By Sunday night I'll have Karina falling into my arms." A nasty glint came into Brian's eye. *"And you know I can do it."*

Daniel went cold. Karina had too much sense to be carried away by Brian's surface charm. But she was in a confused and vulnerable state, and it wouldn't be the first time his brother had dazzled a woman into wanting him.

"Karina's not stupid," he said, his voice rough. "And she's not naive. You can't *make* her love you."

"Care to make a bet on that?" Brian demanded. "Maybe she refused you because she's holding out for something better."

Daniel clenched and unclenched his fists. "Her reasons for not wanting to marry have nothing to do with you or me. If you hurt her, I swear I'll kill you. It's time you thought of someone besides yourself for a change."

"Like you were thinking of others when you ran off with Francine?" Brian pushed forward, forcing Daniel to back up past the cooking island. "You're no paragon of virtue yourself, Danny boy."

Daniel's fist crashed down on the cutting board. *"Don't call me Danny boy!* And stop throwing Francine in my face! I'm through feeling guilty over her. *If she'd really loved you, she would have stayed with you."*

Brian stopped as though struck, his sharp intake of breath audible. "How the hell can you say that? Francine and I were made for each other."

"Then why were you always flirting with other women?"

"Other women came on to me."

"You didn't have to encourage them. How do you think that made Francine feel?"

"No one else mattered to me. *She knew that.*" Brian turned away, his face contorted in pain. "I *loved* Francine."

Daniel stared at Brian's hunched shoulders, his gut twisting with doubt. For once his brother's voice held an undeniable ring of sincerity. Daniel felt himself go hot, then cold, all over. Why had he always imagined Brian incapable of deep feeling? To excuse his own actions? To make himself look superior in his own eyes?

Brian straightened and turned back, wiping a shaking hand down his face. "If I'd known what was going on, do you think I'd have let her go without a fight? You two ran off so fast I didn't have a chance to win her back. And, *you,* Danny, saw an opportunity to do me over and took it." Brian gazed at him with hatred in his cold blue eyes. "I'll bet you loved every minute of it."

"No!" Daniel said. "Of course I didn't."

A thin lock of blond hair fell across Brian's brow as he jutted his head forward. "Face it, you've been trying to one-up me since junior high."

"Don't be a jerk."

Yet somehow he couldn't quite look Brian in the eye. Jamming his hands in the hip pockets of his jeans, he backed off a step. "Since when did you feel threatened by your little brother? You were always the favorite. At school, at home—"

"Are you kidding?" Brian said. "Mom and Dad were hardest on me. I always had to break new ground. You just cruised along afterward, taking it all for granted."

"But it was *you* Dad spent time with. Coaching your team, taking you to ball games…" The old hurt rose in him, sharp and fresh as yesterday. Words he'd never spoken aloud, feelings he hadn't known were trapped inside, burst out of him. "It was *you* he saw as his *real* son."

Brian threw up his hands. "You always had your nose in a book! Or you were off in the woods building a tree fort or something."

"So I wasn't a chip off the old baseball bat. I would have liked some recognition of who *I* was."

"Get real, Danny! Mom and Dad were always telling people how many A's you got on your report card, how you mowed Granny's lawn without being asked, even how thick your goddamn hair was, for crissake!"

Daniel jerked his head in disgust. "Listen to us. We sound like children."

Despite himself, images of their younger days flashed through his mind. Brian, the Number One Son, following in Dad's footsteps on the basketball team, the football team, every damn ball team there was. Brian, the Greek god, offering to get Daniel a prettier date for the prom.

Daniel squeezed his eyes shut, trying to get a clearer picture on the past. He'd never actually wanted to *be* Brian. He'd just hated his brother acting as if he were some sort of crown prince.

Then Francine had come along, convincing him he was so much more interesting, so much more attractive than Brian. He'd been too young to sort out lust from love, vindicated pride from true commitment.

"All right!" he shouted. "I *was* glad she chose me over you. I *enjoyed* beating you at your own game. I was young and stupid. If you want to punch me in the nose for what happened a decade ago, go ahead."

He braced himself for a blow. But instead of bunching up to strike, Brian's shoulders sagged. A cold, sad smile washed over his face.

"You were always so damned noble. All I wanted was to tarnish your gilt a little."

"*My* gilt?" Daniel's hand dropped to his side. "*You* were the golden boy."

"Maybe that's how you saw it. Things looked different standing in my shoes. You were the smart one, the good one. You never seemed to worry whether people liked you or not, but they always did."

Maybe it was a trick of light, or the release of long-pent-up emotions, but suddenly everything was turned around. Daniel had the dizzying sensation of looking at himself through his brother's eyes and seeing all the old hurts and resentments, real and imagined. It made no difference who really was the favorite, or if there'd been a favorite at all. Perception was all that mattered.

Then the moment passed and he was gazing directly into Brian's tortured eyes. He glimpsed the tangled skein of ancient wounds. *God.* They could snarl themselves forever in the past....

Or they could get over it.

He took a deep breath. "Brian, I...I'm sorry." He almost choked on the words and realized it was because, for the first time, he truly meant them. "I'm sorry you suffered over Francine. I'm sorry that for so many years I missed out on having a brother. I'm sorry I hurt you."

Brian's expression turned coldly impassive. "Sorry won't change the past."

"That's true," Daniel said, searching for a way out of their impasse. "But we have to forgive each other or we can forget about the future, as well. We've got to learn to relate to each other as adults, not kids."

"We don't have a future. You decided that when you took off with Francine."

Daniel almost thumped the counter again in frustration. They were going around in circles. "I was in no state of mind to rationally decide anything then. I acted on hormones and impulse. But I'm not the same person I was ten years ago."

"Are you saying you'd do things differently now?" Brian asked with a return to mockery. "Show a little brotherly love? That's convenient."

"For God's sake—" Daniel broke off as the faint sound of Natalie laughing at something on TV filtered through the door. "Look, Brian," he said, "there's a little girl out there who's lost her mother and could do with some family. Whether you like it or not, you and I are family."

Brian turned his back on him, but not before Daniel saw the flash of bitterness in his eyes. "So I should forgive you because of the kid?"

Daniel gripped his arm and spun him around. "Not just any kid, Brian. Your niece. Francine's daughter. You don't have to forgive me, but don't shut us out. For Natalie's sake if not for mine."

Brian squeezed his eyes shut, and stress lines appeared around his mouth. "It's too late. There's too much bad blood between us." He turned away, waving a hand at Daniel. "I'm tired of this. Go on, get out of here."

"Not until I'm finished. I can't stop you from going away for the weekend with Karina, but for God's sake, don't use her to pay me back. She's a good woman, and she doesn't deserve to be screwed around because of something I did a long time ago."

Brian's head shot up. "Francine was a good woman, too!"

"Yes, she was." Daniel took a deep breath and gazed steadily at his brother. "And for what it's worth, I think you would have made her happier."

Something of the old Brian flashed into his brother's eyes then. Not the crown prince or the jaded Rolls-Royce salesman, but the young boy Daniel had caught tadpoles with, the boy he'd raced to the Christmas tree on frosty mornings. The big brother he'd always looked up to but never seemed to catch up with. Daniel's throat tightened and he looked away.

When he glanced back, the spark of boyhood had faded from Brian's eyes. Turning away, Brian crossed to the counter to pour himself another cup of coffee. Daniel watched in agonized silence, hearing the coffeepot clatter on the edge of the cup, seeing Brian's white-knuckled grip on the countertop.

"Brian? Are you okay?"

"I said, get out of here."

Daniel's shoulders sagged and his eyes closed. It was no use. Nothing he'd said had gotten through to Brian. What he thought he'd seen in his brother's eyes had been an illusion created by his own need.

Drained and weary, he turned to go, his footsteps echoing quietly on the marble tiles. His hand was on the doorknob when Brian cleared his throat.

"Daniel."

He paused without turning. "What is it?"

"My golf clubs are in the hall closet."

Daniel went still, not daring to believe what he was hearing. "Your golf clubs?"

"You heard me. Break any and you'll pay."

As an olive branch it was pretty thin, but Daniel was prepared to grasp at twigs. "I...I'll take good care of them." He turned. Brian was stirring his coffee, avoiding his gaze. "Maybe after I bring them back we could catch a ball game sometime."

There was a long silence while the coffeepot bubbled

in the background. Finally Brian said, "Don't push it, Dan."

Daniel forced himself not to mind, to be grateful for what progress they'd made. "All right, Brian. Thanks—"

Brian cut him off with an impatient wave of his hand. "Why are you still hanging around? Karina's waiting."

Daniel nodded. "Okay. I'm going."

He opened the door to the living room, paused and glanced over his shoulder. "But I'll be back."

CHAPTER SEVENTEEN

GOLDEN SUNLIGHT sifted through the chinks in Karina's blind, waking her. She opened her eyes with a smile. Overnight her happiness and peace had grown into a sense of joyful purpose.

Nothing had changed, yet everything was different. Marriage was no longer a thing to be feared and avoided, but a natural progression of her love for Daniel. Her heart sang at the thought of watching Natalie grow up, of someday holding her and Daniel's baby in her arms.

Daniel. She could call him now. Throwing back the covers, she swung her legs over the side of the bed and glanced at the clock. Nine-thirty! How could she have slept in, today of all days?

Dressing quickly, she ran downstairs to the telephone and dialed the number of Daniel's hotel. But when she asked for him, the desk clerk informed her Daniel Bowen had paid his bill and left early that morning.

"He can't have checked out already!" Panic crept into her voice. "He's not moving into his new house for another week."

"Sorry, ma'am, I wouldn't know anything about that."

"Did he say where he was going? Did he leave a forwarding address?" She sensed hesitation on the other end of the line. Not caring how desperate she sounded, she added, "Please, it's really important."

"I probably shouldn't say anything...."

"What? Tell me."

"Mr. Bowen made a couple of phone calls from the desk just before he left. I didn't hear everything because I was busy with another customer, and of course I wasn't eavesdropping...."

"Of course not." Karina paced the kitchen floor. *Get on with it, man.*

"He mentioned the name Brian."

"Brian. Of course. Thank you very much. 'Bye."

"Wait, there's more. I think he was also talking to someone at the airport, inquiring about tickets to Australia."

Australia. "Thank you," she said, and hung up. Karina sank onto a chair, still clutching the receiver. Surely Daniel wouldn't go back to Melbourne without telling her.

Her mind in neutral, she dialed Brian's number. The telephone rang. And rang. On the fourth ring, his answering machine came on.

"Damn," she muttered and hung up before the beep. He was probably on his way to pick her up for the golf tournament. She had to hurry and find Daniel before he arrived.

She called Betty and Kevin, but they'd had no word from him. She tried the hotel again but he hadn't returned, hadn't checked for messages. With little hope of success, she tried to get a telephone listing for him at his new address. No luck there, either.

At least when Brian got here she could ask him if he knew where Daniel was. Her bags were packed and standing by the front door, the golf clubs she'd borrowed propped against them. But unless she sorted things out with Daniel, she wasn't going to any tournament. What had once seemed like the key to a new life now loomed before her as an obstacle to happiness.

Frustrated, she went outside and sat on the top step to watch for Brian's Jaguar to slink around the corner. Then, too restless to sit still, she jumped up and paced the footpath, snapping dead heads off the dahlias. What if she'd driven Daniel away for good? The thought was too horrible to contemplate.

Without him, what was left for her but to climb the corporate ladder? Not so long ago, that had been her top priority. Without a family to help care for, there would be no limit to the heights she could attain. And with success would come the material trappings—a bigger house, overseas trips, clothes, parties....

The thought of another party suddenly seemed inexpressibly tedious. As did the empty house that would await her at the end of each and every night.

Fool. She tossed a shriveled flower aside and strode back up the path to the house. A fool and a coward, that's what she was. She had the address of Daniel's new house. Maybe he was there right now. She'd drive over and camp out front until he showed up.

Karina ran up the steps onto the porch. Forget the golf tournament. Forget the job. Don't think about the look on Brian's face when he showed up and she wasn't there. There wasn't a second to waste.

Next year she'd go to the tournament. But she'd go as CEO of her own company. Yes, that was it. She'd quit procrastinating and install that computer in her basement next week. To hell with Ross and his cronies. To hell with the art department. With Daniel and Natalie around, she'd never be lonely. And if she could poach Kevin from SignCity, she'd be laughing.

Karina grabbed her purse and car keys off the hall

table. She heard the sound of a vehicle and spun around to glance out the door. Brian?

Her heart missed a beat. Not Brian, but *Daniel.*

She came slowly out of the house and down the steps, half afraid she was just imagining that his white pickup was pulling in at the curb across the street.

Then she saw his tall figure emerge from the driver's side and Natalie run around the truck to stand next to him.

Daniel was back.

Now they were crossing the road, Daniel holding his arm in front of Natalie to stop her from running blindly across the street.

Karina ran down the path to meet them. Natalie broke away from Daniel the moment her toes touched the sidewalk. Crouching low, Karina scooped the girl into her arms and hugged her to her chest. Tears coursed down her cheeks, through the creases of her smile.

"I thought I'd never see you again!" Natalie cried.

"I thought I'd never see you!"

"I didn't want to go away, but Daddy said you wanted to live here all by yourself. It's not true, is it?" Natalie pulled back and her tear-filled eyes blazed at Karina.

"No, sweetheart." She wiped the wet streaks away from the child's flushed cheeks with trembling fingers. "It isn't true anymore. I want to be with the two of you."

"Truly?"

At the sound of Daniel's voice, Karina looked up. His eyes, shadowed and grave, searched her face. He was asking for more than confirmation of her words, she thought with a leap of her heart. He was asking for her future. *Their* future.

"Truly."

He took a step toward her and she gently disentangled herself from Natalie. "Oh, Daniel," she said, and went into his arms. He was warm and solid and felt so right. The time for tears was over. From now on there would be nothing but kisses and sighs and loving—

His hands moved to her shoulders, and before she could taste the love on his lips, a gap had grown between them. She swallowed a moan of regret and looked questioningly into his eyes.

"I forgot to give you your birthday present the other night," he said.

She stared at him, startled back into uncertainty. Had she got it all wrong? Had he come back just to give her a birthday present? A sick feeling grew in her stomach as Daniel handed her a wrapped parcel.

"I made it myself," he said.

Karina swallowed hard. "Thank you." She stripped away the tissue paper and stared at the carved ebony box in her hands. "It's beautiful," she murmured. "Just what I needed."

Except it wasn't. What she needed was Daniel and wedding bells and happy-ever-after. And babies. Lots of babies.

She ran her fingers over the polished wood. Despite the numbing cold enveloping her heart, she couldn't help but admire the intricate pattern of paisley swirls and spiraling horns.

"Good grief," she said with a choking laugh. "Is that a *pig?*"

Daniel smiled, but it was Natalie who answered, "Yes. And look, there's a unicorn and your flying ladies. Open it up," she chattered excitedly. "There's a secret compartment and inside is a—"

"Shh, Nattie," Daniel admonished, tugging on the child's braid. "Let her find it herself."

The top of the box lifted easily, but it took Karina a few moments to work out how to open the secret compartment. Her fingers poked and pushed without success until finally she twisted a partition and a thin layer of wood slid back to uncover a small chamber buried in the heart of the box.

Inside, nestled in royal blue velvet, lay a ring.

A ring made out of yellow construction paper. With a red crayoned ruby in the center.

She laughed, and there was a sob of joy in her laughter. "There's an inscription," she said, astonished and delighted but not fully comprehending. Removing the ring, she turned it in her fingers and read, "'I.O.U. one engagement ring'."

She glanced at Daniel, her eyes blurring with tears. "Then you still want me?"

"Forever." His curving mouth was set in a solemn line and his eyes were full of love.

"Oh, Daniel—"

"Wait. Before you answer, there's something else I want to say. If…" he took a breath and cleared his throat "…if you really don't want children, well, that's hard, but I'd rather have you that way than not at all. And so would Natalie."

Karina's heart swelled to bursting at the depth of his sacrifice. He was giving her a second chance, a gift of happiness more precious than all the jewels in the world.

"Marry me, Karina."

She nodded vigorously, her throat too constricted to speak. "Yes," she gasped at last. "Yes. Yes! *Yes!*"

"See, Daddy?" Natalie said, looking up at her father. "I told you she'd say yes."

Daniel gently prised Karina's fingers loose from the jewelry box. "I promise you can have it back in a minute. But I'll need your hand for this next bit."

She laughed, her fingers trembling as she relinquished the box. "I was just scared of dropping it."

Daniel slipped the ring on her finger. It caught on her knuckle and almost tore. By the time it was in place on the third finger of her left hand, her heart was pounding.

She turned her wrist to catch the light in the shiny red crayon, savoring the bliss of wearing Daniel's ring. "I've never seen anything so beautiful," she said, and meant it.

He grinned. "If I'd known you were this easy to please, I'd have asked you to marry me a long time ago."

Though his words were teasing, the look in his eyes left her in no doubt of the depth of his love and the strength of his commitment. And when he pulled her into his arms and touched his lips to hers, she responded with all the joy in her heart.

It was every kiss they'd ever exchanged and more. Longing and love, passion and promise, fulfillment at last.

Finally Karina broke away, her fingers lifted to her mouth. "Brian," she said breathlessly. "The golf tournament."

"Don't worry about it." Daniel pulled her close again and began planting tiny kisses behind her ear.

"Daddy, Karina, let's go." Natalie skipped up and down, tugging on her father's sleeve.

"Okay, okay." He loosened his embrace and glanced down at Karina. "Coming?"

She nodded happily, not knowing where they were going and not caring. Daniel picked up her bags and started in the direction of the truck. She glanced at her watch and felt a pang of guilt. "Brian's due any minute. I'd better wait and tell him—"

"You can tell him whatever you like when we get back from Parksville."

"Parksville?" she said as they crossed the street. "That's where the tournament's being held."

"You didn't really think I was going to let you go with my brother, did you?" Daniel opened the door for her and Natalie, a smile playing around the corners of his mouth.

"Frankly, yes," Karina said. "But I'll pick that bone with you later." She got in beside Natalie and waited while Daniel hoisted her bags into the back of the pickup.

"Does this mean you're not going back to Australia?" she asked as he slid behind the wheel.

His head jerked sideways, a bemused expression on his face. "Whatever gave you that idea?"

"The clerk at your hotel said you were inquiring about flights to Australia."

"Not *to* Australia. *From.* Natalie's grandmother is coming over for a visit and I was arranging a ticket for her."

"Oh." Her relief was inexpressible. She paused for a moment, trying to take it all in. "And is Natalie coming with us to the tournament?"

"No. We're dropping her off at Betty and Kevin's for the weekend."

"They've got a pony," Natalie exclaimed happily, bouncing on the seat.

Karina gave the girl a quick smile before turning her attention back to Daniel. "And have you patched things up with Brian?"

Daniel shrugged. "He lent me his golf clubs. It's a start."

"And you did ask me to marry you?" Best to be absolutely sure.

He laughed out loud. "Yes! Natalie insists on being a fairy princess flower girl. Is that okay?"

"Nattie can be anything she likes," Karina replied with a big smile at the little girl sitting between them. Then she had a worrying thought. "How will you get into the tournament?"

"I reckon D. Bowen could easily be mistaken for B. Bowen. Besides, you're registered as a player. If anyone asks, which I doubt, you can simply say you've got a new partner. For life."

Karina laughed. Then she narrowed her eyes at him. "But can you play golf?"

He started the engine. "I'll fake it."

"I don't think you can fake something like golf."

"Then I'll caddy for you. It'll impress the board of directors no end."

"I don't care about that anymore." At his surprised look, she added, "But it won't hurt to have a few high-level connections when I start my freelance graphics business."

"Good on you." Pride shone in his eyes.

"Oh, and Daniel," she said shyly, "I've changed my mind. I do want babies."

He didn't say a word. Just gazed at her with eyes brimming with love while his mouth slowly stretched into that beloved smile. And time stood still for the space of a heartbeat.

"Hey, what are we waiting for?" Natalie said with all the patience of a six-year-old.

Daniel laughed and ruffled her hair. "We've done waiting, Possum. It's time to get on with life."

He put the truck into gear and stretched an arm along the back of the seat as he reversed out of the parking spot.

There was something truly delicious about his fingers caressing the back of her neck, Karina thought dreamily as they pulled away from the curb. And something both thrilling and comforting to know that very soon they would live together as husband and wife, until death did them part…a very long time from now.

"Wait!" she cried, suddenly. "Go back."

Daniel hit the brakes and the truck screeched to a halt. He glanced at her, eyebrows raised.

"Go back to the house," she repeated. "Please."

"What is it?" Daniel said as he backed down the street. "You haven't changed your mind again, have you?"

She laughed. "Nothing like that. There's something I forgot to do."

He threw the truck into neutral and waited with the motor running while she ran back into the house. The rhythmic beat of a rap tune grew louder and louder as she hurried down the hall to the kitchen.

With a lopsided smile, she reached across the table and switched off the radio.

Silence.

She listened a moment. Not bad. She could get used to it. Maybe in time she'd even get used to her own thoughts.

Daniel gave her a questioning glance as she climbed back into the truck. Karina just smiled and leaned over

Natalie's head to plant a kiss lightly on his lips. She would always love music, but now she didn't need to hide behind it.

Not when she had so much to live for.

READER SERVICE™

The best romantic fiction direct to your door

Our guarantee to you...

The Reader Service involves you in no obligation
to purchase, and is truly a service to you!

There are many extra benefits including a free
monthly Newsletter with author interviews,
book previews and much more.

Your books are sent direct to your door
on 14 days no obligation home approval.

We offer huge discounts on selected books
exclusively for subscribers.

Plus, we have a dedicated Customer Care team
on hand to answer all your queries on
(UK) 020 8288 2888
(Ireland) 01 278 2062.

Medical Romance™

6 brand new titles each month

...medical drama
on the pulse.

Available on subscription every month
from the Reader Service™

GEN/03/RS2